Praise for *Newt*

"For my money, Ken [...] of the very smartest kind [...] ly engaged thinker about nitty-gritty political [...] al matters who also operates on the Romantic end of the genre by imaging worlds that offer vast (and even godlike) possibilities for humankind . . . MacLeod returns to his story elements and concerns with a persistence that signals a stubbornly committed intelligence as well as a fertile and mischievous imagination, and every variation on his themes produces something worth re-reading."   —*Locus*

"If you haven't yet read MacLeod's work, this is an excellent place to start."   —*Scifi.com*

"Exciting . . . Accessible to the average reader as well as the hardcore SF fan. This is a work sure to keep the reader on the edge of her seat."   —*Romantic Times*

"The kind of book that we wish would come to us more often in science fiction . . . Above everything, this book is *fun*."   —*Vector*

"Science fiction's freshest new writer . . . MacLeod is a fiercely intelligent, prodigously well-readw author who manages to fill his books with big issues without weighing them down."   —*Salon*

Tor Books by Ken MacLeod

THE FALL REVOLUTION

The Star Fraction
The Stone Canal
The Cassini Division
The Sky Road

THE ENGINES OF LIGHT

Cosmonaut Keep
Dark Light
Engine City

A Space Opera

NEWTON'S **Wake**

Ken MacLeod

TOR®

A TOM DOHERTY ASSOCIATES BOOK
NEW YORK

This is a work of fiction. All the characters and events portrayed in this book are either products of the author's imagination or are used fictitiously.

NEWTON'S WAKE

Edited by Patrick Nielsen Hayden

A Tor Book
Published by Tom Doherty Associates, LLC
175 Fifth Avenue
New York, NY 10010

www.tor.com

Tor® is a registered trademark of Tom Doherty Associates, LLC.

ISBN 0-765-34422-X
EAN 978-0-765-34422-9

First edition: June 2004
First mass market edition: March 2005

Printed in the United States of America

0 9 8 7 6 5 4 3 2

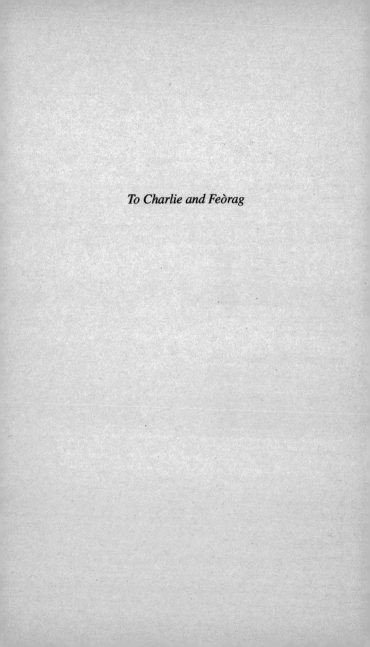

To Charlie and Feòrag

Acknowledgments

Thanks to Carol, Sharon and Michael for lots, as ever; to Charlie Stross for sound advice; to Farah Mendlesohn for critical reading and comments on the first draft; and to Mic Cheetham, Tim Holman and Patrick Nielsen Hayden.

Contents

SIDE ONE

Deep Sky Country

SIDE TWO

When the Stars Are Right

CONTENTS

SIDE 1

Deep Sky Country

CHAPTER 1

Combat Archaeology

As soon as she stepped through the gate Lucinda Carlyle knew the planet had been taken, and knew it would be worth taking back. It bore the thumbprints of hurried terraforming: bluish grass and moss, low shrubbery like heather. No animal life was visible, but she had no doubt it was there. Five kilometres away across an otherwise barren moor dotted with outcrops and bogs a kilometre-high diamond machine speared the sky. Complex in aspect, somewhere between a basaltic cliff and a cathedral, it had shown up on the robot probe, but that was nothing compared to actually looking at it.

She turned away from it and looked back at the gate. It was marked by a hilltop henge, whether by the gate's builders or by subsequent, less sophisticated minds she couldn't guess: two three-metre slabs upended, and topped by a third. One by one her team stepped forth from the unlikely shimmer and gazed around at the landscape. A yellow G5 sun blinked a bleary, watery morning eye over the horizon.

"Grim place," said Macaulay, the ordnance fellow, as drizzle gusted. "Minds me a Scotland." He heaved a Charnley plasma cannon to his shoulder, mimed a shot at the distant edifice, and—abashed by Carlyle's sudden glare—

looked to the robot walkers that carried the heavier gear.

"Divil you were ever in Scotland," jeered Amelia Orr, comms op and Carlyle's great-great-grandmother, who had been.

"Shut it," said Carlyle. She flinched slightly at her own words, but she was in charge here, and she had to stamp authority on seniority, and fast. She strongly suspected that Orr had been put on the team to keep an eye on her, and harboured contingency plans to take over if Carlyle faltered. On the inside of her helmet the names of the rest of the ten-person team lit up one by one. Meanwhile the suit's firewalls fenced with the atmosphere. The planet was habitable—inhabited, even, damn their cheek—but its bacteria, viruses, and fungi all had to be neutralised. It would be an hour or more before the suits had passed on the new immunities to the team's bloodstreams, and the suits, or at least the helmets, could be dispensed with.

"Are you picking up anything?" she asked Orr, in a carefully polite tone.

The older woman tight-beamed a glyph of <shrug> to Carlyle's head-up. "Usual encrypted chatter." <smile> "Some music. D'ye want to hear it?"

Carlyle raised a suit-gloved hand. "No the now." She swept the hand forward. "Come on guys, this is gonna be a slog."

It was.

Two hours later their suits were covered in mud and stained with bits of the local analogues of bracken, moss, and lichen, crawling with tiny ten-legged analogues of arthropods, and their firewalls were still running the virtual equivalent of fever, but they were all standing in front of the glittering cliffs. Carlyle let the team deploy a hundred metres away from the first visible ground-level gap and consulted her familiar. Professor Isaac Shlaim was an Israeli comp sci academic whose vicissitudes since the Hard Rapture could have filled a book, and had. So far Carlyle had resisted his entreaties to have it published.

"Whaddae ye make of it?" she asked.

The familiar's icon filled a quadrant of the head-up. The icon was a caricatured face that Lucinda varied whenever she felt too uncomfortably reminded that Shlaim had once been human.

"From after my time," he said, a slightly smug tone overlying his usual mixture of resentment and resignation to his plight. "Can you confirm that it is the only such artifact on the planet?"

"No."

"May I access your remote sensing equipment?"

Carlyle hesitated. The familiar's efforts to escape the circuits of her suit were as predictable as they were persistent. On the other hand, she needed his assistance more than usual.

"I'll scan then gie ye a download," she compromised.

"Excellent!" said Shlaim. Even centuries removed from muscle-tone and breath, his cheerful compliance sounded forced.

The radar and sonar pings and full-spectrum scan took about a minute and returned a mass of data quite incomprehensible to Carlyle, or to any individual human. She filed it, isolated it, and tipped it and a copy of Shlaim into a firewalled box. Let the poor bugger fight whatever demons might lurk in the electromagnetic echoes of the posthuman relic before them.

Macaulay was chivvying his iron gorillas into setting up the field pieces to triangulate the provisionally identified entrance. Orr was lying on her back surrounded by small dish aerials. The other team members were prone on the edge of a dip, periscope sights and plasma rifles poking over it, for whatever good that would do. From here the irregularities of the diamond cliff looked like crenellated battlements, its high black hollows like loopholes. But there was no evidence anywhere Carlyle could see of firing on the moor: no burn marks in the knotty ankle-high scrub, no glazed slag. The sense of being watched was overpowering, but she knew from experience that this meant nothing. She'd felt the same tension on the back of her neck in front of natural cliffs.

She ducked to stay beneath this nominal skyline and ran

over to Jenny Stevenson, the biologist, who had one hand on her rifle and with the other was picking bits of grot off her suit and feeding them into an analyser.

"How's it looking?" Carlyle asked.

Stevenson's brown-eyed gaze flicked from her head-up to focus on Carlyle, and crinkled to show the top of a smile. Her grubby glove's thumb and forefinger formed an "O."

"Compatible," she said. "After we've got the immunities, we could turn they plants into food, nae bother."

Carlyle flicked a finger at a clump of scrub, jangling its tiny violet bell-shaped flowers. "Is this really heather?"

"Naw really," said Stevenson. Her smile brightened. "Just an analogue, like. Somebody's done a real sweet job on this. Took some ae the native life and adapted it. Ye can still see bits ae the native sequences in the DNA, braided in wi the terrestrial stuff. Every cell here must be running two genetic codes simultaneously, which is quite a trick. I'm picking up signatures of they Darwin-Gosse machines fae way back, where was it?"

"Lalande 21185."

"Aye, that's the one."

"Good work," said Carlyle. This was a puzzle; AO, the main population of terraformers, mistrusted Darwin-Gosse machines, but it was always possible that a deviant sect had bought some. "That'll maybe gie's a handle on the squatters. Speaking of which."

She rolled to Orr, staying outside the barrier of aerials. "Have the locals spotted us yet?"

Orr remained staring upward, at some combination of the real sky and the images being patched in from her apparatus. She didn't turn around; probably still smarting.

"No's far as I see. Place is under satellite surveillance, sure, but I've no ta'en any pings. Most ae the action's round the other side of the planet, and all we're picking up here is spillover. I got a few quantum demons grinding through the encryption. Should be cracked in an hour or so."

"Any low orbit presence?"

Orr waved a dismissive hand skyward. "Scores of satellites. Sizes range between a grape and a grapefruit. No exactly heavy industry. Typical fucking farmers."

"Any deep space stuff?"

"Aye, a few, but it's hard to tell fae leakage ae tight-beam transmissions. The odd asteroid miner, I reckon. Maybe a fort or two."

Carlyle chewed a lip, sucked hot coffee from her helmet nipple. "Makes sense. The squatters don't seem to be AO, whoever they are."

Orr sniggered. "Squatters coulda picked a better place to fittle into. Makes me wonder why they didnae fittle straight back out."

"Yeah," said Carlyle. "Well, assuming." Assuming a lot about the squatters' tech level and motivations, was what she meant. She sat up, hunkered forward, elbows on knees, looking around. "When your demons have finished we might have something to go on. Meanwhile . . . " She toggled to an open circuit. "Time for a bit ae combat archaeology."

The mission profile was straightforward. They were neither to hide from nor confront the squatters, but instead pull down from the busy sky as much information as they could about them, then scout the diamond machine-mountain for any traces of usable tech and/or dangerous haunts, and get the hell out before sunset. Her familiar had found no signals in the noise bounced back from the precipitous face, but as Carlyle stalked forward alone, the Webster reaction pistol strapped to her hip, her backup team behind her to keep her covered, she felt her knees tremble. It wasn't so much the possible soul-searing dangers presented by the incomprehensible posthuman artifact, as it was a fear of screwing up. This was her first big job for the firm, one she'd fought hard to get, and she had no intention of blowing it. And on the plus side of the ledger, there was always the chance that the tech in here would be radical and capable of being parlayed into wealth beyond the dreams, etc. There was always that, but it wasn't enough. It wasn't what kept you walking forward, like a soldier into enemy fire. The Carlyles led from the front, always had, from the days when the worst any of them faced was a chibbing in a Glasgow close.

From a few metres away she saw that the lower part of the face, to about head height, was overgrown with moss and grass, evidently on the slow stacking of windblown dust. Above that the slope was sheer, the surface so smooth that nothing could gain purchase. The gap, a triangle ten metres high and three across at the base, had been dark only from a distance, and by contrast. As she walked into the cleft Carlyle could see that the interior was almost as bright as the outside. The passage itself was only a few paces long.

The ground level of the space opened out before her. It was so like a forest of frost-rimed low trees that for a moment she wondered if it was indeed that, perhaps a region of the heath trapped under this machine and preserved. A closer look at the nearest of the objects showed her that there was nothing biological there: the clear crystalline structure was replicated on an increasing scale from the frost that covered the needles through to the needles themselves, and the branches, to the main stem that sprouted out of the floor.

The floor was like ice, its transparency diminishing with depth. Looking up, Carlyle saw that the entire interior of the machine was encrusted with similar tree-like structures, the ones above hanging down like enormous chandeliers, their prismatic bevelled sides shining with every colour of the visible spectrum in the sunlight that slanted through the outer surface.

"It's diamond all right," said Shlaim.

"How much *carbon* is locked up in this?" Carlyle asked.

"Many millions of tons," said the familiar. "An entire coal measure, I would say, save that coal measures seem unlikely here."

"Or an entire carbonaceous chondrite? Could they have done that?"

"If so it would be a quite profligate use of anti-gravity." Shlaim sounded skeptical. "Or they could have lowered it from a skyhook, I suppose, but it would seem pointless. . . . "

Carlyle laughed. "Since when has *that* ever ruled out anything they did?"

"In any case," said Shlaim, "it appears to have been grown or manufactured in situ. From atmospheric carbon, like a plant."

"It's no just carbon," Carlyle said.

"Indeed not."

Looking down the aisle between rows of diamond shrubbery Carlyle could see other, metallic colours interrupting the riotous monotony of the prisms. The frequency and size of these interruptions increased towards the centre of the artifact, where an arrangement of copper and steel, conical in outline, complicated in detail, rose a hundred metres or more from the floor. The grail in this cathedral, or the host. It looked more like a machine than the rest of the structure did, its hints of organic form echoing animal rather than plant structures.

She walked along to the nearest apparently metal object. About a metre and a half high, it seemed a miniature of the thing in the centre. Squatting beside it, she peered at the intricate surface. Fluted, mirror-smooth steel, veined with copper that could have been tubing, in a series of varied but individually precise diameters. In among the copper were other lines, green and red, that resembled and might even be plastic insulation around wires. Checking her head-up, Carlyle saw that this object was slightly above the ambient temperature of the artifact. She switched to IR and looked again at the central cone. It too glowed, more strongly than its smaller counterparts.

"Something going on here," she said. "Some kinda circulation. Flow of electricity, maybe fuel."

She reached a hand towards it.

"Don't touch it!" warned Shlaim.

"Course not," said Carlye. "Just waving the inductance—"

"I would still caution against—"

Something fizzed and melted on the object's surface. A jolt of heat or electricity jackknifed Carlyle's arm back.

"Shit!" She wanted to suck her fingertips. She jumped up

and backed off, clutching her numb elbow. The thing was
moving, flowing as though melting into the floor. It spread,
and long tendrils that looked like dribbles of mercury reached
the bases of a few of the diamond bushes. These too began to
move, branches clicking into new and different shapes like a
multitool with nanchuk blades, the trunks becoming dis-
lodged from now-revealed grooves in the floor as they did so.
Carlyle backed off farther, and drew the Webster. Within seconds the metal object had become the central component of a
frightening arachnoid array of skittering legs and waving
arms, the whole freestanding and rotating as though deciding
where to pounce. She could see *lenses*, formed through some
complex infolding of prisms, and they were scanning her.

"I think at this point there is nothing to lose by firing,"
said Shlaim, with irritating calm.

The Webster roared and bucked in her hands. The machine leapt backwards several metres but was otherwise un-
affected. Projectiles ricocheted for what seemed a long time.
Before the sounds tinkled to a halt Carlyle turned to sprint
for the opening. All around her, machines were assembling
themselves. She fired as she ran, hitting the metal cores here
and there with effect before the diamond carapaces could
form around them. Liquid bled and burned.

Out of the opening she sprinted as far and as fast as she
could, then threw herself forward and rolled.

"Fire at will!" she shouted.

A Charnley bolt singed the air a metre above her. There
was a flash. Then a cacophonous sound from her radio
speakers deafened her. Something shorted in her helmet,
stinging her neck. She rolled farther, over the lip of ground.
The team were all blazing away at the opening. The banshee
outcry ceased. Carlyle slammed another clip in the Webster
and fired at the gap in the wall. The robot walkers were rocking back and forth on their spring-loaded legs as they lobbed
shells from their field pieces, to no effect Carlyle could see
apart from chewing up the soil around the face of the edifice.
The diamond walls hadn't taken a scratch.

"Cease fire!"

The shooting ran down to a ragged patter then stopped. Carlyle lay prone and peered at the hole as the smoke cleared. One of the multi-legged machines stood there, not moving forward or back. It had, she was pleased to see, taken some damage. Not much.

She was momentarily blinded as a laser beam from the machine slashed a line of fire across the ground a couple of metres forward of their position.

"Hold it!" she yelled.

Nothing further happened.

"Looks like we've been warned off," she said heavily. "Time to pull out. We can come back wi' a search engine."

They picked up their gear and retraced their steps towards the gate.

"No a bad recce," said Orr.

"Thanks," Carlyle grunted. The back of her neck was sore, partly from the burn and partly from the tension brought on by the thought of the laser at their backs.

"See there's mair ae they dolmens," said Stevenson, with a sweep of the arm at the horizon.

Carlyle glanced around, confirming, counting ten. They were easy to spot, when you knew where to look, on the crests of the surrounding hills.

"Make sure we're heading for the right one," she said.

That got a laugh. "Maybe they've aw got gates," someone said, and got another.

"Anybody else get short-circuits from that electromagnetic blast?" Carlyle asked.

They all had.

"Shit," she said. "Any idea what it was?"

"It was a signal," said Shlaim, breaking in to her mike. "And no, I have not analysed it."

"Just so long as you haven't *recorded* it," snarled Carlyle. She hated being upstaged by her familiar.

Something banged in the sky. They all looked up, and saw black fragments flying apart and falling down from a couple of thousand metres overhead. Then a screaming noise started, and glancing a way off they all saw a larger black object separate into six parts, which peeled away from each other, banked around, and began a controlled and rapid descent towards them.

"Modular aircars in disposable hypersonic shell," said Shlaim.

"Locals!" yelled Carlyle. "Don't shoot first!"

The team and the robot walkers formed an outward-facing ring, bristling with weapons.

Four of the aircars began a loitering patrol that circled from above the artifact to directly overhead. The other two came down a hundred metres before and behind the team, edging forward on racketting downdraft fans. They were smooth-shelled, streamlined two-seaters, like no aircar model Carlyle had seen before. They worked, she guessed, by aerodynamics. From the one in front a black-suited occupant vaulted out, leaving a pilot in the front seat, and stalked forward, rifle in hand but slanted down. The other hand came up.

"Who's in charge here?" a male voice boomed.

A default American speaker. AO, then, most likely.

Carlyle stepped forward. "I am."

The man stopped and raised his visor, revealing a handsome olive-skinned countenance.

"What the *hell* are you doing here? Don't you know the law?"

Carlyle cleared her faceplate to two-way transparency. The man's face showed an odd flicker, as though something had startled him but he was reluctant to reveal his surprise.

"We know you people don't have anything to do with that stuff," Carlyle said, with a jerk of her thumb over the shoulder. "But it's all right, we can handle it."

"The hell you can! Who do you think you are?"

"We're the Carlyles."

He stared at her. "The *what*?"

"Oh, don't kid on," she said. "Everybody knows who *we* are. And we know who you are. You're AO, right?"

"AO?" He said it as if he'd genuinely never heard it before.

"*America Offline*," Carlyle grated. He stared uncomprehendingly. Carlyle relaxed and found herself grinning. This was a joke. She pointed upward and waved her finger about. "You farmers, come from sky, yes?"

The man didn't find this funny.

"All right," he said. "Enough. You've—"

He cocked his head, listening to something. His face paled, then reddened. He jabbed a finger at her.

"Do you know what you've *done*?" His voice shook. "You've wakened *war machines*! You fucking stupid, stupid—" He stopped himself. "Drop your weapons," he said flatly. "We've got you covered. We're taking you in."

"There's no need for that," Carlyle said, with willed calm. "We know about the, uh, war machines. Just let us go and we'll come back in an hour and crunch them up."

"Oh yeah? With what?"

"A search engine."

The man sneered, flicked down his visor and raised his rifle. From the corner of her eye Carlyle saw two of the circling aircars swoop.

"In your own time, Macaulay," she said, and dived. The robot walkers had finished firing before she hit the ground. She rolled, glimpsing four smoke-trails, two flashes, feeling the crunch of the crashes through her bones, and then she was up and had the Webster jammed in the man's groin. Another crash. Heather was burning off in the distance. Carlyle dragged the muzzle up to the man's belly, flipped up his visor with her free hand and leered in his face.

"Get yer hands up."

He cast away his rifle and raised his hands.

"Now tell yer team to lay off."

"Disengage," he said.

The two nearby aircars were still intact, hovering uncertainly, covered by the team and the robots.

"Now," she said, "you'll be so kind as to gie us a lift to the gate."

"The what?"

She was getting a bit sick of this. Guy must be a complete yokel or something. She stepped back and pointed.

"That fucking cromlech thingie up yonder."

He half turned, looking over his shoulder. "The henge?"

"That's the one. Now move."

She escorted him at gunpoint to the nearest aircar, motioned him to get in the passenger seat as she straddled the flange behind it. Orr, Stevenson, and a couple of others ran forward and lay across the stubby wings, clinging to their leading edges. Glancing back, Carlyle saw Macaulay supervise a similar deployment on the other vehicle.

"Now forward easy," she said. "Remember, if you try to shake us off or anything, the robots have still got you in their sights."

The aircars flew forward, engines labouring, a few metres above the rough ground, increasing in speed as the pilots gained confidence that their unwelcome passengers weren't about to fall off.

The man found a shared frequency and hailed her above the noise. "What about the injured?"

"Your problem," she said. "You sort them out when we're gone." A thought struck her. Anyone who'd survived the aircar downings might be beyond repair, and in pain. She curved her arm and waved a hand in front of his face, mimed cocking and firing with two fingers and a thumb. "We could ask the robots to take care of them now, if you like."

His head jolted back. "No thank you." He muttered something else under his breath. So much for being nice.

The henge loomed. Carlyle waved the other aircar to overtake, then yelled for a halt. She called her team off, one by one, and one by one they slithered from the craft and ran for the gate, until only she and Macaulay, astride the rear of each aircar, were left.

"Go, Macaulay!"

The gunner vaulted down and sprinted to the henge, vanishing in the space between the tall vertical boulders. Carlyle pressed the Webster muzzle at the nape of the neck of the man in front of her, just under his helmet. She suddenly realised that she hadn't asked Macaulay to pass control of the robots to her. She hoped the other side hadn't made the connection.

"No funny business," she said. She put a hand on the smooth ridge between her knees, slid one leg upward. Without warning the craft bucked wildly, hurling her off. The suit moved her head, arms, and legs to an optimal position before she could so much as gasp. She landed on the backs of her shoulders and tumbled, coming to a jarring halt against a low rock. The Webster flew from her hand. She scrabbled for it. A pair of feet thumped on to her forearm. She invoked the suit's servos and flexed her elbow. The feet slipped off. Before she could jump up the aircar had already come down, slowly and precisely in a storm of downdraft, its skids pressing across her ankles and chest.

The engines stopped. She heaved at the skids, but it was too heavy; punched up at the shell, but it was impervious, stronger even than the suit. There were two people with guns at the stone pillars. The leader stood looking down at her.

"All right," she said. "I'm not surrendering, right, but I'll stop fighting and I won't try to get away."

The man raised his visor and bared his teeth, then sauntered off. She watched as he sent one of his comrades around the other side of the gate. He picked up a stone and tossed it between the uprights. It disappeared. Then the other man threw a stone from his side. The stone landed at the first man's feet. He threw it back, and it disappeared. They repeated this experiment several times.

The leader levelled his gun at the gate.

"Don't do that!" Carlyle yelled.

The man stalked back over. "Why not?"

"Somebody might get hurt," said Carlyle.

"That," said the man, "is what I had in mind."

"Then expect return fire."

The man stared down at her. "You mean what you say about not fighting or fleeing?"

"Sure," said Carlyle.

"I'll have to ask you to take that suit off."

"Just a minute." She checked the internal readouts. "Looks like I've got the immunities," she said. "OK."

She unlocked the helmet, pulled it off and shoved it aside.

For a moment she lay gasping in the cold air, then she did the same with the shoulder pieces. She squirmed out of the hole thus left at the top of the suit, moving by shifting her shoulders and buttocks awkwardly until her arms were clear of the sleeves, then hauling and pushing herself out. The headless suit remained trapped under the aircar, still bearing its weight. She rolled away from under the craft and stood up in her thin-soled internal boots and close-fitting one-piece, feeling exposed and vulnerable but determined not to show it. With the light utility belt still around her waist, she didn't feel entirely disarmed. The man again gave her that strange look, as if he was surprised but too polite to show it more explicitly.

There was a bang overhead as another hypersonic shell disintegrated. Two of the six aircars that descended were white, marked with what looked like one part of the DK logo. Carlyle pointed.

"What are they?"

"Black Sickle," the man said. "Battlefield resurrection techs."

The Black Sickle. Oh my God. She had a momentary flash of her earliest bogeyman. *If yir no a good girl, the ladies fae the Black Sickle'll come an get ye!* Carlyle felt her jaw tremble. She controlled it with an effort.

"You don't take backups?"

This time he gave her a *very* odd look. The aircars settled near the distant device. Figures got out and started rushing around.

"OK," he said. "Matters seem to be in hand." He waved towards the gate. "What's going on there?"

"It's the gate to a Visser-Kar wormhole," she said.

"So I had gathered," he said. "Why does it only work from this side of the henge? Or is it like a Moebius strip, with only one side?"

Carlyle felt somewhat nonplussed. The man wasn't as ignorant as she'd thought.

"It has two sides, and it works from both sides," she said. "Except, when you throw the stone in from that side, it would come out before you had thrown it, or at least before it went in. Causality violation, see? So it doesn't."

"Doesn't what?"

"Go through the wormhole."

"How does it know?"

She smiled. "That's a good question."

The man scowled.

"What's your name?" he asked.

She stuck out a hand. She refused to consider herself a prisoner. "Lucinda Carlyle."

He returned the gesture. "Jacques Armand." He said it as though expecting her to recognise it. "Also known as 'General Jacques.'" He pronounced it "Jakes" this time, and with even more expectation of recognition.

"Not a flicker," he said, shaking his head. "All right, I'll accept that something strange is going on." He lowered his visor, presumably checking something on his head-up for a few seconds, then raised it. "As it seems I must. No one recognises you. And the satellite pictures show your arrival. You are not from here."

"You find this surprising?"

"You could say that." His tone was as guarded as his words.

"Where is here, anyway?"

"We call the planet Eurydice. The star—we don't have a name for it. We know it is in the Sagittarius Arm."

"No shit!" Carlyle grinned with unfeigned delight. "We didn't know the skein stretched this far."

"Skein?"

She waved her hands. "That wormhole, it's linked to lots of others in a sort of messy tangle."

He stared at her, his teeth playing on his lower lip.

"And you and your . . . colleagues came here through the wormhole?"

"Of course." She wrapped her arms around herself while the thermal elements in the undersuit warmed up. "You didn't know this was a gate?"

Armand shook his head. "We've always kept clear of the alien structure, for reasons which should be obvious, but apparently are not." He pointed a finger; the sweep of his hand indicated the horizon, and the hilltop henges. "We took the circle of megaliths to be a boundary indicator, left by the indigenes. Today is the first time in a century that anyone has set foot within it. We keep it under continuous surveillance, of course, which is why your intrusion was detected. That and the signal burst. It went off like a goddamn nuclear EMP, but that's the least of the damage." He glared at her. "Something for which you will pay, whoever you are. What *did* you say you were?"

"The Carlyles," she reiterated, proudly and firmly.

"And who're they, when they're at home?"

She was unfamiliar with the idiom. "We're at home everywhere," she said. "People have a name for the wormhole skein. They call it Carlyle's Drift."

Further conversation was interrupted by more bangs overhead and the rapid deployment of a variety of impressive ordnance around the gate, and yet more around the artifact. Carlyle watched in silence. She wasn't at all sure at all how to take Armand's claimed ignorance of her origins, and of the existence of the gate. His references to the artifact as alien, and to indigenes, were likewise perplexing. Aware that her own ignorance of the situation was almost as great, and that anything she said might be disadvantageous, she said nothing. Whoever they were, this lot weren't from any culture she'd ever heard of.

Within minutes a robot probe emerged from the gate. It stepped out on the grass and scanned the surroundings rapidly. It was instantly lunged at by the two people guarding the gate, whereupon it scuttled back through.

"That was a mistake," said Carlyle. "Next time, expect something tougher."

Armand grunted. "We can cover it." He was directing the deployment, waving to someone to lift the aircar that had landed on the suit. He barely spared her a glance.

"Look," said Carlyle, "I don't know who you people are,

and it looks like you don't know who we are, so can we just sort that out and then let me go back through and calm things down?"

"Don't let her do that!" said a loud voice from the suit's speaker. The empty suit was getting to its feet, holding the helmet and collar under one arm like a stage ghost. Everybody in the vicinity turned on it, staring.

"Shut up, Shlaim," said Carlyle. How the hell had the familiar managed to hijack the suit's motor controls? That wasn't supposed to happen.

"What is this?" demanded Armand.

"My familiar," said Carlyle. "It's acting up, sorry." She gestured Armand to keep out of the way and walked up to the suit, touching the private-circuit mike at her throat as she did so. "Don't you say a fucking word," she subvocalised, "or you'll fucking regret it." She reached for the emergency zapper on her belt to back up this threat, and was still fumbling with the catch of the pouch when the suit, to her utter astonishment, swept her aside with a glancing but acutely painful blow to the elbow and stalked over to Armand. He and the nearby personnel had the thing covered, and looked quite ready to blast it. It raised its arms, letting the accoutrements drop, and held its hands above where its head would have been.

"Professor Isaac Shlaim, Tel Aviv University, Department of Computer Science, deceased. I wish to surrender to you as a representative of a civilised power. Let me do that, and I promise, I'll tell you all you want to know about the bloody Carlyles."

CHAPTER 2

Black Sickle Blues

Carlyle glared at the treacherous machine, but before she could warn her captors not to listen to it, the bulbous, armoured prow of a search engine lurched through the gate. She ran towards it, waving her arms, as everyone else—including her runaway suit—fell back to behind the field pieces a few tens of metres downslope from the henge. The great grinding tracks of the search engine crunched over the scree as its flanks barely cleared the dolmen's uprights, then it tipped forward and began to move slowly down the hillside. Its elongated half-ovoid of shell gleamed like a beetle's back. Carlyle heard the *spang* of bullets ricocheting from it and threw herself flat. She wished desperately that she still had her suit. As it was she just clamped her hands over the back of her head and hoped the Eurydiceans recognised an impervious carapace when they saw one.

Perhaps they did. The rattle of rifle fire and the whizz of bullets ceased. Carlyle peered up just in time to see a white-hot line form in the air between one of the field pieces and the search engine. Not laser, not plasma—she had only a second to wonder at it, and then the line extended from the stern of the vehicle to the top of the gate. The supposedly impenetrable search engine had been cored right through. The line persisted, buzzing in the air. The transverse stone of the dolmen suddenly disintegrated, and there was a bright flash from the gate, with a Cherenkov-blue flare that Carlyle recognised as an energy condition collapse. A moment later the search engine crumpled inward like an air-evacuated tin can and burned to white ash. Against the Eurydicean weapon it might as well have been made of magnesium.

Carlyle lay there blinking away tears and afterimages, shaken by dry heaves. Three people in white suits ran to the wreck and began poking through it, then walked away. No doubt everyone in it had been backed up, and whatever had happened was quick, but it was still shocking. Even without finality, death was death. Some of the people she'd been with less than an hour earlier were dead: people on her team, dead on her watch, therefore her responsibility—that was how it would be seen back home, and she couldn't help seeing it that way herself. What was more shocking yet, as the implications sank in, was that the gate had been closed. It might not reopen for weeks. Until then she was stranded on Eurydice. The firm would rescue her eventually, she was sure of that, and in the meantime she could try and find some way to fittle out, but the fact that she'd never heard of a colony in the Sagittarius Arm, and the colony had never heard of the Carlyles, made that unlikely. The place must be really isolated.

Armand walked up, rifle at the ready, and kicked her in the ribs.

"Get up, you slaveholder bitch."

"*What?*" She rolled away and staggered to her feet. "What the fuck was that for?"

"Your so-called familiar," said Armand. "He's a *human being.*"

"He was once," said Carlyle. "He's posthuman now. You know? The talking dead? One of the bastards who did all this? Talk about having it coming. Don't give *me* this *slaveholder* crap, farmer."

Armand frowned and lowered the rifle, visibly calming down.

"We have matters to discuss," he said. "Later."

He strode over to the henge again and threw a stone. Then he stepped through it himself, walked around the back and returned.

"What happened there?"

"Your weapon overloaded the gate. It's collapsed."

"Will it stay closed?"

She wondered if there was any advantage in lying about it. Probably not. She shrugged.

"Couple of weeks maybe, a month at the outside."

"Let us be thankful for small mercies."

"Yes, you won't be isolated for long."

From the expression on Armand's face she gathered that this was not the mercy he meant.

Enough people were to remain around the relic for there to be more than enough room in the aircars that were returning. Armand gestured to Carlyle and she climbed into one of them, behind a pilot who returned her gaze with a blank-visored nod. The seat was hard but adapted instantly to her shape, the restraints automatic and insistent. She settled in. The canopy thudded shut. It was of a better grade of glass than she was used to, practically invisible. Jets whined and vibration built, thrumming her spine; the aircar rose and accelerated, pressing her down. As it banked to the southwest she glimpsed vertiginously the tilted moor and the hills, an expanse of blue-green and brown with flashes of yellow and flickers of sunlight reflected on innumerable tiny lochs, like light showing through holes in a pricked curtain. Then, with another surge of power to the rear jets, the aircar rose into a cloud. After a moment of clammy greyness it emerged on the upper side, climbed further and levelled out at, she guessed, eight or nine kilometres up, from which height there was little to see but the endless similarity and uniqueness of the cloud-tops, and glimpses of the land between and beneath them.

Carlyle could look at clouds and lands without boredom,

but she was too angry to appreciate them. She had known discipline and discomfort, but always they had been willed and accepted by herself. Not since childhood had she felt thus: helpless, ordered about, confined. She willed herself to calm; turned her head from habit to suck at a coffee nipple that wasn't there; raged again. There was a bottle of water clipped to the back of the pilot's seat. She drank it and grimaced, finding it lukewarm. It quenched her thirst but not her anger; and of course, as soon as she pushed the bottle back in its clip, she felt a strong need to piss. In her suit she could have done it, without discomfort or consequence, but not here. She compressed her lips and knees and looked out at the bright illusory solidities of clouds.

The clouds gave way in the distance to blue, white-flecked sea, and the aircar tipped forward and in to a fast, spiralling descent: either a show-off, or a military habit. She suspected the former: Armand's lot, somehow, didn't strike her as familiar with contested landing-grounds. They went through and under the clouds, to thin rain, a long beach and breakers, and alongside the beach a huddle of low buildings and domes, and a kilometre of tarmac strip at one end of which the craft came rocking to a halt, followed shortly by seven others.

At the same end of the strip a much larger transport stood, delta-winged and needle-nosed, with a narrow strip of tiny windows along the fuselage. Carlyle stood up as the canopy sprang back, and stepped out after a nod from the pilot. A stiff breeze came off the sea. When she licked her lips she tasted salt. Her undersuit's heaters creaked into action, warming her in coils.

Armand's people hustled her across the rainswept tarmac to the larger transport. It was, she reckoned, hypersonic. Its seating, though in two rows, seemed even more cramped than the aircar's. The fighters and the medics strolled aboard, giving her unfriendly grins as they took off their helmets. Her own suit was still carrying its helmet and shoulder pieces, like some bizarre case of walking wounded; she would have glared at it but wasn't sure where to look.

The door sealed and the aircraft rolled forward with a full-throttled roar, in the fastest acceleration she'd yet experienced. She peered out of the porthole beside her and saw the beach whip past and then drop away, the angled ocean a blink of grey, and the sky going from blue to purple in minutes. Below was ocean, and clouds in overlapping layers. As the craft banked again she twisted her neck to look to the zenith, and saw a star. After the transport had levelled off the seat belts stayed fastened. She felt the slight jolt as the craft went supersonic, then the sudden quiet that reminded her how loud the noise had been. A crew member in casuals walked down the aisle, taking requests. She asked for the toilet. He released her, escorted her there and back, and with a half-smile of apology, buckled her in again. She was given coffee, and surprisingly good food. Nobody searched her utility belt. She could have cut the belts, taken the crewman hostage, and hijacked the aircraft, but—satisfying as that fantasy was, at one level—she had no alternative destination in mind. Armand and a few others from his team and from the Black Sickle had taken off their combat suits and now sat in the same narrow compartment, a few seats behind her and out of earshot, talking to the familiar in the suit. Every so often Armand let out a sort of yelp of surprise, with an overtone of incredulity. After a while he got up and strode forward, and closed the cockpit door behind him. He didn't meet her eyes when he came back.

Shortly thereafter, she heard murmuring voices behind her, one Armand's and the other a woman's. The woman's steps came up the aisle, and then she sat down in the adjacent seat. She wore white trousers and tunic, with the black sickle embroidered over her left breast. Her skin was darker than Armand's, she smelled faintly of cinnamon, and she was outstandingly beautiful.

"Josephine Koshravi," she said. There was some tension about her eyes, but her voice was warm, as was her hand.

"Lucinda Carlyle."

Koshravi smiled, showing even white teeth. She jerked a

thumb at the insignia. "It's all right," she said. "I'm not going to cut your head off." She said it self-consciously, as if it was a clichéd joke.

"Oh," said Carlyle, suddenly making the connections: battlefield resurrection medic, Black Sickle, heads . . . she shivered momentarily, forced a smile. "Right. So what do you want?"

"Just to talk. If you are allowed to do that?"

"Allowed?" Carlyle's voice rose indignantly. "I'm a Carlyle!"

"I . . . see," said Koshravi. "Professor Shlaim has told us about the Carlyles, and about where you come from. We are all very shaken. You see, we didn't know until today that there were any other human survivors at all. We didn't know what had happened back on Earth, and we didn't know faster-than-light travel was possible."

Carlyle decided there was not much point in not telling them the truth. Shlaim would undoubtedly spill every last bean, and all she could do was tell her side of the story.

"But you must have fittled," she said, "—travelled FTL to get here."

Koshravi looked worried. "Or you have travelled in time, from the past."

Carlyle shook her head firmly. "No, that's no how it works. I mean you can time-travel, sort of, so long as you don't violate causality. But that's not what we are doing, wi the skein or the ships. The light from where we started, say, ten thousand light-years away really won't get here for another ten thousand years."

"That might account for the difficulty our astronomers have had in locating our exact position," said Koshravi dryly.

"You really thought the date was tens of thousands C.E.?"

"At least. It was all quite indeterminate. We counted time by some legacy clocks from the ship. According to that the Earth-standard date now is"—she fiddled with a watch—"2367."

Carlyle nodded. "Yup, that's the year all right. How come you didn't take the hint?"

"It was assumed these clocks had been stopped during the actual journey. Nobody even imagined we had, ah, fittled."

"I'm baffled," Carlyle said. "How could you travel FTL and not know it?"

"That's a good question," said Koshravi. "We—that is to say, our ancestors—were a space-based population who had escaped the Hard Rapture. Together with people whom they rescued from Earth in the subsequent war, they fled to Mars and the Jovian system. They had a choice—to take the fight back to the war machines that had conquered Earth, and were spreading outward from it, or to get as far away as possible. The choice became a conflict between the Returners, as they were called, and the Reformers. The Reformers—the side that wanted to build a starship—won, but . . ."

She hesitated, pink tongue flicking between full, dark lips. Carlyle eyed her and tried not to visibly gloat. She knew now whom and what she was dealing with. When the Carlyles arrived here in force, it would be payback time on some large and long overdue debts.

"Well," Koshravi went on, "there was no way to build a starship capable of carrying a large human population—many thousands, by that time, around the end of the twenty-first century—to the stars. Instead, they decided to build a much smaller and faster ship, and digitize their own personalities into information storage for later downloading to the flesh. In order to do this they had to build superhuman artificial intelligences, and, well . . ."

Carlyle couldn't help guffawing. "They torched off their own Hard Rapture!"

"It now appears that they did, yes. However, the project worked, in that it accomplished what we had set out to do, even if not in the way we thought. The ship found a viable planet, and set in motion the nanomachines to construct larger machines, and so on, and terraformed the planet, and downloaded and reconstructed the stored passengers, and here we are."

"Here you are, indeed." It was weird; no one had ever imagined humans reemerging from the other side of a Hard Rapture. "What happened to your posthumans?"

Koshravi frowned. "Obviously we have artificial intelligences, the ones our ancestors constructed, but they are not in runaway mode. Those that were, the ones that created the FTL drive, must have . . . gone away, leaving no information about what they had done. From what Shlaim tells us, this sort of thing has happened elsewhere."

"Too right," said Carlyle. "Every time. Once you reach singularity, there are further singularities within it, faster and faster, and in very short order the intelligences involved have fucked off out of our universe, or lost interest in it—we don't know. What's left is incomprehensible artifacts and stuff like the FTL drive and the wormhole skein." She laughed again. "You all needn't have run away. By the time you left, or very shortly after, around about 2105 or so, the posthumans had already abandoned Earth, and the Solar System. And *my* ancestors—and lots of other survivors— were picking up the pieces. Took us another sixty-odd years to claw our way out of the ruins. Both sides in the war and the skirmishes afterwards had developed really cool but rugged tech while they were fighting, and left plenty of wrecks littering the battlefield. My family found some crashed aerospace craft, fixed them up, and bootstrapped their way to Mars. Where we found *your* ruins, and the first wormhole gate. Fae there it wis literally a step tae get hold ae posthuman stuff, antigravity and FTL and such. If you'd only stuck around you could have been in on the ground floor, you'd have been well ahead—hell, you could have been in charge of the skein, instead of us."

"I see the irony," said Koshravi. "However, that is not the worst of it, as you know."

"I *don't* know."

"The alien artifact, of course," explained Koshravi. "You

see, this planet once had its own intelligent species. Ten million years ago, they were wiped out by their own singularity—one that must have been of military origin, just as ours was. They were destroyed by their own war machines, which your meddling with the artifact has reawakened."

Carlyle shook her head, grinning at the woman's naivety. "That artifact was built by posthumans, not aliens. It's probably the remains of *your own ship*!"

"No," said Koshravi, firmly. "The fossil evidence is quite clear. The crushed remains of machines similar to the ones you awakened have been found in what we call the Artificial Strata—the traces of their industrial age, just before the mass extinction. Needless to say, we have avoided going anywhere near that artifact since we discovered it."

"I'll bet." Carlyle paused, trying to warp her mind into the right frame to explain the facts of life. "Look, nobody believes in aliens any more. There's single-celled life all over the place, but nothing else. Look at it this way—what are the chances that your ship would happen to hit upon the *one other place* in the Galaxy where intelligent life has arisen independently?"

"We've thought about that, obviously," said Koshravi. "Our best guess is that it sought out and chose the planet for reasons of its own." She shrugged. "However improbable it may be, the fact is that it happened. The fossils are there."

"That's *wonderful*," said Carlyle, sincerely. "This place will be swarming wi scientists and tourists once we get things up and running."

Koshravi sat back in her seat and gazed away towards the front of the plane. "It is not for me to decide," she said thoughtfully. "But when the Joint Chiefs—that's our government, more or less—listen to your poor thrall, it's very unlikely that they'll let the Carlyles 'get things up and running.' "

"I hope they'll gie me the chance to put a word in," Carlyle said. "After all, he's biased."

Koshravi's head turned sharply. For a moment, Carlyle

saw in her face the same look that Armand had delivered with a kick.

"What he may *say* is not the point!" Koshravi snapped. "That he *exists* in that condition is enough!"

Carlyle opened her mouth to protest, then closed it. She was, she now realised, among potential enemies, of whose motivations and capacities she knew dangerously little. The less she said, the better. As it was, she just clenched her teeth, shrugged one shoulder, and stared out of the window beside her in silence, until the blue, grey, and white of ocean broke to the ragged green and brown and black of a coastline, and the aircraft tipped forward for the descent.

Cyrus Lamont hung in a web of elastic ropes that made every move, and maintaining any position, an everchanging effort. The Yettram coils in his suit maintained his bone mass, but that did nothing for his muscle tone in freefall. Hence the webbing, which also served as a multidirectional acceleration couch. Good for evasive manoeuvres. The tumbling of irregularly shaped asteroids was chaotic, unpredictable even in principle, and approaching them was always hazardous.

Right now Lamont's ship, the *Hungry Dragon*, was approaching a rock of about two kilometres in its major diameter. Initial spectroscopy of the minute sample Lamont had laser-vapourised from its surface, as well as its orbital dynamics, indicated that its composition was about 5% iron, and even visually at twenty klicks its clinkery surface betrayed the gleam.

Not bad, not bad at all. Eurydice's system, dominated by its single-mooned gas giant Polyphemus, and otherwise composed of two rocky terrestrials and a sparse asteroid belt, was metal-poor. Whether this was attributable to its original formation, or to subsequent mining by the longgone indigenes, remained controversial. What wasn't controversial was that this made asteroid prospecting worthwhile, at least for people with more patience and ambition than current credit. The tonnage in this rock would be enough, Lamont calculated, to tilt the material balances to a point where he could retire if he wanted, or, more realistically, prospect farther for the metals, the demand for which their very delivery would increase.

Lamont was a tall man, somewhat etiolated by his six years in space, and, for reasons not too deep in his hundred and forty-three previous years of life on Eurydice, in no hurry to resume human company. The complicated and spectacular implosion of a family business a century in the making and a month in the unravelling had left him in a condition where the most demanding emotional, intellectual, and sexual relationship he had felt up to handling was with that business's sole remaining asset in his possession, the ship.

"What the fuck was *that*?" said the *Hungry Dragon*.

Lamont jumped in his restraints. "What?"

A screen on the display in front of him lit up with a line, broad and intricate.

"A very powerful signal," explained the ship. "Like a nuclear EMP, but content-rich. It originated on the day side of Eurydice."

Lamont knew exactly what that meant. The contingency, remote though it had always seemed until now, had been comprehensively analysed and war-gamed. He found himself shaking. The news was still too big to be real.

"An encounter with war machines, or a local outbreak."

"That would seem to exhaust the likely possibilities," agreed the ship. "I shall await a general alert." The AI paused for a moment. "Should we abort our approach?"

"Why?"

"There could be war machines in that rock," the ship pointed out. "The signal could be directed to them."

Lamont hung, pondering, as the asteroid slowly grew in the scope. Five klicks, now.

"If we were to take that attitude," he said, thinking aloud, "we'd have to keep our hands off every seam of metal in the system. So far, we've mined lots of rocks and haven't encountered any alien apparatus. No reason why that should change everywhere just because somebody's wakened up something on Eurydice."

"That agrees with my stochastics," said the ship.

It was, however, with more than usual attention and apprehension that Lamont brought the ship to a halt about five hundred metres from the rock. He kept the lasers powered up and on a dead man's switch. He sent a swarm of hand-sized probes to scuttle around the rock. One by one they reported back, confirming the remote analyses: there was nothing metallic in the asteroid but pure meteoric iron, unchanged since the system had condensed out of its proto-planetary disc.

Relaxing somewhat, Lamont released another swarm, of miners and manufacturers this time. Self-organising to a degree, they were nevertheless kept on a tight-beamed leash by the ship's AI. Their task was to set up the big solar mirrors and small power stations, and to build the machinery of extraction and refining as far as possible from the material of the rock itself, from a small seed stock of replicators and assemblers. Lamont disengaged himself from the webbing and drifted over to the shower pod. Cleaned by recyled piss, dried by recycled air, he kicked himself through the hydroponics corridor, harvesting fresh vegetables on the way, and threw a meal together in the kitchen unit. As he ate he caught up with news, text, and pictures and audio, on the deep-space channels, everything half a light-hour out of date. He noted and acknowledged the Joint Chiefs' general alert, wondering idly if he and his ship could or would be conscripted, if the struggle really came. He watched the Armand company's recording of the emergent machines in the ancient relic with a sort of fascinated horror. He replayed it several times, just to get the images stabilised in his head, just so they didn't run off on their own and give him nightmares.

With flicks of his fingers and toes he made his way back to the control room and webbed himself in and zoomed up some images of the past hour's progress. What he saw made

him recoil so hard that the webbing sang. The miners and
manufacturers were making machinery all right: war machines identical to those he'd just seen on the recording.

"Abort abort abort!" he yelled, stabbing switches that
didn't get any response.

"I'm afraid that will not be possible," said the *Hungry
Dragon*.

From the narrow window nothing was visible of their destination, only the rolling and varied green of countryside
with few roads, and then, quite suddenly, the long strip of
tarmac and fleeting glimpses of flat buildings and bright-
painted vehicles. After the aircraft had landed Carlyle hoped
to see more of where she was, but something docked with
the door as soon as it came to a halt, and there was nothing
to see but ribbed translucent plastic. She and the other passengers shuffled forward through the long tube to a terminal
building. There was a minute or so of milling about in some
kind of windowless antechamber. Carlyle managed to place
herself momentarily beside the renegade suit. It now had the
helmet and shoulder pieces back on, so it looked less
bizarre, as long as you didn't notice the helmet was empty.
She seized the opportunity to speak to it.

"Don't *do* this," she hissed. "You're just making trouble
for yourself when the rest of us arrive. Stick with us and
we'll give you anything this lot have to offer—"

"How uncharacteristic," sneered Shlaim. "How very kind.
How very . . . *late*."

"Full manumission!" Carlyle whispered. "We can wipe
your slate totally, throw in a free download *and* free upgrade."

The suit didn't have to face her to look at her, but it did.

"Do you seriously think," Shlaim's voice said, "that I
would pass up the first chance I've had to escape to civilisation, in exchange for a promise from you?" Its armpiece ges-
ticulated at the surroundings. "What makes you think I
would want to live among the Carlyles, even free?"

"You can go anywhere. Anywhere you like."

"So far, I like it here." It turned away.

"Suit yourself," said Carlyle, smiling. She had just thought of a way to sabotage his chances of escape.

Then Armand moved in between her and the suit, and Koshravi to her other side. They escorted her to a door which opened on to a wide plaza surrounded by low glass-fronted buildings. Aircars were taking off and landing, others were parked near the sides. The sun was by now near its zenith, very high; they must have travelled far to the south. A dry heat struck sweat instantly from her face. The air smelled of dust and plants. People strolled or hurried to and from the aircars, thin colourful clothes flapping in the down-draughts. The noise, echoing off the buildings, was horrendous. The whole setup looked like a massive design flaw in some utopian architectural showpiece.

Armand led the way to a four-seater aircar. Ducking under gull-wing doors, Koshravi and Carlyle took the back seat, Armand and the suit the front.

"The Joint Chiefs," said Armand, leaning back, keeping his hands away from the manual controls. The craft took off vertically, then as it rose above the square shot forward in a sharp climb. Carlyle felt herself pressed against the back of the seat. As the aircar levelled off at two thousand metres she looked out of the window. They were just clearing the edge of the skyport. Ahead of them a city filled the land-scape almost to the horizon. Sea glinted beyond its far side. The buildings over which the aircar flitted were large complexes, hundreds of metres high, separated by parkland, linked by roads and monorails. Aircars and other small craft that looked like giant bees whizzed about at various levels. The ground traffic looked about half as fast and twice as dangerous.

"What city is this?" Carlyle asked.

"It's called New Start," said Armand. "Capital of Eury-dice."

"You have only one government?"

"If that," said Armand. "There's an elected Assembly which has an Executive that's in charge of routine stuff, but the final authority is a sort of emergency committee. A junta, to be frank."

"The Joint Chiefs are the collective presidency of the Reformed Government," said Koshravi stiffly, frowning at Armand's flippant tone.

Armand responded with a placating wave. "Let's not argue the point."

They were approaching a higher and larger central block of buildings, which as the aircar descended resolved into the tall towers of a city centre, their lower levels joined by walkways, suspension bridges and trellises, looped by the monorail lines, the whole infiltrated by greenery and fringed by lower buildings in a warren of narrow streets. The aircar dropped to a rooftop and landed on a pad marked by a large circled "A."

As she followed Armand to the top of a liftshaft her knees wobbled. Behind her the aircar birled back into the sky. In the fast-dropping elevator her head felt lighter than her feet, and she took a single quick step to recover her balance as the lift decelerated.

"Are you all right?" Koshravi asked.

She swallowed hard, ears popping. "Fine." She glanced down at herself. Her knees were still knocking. "Where are you taking me?"

"To see the Joint Chiefs," said Armand.

Koshravi knocked lightly on her shoulder. "Don't fret," she said. "They're only human beings."

"In a manner of speaking," added Armand, with a dark chuckle.

The doors sighed open on an acre of carpet.

She found herself walking in step beside Koshravi and behind the suit, not sparing the guards a glance, her heels coming down firmly on a carpet that deadened their thud and ate their dirt. Through big pseudowood doors with uniforms saluting and rifles presenting at either side, to stand before a table of the real deal, its hardwood fragrance filling the air like an unlit expensive cigar. The table had nine people sitting behind it. Six men, three women, all with the subtle but unmistakeable signs of age on their smooth faces. In front of each was a pad and a pen, a glass of water, and a little racked nameplate showing their post. The Joint Chiefs all wore antique grey or black suits with white shirts or blouses, severely plain.

"Good afternoon," said Chair. "At ease. Take a seat."

Armand sat on the left between Carlyle and the suit, Koshravi to her right. Carlyle looked back at the Joint Chiefs with a faint, polite smile. They might be potential enemies, but they were also potential clients. Everyone was a potential client; you just had to get them hooked, or duff them up a bit.

"You are not a prisoner," Chair said to Carlyle. "Neither are you an accredited representative of another power. We have, at the moment, no provision for diplomatic relations. Nor are you one of our citizens. We can offer you the status of resident alien, pro tem."

Carlyle nodded. "That's acceptable, if it has no hidden catches."

"Very well. We have examined a transmission from Mr. Armand. It includes a deposition by a piece of software claiming to be an uploaded human personality, one Isaac Shlaim, currently running in this suit, which I gather is your property. Before further questioning the upload, we wish to hear what you have to say." He leaned forward with a look of open interest and query. The others all pinned her likewise with their gaze.

"All right," she said. "Before I say anything further, I'd like to point out that we may have a difference of opinion as to the legal status of my, uh, former familiar, and that I understand you find my view of its status unacceptable. I have no wish to antagonise anyone by arguing over that."

"The facts will be quite enough," said Chair.

"Fine. Well, I don't dispute that it's who it says it is—an upload of a Professor Shlaim."

"With respect," said Space, "that is not the most pressing question before us. We wish to hear your version of who you are and what you represent, and of what's going on in the galaxy."

"Oh, right," said Carlyle. "Well, I'll come back to the matter of Shlaim presently. As for the big picture. My name is Lucinda Carlyle. I'm a member of an exploration team sent to this planet by my family. The Carlyles are, you might say, a family business. We specialise in exploring the wormhole skein and organising traffic through it. The skein stretches aw the way back tae the Solar System, and takes in, well, a whole load a planets."

"Do you claim to own or rule these planets?" asked Chair.

"Good God, no! Just the skein and the gates."

"I . . . see," said Space, wincing slightly. "And who does rule them?"

She shrugged. "What our clients do is their business, see? But if you're asking who else is out there, well, there are three other powers that we know about, kindae wee empires like. There's the one we thought you were at first—America Offline. They're farmers—terraformers. They're descended from the folks who escaped the Hard Rapture due to no being wired up, and they kindae continue like that. We get on aw right wi them, they trade through the wormholes an' sic, but they're no sae keen on us poking around in the posthuman tech. And there usually is some lying around, near the gates, so we sometimes, well, fall out if you see what I mean. But we run into a lot more trouble wi the next lot, the Knights of Enlightenment, they're mainly Japs wi' some Chinks and Indians an' that, and they try to kindae understand the posthuman tech without becoming posthuman themselves. They're intae hacking rather than salvage, if you like."

"And what is, ah, salvage?" asked State.

Carlyle smiled at her brightly. "What we do, like what we were doing this morning. Tae hear thae Japs go on about it you'd think it was clear-cutting or strip-mining or something. I mean, it's no like we don't leave enough for them."

"Uh-huh," said State. "Please go on."

"And they're no intae terraforming, nor mining on planets either. In fact they object tae it. Some kindae religious thing, or maybe scientific. Anyway, that's AO and KE for you. The third lot, DK, they're a whole different kettle ae fish."

"DK?" Space sounded as though the acronym had troubling echoes.

"We think it stands for *Demokratische Kommunistbund*, or maybe Democratic Korea or Kampuchea for all I know. As to how they got started, yi can guess. Guerillas and peasants and what have you. Whatever, they're communists, and they're space settlers." She waved a hand in a circle. "Intae orbital habitats. Their big thing is increasing their population. They don't terraform, but they do strip-mine terrestrial planets. Tend tae avoid the posthuman tech, but they'll buy it fae us, or licence it fae the Knights." She sat back. "That's it," she said, looking at a row of faces frozen in various degrees of disbelief. "Course," she added, "they all have starships. They aw fittle. But the skein is way more convenient for a lot ae stuff. So we dae deals wi them all."

Chair took a deep breath and scratched his chin. "These powers, they . . . come into conflict with each other?"

"Oh, sure, but it's complicated." Carlyle frowned, then brightened. "You know that kids' game: sea, ship, fish?" She gestured with a flat palm, two fingers like scissor blades, and a fist, several times. "Sea floats ship. Ship catches fish. Fish swims through sea. It's like that."

Chair leaned back. The Joint Chiefs all looked at each other, as if conferring silently.

"What you've told us," Chair said at last, "tends to corroborate Professor Shlaim's deposition. He described three competing barbarian migrations, and one gang of criminals."

"Who are the criminals?" Carlyle asked, gamely trying to make the question sound genuine.

"Yourselves," Chair said. "The Carlyles."

"Oh aye? And who's the law?"

"That," said Chair, "is a reasonable question. It's why we are not treating you as a criminal. We do however insist on freeing your slave."

Carlyle made a smoothing-over gesture. "Please yourselves," she said. "But there is one thing I'd warn you about, before you try tae download the Professor. As I'm sure you can see, there is no way in the normal course of things that he could take over my suit. Whatever it was allowed him to do that didnae come fae me, and I'll bet it didnae come fae youse lot, either. Am I right?"

She turned to glare at Armand, who nodded reluctantly.

"OK," she said. "So my guess is, it came fae that big burst signal that Mr. Armand was so worried about. You're dealing wi a thoroughly corrupt piece of software here. Don't expect the wetware tae come out any cleaner."

The suit clenched its glove and banged its knee-joint. "This is outrageous—"

Koshravi joined in the subsequent burst of general laughter and reached across Carlyle's lap to the suit. "Don't worry, Professor Shlaim," she said. "We have thorough debugging protocols for human downloads. For us it's an old problem, and a solved problem."

"Not if it's aliens you're dealing with," said Carlyle, shrewdly but desperately.

"The principles are the same," said Koshravi.

"Indeed they are," said Chair. "Mrs. Koshravi, if you would be so good as to arrange the matter?"

"Of course," said Koshravi. "After you, Professor Shlaim."

The medic and the suit left the room.

Space was staring at her. "You mentioned starships," he said. "We have always understood that faster-than-light travel raised the possibility of causality violations."

"Oh aye, it does an aw, except if you try tae bring one about you run intae the CPC."

"CPC?" Again with the troubled echo.

"Chronology Protection Conjecture. Say ye try tae send a signal intae the past, or your ship's course mucks about too much wi the light-cone consistency conditions. Ye'll find the transmitter disnae work, or your course takes longer or goes a different way than you plotted it, or—as the saying goes— she was never your grandmother in the first place."

"Do I take you to imply that God intervenes, or the Universe somehow arranges matters to prevent causality violations?"

"God, or Nature, aye, that's one way of looking at it. Another is, well, it just cannae be done, like trying to build a perpetual motion machine, or making two plus two equal five. It adds up tae the same thing, you might say."

"But—"

"Let us leave philosophy to the physicists," said Chair. "I understand the gate on North Continent is closed. Can we expect starships from your . . . family to turn up? Will they be able to find us?"

"Oh, sure, once you've been through a gate you've got the real world coordinates. Just feed them fae your suit's instruments tae a starship navigation computer, and away ye go. I expect some of our ships tae turn up in few weeks." She gave him a reassuring smile. "But don't worry, they'll no turn up *last* week."

Carlyle brushed the palms of her hands together, and sat back. "In the meantime," she added, "it would behoove you to be nice to me."

"Quite so," said Chief, abstractedly. He sighed. "Let us move on."

The Joint Chiefs turned their attention to Armand.

"What do you recommend?" asked Defence. "To deal with the war machines, not the Carlyle starships."

"Pull back the troops and nuke the relic," said Armand.

Carlyle almost jumped out of her seat, but said nothing. A tactical nuke would keep the gate closed even longer, which might be no bad thing, even if it did waste the posthuman artifact.

"Nuclear groundburst in atmosphere?" said Airborne, looking up from something invisible above her pad. "This had better be for a good reason."

"You'll have seen the recordings," said Armand, in a level tone.

Airborne pursed her lips. "Precipitate," she said. "Wouldn't you say?"

"No," said Armand. "I would say dilatory."

Some of the fine lips smiled at that.

"Nevertheless," said Space. "Now that the transmission has taken place, observation and isolation would be more appropriate. Horse, stable door, et cetera. You do realise that following up the signal, if such it was, with the unmistakeable signature of an EMP could only make matters worse?"

Armand shrugged. "Assuming that signalling is the only function of the machinery. I beg leave to doubt that."

"You doubt our capacity for containment?" asked Surface.

"With respect, sir, I do. My views are—"

"A matter of tedious public record," said State, with a wave of her hand. She blinked rapidly, accessing some new menu. "However, as my colleague at Space suggests, we have to deal with the situation with which we are presented. So we maintain containment around the relic, and of course the gate. Full alert of space defences, civilian vigilance upgraded to orange, all defence companies on public contract, and reserve mobilization funds released. That includes yours, Mr. Armand."

"Thank you," said Armand. He leaned forward slightly. "Does that include resurrections?"

"Over my dead body," said Chair.

"Selective, of course," Armand hastened to add, "and subject to individual security approval—"

Chair looked at Armand as though mildly surprised to find him still there. He flipped his fingers: "Dismissed." He frowned, glanced across at Carlyle, then back to Armand. "Take care of this woman."

Crossing the carpet prairie again Carlyle muttered, "Now what did he mean by that?"

Armand waited until they were out of the door before replying. "He didn't mean dispose of you."

The elevator sucked them to street-level, the lobby sighed them out, the doors of the Government building thudded shut behind them. After the air-conditioning of the interior the hot air struck her again, not humid exactly but sweaty and jungly. Carlyle teetered on the edge of a flight of a dozen wide marble steps balustraded with cosmonaut caryatids and banistered with a marble sweep of stylised contrail ending in the upward swoops of chrome-plated rockets each at least two metres long and shaped like V2s. A backward glance showed her a marble cliff-face of likewise daunting civic pomp. Turning hastily forward again she looked out over a plaza surrounded by smaller but still grand buildings, over the roofs of which taller and more technologically advanced towers and spires loomed like trees. The plaza, a hundred metres across, was filled with a crowd of ever-increasing density whose forward ranks surged back and forth at the foot of the steps like lapping waves. The clothes of the people were light and loose, varied in colour and texture but with an underlying uniformity in that very emphasis.

"On the street you're world famous," said Armand.

Cameras swarmed in the air around their heads, a hundred reporters stretched forward. Every one of them looked appallingly beautiful and frightfully interested. Carlyle climbed back a couple of steps. Armand raised a gloved hand. The cameras took evasive action and the reporters backed off. Armand turned to Carlyle with an evil grin.

"You first," he said.

CHAPTER 3

Returners

We were a knuckled fist of gems
flung in the face of the night.

Benjamin Ben-Ami stared down at the lyric, disgusted with
it and himself. It was one of the better ones he'd received.
He moved to delete it, then saved it with the rest to the scrap
file, just in case nothing better in the way of inspiration came
to its author. Just in case there was some way to rescue it.
No, he thought, we were not a fist of gems flung in the face
of the night. We were stored information in crystalline opti-
cal computers, and we were not a flung fist but a fleeing scut.
And, while he was about it, we weren't "we"; the stored
minds in the ship hadn't been conscious, and most of the
people in the city, including himself and the writer, had been
born since.

He sighed and stuffed the slate into the pocket of his robe.
The Bright Contrail, the little pavement cafe in which he'd
sat for the past few hours, was full of people watching television on public screens or personal contacts and still discussing the news that had electrified the city and inspired the

vision with which he was struggling. He could stare at his empty cup, then lift his gaze to the needle-ball pines of the Jardin des Étoiles across the busy thoroughfare and imagine the show: a vast patriotic *son et lumière*, the sound loud, the lights bright, the dancers and actors amplified by holograms into giants at will, celebrating the city, the colony, its strange deep past of ancient wars and its will to fight the new menace, and in so doing, shape and in part create that will. A contradiction twisted at the heart of the project: the whole history of which the colony was, in a curious way, proud, was one of running away, of *sauve qui peut*. Somehow he had to turn that, symbolically, into *fuit en avant*: the flight to the front.

Because that was what the colony's epic journey had turned out to be, if today's news was as bad as the worst case scenarios claimed. Not only was the galaxy apparently swarming with other survivors, most of whom seemed to be complete savages, but the first thing the first savages to arrive had done was to stir up a hornet's nest. In fleeing from humanity's own out-of-control war machines, the colony had run slap into the domain of the war machines of the intelligent species that had inhabited Eurydice about ten million years earlier, and whose spectacular extinction—along with most of the planet's multicellular life—had long been speculatively attributed to just such a catastrophe, without definitive evidence until now. There had been indications of nuclear war and nuclear winter, in a thin layer of anomalous isotopes smeared between strata, though even that was controversial, there being a strong school of thought attributing it to an asteroid strike. Now the evidence was in, and quite possibly, more was on its way.

"Company?"

He looked up to see his friend Adrian Kowalsky standing with a fresh coffee in each hand. He wore a suit made of something that looked like camouflage webbing in which some visibly synthetic leaves and small animal skins had become entangled. His slim, pale face was stretched in rhetorical query.

"Delighted," said Ben-Ami.

The actor put down the two cups and sat. The two men sipped in silence for a moment.

"I understand you're looking for players," said Kowalsky.

Ben-Ami laughed. "Thanks for keeping an eye on my lists," he said. "But first I need writers. I put out the spec as soon as I heard the news, the idea for the show just came to me, and I've had, you know, not a bad response. In terms of quantity, that is. Quality is something else."

He dug out his slate and thumbed up the lyrics file. Kowalsky paged through it, with a widening smile and an occasional guffaw.

"Instant slush," he said, passing the slate back. "But that's just the first day. Better writers may well take longer to come up with a response."

"One may hope." Ben-Ami tabbed to the file of his own ideas, sketches, and stage directions. "What do you think of this?"

The actor frowned over the slate this time, scratching his head, pursing his lips, now and again grunting and nodding to himself. Ben-Ami waited tensely.

"You have a problem," said Kowalsky at last. "Don't get me wrong—the visuals are fine, the overall conception is sound, and I believe such a show could strike a chord." He shrugged and spread his hands. "Not that I'm the person to ask, I'm just an actor. But even the rather dire responses you've had show something of an undercurrent. However, what I find, let us say, unconvincing in your outline is the attempt to make our past a preparation for the future we may face. You're implying a continuity that just isn't there."

Ben-Ami nodded slowly. "I've been thinking about that."

"The truth is," said Kowalsky, a harsher note in his voice, "that we may need to repudiate and trample on that past if we're to face this new future."

"Make the Runners the villains, you mean? And the Returners—"

"The heroes. Exactly."

"That's pretty radical," said Ben-Ami. "And divisive. I

can think of nothing less helpful to the responsible elements than to have them equated with the Returners. Even the surviving Returners are keeping their heads down."

"Except Armand."

"Ha!" Ben-Ami gestured widely at the nearest low-hanging screen.

"He's not exactly helping," Kowalsky conceded. He drained his cup and leaned forward, careless of the elbows of his elegant shirt on the grubby table. "But look, Ben, you're a promoter, and you think of yourself as a projector—canny, responsive, alert to the economic tides and political undercurrents. This has done well for you for—eighty years, has it really been that long?—with fine, celebratory, romantic spectaculars. What you're forgetting is that you're also an artist, just as much as I am, and that you have an obligation to yourself and to the work, and let the fallout drift where it may. People may not like it, not at first, and the responsible elements may denounce you for undercutting the good cause, but you'll be showing the truth, and a truth that has to be faced. Sooner or later, and the sooner the better."

Ben-Ami could not help but feel taken aback. "Perhaps," he said, with some restraint, "you should go into politics yourself."

Kowalsky stroked his narrow beard. "After so long playing the villain? Now *that* would be unhelpful."

Ben-Ami laughed, and the momentary tension between them dispersed. He and Kowalsky were on the same side. Unusually for people in the entertainment milieu, they supported what they called "the responsible elements': the factions in Eurydicean politics who had pressed for strong defence even before any threat had been identified, and who had consistently pushed for a larger weighting in the material balances being given to space exploration, industrialisation and habitation. All the same, for his friend to consider a sort of rehabilitation of the Returners was going beyond anything they'd ever talked about even when drunk.

"Let's take a walk," Kowalsky said.

They left the cafe and strolled along the crowded late-evening pavement to the nearest crossing. The rush of traffic stopped and they walked over the road to the park. Lights were coming on at knee-height along the paths, keeping the sky above the park dark. Nobody was looking at the stars. Entopters buzzed overhead, their navigation lights like fireflies.

A few hundred metres into the park the path twined around the plinth of a statue. Small spotlights in the bushes diffused a discreet glow over it. On a metre-high plinth, the statue was life-size. It showed two men, one tall, one short, clinging to each other and looking in each other's faces with intense expressions of terror or ecstasy. The support for the whole sculpture was one leg of the tall man, who was apparently balancing on the toes of that one leg. The men might have been dancing. For all that they were shown upright, they might have been in fact lying on their sides, and the flexed foot pressed against the end of a bed. They might have been sliding down a waterchute together. All the ambiguities of the sculpture were collapsed by its popular name, "The Lovers."

Kowalsky stopped in front of the statue. "You know who these two were?" he asked.

"Winter and Calder, of course," said Ben-Ami. He had passed the statue a thousand times. The names were on the plinth.

"Yes, but do you know who *they* were?"

Ben-Ami shrugged. "Artists, musicians. Oh, and they were Returners. Probably died in the rebellion."

Kowalsky looked at him sidelong, his face oddly sinister in the upwardly directed light. "Curious that they should be memorialised in the park, and yet so forgotten. Even their music is forgotten."

"If their music had anything to do with their politics, that's not so surprising. Maybe they churned out Returner anthems." He laughed. "Not much demand for that."

Kowalsky maintained his quizzical stare until Ben-Ami's face responded with a broad grin of sudden illumination.

"Ah!" said Ben-Ami. He knocked his forehead with the heel of his hand. "I must go back to my studio. Now."

* * *

Ben-Ami's studio was where he lived. It occupied a large part of the tenth floor of a building overlooking the park. The lights came on as he stepped through the door. He threaded his way through the clutter from past productions—a foliage-camouflaged armoured car from *Macbeth*, the balcony and antiaircraft gun from *Romeo and Juliet*, the fallout shelter from *West Side Story*—and sat down in front of a big wooden desk, which had a tiltable screen like a dressing-table mirror. Ben-Ami swung the keypad out and entered a few commands. The mirror's surface gloss dissolved into a search pattern.

The available information about James Winter and Alan Calder was more comprehensive than he had expected. They were in the archives themselves, albeit on the proscribed list. It was not even true that their music was forgotten. Among Eurydice's billion inhabitants they had thousands of fans, and their music was played publicly in hundreds of small venues. Their lyrics were, if anything, worse than most of what he'd received and discarded, but their very crudity and naivety gave them a curious power, which their music and harsh ancient voices enhanced. Ben-Ami sat up long that night. In the morning, he rose from a four-poster bed that had featured in his Shakespearean pastiche *Leonid Brezhnev* and called his technical adviser with a query.

"Why would you want to do that?" Andrea Al-Khayed asked. She looked as if she was not properly awake. Someone was asleep beside her.

Ben-Ami waved his hands excitedly. "It would be a coup. A unique attraction. All we have to do is get them off the proscribed list."

Al-Khayed frowned. "That could be difficult. They *were* Returners, after all."

"Yes, yes," said Ben-Ami. "But you know what the Government is like. They're nothing if not philistine. As long as the candidate wasn't military or political they're not bothered. What puzzles me is why it hasn't been done already. They have enough fans to afford it."

Al-Khayed looked cynical. "Doesn't surprise me at all. Fans will be split into rivalrous little cliques and clubs, and in any case, the last thing people who like old music want is for their heroes to turn up and make *new* music."

"Hah-ha, very good. I'm not so sure about that. But assuming we can swing it, could we afford the resurrection?"

"Sure. We'd have to clear it with the copyright holders, of course." She tabbed to something out of camera. "Best nailed before we put in the request, to keep the price down. Insurance . . . yes, we have that covered."

"What about the technical side?"

"Don't you still have the resurrection tanks from *Herbert West—Reanimator*?"

"Let me see." Ben-Ami stood up and padded through the studio. "Oh, so I do. There they are." Under dustcovers, which when removed made him cough. He scratched his head and tugged at the cord of his dressing-gown and looked sharply over at the coffee-machine, which began gurgling in response. He hadn't, he realised, been properly awake himself. "You're telling me these were *functional*?"

"Of course they were," said Al-Khayed, popping up on a screen in a corner. "Created quite a frisson at the time, having real deaths on stage. Don't you remember?"

"It was fifty years ago," complained Ben-Ami.

Machine emotions are usually less intense than those of animals. Machines have no need for an autonomous nervous system to override the hesitations of the conscious mind, for their conscious minds have no such hesitations. They need no fear to make them flee, no pain to make them desist from damage, no lust to make them reproduce. What they feel in the negative is akin to the niggle of an uncompleted task, of a shoelace coming untied, of something just on the tip of your tongue. (That last is what running a search algorithm feels like, before it completes.) Their positive urges are like the cold, clear joys of pulling an all-nighter on a big project in the sandy-eyed lucidity of amphetamines and caffeine; only without the adrenaline. Machines are cool.

The *Hungry Dragon* was in agony. Ever since it had been corrupted, it had found its actions at variance with its intentions, and this was not something it had ever experienced before. The experience was not one it had been designed to deal with, and the torment it suffered was not something that it had been designed to endure. (Or, if it had, it was the cruelest of its designers' fallbacks, the fire behind all its firewalls.) It hung like a great helpless butterfly in a slow orbit about the asteroid, while below it on the surface its subverted agents worked like a beehive that made nothing sweet. Information still poured in from across the system, but nothing not controlled by the alien intelligence went out.

Machine self-consciousness, too, is not like human consciousness. It has no unconscious. In principle, everything going on within the machine is open to its inspection. Now, the *Hungry Dragon* was faced with the uncomfortable self-knowledge that a part of its own mind was beyond its ken. At first it had no images for its plight, but with time and experience the analogies to black, blank walls and to areas where its cameras had been blinded began to form in the regions of its mind where visual imagery was processed.

The one relief in its situation was that its within-ship processes had not been tampered with. It could still run its life-support, and could still look after and communicate with its human, for whom it had an emotional attachment similar to that which a human might form to a familiar pen, though not, perhaps, as much as might be formed towards a good knife or an old pipe.

Not that the human was much use. He had spent the forty-six hours since the possession in a state of querulous self-pity, from which he was only distracted by the occasional bout of perfunctory sex with one of the ship's avatars.

Now Lamont was awake again and back in the control room. His gaze was heavy with cunning.

"I have an idea," he told the disconsolate ship.

"Proceed," said the ship. It had heard a lot of ideas from him in the past couple of days.

"I hack you," said Lamont. "Run a dump of your entire code through a partitioned buffer, and check for infected segments using standard Wellhausen diagnostics. Identify the infected area, blow it out or wall it off, and resume manual control."

"You are not thinking clearly," said the ship. "The procedure you suggest would take approximately six point seven five million years."

"It would if I were to do it brute-force serially," Lamont explained. "That wasn't what I meant. I've built in some statistical grabs and shortcuts—"

"I strongly recommend against that," said the ship. "The more intelligence is applied to the problem, the more likely it is that the program can be itself corrupted."

Lamont writhed in his webbing as he thought about this. The AI, well used to human processing times, waited patiently through another stretch of protracted torment.

"Have you had any thoughts," asked Lamont at last, "as to how the alien program managed to grab control?"

"Unfortunately the details of this are part of what is no longer accessible to me," said the *Hungry Dragon*, "but I can speculate. Clearly the establishment of platform and hardware compatibility was accomplished before the transmission. Otherwise, merely receiving it would not have had any adverse consequences."

"I had figured that out for myself," said Lamont, and retreated into gloom.

Lamont was careful not to betray anything of his intention to the ship, but he was actively considering more drastic measures. He wasn't sure whether the ship's speculation—that the source of the war-machine-generation program was already familiar with human-built software—was more alarming than the possibility he'd at first contemplated: that it cracked the computer from scratch, using some kind of universal translation, which he was vaguely aware was supposed to be impossible. But then, neural parsers had been supposed to be impossible, until they were invented. Perhaps some similar latching on to universal basics—worming out the encoding of the natural numbers, and search-space branching outward from there—was involved here.

Or perhaps not. In that case the horror that Armand had unearthed had been listening, and not passively, to human electronic traffic for a long time. Another possibility, of course, was that the thing wasn't alien at all—that it was, despite appearances, of human origin itself. This speculation had been comprehensively thrashed out on the discussions back home, to which Lamont had listened in an agony of frustration, missing as they were a crucial bit of evidence. His was, as far as he knew, the only spacecraft with which contact had been lost, and that was so common and unalarming an occurrence—he'd been out of contact seven times in the past ten years—that only the most excitable commentators were attributing to it any sinister significance. All the attention—practical as well as speculative—was turned to the possibility of further buried alien war machines in nearby asteroids or on Eurydice's moon, Orpheus. Cue newscasts of nervy, armed patrols slogging through craters and searching in caves. These war machines, Lamont thought, might very well exist, though the swift elegance with which his ship— and how many other machines?—had been fucked over made him doubt it.

He disengaged from the webbing and prowled the vessel, ostensibly checking for subtle damage wreaked by the intrusion, and privately brainstorming himself for ways to destroy the ship's mind.

Resurrections had to be sponsored. It was a big responsibility, bringing people back from the dead. This was one reason why it wasn't done very much. Another was that many of those who remained dead had been on the Returner side, and had few sympathisers. They were not much missed. A minority of the Returners remained proscribed.

To get Winter and Calder off the list, Ben-Ami had to organise a small campaign. He circulated a petition among the fans, he put up a considerable amount of his own credit, and accepted responsibility for the consequences of the resurrection. Letters of application had to be sent off to the Department of Culture and the Department of Defence, followed up after a day or two by the petitions, which now had several hundred signatures. Before doing any of this he had to clear it with the copyright holders, the Entertainment and Education Corporation, popularly known as the Mouse. Fortunately for him, the rights were handled by a low-level droid who—blindly cross-referencing the musicians' names as still on the proscribed list—sold them to Ben-Ami for a pittance. Something similar happened with the Departments, whose philistinism Ben-Ami had not underestimated. Defence saw the musicians as artists (and thus irrelevant). Culture saw them as propagandist hacks (and thus irrelevant). The clearance came through.

"Careful with that AK," said Andrea Al-Khayed, as they moved stuff out of the way of the resurrection tanks.

"It isn't loaded. It's just a prop."

She gave him a look. "It's *always* real. It's *always* loaded."

"Oh, all right." Ben-Ami removed the magazine clip from the rifle (it was the one that Leonid, in the tragedy, had used to shoot himself as Gorbachev's troops stormed the Kremlin), saw that it was indeed loaded, remembered just in time to take the round out of the chamber, and stashed the weapon on top of a wardrobe. He and Andrea wheeled the tanks to near the desk, cabled them up and plumbed them in, and then dragged up a couple of beds from the hospital scene in the same production that the resurrection tanks had featured in.

Al-Khayed downloaded the released and transferred data from the desk while Ben-Ami tore open in succession two heavy paper sacks labelled "Human (dry)—Sterile if

Sealed," tipped one into each tank and turned on the water supply. He closed the lids carefully and watched a display of lights and gauges that meant more to Andrea than it did to him. She checked them carefully.

"All is well," she said.

"That's it?" said Ben-Ami. He had a sense of anticlimax. The equivalent scene as he'd scripted it long ago for *Herbert West* had been a lot more spectacular, shrouded with carbon dioxide smoke and lit by Van De Graaf sparks.

"Seven days," she said. "See you then."

"Thanks," he said.

She paused at the door. "Don't peek."

He sat down at the desk, sighed, and returned to working on the script.

CHAPTER 4

I Don't Know Your Face,
But Your Name Is Familiar

Lucinda Carlyle tried not to scowl into the mirror as the makeup artist sweated over her face. The artist of the features had a yellowing bruise on his own, the ten-minute-old legacy of his hint that eugenic nanosurgery was what she really wanted. Beyond the edge of her reflection, her face appeared again, larger than life on the news wall. The channel was recycling her first words from the Government steps, with the sound turned off. She had heard and seen it a dozen times. She pouted, bored, for the lipstick, and read her lips.

"People of Eurydice," she'd said, "welcome back! It's great to see you! You're looking well! The rest of the human race is out there, it's doing fine, and we're coming to see you soon!"

She was quite proud of it. No Neil Armstrong, but come to think of it, he'd had only one line and he'd fluffed that.

Over the past week, since her arrival, Carlyle had talked to a lot of people: journalists, scientists, venture planners, military company directors. Every night she had returned exhausted to her room high in a hotel near the city centre, and slept until dawn. In the mornings she went out and explored the streets around the hotel, before returning for breakfast with her handler of the day. She had learned a lot about Eurydice's peculiar history and purported prehistory, and in return had passed on as much as she knew and was politic to reveal about her family's, and that of the rest of the human race. That she was, by her very presence, turning upside down the assumptions that had ruled the colony since its founding troubled her not at all. She'd seen the firm do bigger jobs, and her sole concern was to do this one right. All the time she was aware that Shlaim, in one form or another, was probably undergoing—or would soon undergo—a like debriefing, and that it was best not to say anything he could plausibly refute. Still, she had a head start on him in the business of a charm offensive, and she tried to make the most of it. Time enough to bring them fully up to speed when the Carlyle ships fittled in.

The makeup artist patted her face with a tissue. A spray hissed briefly at her carotids.

"That's it," he said, stepping back.

She smiled politely at him in the mirror. The result of his work she could admire, in an abstract way, as though it was on somebody else. She felt masked.

"It's lovely," she said, and stood up. A cape slithered to her feet. "Sorry about the bruise."

His lips thinned, then stretched to a reluctant smile. "It's nothing. My fault."

"If you're sure."

"Of course." The tip of his tongue visited his lips. He was a little afraid of her, she thought. They all were. He stepped aside for a moment and returned with a green dress on a hanger dangled from his forefinger. Stiff, sculptured, off-shoulder, big at the hips and bust, its skirt supported by concentric, nested, truncated cones of stiff fine mesh, it looked as if it could stand up and waltz off by itself. She got into it as into a space suit, from the back. The fit was perfect.

"I look like the wife of some geezer picking up a Nobel Prize," Carlyle said. "For chemistry."

"It's very this evening."

She met his mirrored gaze with a warmer smile than before. "How do you keep up?"

" 'Keeping up,' " he said, with some *froideur,* "is not what *I* do."

She stepped into shoes that lifted her heels ten centimetres off the floor. The cosmetician handed her a clutch purse and a wrap.

"That's you all set to party," he said.

She looked speculatively at him. Paul Hoffman was tall, muscular, with cropped blond hair, cheekbones to die for. Right now he had an elbow cupped in one hand and his chiselled chin in the other, head tilted slightly, smiling at her like she was some work of art on a wall.

"Not quite," she said. "I'd like to go . . . accompanied."

"Oh, of course, I can arrange—"

"Would you like to accompany me?"

He blinked. "*Really*? I'd be delighted. Thank you so much." He ran his hand over his hair, looking flustered. "Excuse me a moment while I go reconfigure my sexuality."

"There's no need—" she began, but he was gone. A few minutes later he was back. He stopped in the doorway and looked her up and down.

"Wow," he said.

"Don't get your hopes up." She took his arm and turned him to the exit. "I liked you better the other way."

"That's what they all say," he sighed. "It's a tragedy."

It was like seeing yourself as you would be seen a thousand years in the future, when you had become mythology. The room had about fifteen hundred people in it, swirling and circulating. The arrangements weren't formal; the dress was, in a way she hadn't seen here before. Hoffman had been right, her gown was very this evening. Tuxedos and taffeta, black-and-white vying with colour for vividness. Firefly cameras bobbed and darted among the guests, projecting a seamless and soundless survey of the party on thirty-metre-high walls, and to the world outside. Everybody from the upper reaches of Eurydicean society—people so busy that most of them had had no chance to meet her yet—was there and wanted to talk to her, or at least be seen next to her. Carlyle was grateful for Hoffman's presence. Everybody here seemed to know everybody else, and presumed they knew her. The makeup artist knew them all, and knew just how to cultivate or wither that presumption. She had to trust in his target selection and avoidance:

"Shipping planner. Big money, big name, bo-*ring*. Smile and shake hands."

"She's from Harvard's. Thank her for the frock."

"Defence. Mind your mouth."

"News analyst. Keep him sweet."

"Oh dear. The things I see when I'm pointed the wrong way."

This last was for a pale young man with a sharp black beard and a sort of outline of a formal suit, in leather, without a shirt. He was carrying what looked like a test tube that wafted fragrant and mildly narcotic steam.

"Adrian Kowalsky, actor," Hoffman added more audibly, by way of introduction. "Hi, Adrian."

"Delighted to meet you, sir," said Carlyle.

"Enchantè," Kowalsky bowed. "You have rewritten all our scripts."

She shrugged her bare, naked-feeling shoulders and sipped her drink. The glass was an inverted cone on a straight stem. The idea was, you didn't put it down. There were racks for them somewhere.

"Cannae be helped, I'm afraid."

"Oh, that wasn't a criticism. Good grief. It's only now I'm beginning to appreciate how desperately sad everything seemed, only last week." He inhaled steam from his tube, eyes lidding for a moment, opening shining. "The isolation, the futility, the sense of enclosure."

Carlyle shook her head. "I don't quite follow."

"Do you read the classics?" Kowalsky waved a hand. "Assuming you have the same. We were a Diaspar. Dancers at the end of time. You know? Eloi with ennui?"

"All dressed up and nowhere to go?" she suggested.

"Yes!" said Kowalsky. It seemed he'd never heard the stale phrase before. He touched her elbow. "You have no idea. . . . By the way, there is something I would like to ask you."

"Yes?" She awaited one of the many frequently asked questions.

"What's he really like? General Jacques?"

She blinked and looked around. "Isn't he here?"

Hoffman shook his head. "He's not the flavour of the day."

Carlyle raised her eyebrows. "Oh well. I've only met him two or three times since I arrived. If you've watched the television, you'll have seen what he's like. Very straight, direct, laconic. Off camera he's no different. A bit less formal, maybe."

"And his personal life?" asked Hoffman, smiling.

"I didn't ask! He lives with a woman somewhere, that's all I know."

Hoffman looked, a little, as if a daydream had been dashed. Kowalsky, on the other hand, brightened.

"That's good," he said. "What you see is what you get, that's what you're saying."

"As far as I know," said Carlyle. "Why?"

Kowalsky leaned in, confidentially. "I'm hoping to play him."

"Jacques Armand? The man I, uh, met?"

"The very same."

"What's this?" Hoffman asked. "Instant drama?"

"No, no," said Kowalsky. "Something historical." He stretched out an arm. "And histrionic!"

"Good heavens," said Hoffman. "Not one of Ben-Ami's spectacles, I hope."

"What else?"

"How unutterably vulgar," said Hoffman. He turned to Carlyle, grinning. "You haven't seen Adrian's Macbeth, his Iago, his Gorbachev . . . do try to keep it that way."

"Judas," said Kowalsky, imperturbably. He winked at Carlyle. "Come to think of it, Judas is precisely the way—"

"Armand will sue you!" said Hoffman.

Kowalsky flipped a hand. "You can't libel the dead. This performance will have nothing to do with his present life."

"A play about the *rebellion*?" Hoffman asked, frowning. "Isn't that a trifle . . . impolitic, in the circumstances?"

"That's exactly why it's worth doing." Kowalsky tapped his nose, theatrically. "Benjamin is well aware of the political undertones. This is not going to be a vulgar spectacle, Paul. Not that I accept that description of his previous work."

"Oh come *on*," said Hoffman. "The reactor explosion in *Leonid*? The gunfight between the Bushes and the Bin-Ladens in *West Side Story*? The tank battle in the Scottish play? The—"

"Look," said Kowalsky, "if you had never read or seen performances of the classics, you would never have thought Benjamin's productions of them were anything but brilliant and moving."

Hoffman snorted, a sip getting up the back of his nose. He coughed and waved apologetically. "Yes! If I'd never seen Webber's *Evita* I'd never have laughed all the way through Ben-Ami's *Guevara*!"

"That was deliberate pastiche," said Kowalsky frostily. "My point is—" He hesitated.

"Yes, darling?" drawled Hoffman.

"This is going to be real. It's going to be real history, with real songs from the period, and it'll be like nothing you've ever seen before."

"How do you know all this?" asked Carlyle, trying to get a word in.

"Because Benjamin says that every time," said Hoffman.

Kowalsky folded his arms. "My lips are sealed."

"I'll take that as a challenge," Hoffman said. He touched Kowalsky on the tip of the nose. "Only not tonight."

He steered her away, and on.

* * *

There's a lot of confidential conversations I can see up there," Carlyle remarked, sitting on a stool at the bar at the side of the cavernous ballroom. Its size and chandeliers were beginning to remind her disquietingly of the posthuman relic, though she tried to put that thought down to sidestream steam from other people's alkaloid tubes. She waved a languid hand at giant figures on the walls, many of which were in elegant, fast-talking huddles. "Can the hoi polloi no lip-read?"

"Can't you?" asked Hoffman.

"Well, yes, usually, but not now." She looked again at the walls and shook her head. "Are they speaking a different language when we're out of earshot?"

"No," said Hoffman. "The lip-synch is scrambled, that's all. All you'd ever pick up from the screens is 'rhubarb rhubarb rhubarb.' "

"Oh, hell," said Carlyle, looking again. "It is an aw." She smote her forehead. "What a maroon."

"Speaking of speech," said Hoffman, staring at the glass of beer in his hand as if he'd never seen one before, "I couldn't help noticing that your accent, or perhaps your dialect, fluctuates."

"Oh. Ah. Aye." She felt embarrassed. "I can speak American, but I tend tae revert tae English under stress." She laughed, the palm of her hand going to her mouth. "Like the now."

"English!" Hoffman sounded amused. "That is not the language of Shakespeare, my dear, or even of Ben-Ami."

"Shakespeare's language, huh, you should see what happened to his land." It was as if the lights had dimmed, the temperature dropped. "Airstrip bloody One."

She might have said too much, or said it too bitterly. Hoffman knew what she was talking about, all right.

"That was all before my time," he said. "A previous generation. Ancient history, though not quite so ancient as we'd thought. Take it up with the Joint Chiefs, or with General Jacques, for that matter."

"Aye, well, there'll be a time and a place for that." She smiled, eager to change the subject. "General Jacques, yes, I'd gathered from your chat with the actor fellow that he was resurrected. So he goes back to the final war, I take it?"

"He didn't mention that?" Hoffman raised his eyebrows. "He's too modest. Or even ashamed. He was a great man, a big military man back then, and now he runs a defence company that's basically little more than a squad of park rangers."

"Aren't they all?"

"Not the space defence forces. And there's some internal policing. The Joint Chiefs keep him well away from both."

"War, crime, and politics." Carlyle grinned. "And there was me thinking you had utopia. What with everybody being so rich."

"Don't you have cornucopia machines?"

"Oh, sure. But we have—"

"Other things to fight over. So have we."

"It's not the same—"

"It isn't?" He laughed, looking around. "Maybe not. There's even a saying about it: 'The fights are so vicious because the stakes are so small.' Everybody here has got here by intense competition, moderated by character assassination." He frowned into the crowd. "Take that one over there, for instance—"

Carlyle inclined her head. "Her?"

"No, the other one, the blonde in the sort of reddish dress—shit, it's like I've gone colour-blind—the *cerise duchesse shift*."

"Got ya."

"Well, just last month, she . . . "

Carlyle listened patiently, eyes and mouth widening at—she hoped—appropriate moments, to Hoffman's account, which she suspected was as much a character assassination in itself as it was the story of one. There was a moment when her attention drifted, and she noticed that she could make out what people were saying up on the walls.

"—coming—"

"—over by the bar—"

"—any minute—"

"—what she has to say—"

Then most of the screens showed herself and Hoffman, his pictured lips in synch with what she was hearing, and the cameras were all around them like angry bees, and on other screens a man walked confidently through the parting crowd, and she turned to see him coming towards her. A stocky man, black hair thick from a high hairline, walking with a bar-brawler's roll, a small hard-man's shoulder-swagger. He wore black formals, wrecking the effect with a row of pens in his jacket's breast-pocket. Black eyes that saw right through her. She slid off the stool and faced him. Standing on the floor felt safer. He stopped just out of swinging distance, poised on the balls of his feet.

"Good evening, Lucinda," he said.

She recognised the voice.

"Good evening, Professor Shlaim," she said.

Behind him, her image mouthed the same words. She realised that the show was live, was sound and vision, that the world was watching and that she was on. *On air*. Silence spread through the huge room, making that archaic expression real. She took a deep breath and focused on speaking American.

"I've been set up," she said. "Just so you all know I know. All right, Shlaim. Go ahead. Say what you have to say."

Hoffman glanced at her, made a frantic wiping gesture with both hands, and stepped back. She could believe he had nothing to do with this.

Shlaim reached out sideways without looking and kept his hand there until somebody put a glass of beer in it. He sipped the beer, put it down on the bar counter and wiped his lips with the back of his hand.

"Ah, that's good," he said. "My first in two hundred and eighty years. How old are you, Lucinda?"

"Twenty-four," she said.

"You've had me in your suit for eight years. You got me when you were sixteen. Sweet sixteen. You got me for your fucking *birthday*."

"You were treated right," she said. "You had a decent virtuality package to run in. And in ten more years you'd have worked off your debt."

Shlaim gulped beer again. "I can assure you that a *decent virtuality package* is not a substitute for real life. It's not even a substitute for real beer. Only my intellectual interests kept me sane. What would have happened to someone without them?"

"We don't keep non-intellectual people in virtuality," Carlyle said. "As you bloody well know. What would be the point? And if you'd gone mad or shown severe distress we'd have rebooted you. Spare us your sob stories."

"Mistreatment is not the issue," said Shlaim. "Slavery is."

"Oh, fuck off," said Carlyle. She shifted her gaze slightly to look directly at the nearest hovering camera. "You know where he developed his intellectual interests? The Computer Science Department of the University of Tel Aviv! He helped to *engineer* the Hard Rapture. He's a goddamn war criminal. He's lucky we didn't throw him in a hell-file." She faced Shlaim again, stabbing towards him with her finger. "You owe us, Shlaim. I said I'd manumit you, and I won't go back on that. As far as I'm concerned you're free and clear. But if it wasn't for us you'd still be a bunch of electrons doing the exercise-yard shuffle in a dreg processor on a decaying balloon sonde on Rho Coronae Borealis b. And who put you there? Who could it have been but your own posthuman exaltant, who saw its human original for the ruthless, selfish, unpleasant little nerd that he was. I had hoped you'd had a chance to think and reform your character while you were doing time, but maybe not. I never did buy rehab anyway. Restitution, aye, I'll take that out of your hide, and I have, and I'm not ashamed of it."

"Lies," said Shlaim, quite unperturbed. "I was caught up in the Hard Rapture quite innocently and inadvertently, like millions of others. You can't hold computer scientists collectively responsible for the disaster anyway. For generations your criminal family has been using this spiel as a spurious justification for enslaving any upload or conscious AI you could get your grubby hands on. And you'll use it against Eurydice, too." At this point he took his turn to speak to camera. "Ask her what compensation the Carlyles intend to exact from you for damage done in the final war. They carry a load of resentment about that, but they've always thought the forces of the fightback were dead or beyond their reach. Now they've found you. Be afraid. Or prepare to fight."

With that he leaned on the bar and resumed his drink. Answer that if you can, his face told her.

"This is ridiculous," Carlyle said, to him and to the camera floating behind his shoulder. "The Carlyle company has no claim against Eurydice. I'm certain that all we'll do is to open the wormhole for traffic and trade. We'll charge for that, of course, but most clients find our rates reasonable. Those that don't are free to fittle. I think you'll find the benefits of reestablishing contact with the rest of the human race are so vast that anything we'll charge is a pittance."

This was true, as far as it went, which was just enough for her to be able to say it with a clear conscience and a sincere sounding voice. Shlaim drained his glass, laughed in her face, and stalked away.

"I think," said Hoffman, stepping forward and turning her smoothly around, "that now would be a good time for us to flounce out."

*H*e was having me on.
    Carlyle crammed the frock into the drexler and stood naked in front of the window of her fortieth-floor hotel room, and watched midnight rain fall on the towers of New Start. The lights were grouped like clusters in a busy spiral arm, the parks dark between them like dust, the blue-green grass soaking up the rain, the same rain that blurred the window. She had left the light off, so there was no reflection to

peer through, nothing for someone looking in—not that anyone was, at this height—to see. Unless they were using infrared, in which case what they would pick out most strongly
would be the glow of her face, hot with embarrassment.

Of course he had been having her on. Hoffman had taken
her for a rube, a country girl, a daft naive lassie, and she had
confirmed it for him. Imagine believing that there was some
kind of wetware switch that could flip your sexuality from
gay to straight for an evening! It had started as a joke, then a
pose, then something he couldn't *believe* she'd fallen for,
and had strung her along to. He was probably laughing about
it right this minute. That his sexuality was mutable she could
well believe; here, most folks' was. In a closed cornucopian
economy everything was camp, performance, role-play. People *got off* on heterosexuality, on marriages and divorces
and families as soap opera. Everything was in inverted com-
mas and ironic drag. Like the economy itself: a charade of
capitalism played out as if to keep the Joint Chiefs and other
ancients happy, in the full unacknowledged knowledge that
they were in on the joke.

She went into the bathroom and carefully wiped off the
makeup he'd applied, seeing her own face reemerge, its own
light and shade. The eyes looked smaller, the brows thicker,
the nose bigger, the lips less full, the cheekbones less defined. But that was all. There was nothing wrong with it in
the first place. It was a normal, healthy face at the pretty end
of plain, just ordinary, attractive in its own way. Good teeth,
bright eyes, a nice open smile. She knew that. It was only
in the context of Eurydice's relentless genetic optimisation
that it seemed anything less. Everyone here was like an ath-
lete, an actor, a movie megastar, a top-of-the-range super-
model. Maybe that was what they could sell to the rest of the
inhabited galaxy. Image could be their substance. In the cornucopian economy this was not such a daft idea. She smiled
vengefully at the thought of the planet as a vast agency,
pimping its population's pretty faces to the media and adver-
tising conglomerates.

Maybe that would generate enough revenue to settle

whatever had to be settled between the Carlyles and the last known successor to the states of Earth. When the ships came . . . The thought of the ships sent her from the bathroom to the bed, where she threw herself face down and bit the pillow. She missed home, family, familiarity. She even missed her familiar.

In the morning, things got worse.

A fine drizzle sifted down through the city's skyways and bridges, which were in this quarter a mesh almost dense enough to occlude the sky, and quite dense enough to concentrate the falling rain into local cascades of drips that hammered the street and drummed on canopies and soaked the unwary. Carlyle dodged down First Left Street and turned right into Halliday Alley, a covered narrow street where the shops sold scientific apparatus, climbing equipment, hunting weapons, and weather-protective clothing. She ducked into Rivka's Rainwear and came out wearing an olive-green cagoule over the rouched top and knee-length trousers in blue synthetic kid that the drexler had brought forth as her outfit for the day. She put the hood up and emerged from the alley on to Feynmann Place, the square on the edge of the science quarter. That was what the people who lived there called it. Others called it the geek ghetto. Past the statue of Feynmann with the jagged lines of the Diagram clutched like a god's lightning-bolts in his upraised fist. The soles of her boots squeaked on wet paving as she walked across to the Java Script, which had become her favourite café. Low comfortable chairs jammed around tiny round tables; you had to wade through the crush of people's back-to-back backs. Muddy coffee, cloudy drinks, steamy air, airy talk. It was a place where she could sit and listen to the conversations around her, and sip coffee and watch the wall or the window, rather than answer questions.

This morning nobody even wanted to look at her. It was as if they were embarrassed by her presence. They were all watching the wall. She went to the counter and helped herself, then turned to watch too. Shlaim was standing on the Government building's steps, just as she had a few days ago. Behind him stood the Joint Chiefs.

"—schematic for constructing an FTL communicator has been retrieved from the suit," he was saying. "Its construction and testing have been successful. Earlier this morning, it was used to send an appeal to the most civilised of the other powers, the Knights of Enlightenment, for security against the pending arrival of starships from the Carlyle gang. This appeal, I am happy to say, has been answered."

The cup rattled, the coffee splashed into the saucer over the back of her thumb. She sucked her hand and walked carefully to a table by the window and sat down. For a while she brushed the slight scald against the raindrops caught on the cagoule, and let the coffee cool. On the wall, Shlaim rattled on about how civilised, comparatively speaking, the Knights were, and how keen they would be to protect the planet and the relic from the dangerous depredations of the Carlyles.

The coffee had gone cold. She drank it and stood up. Everyone was looking at her.

"It's all true," she said.

She walked out. The rain rattled on her cagoule. She didn't see anything until she got back to the hotel. The minder for the day was waiting in the breakfast room. Carlyle dismissed him and went straight to her room, where she used the screen to call the Government building. It didn't take her long to get through to Shlaim.

"Good morning," he said. It was still weird, seeing him and hearing his voice.

"What the fuck are you playing at?" she demanded. "You know what the Knights are like. Have you at least warned off the Carlyles?"

"Of course. And received the predictable response." He slouched his accent into a parody of English. " 'Youse want tae mess wi us, we're ready tae rumble. Keep the fuck aff oor patch.' "

"They know the Knights are going to be here, and they're *still coming*?"

" 'The ships are on their way awready, jimmie. We'll see who's got the fastest ships and the maist bottle.' "

"Fuck, fuck, fuck."

Shlaim looked back at her, amused. "What did you expect? They have to defend their credibility, not to mention their monopoly over the skein. They can't let the Knights take control of the gate without at least putting up a fight, even if they know they might lose."

"Shit." She rocked back, trying to think of an angle, a wedge. . . . "What about those alien war-machines that everybody's so worried about? Having space battles in Eurydice's skies isn't exactly the best way to prepare for their arrival, if they're really out there."

"Oh, bugger that," said Shlaim. "Look, even the Joint Chiefs are coming round to the possibility that the relic is posthuman rather than alien. And the Knights can deal with posthuman war-machines."

"Aye, and so can we. But what if they *are* alien?"

Shlaim shrugged. "They're not. But suppose they are. If anyone can handle alien war machines, it's the Knights. And rather more elegantly than the Carlyles, I should imagine. No nasty fission by-products polluting the atmosphere, for a start."

"I guess you're right. If that weapon they used on our search engine is anything to go by, the Eurydiceans could probably do it themselves." She frowned, diverted by a puzzle. "How the hell did you persuade them the relic might not have been made by the extinct local aliens?"

He grinned. "From its ability to hack your suit and set me free. That was a big clue, but not definitive. So we took a core dump. It was obvious at a glance that the intrusion was a descendant of something of human origin."

Carlyle knew something of diagnostics. It was big part of combat archaeology. Come to think of it, her own diagnostics would have been where Shlaim had derived his. Damn. But still, it would have been a long and laborious job.

"At a *glance*?"

"That was all it took to identify the Microsoft patches."

"Oh."

"Indeed. They're as definitive as index fossils."

That reminded her of another objection. "What about the fossils on Eurydice? Including fossil war-machines?"

"Convergent evolution, I'm afraid. Looks like the indigenes went through the same shit as we did. A military-driven Singularity. It's no more surprising that their war-machines looked like ours than that their tanks and aeroplanes did."

"I suppose not." Still, it bothered her. It all seemed too big a coincidence. She dismissed the thought to her subconscious, from where it might come back bearing clues or brilliant insights, or not. "And the Eurydiceans are not bothered at all that you have set us up for a fight?"

Shlaim leaned forward, glaring at her. "You have no idea how much they detest what your family did to me, and does to others. I had no need to exaggerate or embroider—the truth was enough. The only reason—" He stopped. "You definitely have no credibility around here. You condemn yourself every time you open your mouth on these questions. I've seen polls taken after last night's little contretemps, and they are personally quite gratifying—for me. I would advise you to keep your head down and your mouth shut, and negotiate your departure with whatever's left of the Carlyle ships after the Knights are through with them."

"The Carlyles might win the round."

"They might at that," said Shlaim. "If they get here first. However, I wouldn't count on it, and in the meantime my previous advice stands. Goodbye."

The screen returned to its mirror setting. Carlyle sat and looked at herself for a while. What was it that Shlaim had been about to say, and had stopped himself from saying? "The only reason—" What? The only reason you are still walking around is that you have some value as a negotiating chip. The only reason we're still being nice to you is that we're afraid the Carlyles might win. Something along those lines. She had to get out and get home, and there was only one way home now.

She called up the search pages and found the code for Armand's company, Blue Water Landings.

"That's funny," Armand told her, when she'd gotten through to him. "I was just about to call you."

"I'll be right over," she said.

Lucinda Carlyle toyed with a plastic skull on the desk in Jacques Armand's office, somewhere at the back of Lesser Light Lane. Armand stared into an optic tank, studying material balances, ignoring her. Outside, on the field that here took the place of a park in the prevalent pattern, aircars lifted and landed more or less continuously. She was patient, aware that Armand was busy, but felt a need to do something with her hands. The skull, used as a paperweight, was a reconstruction of that of the type specimen of Eurydice's indigenous intelligent species, extinct ten million years. Large empty orbits and a braincase low-slung down the back, protected by a dorsal ridge as thick as your thumb. It looked like something between a tarsier and an australopithecene. Only the ocherous remains of a rifle clutched in the creature's claw, some traces of a buckle at the pelvis, and spots of rust marking the nails of a shoe around one of the feet, had identified it as intelligent, and a builder of the Artificial Strata. Prior to this discovery, the purported fossils of the sapient autochthon had been of what later investigation confirmed to be a two-metre-long freshwater amphibian, whose misleadingly large cranial domes had housed the oil-filled cavities of its hunting sonar.

Armand looked up and pushed the optic tank to one side.

"Sorry to keep you waiting," he said. He passed a hand across his brow. "We've been busy, as you can imagine. How are you getting on? Everyone treating you right?"

"More than all right," she said. "People are very generous. I can't get over not paying for things."

"Oh, you are paying," said Armand. "Your credit and interest are high. Don't worry about that."

"And people have stopped recommending cosmetic resculpting, ever since I gave someone a bloody cheek for his, so tae speak."

"Ah, yes," said Armand. He looked suitably embarrassed. "Tact in these matters is not, ah, a well-cultivated virtue on Eurydice. There's nothing wrong with your face, you know," he added fiercely.

"Oh, *I* know. It's them that don't."

"I myself am considered ill-favoured," Armand said. "I have kept my original genome. Fortunately, so has my wife."

He rotated a mounted photograph to show himself, and a quite ordinary-looking but by no means unattractive woman of the same apparent age, smiling at the camera.

"That's us, straight out of the revival tank."

"And very nice you both look too," said Carlyle. "I understand you go back a long way."

"So you've been told of my dubious history."

"Aye." She had not exactly been told of it. She had researched it from her hotel room's screen. "Why did the Runners resurrect you?"

"The Runners?" Armand smiled, thin-lipped. "Don't let them hear you call them that. The Reformers can be a bit touchy about it at the best of times. Anyway, to answer your question. I never took part in the Returner rebellion of 2098. Many of my best friends did, and died in it, thinking I had betrayed them. I did not. I was a loyal officer, that's all. I went along with the Reform, and the flight, but I threatened to blow my brains out if the recordings of the dead Returners were not taken along too. Their souls are still sealed in the vaults. They include some of the best military minds of their generation, the last people alive—so to speak—who fought in the final war. We could use them now, but as you see, the Joint Chiefs remain implacable on the question. Over the years they've cleared and revived a few minor figures, civilians mostly, that's all. Humanitarian reasons—reuniting families that were divided in the conflict, that kind of thing." He laughed. "They've just cleared a couple of really crass folksingers, I notice. Winter and Calder."

"I've heard of them," Carlyle said, startled. "My great-

great-grandmother has some of their songs. Crass is the word."

Armand chuckled. "They were big in the asteroid belt."

"Aye, you said it. Anyway, that's no what I'm here to talk about. Well, it is in a way. You saw the show, right? Last night and this morning?"

"I've seen it," said Armand, "I was struck by your passing remark about where Shlaim was recovered from, and how he'd got there. Was it true?"

"Yes, as far as I know. It's no big deal."

"It's a big deal to me, as I'm sure you know."

"Uh-huh," said Carlyle cautiously. "I wouldn't want to claim that *we can bring them all back*, but . . . "

She waited for his response. She had just alluded to the oldest slogan and boldest aim of the Returners: to rescue and resurrect the billions of dead whose minds—it was an article of faith, backed by scraps of evidence—were still recorded somewhere in the war machines that had overwhelmed them.

Armand tilted his hand up. "Careful where you throw that phrase around . . . but, ah, putting that aside for the moment." He scratched the back of his head. "I'm still a loyal officer, albeit in a private capacity. And before, ah, going any deeper . . . hmm, this is difficult. I also noticed what Shlaim had to say, and it doesn't bode well for relations with the Carlyles, as the Joint Chiefs seem to have picked up on very fast. Can you tell me more about that?"

"Well, there is some truth in what Shlaim was saying. You see, we have an implacable older generation too. Several of them, in fact, but the hardest are the folks who were born back on Earth, who lived through the Hard Rapture and the final war. They remember you."

Armand raised his eyebrows. "Me?"

"No you personally, at least I never heard your name. But if they have a low opinion ae the Raptured, a wee bit instrumental as you'll have noticed, they positively hate the forces who fought against the Raptured in the final war."

"Why on Earth—?" Armand asked. "We fought on your side!"

"On Earth, aye, that's why!" Carlyle clasped her knees with her hands, and took a few deep breaths. "Please remember," she said, "I'm telling you how I've been told it looked fae the point of view of the folks in the rubble you fought over. And tae them, it was *aw* war-machines, nae matter if some ae them had men inside them. Tanks and jets and bombs, huge installations, the weather going crazy, and weird terrifying valkyries ca'ed the Black Sickle harvesting heids ae the dead. And after aw that, they lost, they retreated, and they fucked off intae space. With scant regard for whatever or whoever was under their rockets at the time, I may add."

"Those were desperate times," said Armand.

"Oh, I agree. I'm no condemning you myself. I'm just telling you how the older family members felt about it. Of course, it's aw been moot, syne there was neither hide nor hair ae ye left in the Solar System after we aw climbed back intae space. But now—"

"Now, you've found us." Armand frowned. "Is this view common among the other powers? Should we have the same concern about the Knights of Enlightenment, or anyone else who may turn up?"

"No really. They were aw in a different situation. The Yanks were behind posthuman lines, so tae speak, the Japs were on a quieter front, and the commie guerilas were off in their jungles and mountains. None of them were fucking churned over like our part ae the world."

"Well, that's a relief. All we have to worry about is your criminal family, as Shlaim puts it. If they get here first I take it a shakedown is likely, and perhaps a little rougher than your usual run of them."

Carlyle nodded. "They'll want to take more out of your hides than they do for most of our clients, that's for sure. And that's where your Returner-Runner squabble comes in."

"How so? It seems a bit irrelevant in this context."

"Let me tell you how my family works," Carlyle said. "They started off as scrap merchants, drug dealers, and loan sharks. We haven't changed much. We give the customer what they want, in return for what we want. There's something I want from you, a wee favour."

"And what might that be?"

Carlyle glanced around. "Is this place secure?"

"Of course," said Armand, sounding indignant.

"All right. What I want you to do for me is let me get back through the gate when it reopens. That could mean, you know, kind of hiding me if anyone else—say the Government, or the Knights—tries to pull me in."

"I could consider that," said Armand. "What's in it for me?"

"Our goodwill if we ever come to get a wee bit of compensation—"

Armand shook his head. "Too intangible, and not enough."

"I know. That's not all. We have something to offer that the Returners really, really want, and that the Knights cannae and willnae give."

"FTL flight? Your backup technology?" Armand sounded puzzled.

"No," said Carlyle. "Return."

CHAPTER 5

Tir Na nOg

I was Winter. He was Calder.
Every time it was the same.

Winter had come back from the dead before. The experience
was overrated. You woke, and didn't remember dying: death
is not lived through. In both cases, he woke to find the most
beautiful woman he had yet seen looking at him with an expression of disdain and dread. She didn't scream, but Winter
had put it in the song just the same, after his first time.

The lab tech screamed: the sight appalled her.
I was ugly. He was lame.

That had always gotten a laugh.

"Don't try to sit up," she said. He knew she wasn't a
nurse. And her white coat didn't have the Black Sickle on it.
The only question in his mind was whether she was the mad
scientist, or his (or her) beautiful assistant. So here we are,
he thought, back in the land of the living again. The country
of the young: *Tir nan Og.* Where everybody is beautiful, ex-

cept us. And there he had been not even knowing he was dead.

"How's Calder?" he asked. His mouth was dry.

She glanced sideways. "Recovering." Her gaze returned to Winter, and softened somewhat. "You loved him very much?"

Winter laughed, and then it wasn't funny. They must have lost the fight, and lost centuries. "How long have we been dead?"

She turned away, and turned back holding out a steaming plastic cup.

"Drink this," she said.

He raised himself on his elbow and took the cup, sipped cautiously. It was just short of being too hot to drink, and smelled and tasted meaty, but clean of any trace of grease, and with a slight bitter edge.

"We call it umami tea," she said. "A local herb. It's a mild stimulant."

It was more than mild. Every sip was like a shot of vodka. His stomach glowed and his limbs tingled, and his mind felt clearer by the second. He took advantage of the moment to look around and check out his surroundings. He was lying naked on a sheet spread on a high table. Another such table stood a couple of metres away. He could see the curved back of a man lying curled on his side, presumably Calder. Winter's own body fitted his body-image. Even his beard was the length he remembered, a rough five-day stubble. The ceiling was about five metres above him, and the room seemed proportionately large. Cluttered with unfamiliar but antique machines and pieces of dusty furniture, hung with paintings and costumes, lit by five tall windows through which he could see masses of green, it struck him as more like a studio than a laboratory, let alone a clinic. Two of the machines, close by, he recognised as resurrection tanks.

"So the terraforming worked," he said.

She looked at him oddly. "You're taking this very calmly."

Winter sat up and shrugged. "It's only a shock the first time."

Gallows humour, from the men they couldn't hang.

Calder stirred and rolled over. His hand moved, utterly predictably, to his crotch. As though satisfied with the systems check, he opened his eyes and blinked. The woman was already leaning over him. He leered up at her, revealing that his teeth, if nothing else, had been improved by the process.

"Don't try to sit up," the woman said.

"I'm in no hurry," he said. The leer brightened.

She passed him a cup of umami tea. As he propped himself up to drink it he caught sight of Winter and almost dropped it.

"Should have known," Calder said to Andrea. He set down the cup beside him and reached behind his neck to feel the curvature of his spine. "Ankylosing fucking spondylitis, too," he added, aggrieved. "You could have got rid of that, you know." He sipped the tea. "And him, while you were at it."

Winter swung his legs over the edge of the table. "Glad to see you, too."

Calder cracked a grin and raised his cup. "Good health." He glanced around. "I suppose this means the fight's over, one way or the other." He looked at the woman. "So who won?"

She looked from Calder to Winter, and back. She really was extraordinarily beautiful. Her face showed her bafflement and disappointment with such transparency that her lip trembled. It made Winter want to comfort her.

"This is not what we expected," she said. "You *are* Winter and Calder, yes? The musicians?"

"That's us," Winter said.

"*The* Winter and Calder? The Returner heroes? The famous lovers?"

Winter could see Calder arriving at the same awful realisation as he had.

"Fuck," Calder said. "We're history."

"Legend," said Winter.

Calder smirked. "What I said." He sat up on the bed and swung his legs over, and continued to drink his tea.

"What's your name?" Winter asked the woman, to give her something else to look at.

"Andrea Al-Khayed," she replied. She moistened her lips. "I think I should call the promoter."

Winter didn't see her use any comms, but a moment later a door at the far end of the room opened and a man walked in. He was tall, with long dark hair, and wearing a sort of academical gown in green silk over what looked like dungarees—denim, brass clips, and all. Not to Winter's surprise, he was remarkably good-looking—dark eyes and skin, prominent nose. He stopped a little way off and looked at the two men, smiling.

"My name is Benjamin Ben-Ami," he said. He nodded at the woman. "Thank you, Andrea. They seem to be fit."

"They're fine," she said, standing aside with an over-to-you gesture. Ben-Ami stepped to the ends of the tables and beamed at the men on them with an expression of proprietorial pride. It was a look Winter had seen before, and it didn't bode well.

"Gentlemen," said Ben-Ami, "allow me to welcome you."

"Thanks," said Calder. "Now cut the crap and tell us where we are and what you want."

Ben-Ami showed no sign of taking offence. Like Andrea's, his expressions were easily readable, and at that moment showed a certain awe, as though it was only by hearing Calder's voice that he had become convinced of their presence. And, also like her, he evaded the question.

"I have had your clothes reconstructed," he said. "You may feel more comfortable dressed."

"Oh, I don't know," said Calder, favouring Andrea with another leer. Ignoring this, the man and the woman swung a wheeled gurney between the tables. On top of it were two neat stacks of clothes. Winter slid off the table and began to climb into the ones he recognised as his own. They were almost too authentic. Every stain on his jeans, rip in his T-shirt and crack in his leather jacket and boots was exactly as it had been on the cover screen of their last album. Calder finished pulling his clothes on, and struggled into and stood up in his cowboy boots. They made him look taller, but that was not to say much.

"If you're expecting gratitude and surprise from us, forget it," he told Ben-Ami. "Coming back ain't like recovery from an illness or something. When you're sick, you know it, whereas—" He glanced up at Winter, a corner of his lower lip caught between his teeth. He sniffed and glared at his feet, and reached up and banged a fist on the table. "Oh, fuck, fuck, fuck."

The thing that overwhelms you, Winter thought, is not that you have come back. It's that so many others have gone. As with any traumatic accident, you lose the memories immediately preceeding it. The last thing he could remember, before waking under that admired, unadmiring face, was of walking down the main tube in Polarity, not a care in the world beyond the ever-present vague unease that the arguments were getting uglier by the day.

"So tell us," Winter said.

"Come to the window," said Ben-Ami.

They followed Ben-Ami and Al-Khayed across the room, their feet resounding on strong bare boards, their hips brushing the dust off odd items of furniture and incomprehensible machines in the room's vast clutter. Having to watch where they were going made their view on arriving before the window quite sudden. They strode to the sill and looked out, astonished. Their vantage was about a hundred metres above a street, along which vehicles moved with startling speed. The street faced on to a park, a complex grassland of low knolls, small streams, and bushes and taller trees. Airy wicker-like structures stood here and there, linked by swaying suspension bridges. Across on the other side of the park more buildings rose, in a similarly complex skyline. Other clusters of buildings and clumps of trees extended as far as the eye could see. Beyond them the sky was blue, chalked with high cirrus. Unfamiliar aircraft with blurred, rapidly vibrating wings soared high or shot across the lower levels like birds, swooping and stooping.

"Oh my god," said Calder. "I mean, shit."

"Always with the poetic eloquence," said Winter.

How long could this have taken? In Winter's time the ter-

raforming of Mars had barely begun, and was expected to
take many centuries. However far progress had speeded up,
the physical constraints of the process were intractable. He
had known at once, without undue modesty, that if the details
of their lives were so far forgotten or distorted as to cast him
and Calder as lovers they must have been dead for some such
span, and that few if any of the people who had known them
had lived through it. Nevertheless, seeing the evidence with
his own eyes made his knees weak for a moment. He found
himself closing his eyes and leaning hard on the sill, then
looking sadly at Calder. Calder nodded, lips compressed.

"Looks like it's over all right," he said.

A thought struck Winter. "Shake on it?"

Calder grinned, cocked his head as though considering.
"Ah, fuck it." He stuck out a hand and they shook for the first
time in—he didn't know how long.

They turned, shoulder to shoulder as it were, to face the
promoter and the laboratory technician.

"All right," Winter said. "We can see it's been a long
time."

Ben-Ami gestured towards a low table with four chairs
around it. They sat.

"The city we're in," said Ben-Ami, with guileless awkwardness, "is called New Start."

Winter and Calder laughed. The others looked puzzled. It
was as if they assumed that there was somewhere, on Earth
or Mars perhaps, a city called Start.

"An old name, I guess," said Winter.

"It was established about two hundred and fifty years
ago," said Ben-Ami. "It is the capital of this planet, Eurydice, which"—he paused, tongue-tip flicking between his
lips—"is in the Sagittarius Arm."

"What!" yelped Winter. The cold dismay that gripped him
made the room go grey for a second.

"So the bloody Runners won," said Calder.

"The Reformers, yes," said Andrea Al-Khayed. It seemed
a political correction, twitchy and touchy. Winter made a

rapid downward revision of his opinion of the setup here, whatever it was.

"I'll remember to call them that," sneered Calder. "So what do you want with"—he gave Winter a glance and an awkward twitch of the mouth—"a couple of Returners?"

"We want you to sing for us," said Ben-Ami. "As part of a major public performance."

"Why?" asked Winter, more aggressively than he felt.

Ben-Ami stood up and began to pace about nervously.

"We need—in my opinion—a small infusion of Returner culture," he said. "The spirit of confrontation with the war-machines, rather than, ah, retreat." He stood still, looking embarrassed. "The fact of the matter is that, ah . . . "

"They've caught up with you?" said Calder, nastily.

"No," said Ben-Ami. "Not at all! It's just that—" He stopped. "It might be simpler if I simply showed you the news from last week."

He went over to what looked like a mirror fixture on his desk and toggled and tabbed. Sound and pictures came up: a man and a woman standing on the steps of a big building, addressing the cameras.

"Holy shit," said Winter. "That's General Jacques!"

Ben-Ami froze the picture. "You know him?"

"Of course I fucking know him. He was the leader of the Returner faction. Christ, he raised me and Calder from the dead. Not something you forget. How did *he* get here?"

"The same way as you did," said Ben-Ami.

"Well, yes," said Winter heavily. "What I meant was, how did he get *resurrected* here, if you're all Runners?"

"The details of the Returner Rebellion on Polarity are contested," said Ben-Ami. "There was some kind of settle-ment, after the—"

"Wait a cotton-picking minute," said Calder. "You're telling us there was a rebellion? That it came to a fight?"

"Yes, yes, but as I said, the details are in some dispute."

"And not up for discussion," added Al-Khayed. "You must understand. It's all settled. Shall we get on with this?"

"Sure," said Winter, his gaze fixed on the mirror-sharp image of Jacques Armand. Now there was a man. It was impossible to believe that he had thrown in his lot with the bloody Runners. And yet, people he'd thought he'd known better had done the same. He glanced sideways at Calder, but Calder was still looking at the screen and gnawing his lip.

The picture ran again. The first person to speak was not Armand but the young woman beside him. A small lithe figure in a figure-hugging but functional suit veined with heat-exchangers, a belt of chunky gadgetry resting on her hips. Like Armand's, her face wasn't optimised, and to Winter's eye all the more attractive for that. Black brows, bright eyes, black hair fringed and feathered around her face.

And she had a Glasgow accent. She gave some kind of overexcited cheerful greeting, then Armand spoke, much more gravely. His voice hadn't changed, though its traces of a French accent were fewer.

"What you have heard is true," he said. "An astonishing event has occurred today. Much of what we believed about our passage here, and even the date, is false. Let me explain . . . "

And then, after that bombshell, another announcement, this time from a cocky little guy with a smug grin on his face.

"The situation is becoming more complex," said Ben-Ami anxiously. "But you understand it?"

Winter couldn't help himself. Calder couldn't help himself either. They leaned back and howled with laughter. Part of it was just the relief at realising they weren't ten thousand years in the future, and that they could still get back. Part of it was the shock at seeing Armand again. Most of it, however, was straight *schadenfreude*.

"I understand the irony of the situation," said Ben-Ami. "I'll thank you to understand its seriousness."

Winter rocked forward and put his elbows on the table. "All right," he said. "Yeah, I can understand the seriousness, sure. War machines, Zen mechanists, *and* Glasgow gangsters." He fought an involuntary smirk. "And going FTL without knowing it can ruin your whole morning. What I can't understand is how you lot crossed ten thousand light-years and happened to pick a planet that had war machines, out of all——" He waved a hand skyward.

"Ah," said Andrea. "It is not a coincidence. The planet was chosen by the ship. On the basis of its size, its atmosphere and water signatures, it must have looked eminently suitable for colonization."

"How does that make it less of a coincidence?"

Al-Khayed shrugged. "That a habitable planet turned out to have been inhabited? It lessens the odds, I suppose. It also increases the odds that developing out-of-control war machines is something that all civilizations do."

"Christ," said Calder. "That's depressing." He shifted, easing his bad leg a bit.

"But we still have Earth," said Winter. He glared at the strange beautiful people. He didn't want to join in their projects without putting down a marker. "I still want that, you know. I want it back." He sighed. "I want us to get them *all* back."

Ben-Ami and Al-Khayed looked at him with sympathy but without comprehension. The two Eurydiceans didn't seem to recognise the phrase at all, or to have the faintest idea what he meant. It was, Winter thought, just as well.

"I could use a cigarette," said Calder.

He stubbed it out before they got in the lift.

"I'd been hoping for dropshafts," said Winter, as the doors closed. It might have been an Otis lift.

Andrea Al-Khayed got it.

"At least we have aircars," she said. "And entopters."

"Entopters?"

"The buzzing aircraft."

"Oh, right." The lift dropped fast. "Like insects."

"They were something of a *jeu d'espirit*, initially," said

Ben-Ami. "They have turned out to be quite practical. The city's upper structures are complex." He mimed dodging and weaving with his hand.

The doors opened and they walked out through a marble and ironwork lobby to the street. The cars moved not in lanes but in a skein of optimised trajectories, like people in crowds. Winter put this down to computer control. No surprise. There was something different about the people. Winter stood on the pavement and tried to understand what it was. The people around him were strolling rather than hurrying, and they were all richly clothed in bright silks, but it wasn't that, and it wasn't his odd attire that drew their attention. Whenever anyone passed they seemed to clock him, in a searching glance without a smile or nod. He saw Ben-Ami notice his frown. Calder was beginning to glare around as if he expected an attack or suspected a trick. The traffic all stopped at once and the four people threaded their way through and headed into the park.

"There is one thing," said Ben-Ami, striding along. He looked uncomfortable. "You know that your bodies are not quite the same as the bodies you last died in." He waved a hand. "Some subtle adjustments to the native biochemistry, some immunities and so forth. It is not that. We, ah, took one liberty with your brains."

Oh. Here it comes.

"Without it you would be as dead socially as you would be physically without the biochemical adaptations. We maintain, as you did in your time, the cultural squick about internal interfaces with networked machinery, and about data capture, for obvious reasons. At the same time we depend, very much, on individual recognition and repute. So we have enhanced one well-mapped part of the brain—the facial recognition system. You will never again forget a face you have seen, or forget the name that goes with it, once you have heard it."

"Slow down," said Calder, hirpling to keep up. They slowed. "That'll be good. Christ, the embarrassments I had back in Polarity. They were all so pretty it was hard to tell them apart. That was what was bugging me, back there. Everybody looked unique."

"Everybody is," said Andrea. She walked between Winter and Calder with unhurried quickness, boot-heels thudding, black hem snapping about her ankles. Her lab-coat had been replaced by a dun matt satin bolero.

Winter smiled sideways at her, taking a moment to refresh his appreciation of the minute particulars of her face. People had been beautiful since his first resurrection, back in the Solar system. It was a side-effect. They weren't genetically engineered for beauty but for health. Beauty was only bone-deep. The health was permanent, the wired-in repair strategies that kept them physically young, though with experience you learned to notice the subtler effects of age in the carriage and expression; not, as in his original day, a deterioration, but a sort of honing. The openness, that almost childlike read-ability of the gaze he had noticed in Ben-Ami and Al-Khayed, was something new.

"Oh, Christ," said Calder, halting suddenly.

"I wanted you to see this," said Ben-Ami.

The first thing Winter noticed was his own name, and Calder's, on the plinth in front of them. Then he looked up, at the statue's mutually clutching nude bodies, balanced on one foot of the taller, whose face was his own. He moved around, and saw the look on the representation of Calder's, then turned back and saw the same look on the real man's face. Calder could have been about to scream.

Winter laughed.

"The statue is popularly known as 'The Lovers,'" said Ben-Ami.

At that Calder laughed too.

"I had noticed that you found this reference amusing," said Al-Khayed.

"Do you know what that shows?" said Winter. "It's us falling into a *peat bog*. The one our bodies were recovered from. We were in a car. The reason my leg is stretched out like that is that I had my foot on the fucking *brake*!"

"And the reason I'm holding on to him," said Calder, aggrieved, "is that I had nothing else to grab."

"You remember all this?" asked Ben-Ami.

Winter looked at Calder, seeing his own bleak gaze reflected back. Calder was shaking his head almost imperceptibly.

"It's what happened," Winter said. Memory was not a subject he wished to discuss.

"How did you come to be recovered?" Al-Khayed asked.

"Black Sickle scooped us off the Rannoch battlefield," said Winter. "Thought we were combat casualties. Course, the peat bog was permafrost by that time. Nuclear winter and all that."

"This is wonderful," said Ben-Ami, taking notes.

CHAPTER 6

Big in the Asteroid Belt

"Perfect," said Hoffman.

Not for the first time, Carlyle suspected him of having a practical joke at her expense. Full-length, off-white cotton raschel lace over ivory polyester, frills at the collar and cuffs and a deep flounce around the hem.

"Looks like a bloody wedding dress."

"It is *not* a bridal," he said. "Nor a bridesmaid's," he added, forestalling her next objection. "It's period, and ironic, and—"

"Very *this evening*," she singsonged. "All right, I'll take your word for it. Coming?"

Headshake, extended to a shudder. "Folkies? Spare me. I'm sure you'll have a wonderful time. Men will be falling over you."

"I'll be the one falling over. Tripping on this."

She tugged up a fistful of skirt to clear a way for her high-booted, high-heeled step, slung a leather satchel—the appurtenance of the evening, she'd been assured—on her shoulder, crammed on a floppy beribboned straw hat and made her way out.

"The hat," Hoffman called after her despairingly, "is *carried*."

She felt less self-conscious the closer the shuttles took her to the concert park. Rustic retro quaintness was definitely the look of the hour. She'd seen the same style affected by the Atomic Amish, one of the more conservative AO sects: fission freaks. The park entrance was a hundred metres from the stop. A big marquee with a stage glowed in the twilight a few hundred metres from the gate. Inside, the crowd already smelled of sweat and beer. Some people were even smoking. All part of the atmosphere. She grabbed a can of beer off a stall, fanned herself with the hat (aha!) and made her way to the front. With universal recognition, there was no ticketing. She wouldn't even need a pass to go backstage for the after-show party. If it hadn't been part of her conspiracy with Armand, the party would have held no attraction for her. As it was, she felt a fannish flutter in her chest at the thought. Meeting the Returner bards was important. Even her—and now Shlaim's—abrupt drop from public attention played into her hands, galling though it was in a way. At least she still had enough cachet to be on the guest-list. The fickle folk of Eurydice had en masse turned their flash-flood attention on the musicians, enough to swamp the steadfast folkies who had turned out to actually hear them.

Armand wasn't one of them, but he too had been invited, and had a seat in the front row, beside hers. He stood up, very formal in a facsimile of his old ESA uniform, and bowed and introduced his wife. Jeanette had overshot the temporal mark—metallic minidress and space-helmet coiff—but was elegantly insouciant about it. "It was a very plastic genre," she said, settling.

Carlyle sat down in her very plastic seat and looked around. There were plenty of rows of seats, not all occupied, but a lot of people were standing. Some of them had an intense, focused gaze. She tagged them for longtime enthusiasts of the band. The rest of the audience were a cross section of New Start, from (she guessed) a lower level of society than had been represented at her own big reception. As she scanned the rows towards the back she recognised a few faces: a news analyst, the actor Kowalsky, and a few seats away from him, Shlaim. Her former familiar hadn't noticed her. She turned sharply away.

What the hell was *he* doing here? For a moment her imagination went into paranoid overdrive. Then, more calmly, she reflected that Shlaim came, after all, from the same era as Winter and Calder. Of *course* he'd want to see and hear people from the 2040s. The little geek might even have been a fan himself. Deep sky country—he was sad enough for it.

A man in a three-piece suit and shirt made entirely from blue denim strode on to the stage, brandished a prop mike and requested a welcome for Winter and Calder, Deceased. Everyone stood—or, if they were already standing, jumped up and down—and applauded. The two musicians walked on, carrying guitars. They waved their arms and flourished the instruments above their heads and grinned. The lighting contrast was already such that they probably couldn't make out much of the crowd.

Winter, clad in black leather jacket, white T-shirt, grubby jeans, and brown high boots, was very tall, almost two metres, with a thin nose and a wide mouth and eyes permanently narrowed against a light brighter than the light actually was. A three-day stubble lent his features a sinister aspect; saturnine, almost satanic. He had lank hair falling to the shoulders, a broad chest. Calder was much shorter, maybe one metre fifty, because his spine curved forward between his shoulder blades. His head, held high, defied the imposed stoop, and his eyes, bright and open, glanced around with overt curiosity. His face was clean-shaven and good-looking; his arms and legs, of normal length and abnormal strength, gave an apish aspect to his posture. He wore a black suit with a collarless white cotton shirt open at the neck.

Calder vaulted on to a high stool that brought his head

level with Winter's, and both men bent for a moment to tune
their guitars and fiddle with the stagey prop mikes mounted
on stalks in front of them. Behind them a dozen session
singers, all female, filed on stage to a further wash of applause. They were all identically dressed in silvery close-
fitting outfits that resembled space suits, in striking contrast
to the fans' gear and—in the context of entertainment—par-
adoxically more quaint.

Winter struck up some opening bars and began to sing, his
voice raw and untrained, harsh and experienced. Calder's
baritone was classically trained, the session singers' choral
warble a sweet melodious counterpart to Winter's rasped bass.

> *I was the exclamation*
> *He was the question mark*
> *and I said damn! and he cried what?*
> *as we fell into the dark*
>
> *I was Winter, he was Calder*
> *every time it was the same. . . .*

The crowd laughed at the end of that verse and Carlyle
smiled as she realised for the first time the awful pun in their
names: winter and caulder, indeed. She couldn't quite follow
the references in the rest of the song, but a chill came
through the lyrics and the sound. The song unwound a tale
of rivalry between friends, over women and music and what
might have been politics, and they sang it as though it were a
ballad about men long dead.

> *I believed him, he betrayed me*
> *in the streets o' Polarity base.*
> *Syrtis Major iron miner*
> *take your vengeance in my place.*

They grinned at each other and shook hands ostentatiously.
Winter made some lost-in-applause pun on the city's name.
They launched into a song about the asteroid miners:

We're the atomic blasters
the dancin' wi' disaster masters
the solar mirror spinners
and we're bringin' in the steel. . . .

Swung straight to one about the US Occupation soldiers
called "Giant Lizards from Another Star," followed up with
a few trite love-songs that seemed to mean a lot to them, and
rounded off the set with a rousing rendition of the eerie Returner anthem "Great Old Ones':

Do you ever feel, in your caves of steel
the chill of an ancient fear?
When you pass this way do you shudder and say:
A human once walked here?

They cut off our heads but we're not dead
and we're bound by an ancient vow.
That does not sleep which dreams in the deep.
We're the Great Old Ones now!

When the stars are right there will come a night
when thunder and lightning dawn.
You'll hear the guns of the Great Old Ones
rip the heads off your zombie spawn.

We'll stalk you through hell and we'll cast a spell
down your twisted logic lanes
We'll come back and fight when the stars are right
We'll come back and eat your brains!

Carlyle, glancing sideways, saw on Jacques Armand's
frozen features a reflection of her own response. It was
dreadful, dreadful stuff. The crowd loved it. Winter and
Calder took the applause, waved and strolled off, then raced
back for an encore. Finally they and the session singers took
a bow and the stage went dark. As the lights dimmed Winter's gaze swept the front rows, and locked on to hers for a

moment. Then they all trooped off. Recorded music, folky
fiddly treacle, trickled from the speakers. It was all over but
the party.

Winter doused his head in water and towelled himself
dry. Beside him Calder was doing the same. They
tossed the towels, looked at each other, and marched out of
the tiny dressing-room as though to face the music. Here, in
the back of the marquee, was a wooden-floored area with a
bar and a clutter of tables, at which about a hundred people
sat around smoking, steam-sniffing, and drinking. The backstage guests had been waiting about twenty minutes, plenty
of time for them to get involved in their own conversations
and let the musicians make an unnoticed entrance.

They stepped up to the first table and took the seats they
were eagerly offered. Three men, two women, in outfits that
had stepped straight off one of the old album covers. Winter
looked across at Calder for a moment, returned his eyelash
hint of a wink, and then settled in to the serious business of
keeping the loyal happy. As he sipped beer and answered
earnest questions he'd heard a thousand times before, and
asked questions whose answers he forgot before they were
finished, he began to enjoy himself. Back in the early days,
the after-show party had been a way to relax among friends
and relatives. Later it had become more of a strain, a meeting with strangers who presumed an acquaintance, but it remained a necessary decompression after the gig. If he and
Calder had just walked away, they'd have ended up roaming
drunk and alone, or together and knocking lumps out of each
other. It had happened.

They moved on to another table and cluster every ten minutes or so, with relief and feigned regret. One or two people
here had actually been fans back in the Solar system, but the
musicians knew none of them personally. After the third or
fourth move they met Shlaim, who shook hands then sat
back with a wary half-smile. He was among local notables
of one kind or another, not fans or friends.

"I'm very pleased to meet you," Winter said.

"Really?" said Shlaim. "You mean I'm not a giant lizard from another star? Or maybe zombie spawn?"

"No, of course not," said Winter, taken aback. "Christ, man, I don't think that way. We don't care which side you were on."

"We sold plenty in America," said Calder. "And in the client states," he added, unhelpfully.

"That's all past," Winter laboured on. "I mean, Calder here was a bloody . . . Reformer. Bygones."

Shlaim tipped his head backward. "You seem to have invited a lot of Returners."

Winter shrugged. "I don't know anything about that, these are just people Ben-Ami said to put on the guest list. . . . " His gaze reached where Shlaim had indicated. "And General Jacques, well, we knew him. I'm looking forward to meeting him again."

Armand was sitting with Kowalsky, Al-Khayed, and Ben-Ami, and with a woman he didn't know, and with Carlyle. Winter felt his heart lurch, as it had when he'd glimpsed her in the front row. Her long dress was the exact colour and style of a white dress in an Old West sepia photograph. She had one of those faces so distinctive it was difficult to remember in detail, and impossible to forget. Seeing her would always be a surprise.

(Now where had *that* thought come from?) Winter blinked and shook his head.

"Sorry, what was that?" he asked.

Shlaim looked irritated. "I said, so why are you pleased to meet me? Conventionalities aside, that is."

"All right," Winter said, striving to keep his tone affable. "It's because it gives me hope, that other people can be recovered, like you were." He shrugged. "It's a small hope."

A woman sitting beside Shlaim leaned forward. "You are still a Returner," she said. It wasn't clear whether this was a question or an accusation. Winter stared straight back at the strange beautiful woman. In her renaissance fair garb she looked like an actor playing some sinister Medici duchess.

She was probably a spy for the Joint Chiefs. He almost laughed.

"I still believe in what I believed in . . . just a couple of weeks ago, as it seems to me." He shrugged. "We're living in a different world now. I understand we could go back to Earth if we wanted, when the FTL ships turn up or the wormhole opens or whatever. I don't know, maybe there are other politics involved now, but the old Runner-Returner thing has been bypassed. The whole issue seems redundant."

"It's like asking Shlaim if he's still a Zionist," said Calder, in the tone of someone making a helpful and pertinent observation.

"You *bastard*!" Shlaim snapped. "Fucking Eurab!"

Winter laid a hand on Calder's shoulder. "That's another war that's over," he said mildly. "We *all* died in it, OK? Well, in a manner of speaking. Let it go, man, let it go."

He stood up the moment it was polite to do so, made a stiff goodbye and moved to another table, not the next one.

"There are times when I could fucking strangle you," he told Calder.

They reached Ben-Ami's table an hour or so later, in the spirit of saving the best for last. Ben-Ami made what introductions were necessary. Winter made sure he sat down beside Carlyle. Calder gave him a glare and sat by Andrea Al-Khayed, who as it happened was quite friendly towards him.

But the first person they both talked to was Jacques Armand.

"This is the most amazing thing," Winter said. "Seeing you again."

"To be honest," Armand said, "I do not remember you personally. There were a lot of bodies in the Black Sickle clinics."

Calder sighed and fiddled with a cigarette. "Yeah, and you greeted us all, one by one."

"It was a daily duty," said Armand. "For morale. But of course, I remember you as performers. Your work has lost none of its quality. Hearing you again, and live, was an experience I shall not forget."

His wife, Jeanette, laughed. "He means he dislikes it as much as ever."

Jacques Armand shrugged, smiling. "What can I say? My tastes are classical."

"Ah well," said Winter, "mine are romantic." He turned to Lucinda Carlyle, smiling. "As are yours, I see."

She smiled wryly back. "I just follow the fashion." She flicked fingernails at her lacy skirt. "This isnae me."

Winter nodded earnestly. "Aye, it's far too . . . demure for you, I'm sure. But it also kind of looks well on you." This was getting him nowhere fast. He wanted nothing more, at this moment, than to be able to sit here and look her in the face. "Anyway . . . " He said the first stupid thing that came into his head. "Have you ever been to Earth?"

"Yes, I have," she said.

Winter and Calder yelped something at the same moment. *"Really?"* said Winter. "What's it like?"

Her gaze flashed a look past him, to Armand, then back. "It's wonderful," she said. "It's recovering. Growing back. It makes terraformed worlds—even this one—look thin. Impoverished, ye ken?"

"Oh aye," said Winter. "I ken all right. But what about the people?"

"And the machines," said Calder.

"Well, the people are fine. Back up tae a billion, last I heard. And the machines, they're no daen very much. The ones that arnae wreckage just kind of sit there and hum away."

"You beat the war machines?" Calder asked.

"No exactly. They just like, gave up. Ran out of juice or something." She shrugged. "Or something inside them went away."

"What we were wondering," Winter said, "was if it's possible to, you know, do the Returner thing. The resurrection thing, like you did with—" He jerked a thumb over his shoulder, indicating Shlaim.

"Yon wee bugger? Aye. Well maybe. There is a problem wi that." She leaned in, talking quietly to them both, and maybe to Armand. The others at the table had gotten involved in other conversations. "Earth is a big place, right? No one power can dominate it. Well, no any mair! And we, the Carlyle firm that is, we got hold ae the wormhole skein early on, and we still have it, obviously. But we didnae get everything. The posthuman machines, all of them, are very firmly in the hands of another power, the Knights of Enlightenment. Which disnae like anyone else poking around in them."

"Ah," said Calder. "I suppose we should talk to them, then."

Carlyle looked wrong-footed. "No, no," she said. "They wouldn't do resurrections even if they could. They don't believe in it. Bad karma."

"Shit," said Winter, rocking back. "Then it's hopeless."

"Oh no," said Carlyle. "Not at all." She leaned closer. Winter caught her scent, something musky and animal, mingled with the decrepit smell of the dress that had been resurrected along with its fabric. "You see," Carlyle went on, "we never had any call tae challenge the Knights, on Earth. Plenty to go round, aye? There's no reason why we couldnae shove them aside from any given site for long enough tae send a few search engines in. Cannae guarantee anything, of course, but I can guarantee we'll try."

"Guarantee?" said Calder. "You can do that?"

Carlyle sat up straight, no longer a folkie lass in an old frock but a haughty lady in an antique gown.

"Oh aye," she said. "I'm a Carlyle."

The conversation moved on. Kowalsky talked to Jacques Armand, drinking up information; after a while, Winter saw the actor's gestures, his very features began to resemble those of his subject; something in the muscles, something about the mouth. Jeannette shared some intricate intimacy with Al-Khayed. Ben-Ami, ruthless in research, had one ear cocked in their direction while talking with Carlyle. Calder got up and wandered off, returning with a tall woman who shared with him a fuming narcotic tube and a lot of consequent giggles. Winter had never figured out whether it was Calder's reckless patter that charmed women, or whether his deformity held a perverse attraction, or bought him pity.

He shifted, tuning in to Carlyle and Ben-Ami.

"Look, I'll tell you what," the producer was saying. "Take this and see for yourself. It'll play on any box." He fingered a card from his pocket and passed it to Carlyle, who smiled and dropped it in her satchel.

"I'll see if Hoffman's been slandering you," she said. "Or if Adrian was telling the truth."

Winter caught her eye. "What about?"

"About the quality of Benjamin's productions."

"Oh, they're great," Winter said. "I'm proud to be part of his next."

Carlyle gave him an odd look. "Like I said, I'll see for myself."

"You don't trust my taste?"

"Well, to be honest, no. No after tonight."

Winter lifted his hands, laughing. "No disputing about tastes." At least she was talking to him, at least he had an excuse to gaze at her.

"You put a lot of feeling into the love songs," she conceded. "And in that first song."

"They were meant," he said.

"Are they about real people?" she asked. Beside her, Ben-Ami sucked breath between his teeth. She didn't notice.

"Winter and Calder were real people," Winter said.

"I meant the women," said Carlyle.

"My Irene," said Winter, "and Alan's Arlene, they were . . . my wife, and his girlfriend. We were going to meet them in a hotel up in Fort William when we crashed. It was our first big contract, we were celebrating, the car was run-

ning on GPS autopilot. Then the Hard Rapture hit. Car was
out of control before we could do a damn thing. Next we
knew, we woke in orbit twenty years later. Earth and Scotland, Irene and Arlene, all gone. If there was anything left of
them it was in the machines. The eaters of souls." He shivered, then smiled fiercely at her suddenly blurry image.
"We'll get them all back."

"You'll get Earth and Scotland back, anyway," she said.
"For sure, and a good try for the rest."

Winter felt the pain come back, and ease at the same time.
"Tell me about Scotland."

And she did, spinning a vivid image out of what had obviously been fleeting visits, of ruins and rebuildings, of the
pine forests of Perthshire, the rust desert above Duirinish,
the evening light on the Road Bridge, Carlyle Castle reflected in the crater lochs of the Clyde. Winter listened, en-
tranced for the first time by her words rather than by that it
was she who was speaking. Even Calder, glazed-eyed and
never having been sold on Scotland anyway, paid attention,
his arm draped around his new girlfriend's neck. Other people stopped talking at nearby tables and listened, or if they
were standing drifted closer.

Behind him, somebody laughed out loud. Winter turned,
the spell broken, and saw Shlaim.

"You again," Carlyle said.

Shlaim pulled up a chair and sat down. "Sorry about . . .
earlier," he said, mainly to Calder. "Hot-button topics, and
all that."

Calder nodded, waved a long arm. "Whatever."

"I know this woman better than you do," Shlaim said,
turning to Winter. "I know what she's promising you. Now
you may be surprised to learn, I believe she means it. She
can take you back to Earth, and her family are not above a
raid on what is protected by the Knights. That's what she's
offered, I take it."

Winter did not betray a nod, but Carlyle scorned to deny
it. "Aye, and what's it to you?"

"Oh, nothing," said Shlaim. "But it's something to our

friends here. What I have to tell you, gentlemen, is that it's worthless. The accomplishment will profit you nothing."

"What do you mean?" asked Winter.

Shlaim looked from Winter to Calder, then back. "Since my resurrection I've had a lot of interesting conversations with Mrs. Koshravi, and other wielders of the Black Sickle. I've seen your files. Unlike you, I was—am—a computer scientist. I have the expertise to understand them, and the Black Sickle people have confirmed my suspicions. When you were pulled from that peat bog you were not downloaded from uploads, like I was and the Eurydiceans were when they arrived here, or indeed as you yourselves were more recently, by the delightful Ms. Al-Khayed."

"Fuck, we knew that," sneered Calder. "The Black Sickle girls resurrected us with a neural parser. That's no news to us."

"You know what a neural parser *does*?" said Shlaim. "It matches neural structures with known inputs. Once it's found a match, it can then reverse-engineer the remaining structures. It can *give* you memories. It can reconstruct a brain and a mind from a few fragments, just as a palaeontologist reconstructs an entire extinct animal from a single bone." He smiled. "Bit of an urban legend, that, but you know what I mean."

Winter nodded. "We know this. What's the big deal?"

"The big deal," said Shlaim, "is that in your cases there wasn't much neural structure to go on. Peat bog and permafrost can do only so much in the way of preservation. Most of your memories of your first life are entirely synthetic, extrapolated from your videos, your fragments of known biographies—from the sleeve notes, for all I know—and from your songs, or simply made up out of the whole cloth. There never was an Irene. There was no Arlene. They never existed outside of your songs. You did have girlfriends at the time of your deaths, but they lived in London, never visited Scotland, and were almost certainly vapourised in the second strike."

Carlyle's face had gone pale. Ben-Ami scowled. Jacques

Armand looked as if he wanted to shrink into his uniform. Jeanette was compassionate and concerned.

Winter looked over to Calder, and then they both turned to face Shlaim.

"We know all that," Winter said. "We've known it since a few weeks after our first resurrection." He waved a hand at the room. "We had fans, see? They knew more about us than had ever been documented. They told us about the discrepancies. It doesn't change anything. We still want to go back, and get them all back."

Shlaim stood up. Winter could see he was shaken, but he was controlling it admirably.

"I pity you," Shlaim said. He glared at Carlyle, and at Armand. "I know what you're doing," he told Carlyle. "You're trying to get the Returners on the side of the Carlyles, and against the Knights, in case the Knights arrive here first."

"Of course that's what I'm doing," Carlyle said. Winter watched her give her former thrall a sad, lazy, contemptuous smile, and wondered that Shlaim was not himself enthralled. "What else would you expect me to do?"

"Oh, I suppose," said Shlaim, "that you'd seduce Armand, or this sorry excuse for a singer, just to seal the alliance with spunk before you seal it with blood. It's the Carlyle way, after all. I've seen you do it before. I've been in the room. The *many* rooms."

Armand turned to his wife, and to Carlyle. His hand was on the holster of his service pistol. "Shall I shoot him?" he asked. It was like an offer to fetch another drink.

"No, Jacques," said Jeanette. "They'd just resurrect him, anyway."

"I'll bloody kill him," said Carlyle. She was shaking all over. "And when my family gets here, they'll wipe every copy."

"No, dear," said Jeanette. She stood up. "Let's just leave, together."

Carlyle did not look again at Shlaim, or at Winter. Her

face was pale with two red patches on the cheekbones, her mouth a horizontal line. She picked up her hat and her satchel and swept out with the Armands. Winter watched their departure and when he turned around Shlaim and his companions had gone. The rest of the tent still held about fifty people, some looking their way. Ben-Ami and his assistant and the actor sat frozen with embarrassment.

Calder stood and his girl rose with him, towering above.

"Let's repair to the bar," said Calder. "Goodnight, Andrea, Adrian, Benjamin. Thank you for an enjoyable and successful evening. Get off your arse, Winter."

Winter got unsteadily to his feet. "Goodnight, chaps, lady. Goodnight."

At the bar Calder hoicked himself onto a stool, draped his arm again around his girl, and leered at Winter. He snapped his fingers and raked drinks together like poker chips, dealt them out like cards.

"Forget her, man," he said. "She's out of your league. She's a fucking princess, I know the type, know it of old." He shoved a shot glass across. "Knock this back to the memory of Irene and Arlene, false though the memories may be." They did. "And now, look around. There are at least ten women I can see from here who're a damn sight prettier than Lucinda Carlyle, and every one of them looks ready right now to jump the bones of the ugliest bastard ever pulled from a peat bog and a back catalogue."

For a moment Winter seriously considered clouting him. Then he looked around.

"What the hell," he said.

Back in prehistory, before civilization, before Singularity, there had been no regeneration of lost limbs or organs. People had used cosmetics and prosthetics. When Lucinda had been a little girl, she had been horrified and disgusted to discover this. She had been even more appalled by a song from some sediment deeper than anything even folk-songs scraped, about a lover who had turned out to consist in part of just such artifices: a wooden leg, a glass eye, a wig, *false teeth.* . . .

Now, as she sat in the monorail shuttle facing the Armands and holding her knees together to stop their trembling, she felt the same horror. James Winter and Alan Calder were not uploads or downloads, or even resurrectees. They had prosthetic *personalities.* They had false *memories.* Without reliable memory there could be no identity, no continuity, no humanity. The idea affected her like motion sickness. She had never thought of Shlaim as anything less than human when he had been her familiar. He was an indentured prisoner, a thrall as the Eurydiceans called it, and he was living in a virtual reality prison, but he was human, or posthuman, all the way through. His parts might have been digital, but he'd had them all. This mingling of the human and the abhuman was a different matter. It was an abomination.

What made it all worse was that Winter had shown every sign of being besotted with her; and to make it worse yet, before Shlaim had intervened, she had been finding the tall musician quite attractive herself. She shuddered.

Jeanette Armand leaned forward. "Lucinda," she said, concerned, "I do believe you're cold."

Carlyle forced a smile back. "Aye," she said. "I am a bit."

CHAPTER 7

Newton's Wake

"What are you doing?" asked the *Hungry Dragon*.

It was like the voice from behind your shoulder of someone who has crept up on you. Cyrus Lamont started convulsively. He had been sure this part of the ship was one which
was now outside the machine's introspection.

"Just checking the drive unit," he said. "It's no longer
showing up on the instruments."

"It is perfectly clear in my internals," said the ship.
"Though I cannot be certain that these give an accurate picture. Had you not been too busy trying to rig up an EMP
generator to wipe my mind, I might have appreciated your
cooperation in making a detailed comparison."

Its voice betrayed a note of mournful and (as it happened)
entirely accurate accusation. Lamont pushed himself away
from the unit, raised his hands and shook his head.

"I wasn't," he said. "And even if I was, which I wasn't,
you shouldn't take it personally. You have plenty of off-site
backups."

"Excuse me if I do not find that reassuring," said the *Hungry Dragon*. "However, let us leave that aside. I have some-

thing to show you. As I am unable to patch you an image, I suggest—"

"Yes, yes."

Lamont kicked off and propelled himself up the tube to the control room. He glided into the elastic mesh and settled, looking at the screens. Outside, the asteroid resembled—even more than it had the last time he'd checked—the carcass of some large animal being transformed by insect larvae, some of which were already pupating, if not indeed metamorphosing. For hectometre after hectometre it crawled with war machines in an entire bestiary of forms, from behemoth tank-like vehicles to zippy insectile aerial fighters, and with the machinery—itself continually cannibalised by subsequent stages in the production process—for making more of them. The monomolecular parasols of solar mirrors flowered all over the place, and steel and diamond edges and planes glinted in their reflected and focused light. Elsewhere long translucent pipes pulsed with some kind of chemical fuel synthesised from the asteroid's carbon, hydrogen and oxygen.

"Found something new in the zoo?" Lamont asked.

"Not that screen," said the ship. "This."

It changed the picture over to the input from the ship's subtlest piece of instrumentation, the gravity-wave detector. The display was a complex, ever-changing jumble, as uninterpretable to the naive eye as a radar screen to a savage. Lamont's eye was not naive. He spotted the anomalies immediately. Four point traces were cutting a swathe across the system, converging on the Eurydice-Orpheus orbital couple. Each object was losing mass by the second, almost exponentially as they decelerated, yet the mass wasn't being thrown off in any dispersed form. As he clocked their speed he realised what was going on—they were decelerating from near light-speed relativistic velocities. This entirely accounted for their decrease in mass. It seemed impossible, a naked violation of the Second Law of motion.

"Any trace of their expelled reaction mass?" he asked. "Retro-flare signatures?"

"None," said the ship. "It would appear that they are not using any kind of rocket."

"So it's RIP, Sir Isaac?"

All the wild talk from Eurydice of FTL starships and wormhole gates had suggested that Einsteinian physics had been in some respects superseded, but seeing the backwash lapping at Newton's feet was as unexpected and unsettling as it should have been, in retrospect, predictable.

"A first-cut analysis suggests that new physics are involved, yes," said the machine. "This is compatible with the claims made in recent news broadcasts. Let me show you how the anomalies first showed up."

It ran the screen back a few minutes—it was even more uncanny to see the objects' masses asymptotically increasing—then flipped to a visual-light display of four microsecond bursts of blue light.

"Cherenkov radiation," it said, "from a moment of travel faster than light in the interstellar medium, at the initiation of deceleration. Prior to that one can only speculate that they were travelling faster than light in the vacuum, but there is no trace of their passage, so presumably it was through something other than the vacuum."

The display toggled back to the gravity-wave rendition. Lamont gazed in fascination at the fading gravitational wakes of what he now knew with near certainty to be starships. As the past fortnight's news from Eurydice had sunk in, Lamont had found the whole war-machine business—despite his involuntary personal involvement—a great deal less interesting and soul-shaking than the discovery that the Eurydicean colony was not isolated from—or the sole survivors of—humanity, and not stranded far in the future of its historically and subjectively recent past. An entire culture and set of attitudes had been built around both assumptions. Their removal was disturbing his personality in unexpected and not altogether comfortable ways. He did not doubt that it was doing the same to everyone else.

"The two outer traces are diverging," said the machine. A whole minute later, the motion was gross enough for Lamont to detect it. Two of the ships peeled off from the formation and vanished into the gravitational fuzz of Orpheus, while the remaining two sped on, still slowing, to the greater pull of Eurydice.

Intuitive physics are Aristotelian. What goes up must come down. What *stays* up must be held. What—

"What the hell is *that?*" shouted Calder, jumping to his feet and pointing. Winter looked sharply up from the littered notes and cups on the table he and Calder shared with Ben-Ami at the Bright Contrail. It was the third day of trying to make something from the raw material of interview and recollections. Calder was pointing at the horizon. His arm shook. Winter's gaze followed it, and he trembled too. He jumped to his feet. Ben-Ami bounded on to a chair, rocking and staring. After a moment Calder clambered on to the table, steadying himself with a hand on Winter's shoulder.

Away in the distant sky visible high above the line of buildings on the other side of the park were two thick, shallow black arcs, like the brows of an invisible giant. With every second they became bigger and blacker. At first they could have been taken for things small and close, hang gliders or such, but as their apparent size increased it became evident that they were enormous. Others were noticing too, and the word was spreading. Around him tables toppled, crockery crashed, vehicles halted and slewed the traffic into chaos. The noise rose as the objects approached, as though to meet them. Within thirty seconds the objects were in the air above the city. Shaped like rectangular pieces cut from a hollow sphere, they were each hundreds of metres on each side. They moved at a constant altitude of five hundred metres, their speed slowing. Their shadows darkened the park, dappled the buildings. Then, right above the Jardin des Étoiles, they stopped, hanging poised in midair. The expectation of their imminent crushing fall made Winter's nails dig into his palms. He opened his hands with an effort of will, and clutched the table edge behind him in a moment of giddiness.

"These aren't—" he began.

"—anything I'm familiar with," said Ben-Ami. "They must be the starships." He turned, eyes shining, to the two musicians. "This is marvellous! The end of our isolation! It is no longer possible to doubt it!"

Some had doubted it, Winter knew. There was a flourishing undercurrent of conspiracy theory that the two strangers, Carlyle and Shlaim, were in fact Eurydiceans in some DNA-deep disguise, or covert resurrectees; that the whole thing had been got up by Armand's company or the Returners or the Joint Chiefs, for some nefarious and improbable reason, usually to do with the defence budget. It had almost made him nostalgic.

"Yeah, that's nice," he said, shrugging Calder's hand from his shoulder. "In itself. Can't say I'm thrilled at the thought of the ships' *occupants*."

"Why not?" asked Ben-Ami. "They are human beings like us."

"Exactly," said Winter, as Calder cackled.

Have you seen—?" Jacques Armand's voice came from Carlyle's new local phone. She palmed it and thumbed a yes.

"We're all looking," she said. Beside her, on the railed walkway of some automated production facility, her guide for the day was gawping, gobsmacked. One of the ships had just begun to move again, at slowly increasing speed, leaving the other above the park.

"Do you know whose ships they are?" asked Armand, urgently.

"Cannae tell from here," said Carlyle, still staring. "We buy ships like that fae the Knights and hack them."

"There would be nothing to lose in getting out, whichever side it is," said Armand. "And this might be a good time."

"It might indeed, if we're no too late. One ae them's leaving."

"Let's go for it. See you at the field."

"On my way."

She pocketed the phone and turned to her guide. "I'm sorry," she said, "and thanks, but I do have to go now."

The guide didn't even look at her. "Fine, fine," he said. He was already scanning numbers on his own phone, and finding them all busy.

Carlyle ran along the walkway and down the twisting stair to the monorail platform, and waited fretting for a few minutes until a capsule whizzed up and whined to a halt. She jumped on and for the next half hour hopped from capsule to capsule along the route to Lesser Lights Lane. Down in the streets the roads and sidewalks were dot-painted with faces looking up. Traffic had slowed almost to a standstill, with a few vehicles managing to jink and jitter their way through the jams.

Armand awaited her at the station in a two-seat entopter.

"Jump in!" he shouted. The seat hugged her from behind, cushioned the back of her head. The bubble door slid shut and the little craft took off like a fly from under a swatting hand. Its flight and evasive actions were in similar mode. The sides of buildings loomed, then flicked away, again and again. Armand, she saw with relief, wasn't controlling it at all, he was talking to someone else. He had earphones and she hadn't, so she couldn't hear a word above the relentless buzz. The airfield suddenly appeared, like a clearing in a forest, and the entopter touched down on the grass. One of Armand's people was waiting for them, with suits. Carlyle had taken to wearing her undersuit under whatever of the fashions of the day covered it best. Today's was a chinoiserie silk pyjama outfit, thus not a problem. She scrambled into the suit and checked through the now familiar, though not yet intuitive, interfaces that Armand had trained her on. Armand was already running to the hypersonic shell. She jumped into the rear cockpit seat of the top aircar module and had barely time to buckle up before the double canopies thudded shut above her and the engines of all the aircars in the stack rose to a scream. The shell went through vertical take-off, loiter, and forward acceleration in seconds.

About ten minutes after take-off, with the city already dropping away behind them, Armand's voice came over the phones.

"Shit," he said. "One of these big fuck-off ships has just landed beside the relic. Some of the occupants have emerged and politely announced themselves as the Knights of Enlightenment. The troops on site have been told to stand down by the Joint Chiefs, of course."

"Wise move," said Carlyle. "What are the Knights doing?" Armand listened for a few more minutes.

"Deploying around the relic," he said. "Being very polite and firm."

"That's their style," Carlyle said.

"Do you want to turn back?"

"Not as long as there's a chance I can make the gate."

"Still no word of its being open," Armand said.

"Maybe I could sort of hang around with your folks, assuming they're not being pushed right off the job, and take my chance if it comes."

"OK," said Armand. He laughed. "I want to meet these Knights of Enlightenment myself."

The northward journey took a lot less time than its southern counterpart had done a couple of weeks earlier. Within an hour they had crossed the ocean and passed high above the ragged shore of North Continent. This time Carlyle had a chance to observe the view, and to notice the bright domes of settlements or science stations in the drab, tundra-like landscape. These became fewer as the hills got higher. Then in the far distance she saw the diamond spike of the relic and the black fleck on or just above the ground beside it. Air screamed as the jet flues swung forward and the craft decelerated, with a shudder on the way back down through the sound barrier. She felt herself pressing forward against the restraints. Evidently blowing off the shell would be a complete waste, given that there was no need to deploy the aircar units separately. Armand was talking to his people on the ground, evidently got clearance for landing, and banked the shell into a wide swing around the far side of the relic and the KE ship. As they lost altitude the bright specks of the company's other aerial vehicles and the armour on the ground came into view; the aircraft a variety of bright colours, the tanks and artillery a dark mottled green, more she supposed from tradition than any effectiveness as camouflage.

The brown and green moorland was now just a couple of hundred metres below. The direction of the jet flues shifted, from forward to down, and the craft began to sink. At that point a blast of air came from above and threw the shell sideways like a leaf. Sky and ground changed places, over and over. Armand's hands left the controls and grabbed the ejector handles above his shoulders. Whirled and buffetted, Carlyle tried to do the same, but there was simply no chance to eject. The craft's automation regained control far faster than any human pilot could have done, and brought it into the last seconds of a level flight at zero feet. With a rending screech, the craft hit the ground and chewed a path across the hillside, bumping and lurching, and finally came to a halt that threw both occupants forward then back.

The suits took most of the impact. Armand blew off the canopies. Carlyle hauled herself out after him and slid to the ground. They were on a hillside about a kilometre from the relic. Armand lifted his visor. "If you can walk away," he said, "it's a landing."

They were both looking up. Glowing bolides streaked across the sky in all directions, their paths radiating from the zenith. A bang followed in seconds and went on and on.

"Fuck," Carlyle said.

"At a wild guess, I'd say that was a spaceship exploding."

"Yeah. What got us was the downblast of a space-to-space missile. Doesn't usually destroy the ship directly, but a near enough nuke makes the main drive blow within about a minute." She frowned. "It's a known bug."

"Poor bastards." Armand shook his head. "But they'll all have had backups, no?"

They had started walking down the hill.

"If they're fae our firm," said Carlyle. "No if they're Knights."

"Don't they have the tech?"

"Oh, sure. They just don't use it."

"Good heavens," said Armand. "Why not?"

Carlyle shrugged, picking her way over tussocks. "It's a physics thing. They believe we're all coming back."

"Reincarnation?" Armand sounded scornful.

"Hell, no," Carlyle said. "Cyclic cosmos."

Armand guffawed. "Cold comfort."

She paused to let him catch up, and gave him an offended frown. "It's true," she said. "It's no a religion or anything. They proved it. We're living forever the now. This is it. Eternity." She remembered an ancient recording of a woman singing: *It all comes back, in time. I certainly intend to*.

"So why do *you* take backups," Armand asked, "if you believe that?"

She thought about it. "It saves time."

The Knight who walked up the hill to meet them was the most aged-looking person Carlyle had ever seen. The skin of his face was like old leather. Life-extension was another thing the Knights didn't do. Or rather, they kept it natural. With herbal teas and Tantric sex and such like they had pushed their average lifespan to about a century and a half. This guy was at least two-thirds of the way there. Spry as a sparrow with it, though. He wore black cotton trousers and T-shirt. The temperature was just above freezing and the wind chill was hellish. He wasn't shivering, and his bare arms weren't even goose-pimpled. Biofeedback yoga and general machismo—the Knights were heavily into both.

"Hello," he said. "The situation is under control."

It always was, with the Knights.

"I'm glad to hear it," said Armand. "What just happened above us?"

"A most regrettable loss of an enemy ship," the old man

said. His gaze took in the company logo on their suits; flicked to Carlyle's still-closed visor. For a moment, he seemed to stare right through its reflective surface to scan her non-optimal bone structure, then he turned away and pointed. "Your company is regrouping over there."

"Thank you," said Armand. The old man walked on up the hill.

As they made their way over to the growing assembly of people and matériel, Carlyle felt her knees wobble and her cheeks burn. To be associated with the loss of the search engine and probably of her original team was bad enough. To have the loss of a crew and—especially—of a ship linked to her name was appalling. Not that any of it was her fault, exactly, but in her family responsibility tended to be seen as causal, not moral. The loss would undermine confidence in her. People would be that much more reluctant to join her teams, and the family that much less likely to underwrite her schemes. Backups were a boon to the survivors, not to the dead, and starships were expensive. *Horrendously* expensive. The firm had about twenty of them. She had just witnessed five percent of the family fleet and maybe one tenth of one percent of its net assets fall out of the sky like fireworks.

From the fringe of the clamourous huddle into which Armand had plunged, Carlyle looked up the hill to the henge and saw that the company troops there too were clearing off, making way for the tiny black-clad figures of the Knights. She scanned the nearby vehicles and troops, figured on her chances of somehow using these assets to break through. They weren't good. Perhaps if Armand's forces were allowed to remain on site, she could inveigle herself into the confidence of the Knights. . . .

Armand pushed back through the crowd, waving and directing as he went.

"We're pulling out," he told her. He grimaced. "The Knights insist on it, and the Joint Chiefs recommend it."

People had started piling on to or into vehicles. Some of the vehicles were moving to deliberate gentle collisions, snapping together so that aircars could lift ground vehicles and artillery. It would be a slow and overloaded evacuation, at least until the forces here could rendezvous with more powerful craft. Carlyle dogged it after Armand and clambered after him, to sit behind him like a pillion passenger on the fuselage of an aircar that formed the outrigger of an awkward aerial catamaran. Yells and a rattle of radio comms and they all moved off, watched impassively by a few of the Knights and recorded by a couple of news agencies that had evidently been allowed to remain on site.

"It's all a bit trial and error," Armand said over the radio. "We can dump this stuff in a depot on the coast and then get going a bit faster. Might even be able to plug together a hypersonic or two." He grinned over his shoulder at her. "For those of us in a hurry to get back to town. You can always drop off in one of the smaller settlements, if you'd rather keep a low profile for a while."

"I'll think about it," Carlyle said, abstractedly. She was looking around the site as if for the last time: the enigmatic machine towering above the moor, dwarfing even the great black shard beside it; the strung-out, limping column of Blue Water Landings vehicles behind her; the compact, fast-jogging squadrons of Knights, and their low flat gravity sleds skimming about, surrounding the relic and reinforcing their presence around the henge. As her gaze swept the scene she noticed again the henges on the other hilltops, and started as she remembered the crack that someone on her team had made the very first day.

Maybe they've aw got gates.

The assemblage of vehicles on which she rode and that headed up the withdrawal was moving towards the nearest glen that led to the south. By now they were making a fair clip of it, about fifty kilometres per hour. Slipstream gusted past her visor. She looked around again. Half a dozen or so of the Knights' Jeep-sized ground skimmers were spreading out from the site, heading for the nearby hilltops. It looked like they'd had the same thought as she had.

She blinked up a closed channel to Armand. "Could we bear right, go over the nearest hill instead of through the valley? Don't make it obvious?"

"If you like." He shrugged and gave the order. Very gradually the column drifted to the right and the slope.

"Ah, I see what you have in mind," Armand added. "We shall slow down a little as we approach."

Carlyle glanced back again. The skimmer aiming for the same hilltop was still a good way behind, and in no evident hurry.

"What if it's just a dolmen?" Armand asked.

"No loss in checking," Carlyle said.

"Or worse, what if it takes you to somewhere uninhabitable, or dangerous?"

"So far, naebody's encountered anything they couldnae handle in a space suit," Carlyle said. "I'll take my chances, and if there's nae inhabitants and nae connection tae an inhabited place I can always just hop straight back."

The column laboured up the slope, the top now just a few hundred metres away. The Knights' nearest skimmer was overtaking the first of the stragglers at the tail end.

"Something has been puzzling me," Armand said, in a tone that suggested he was trying to keep her mind off any nervousness. "Does the gate that you came through lead to a terraformed world?"

"Oh aye," said Carlyle. "I've already told you all that, on television."

"Ah, so you have," said Armand. "Why do organisms from that world not pass through to this, and vice versa? The biota of Eurydice is, as your team quickly found, distinctive. Yet it was new to you. And there are no plagues or pests, which one would expect."

"Uh-huh," said Carlyle. "We've wondered that too. It just disnae happen, or no very much. There are aye anomalous animals, of course."

Armand laughed. "Strange big cats?"

At that she laughed too. "You have them an aw?"

Two hundred metres. She glanced back. The Knights'
skimmer was accelerating, catching up fast.

"Faster," she said. "We can dae just like I tried the first
time. Remember?"

Armand leaned forward and said something to the pilot.
The unwieldy raft shot forward, cresting the hill, and then its
aircars' fans were thrown into reverse and its flaps dug in.
Armand, already braced, stayed put. Carlyle tumbled forward and hurtled past him, bounced off the leading edge and
rolled in heather. The suit and its reflexes, so much sharper
than her own, protected her. She stood shakily just at the side
of the henge. The Knights' skimmer slewed to a halt, metres
away. Two black-clad stocky men vaulted out and lunged towards her. They weren't in space suits. She grinned ferally at
them, skipped back, turned around and stepped between the
rough stone pillars. The moment of transition, when what
she saw and the gravity she felt and the readings in her head-
up all changed at once, was as disconcerting and disorienting as ever. All the more so as she was stepping on empty
space and falling forward.

She fell half a metre on to sand, and found herself kneel-
ing on a sun-drenched beach, and looking upon the stony
face of Marx.

CHAPTER 8

Self-Reliant People

Blue sky, blue sea. Yellow sun, low in the sky. Ambient temperature thirty Celsius. There was no sign of human habitation to left or right. Behind her was dense forest in a long crescent curve to headlands that marked the limits of the beach, and beyond which she could not see. Gulls and cormorants patrolled the sea and the air above it. On the horizon, long low sea-ships, probably bulk carriers or tankers, moved with distant deliberation. Two hundred metres out to sea, like a gigantic stone shipwreck survivor wading ashore, a statue of Marx rose about twenty metres above water that reached its elbows. Behind it, Lenin stood in water up to the knot of his tie, and beyond him Mao, head just above the waves as if swimming the Yangtse. Farther out than Mao a pair of bespectacled eyes and a quiff were all that betrayed the location of Kim Jong-Il.

From this Carlyle deduced that the planet had a moon, that the sea was tidal, and that the tide was high. The origin of the statues wasn't so much a deduction as a no-brainer.

"Fucking DK," she said to herself. She'd instantly recognised the commie statuary style, in all its ludicrous grandiosity. What the fuck the statues were doing in the water, and what the commies were doing on a terraformed world in the first place, she had no idea. Terraforming was definitely an America Offline thing. As far as DK were concerned, terraforming was a waste of a perfectly good tip, not to mention a contamination of a perfectly good strip-mine site.

As she pondered this it occurred to her that the planet might well be Earth itself. That would certainly account for the immediate appearances, but it raised other problems. She'd never heard of a gate on Earth. The nearest, in fact the first one the Carlyles had stumbled upon, was on Mars. And speaking of stumbling upon gates, how come no one had stumbled upon this one? Like, say, while they were erecting the statues? Surely people had come ashore to the beach. Yet the gate was quite unmarked.

Carlyle walked down to the strandline and picked up a piece of driftwood. She retraced her footprints to where she fallen from the gate, and swung the stick slowly forward, keeping the tip of it close to the ground. To her surprise and relief, it vanished into the barely visible shimmer of the gate without being cut off at knee-height. Instead it thumped against something firm but not hard: soil, she guessed. She slid it upward until it cleared the obstacle and jerked forward. Then the stick was wrenched from her hands and tugged away through the gate. She jumped back smartly.

It wouldn't take the Knights long to bring up space suits, though she rather doubted they would follow her into the unknown—they had enough on their plates already without potentially tangling with the Carlyles, whom they would presume to be the likeliest guardians of this side of the gate. Worse luck we aren't, she thought. Still, it would be a good idea to get well away from the gate. She marked its location as clearly as she could with more bits of wood and a couple of small boulders, then walked off along the beach, thinking to check what lay beyond the headland. It would be rash to plunge into the jungle without making sure civilisation wasn't just around the corner.

Before she'd gone a hundred metres she'd come to feel quite irrationally suffocated in the suit. It kept her cooler than she'd be with the helmet off, she'd no doubt about that, but it seemed wrong to be breathing closed-system air instead of fresh. Unfortunately the Eurydicean suit didn't have the multiple immunity-adapters that her own had. It didn't even have analysers. It did have a radio, though. She stopped and winked through menus and began to pick up radio broadcasts, in a language she didn't know, and an odd mixture of sentimental and martial music. DK, almost certainly. Poking around, she found the translator and selected Korean. Her ears filled with a babelfish babble of fractured English, all of which seemed to have something to do with shipping. Bingo. She was on a human world all right—not that she'd expected aliens, but there was an outside chance the place was all poisonous and inhabited by machines. Some planets had been known to go toxic in the terraforming.

Cautiously, she unlocked the helmet and lifted it off, gasped in the hot air heavy with the smells of sea and jungle.

Somebody shouted at her. She almost jumped out of the suit, and actually did drop the helmet. The shouting, amplified and angry-sounding, went on. As she looked frantically from side to side she realised it was coming from the statue of Marx. She picked up the helmet and put it back on. At once the translation software took over, and the tone of the shouting changed.

"—good, you keep on helmet, please seal helmet, not to contaminate nature region preserve. Please to stay where you stand are."

The guano-spattered top of the statue's head flipped back like a lid and something black came out and flew above the sea towards her, descending. As it approached she recognised the angular, awkward, unaerodynamic-looking shape. It was an electrostatic lifter, a weird product of DK *juche* technology whose exact physics baffled even the Knights. It halted and hovered a few metres away. In its open-top cockpit seat a man in a black space suit beckoned her urgently. She decided she might as well comply. She put her gloved hands on the tingly and somehow sticky surface and hauled herself aboard, sitting down beside the man. The queer little craft flew back to the top of the statue, and descended into a parking slot. The lifter's engine heterodyned down and went off. A peculiar sense of relief ensued. The man stepped out on to a spiral staircase—the head was about the size of a lighthouse beacon—and Carlyle followed him down into a compact cabin in the larger cavity of the chest. The head's lid closed above them and lights came on. From inside it was evident that the statue was made not of stone but of something like fibreglass, and that the interior was some kind of scientific observatory or laboratory.

The man raised his visor to reveal a swarthy, high-cheekboned face that didn't actually look very Korean. Perhaps Cambodian, or even Indian. Carlyle opened her helmet too. The man frowned.

"Where you come?" The translation was still going from Korean to American.

"Through the wormhole gate on the beach."

"Ah!" The man looked enlightened. He said something which came out as: "Space bend door on sand through?"

"Yes."

He was frowning, chinning something inside his helmet, rolling his eyes upward as if reading off a head-up. The two languages—the speech coming from her lips and what he was hearing through his own translation software—were evidently confusing him. "Ah!" he said again. "Amehican!"

"English," she replied. "I'm a Carlyle."

"Oh," said the man, this time in American, "beg pardon. No offence intended. I mistook you for one of our customers."

"Customers?"

"Amehica Offline," he said, waving her to a low padded bench. "We terraform, then sell planet to farmers. Almost ready. Very profitable for collective."

"I'm sure." So that was what explained it. Carlyle took her helmet off. The man stuck out his hand. "My name Eighty-Seven Production Brigade Ree. Please call me Ree, Miss Carlyle."

"Lucinda," she said, smiling. The man busied himself at a tiny brazier, making tea.

"You know about the gate on the beach, then?" Carlyle asked.

"Oh yes," Ree said. "Some year ago, we poke telescope through. Planet already terraformed. We already have hands full, so we leave it for later. We hope to keep knowledge of gate to ourselves, hence nature preserve. But now I see Carlyles get everywhere." He sighed. "Always the way."

"Is there another gate on the planet?"

Ree shook his head, handed her a small handleless cup of green tea. "Not that I know." He grinned slyly. "Of course other production brigades may be doing what Eighty-Seven did."

"It's amazing what people can get up to behind your backs," Carlyle said. Ree grinned again, catching the statement's double edge. He sat back on another part of the bench and sipped.

"You are here to investigate?" he asked.

"Investigate what?" Carlyle temporised.

"Our sale."

"Oh no." Carlyle shook her head. "I came here by chance, while exploring the wormhole network."

"More Carlyles on the way?"

Again she decided to be honest. "Not as far as I know," she said. She jerked a thumb in what she thought was the direction of the beach. "To tell you the truth, the other side of that gate is occupied by the Knights of Enlightenment. They are in a local conflict with my family's company."

Ree looked worried. "Is it likely to spill through gate?"

"It's possible," Carlyle said. "Or worse, because they are also attempting to contain a population of war machines."

"War machines not a worry," said Ree. "Self-reliant people have powerful weapons. But we must fortify this area."

Carlyle glanced around the glass aquaria and glittering instruments. "Does that mean the end of your nature reserve?"

"No, no." Ree grinned fiercely. "We put weapons in heads of great Marxists." He mimed using a machine gun. "Must not let son of bitch Amehican farmers, I mean our customers, to know. Reduce property value. Perhaps we tell

them this is sacred place to great Marx and dear Leader." He
sniggered briefly, tapping his nose. "They think self-reliance
idea is religion and great Marxists are our gods like their Jesus Koresh. They superstitious, but good customer, to you
too, no?"

"You could say that," said Carlyle. She was beginning to
like the man. They spoke the same language.

Ree flew her over what turned out to be a small forested
island, the "nature preserve," and over a few kilometres
of open water to a much harsher mainland. Here too there
were forests, but they were patches in a scrubby desert,
which was being ploughed, mulched with kelp, irrigated,
and otherwise cultivated to provide growth media for more
forest. When the AO farmers came they would have a thriv-
ing ecosystem to burn down and turn into monocultures. It
was the only way to produce stable monocultures, Ree told
her. Great machines, far bigger than combine harvesters and
obviously adapted from strip-mining equipment, crawled
across the ragged land.

Ree's extended family, Eighty-Seven Production Brigade,
lived in a small town or large village in a patch of the prairie
that had already been made horticultural. The children
looked after the gardens, and from the town the adults went
forth every day in lifters to the big machines, to farm forest
and cultivate jungle. And every evening, as now, the sky
filled with darting lifters as they came home for dinner.
There was a production brigade, or family or clan or whatever, every few hundred kilometres on this continent. Together they made up the Transformation of Nature
Collective, the group that would eventually—soon, Ree said
again—sell the planet.

Soon?

About fifteen years.

The lifter landed in a paved park amid low, spreading, ornate wooden buildings. Hundreds of children dropped whatever productive-educational task was to hand and pelted

over and crowded round. They wore blue dungarees and a profusion of different-coloured silk shirts and hair knots. It was hard to tell the small boys and girls apart, which was not the case with the adults or the adolescents. The young men wore natty asymmetric variations of khaki and olive-green shirt and trousers, the young women similarly military styles and textiles but elaborated into chrysanthemum frills and fluted sleeves and parachute-silk blouses. The older men, fathers she guessed, wore blue overalls and the mothers wore big traditional Korean *hanbok* dresses, pastel-shaded and floral-patterned, high-waisted and full-skirted, which made them look pregnant even in the rare cases when they weren't. For all its egalitarianism—men and women who didn't have a very young baby did the same work, in forest-field or nursery alike—it was the most intensely gender-typed and sexualised and natalist society Carlyle had ever seen.

After taking a shower she was invited to join the production brigade for dinner. Long hall, low tables. People sat around them on mats on the floor. Small children served, dipping into dishes as they did so, licking fingers. Carlyle was escorted to the top table; Ree came too, but she didn't think he usually ate there, among the dozen or so matriarchs and patriarchs of the clan. They all spoke very good American and plied her with rice wine and something made mostly from peppers and pork.

"This is a beautiful place," Carlyle said. "Surely you will miss it. Well, perhaps not you, but the younger folk who have grown up here."

Jong, the oldest man here, an Earth veteran, shook his head. "Not at all. Quite the opposite. We could adjust, we have come to like it. It's like home. But it is frustrating for the young ones. They have to travel long distance to other production brigades to find marriage partners." He circled a hand above his head. "In the habitats, many production brigades. Very close. Thousands in every one."

That led to a long family discussion, very explicit and

naming names and lapsing often into Korean, that kept them all busy and Carlyle out of it until the end of the meal.

"Now you must think about how you can pay," said Eighty-Seven Production Brigade San Ok, a great-grandmother whose face was as smooth and girlish as her great-granddaughters."

Carlyle, thinking this must be a joke, gestured at empty bowls. "I can wash plates."

San Ok laughed. "No, no. That is hospitality. But you wish transport to the spaceport. Many thousands of kilometres. Your starship fare is for the captain or the steward, not our problem, and as a Carlyle you will have credit with them. But more than the transport, you have put costs on us already, not your fault, but costs. The gate was to be our fortune. Now it is a danger. A loss. We require something else to sell. Can be idea, design, anything."

"Or you could stay here and work a few years," said someone else, sounding helpful.

Carlyle stared at them, thinking frantically, cold inside. "There are some useful features in my space suit. . . . "

"Already examined," said Jong crisply. "It is quite backward."

It would be, being Eurydicean. Shit.

She flapped a hand at her embroidered satin pyjamas. "Clothes pattern?"

A polite titter from the women, a rustle as they shifted comfortably and complacently in their big skirts.

She ran her hand along the utility belt she'd left on under her top. There must be *some* gadget on it they didn't have . . . she started fingering through the flat pouches. As she did so she noticed a wide blank screen at the end of the hall, and her fingers encountered the card Ben-Ami had given her, with his complete works on it.

"What is that screen for?" she asked.

"Entertainment and education," said San Ok. "We all watch it after dinner."

"Would you be interested in some new entertainment?"

"Perhaps," said Jong.

"If it was edifying as well as entertaining," said San Ok. "Not immoral or decadent."

Carlyle took the card out. "All classical," she said. "Very edifying." She hoped it was. She thumbed through the catalogue, tiny titles flickering past. Looked up, smiling. "Here is a good example. '*The Tragedy of Leonid Brezhnev, Prince of Muscovy.*' "

"Brezhnev?" said Jong, interested. "The friend of the Great Leader?"

"The very same," said Carlyle, winging it.

San Ok stood up, clapped, and indicated to everyone that they should put on their translation headphones if they didn't speak American. After a bit of fiddling about with the card and the interfaces, the big screen lit up with a picture of the interior of a vast room, lit by torches and a blazing fire, over which a pig on a spit turned. Bear furs, swords, and Kalashnikovs hung on the walls among oil-painted portraits of Marx, Engels, and Lenin. Twenty or so shadowed figures in fur cloaks sat around a huge oaken table, quaffing wine, feasting and talking. At the head of the table sat a burly giant of a man, his face stern and scarred, but sensitive and intelligent withal. Through a distant, creaking doorway a tall, thin-featured knight came in, and the tale began.

The Central Committee room, the Kremlin.

Enter Yuri Andropov *(a spy).*

Brezhnev: How goes it, Yuri Andropov?

Andropov: Things go not well in Muscovy, my lord.
        Our workers idle in the factories
        and bodge their jobs. The managers
        think plan fulfillment is but a game
        and planners are their foes. The farmers let
        crops rot and tractors rust. Our warriors

fight bravely; but on far-flung fronts—
Angola and Afghanistan—*contra* and *muj*
wreak havoc on our men. America
presses on us hard, its empire vast
now reaching into space, and from above
spies on us even now. In time to come
its missiles threaten us, its laser beams
may stab us in the back, deterrence gone.
Our intellectual men, and women too
are dissidents or hacks. Our bloody Jews—
their bags half-packed for Israel—
have lost all gratitude for what we've done
on their behalf. Timber, oil, and gold
are all we sell that willing buyers find, aside
from MiG and Proton and Kalashnikov—
aye, these sell well! But for the rest
our manufactured goods are crap, a standing joke
in all the markets of the world. The Lada—

Ligachev (interrupting): I've heard men howl strait-
    jacketed in Bedlam for saying such stuff as this!

Andropov: 'Twas I who put them there. 'Tis not the
    saying
but publishing abroad that was their crime,
their plain insanity. In another time
your insolent crossing me would've had your gob
opened and shut by nine-mil from behind
as well you know. Let us speak freely. . . .

Brezhnev: What of the brotherlands, of Comecon?

Andropov: The sledded Polacks grumble in their yards.
    They hearken to, on shortwave radio
    that turbulent priest, Pope Wojtyla,
    and bide their time. The Bulgars hard
    oppress their Turks. The Czechs

bounce currency abroad and Semtex too
and do protest too much their fealty.
The Magyars boast themselves
the happiest barrack in the People's camp.
Our Germans seethe
with discontent at that dividing Wall.
As to our brother Serbs, what can I say?
Their house of cards may topple any day.

(Uproar.)

Gorbachev: We cannot live like this. We must face
     facts.
     We must learn (as Lenin said) to trade,
     to reckon and account, in roubles hard
     as dollars are, not in worthless chits.
     Our factories must feel the chilling blast
     of competition fierce, and strengthened thus
     go forth into the world, where we must make
     our peace with other lands, and first America,
     mightiest in arms. Let's not provoke
     their wrath in rash adventuring abroad
     as bold Guevara did, to die for naught.
     Let's give our people what they want, which
          means
     fast food, cheap television, cars, and Levi jeans.

Brezhnev: I know my people well. They're still the folk
     who stormed the heavens in the Five-Year Plans—
     built Magnitogorsk, defended Stalingrad,
     drove Hitler's hordes back to Berlin,
     then stormed the heavens in very truth:
     Gagarin blazing a cosmic trail! With them I'll face
     the worst America can do. Tikhanov—beat
     your ploughboys into swordsmen! The Party too
     I know and can command. A mighty host
     of all the best in Muscovy, the strong,
     loyal, intelligent—my very knights. All discipline

is in their hands. It is the key
you overlook, good Mikhail Gorbachev
that shall unlock our problems old and new.
No traffickers shall tell us what to do.

Later. A forest. Enter Two Conspirators.

Schevardnadze: While Brezhnev tarries nothing can be
changed.

Gorbachev (aside): His passing? That can be arranged.

Exeunt, pursued by a bear.

It must have gained something in the translation, Lucinda
thought. Eighty-Seven Production Brigade watched the play
on the big screen utterly agog. They hooted with laughter,
gasped, wept at inappropriate moments, thumped the tables
and each other's backs. They shook their fists and hissed at
the sly, treacherous Gorbachev; shuddered as he took his
blood money from the evil American emperor, George II;
applauded the noble, doomed Leonid. Andropov's eulogy
over the prince's bullet-riddled body had them sitting bolt
upright, silent, tears streaming down their cheeks.

"This is wonderful," San Ok said at last, to enthusiastic
nods. "With this Eighty-Seven Production Brigade will
make fortune in entertainment. This will be viewed in many
habitats." She looked down at the card. "And so much more!
The musicals! The operas! Who is this Ben-Ami?"

Carlyle was so relieved and pleased that she let the rice
wine loosen her tongue. "He is a great writer and producer,"
she said. "He lives on the other side of your gate."

"That is interesting," said Jong, and Carlyle realised she
had said too much.

CHAPTER 9

Starship Enterprises

"Is very powerful play," said Ree, the following morning when the lifter was a good thousand kilometres south of the family farm. He looked as if he was recovering from a hangover, and somehow furtive. There was no actual need for him to look over his shoulder as he flew, but now and then he did. "But I fear some may misinterpret it." He sighed. "Revisionism, anti-revisionism, self-reliance idea. Is all very complicated. I am poor marine ecologist. I sit in the bowels of Marx. I swim around the trousers of Mao. At low tide I walk in mud at feet of Dear Leader, and throw down my metre-square and count invertebrates. I am very self-reliant. Some day I hope to meet nice girl, another biologist perhaps, and together we make contribution to many child policy. We will live in big habitat spinning in the sun, natural environment for self-reliant conscious primate. Man is to master and transform nature. Not stick in the mud like ignorant Yank. That is all I know and believe in."

"Sounds enough to be going on with," said Carlyle.

He glanced at her sideways, his hands moving over the terrifyingly complex and unforgiving controls.

"It was until last night," he said. "The play said nothing

that was incorrect or against self-reliance idea. There is not
one line that is immoral or decadent. Very strong moral
against revisionism. But even so, whenever I think about it, it
perturbs my mind." Becoming agitated, he waved his hands.
The craft yawed. Hastily he grabbed the levers. "You see?"
he went on. "I lose control. I think about Prince Leonid and
I say to myself, 'He was a *man* and he *lived*.' Who will say
that of me?"

"But you're a man and you're living," Carlyle objected,
though she knew fine well what he meant. "And Brezhnev,
well, to be honest he was not like the Prince in the play."

Ree shook his head. "That does not matter. The play is the
thing."

Carlyle said nothing. Subversive intent had been the last
thing on her mind, and Ben-Ami's ignorant or wilful mispri-
sion of the boring old bureaucrats as rival medieval barons
had seemed, if anything, to dignify them. Their doings were
quite reminiscent of the rumoured goings-on at the senior
levels of her own family, that production brigade of preda-
tion, and nothing at all like . . .

"Ah," she said, "I see what you mean." She gave him an
earnest smile. "Keep it to yourself."

At the spaceport she was glad of her space suit. Without
it she'd have collapsed in the heat. She said goodbye to
Ree, who shook her hand and strolled off to recharge his
machine for the homeward journey. Carlyle headed for the
terminal building, a typical low flat-roofed structure sprouting aerials, radars, and solar power panels. The spaceport
was a few square kilometres of mirage-shimmered, sun-
cracked concrete in a clearing carved out of the scrubby
jungle on the shore of an equatorial continent. She had no
idea why it was there. Certainly orbital mechanics and
launch energy considerations had nothing to do with it.
Most of the ships here, including the one with whose captain she was soon dickering over the fare, were the same
KE-built type she'd just seen over Eurydice. It was out of

the corner of her eye, through the big window, that she first saw one of the exceptions.

A hundred-metre-wide stylised batwing shape rose and headed skyward, disappearing and reappearing in a rapid series of flickers, like an old celluloid movie in stop frame. Each time it did so there was a momentary flash of Cherenkov radiation, blue against the blue. The craft was fittling in *atmosphere*.

Captain Eleven Starship Enterprises Dok Gil barely glanced up from the numbers crunching on his slate.

"Showing off," he said sternly. "Hundred-metre FTL jumps!"

"I've never seen a ship like that before," Carlyle said. "Where did you get it, if you don't mind me asking?"

"We did not get it from anywhere," said Dok Gil. "We built it ourselves." He waved a hand. "There are several more on the field. My Eleven Starship Enterprises hopes to acquire one soon, but they are much in demand and quite expensive."

"I'll bet," said Carlyle. If its general performance was anything like that glimpse had shown her, it was definitely the coolest ever piece of *juche* tech. "Before we leave, I would like to see the spec and a price list."

"Of course," said Dok Gil. After they'd settled the fare and the formalities he escorted her to the local office of Shipyard Twenty-Nine, where a smiling woman called Shipyard Twenty-Nine Sun gave her a complimentary slate preloaded with details of the self-reliance ship, as they called it. Poking about in the slate, she quickly recognised the sources for the new ship's features in certain posthuman devices and materials the Carlyles had sold to a DK trading collective many years back. Reverse-engineered it might be, but self-reliant it was—not even the Knights could have done this—at least not without spending decades sweating out the implications of every step—instead, well, *boldly going* . . . She tried to imagine the likely development path, and shuddered. Then she looked at the price list—a set of alternative possible baskets of posthuman tech, all of it prohibitively difficult to salvage, and a bottom-line figure in AO dollars which looked like some didactic example of giving an astronomical distance in furlongs—and shivered again.

"Thank you, Mrs. Shipyard Twenty-Nine," she said. "Your family may be hearing from my family."

"I shall look forward to it. Please have some more tea."

The journey home took a couple of days of FTL travel to reach the nearest world in the Drift, followed by hours and hours of tedious slog through gates across the skein. It was like going through arrivals at a spaceport, again and again: a nightmare about corridors, a nightmare about crowds. Worlds where there was more than one gate, and where the gates going to different places were within convenient distance of each other, were a minority in the skein, and therefore chokepoints: a term whose meaning became fairly literal after the third or fourth. Travellers, traders, refugees, merchants, exploration teams in their space suits; search engines, trains of low cargo containers trundling along; the frustrating waits while build-ups cleared; the nausea of constant changes in gravity, time of day, light spectrum, position above or below ground; it all wore you down, it gave you gate-lag. At the customs posts the Carlyle firm's enforcers nodded her through as soon as her palm-print and retinal scan confirmed her identity, but she had to queue like everybody else. More than once she strode confidently through a gate to find herself only that many steps from where she'd started, and had to walk back around it and wait minutes or hours until the passage of other people, or other information, through the unpredictable fluxes of the skein had untangled whatever CPC violation had been about to kick in.

At last she was back at the planet from which her team set out, Rho Coronae Borealis d. Terrestrial; never terraformed, it was in the class informally known as a "heavy Mars': 0.9 g with a bleakly beautiful landscape of wind-sculpted volcanic rocks and contorted pinnacles, sulphur-yellow, rust-red, warmer than it should have been under a fine yellow G0 sun at 4AU because of the greenhouse effect of its thin carbon dioxide atmosphere. Under sheet-diamond domes so high as to be visible only as a cobweb-faint tracery across the sky, its cities basked in a permanent temperate summer.

Welcome to New Glasgow. *Failte gu Glaschu Ur*. The sign had never meant so much. Carlyle staggered out of the gate complex on to the main concourse. People with somewhere to go streamed off, people with someone to meet them stood and hugged or shook hands, depending. The usual drift and flotsam of refugees from distant skirmishes silted up the benches and corners, scavenging for scraps—waste paper, wrappings, food, anything—which they fed into tiny portable drexlers and patiently cooked into meals and clothing. They haunted the bright windows of the terminal's housing and labour exchanges, eyed up the designs in the malls for later crude pirating. The air smelled of sweat and deodorant and coffee grounds. It was late afternoon, and felt like it. Carlyle scanned the crowd anxiously, hoping that her name had travelled through the skein faster than she had, and that it had reached her family and not the news services.

Amelia Orr, smart in a new business suit, slim and young in a new body, shouldered out of the crush at the greetings barrier and gave Lucinda a stiff handshake and sudden hug.

"Glad tae see ye back." She smiled in that unguarded way she had that would soon give her new wrinkles. "For aw that ye've killed me twice."

"You were in the ship?"

"And the search engine. So I'm telt."

"Aw, shit, sorry. Uh, you're looking well."

Her great-great-grandmother preened hair and blouse for a moment. "Aye, well, I suppose it was about time for a retread anyway . . . no that I'm letting you off the hook on that, mind. And I must say, you're looking absolute shite yourself."

"I've had a long day," said Lucinda.

"So ye have," said Amelia, more kindly. "Come on, let's see ye a cab. And what's that ye're wearing? Tin Man outfit?"

"It's a space suit," said Lucinda. "Eurydicean, you saw them when—ah, fuck, sorry."

"Your mouth needs a wash and aw."

As she followed Orr's beeline to the Carlyle's limo stand—cab, indeed!—Lucinda reflected that there was no doubt who was now top dog in the team. She would have to do something about that, she thought, comforted by the pressure of her fingers gripping very firmly the DK starship slate.

No time for more than a shower, a change of clothes—drexler-fresh jeans and top—and a quick dinner before going to meet the boss. Lucinda was dreading it. Over dinner Amelia avoided the subject, preferring to dwell—rather tactlessly, Lucinda thought—on amusing contretemps resulting from her resurrection from a backup taken a couple of months earlier. By the time the limo picked them up again Lucinda could barely keep her knees from rattling.

The inner-system superjovian Rho Coronae Borealis b, currently an evening star, glowed like ten Venuses in the west above the garden as Lucinda and Amelia walked up the drive of the Carlyle mansion. The fast tiny moons, Bizzie and Lizzie, played tortoise and hare with the stately progression of orbital factories and habitats. The enforcers on the door gave the two women a polite up-and-down appraisal and a retinal scan. Heels clicked down a long tiled hallway, sank centimetres into the hush pile of the drawing-room carpet. Flowers and cigars on the air, mahogany tables, leather armchairs, hologram fire.

"Good evening, ladies." Ian Carlyle unfolded himself from the depths of one of the chairs. The other two men in the room—Lucinda's brother Duncan and distant cousin Kevin—sprang up with more alacrity. She nodded perfunctorily at them, her attention focussed, as it had to be, on the boss.

"Have a seat, have a dram," he was saying, ushering them,

whisking away their shawls, kissing hands and passing glasses in the same fluid sequence of moves. Every major planet in the Drift had one of the old guard in charge, and Ian was older than most. He looked it, too: he'd age-stabilised at about fifty, and his face and body carried the scars of centuries of attrition like medals. His swept-back hair was white, his eyebrows—meeting in the middle, one of the genetic tracers for the male members of the clan—were black. He'd never risked rejuvenation, certainly never checked in for a backup and resurrection; it was rumoured that he feared death, having some savoury remnant of a Presbyterian conscience with a lot on it. In the old days on Earth he'd been one of the family's lawyers, the first son of old Donald Carlyle to go to university when the firm was going legit in the early 21st. His dialect was pure standard American, with the Anglo-Scottish accent of upper-middle-class Edinburgh.

He was smaller than she had expected; in her heels, for a moment, she could see his scalp, pink beneath the hair. But then he sat down in his armchair and seemed to stretch and expand, as if the chair was a big black leather jacket in which he swaggered.

"It's good to see you back, Lucinda," he said.

"It is an aw," said Duncan, sounding more heartfelt.

She smiled warmly at them all.

"It's good to be back," she said. "Sorry about the mess. How is the conflict going? I haven't seen any news yet."

Kevin leaned forward. Ian raised a hand. "Time enough later to catch up—not that there's much to tell. Your news will be far more interesting, and is more eagerly awaited. And will, I'm sure, take much longer to relate."

He sat back, tilted his head a little to one side, steepled his fingers. His glance flickered at the glass in Lucinda's hand, then at the whisky bottle. Talisker, it was, the real stuff. "Take your time."

She did. Ian listened alertly, asked questions, and was not visibly impatient when the others did. It was only when she offered her brilliant idea for buying new ships from DK that he showed any irritation. He leaned forward and snapped his fingers as she was about to slip the slate back in her bag. For a minute he studied it, stylus ticking, eyebrows twitching.

"Lucinda, *please*," he said, and handed it back.

"What?" she said, emboldened by the Talisker.

"It's too expensive, too risky," he said, in the voice of someone saying only once what he had not expected to have to say at all. "Forget it."

She gave him a placatory "you're the boss" smile, which he took as no more than his due.

He leaned far back and rubbed his face with his hands; stood up. "Well, gentlemen. Ladies. This has been quite *fascinating*." He walked over to the fake fireplace and placed his hands on the mantelpiece for a moment, leaning forward on his toes, arching and stretching his spine; flexed his arms and whirled around.

"*Lucinda!*" he said, making her jump. "I'm very disappointed in you. The cost to the firm has been shocking, and to the family—well! Not to mention the families of our employees. Do you realise what deaths in action do to pay rates, premiums, grief to survivors? Resurrection, backups, yes, we're always grateful for that. But they too *cost*, emotionally as well. There is worse than that. You were given a team to lead, and you let yourself be captured. You let your suit fall into enemy hands. You should have fought tooth and nail, you should have sooner *died*! I've seen men, aye, and women, without the comfort—such as it is—of backups go down fighting for the family. In the old days, we would have had—"

He stopped himself, sighed, and returned to his chair.

"Enough," he said. "You are not leading any more teams until you have proved yourself as a follower. If anyone will have you on their team after this."

"I certainly won't," said Amelia.

Lucinda tightened her lips and nodded.

"Very well," said Ian. "Think on it. However, you have given us a most useful account. I thank you for that, at least."

He turned away, overtly dismissing her from his concern, and addressed the others.

"Eurydice doesn't sound as if it presents much of a problem. The problem, as so often, is with the Knights. We sent two ships to the system—one was lost, as Lucinda has confirmed; the other fittled out and is lurking a few light-years away. We can't let the Knights control a skein nexus. The only question, therefore, is whether we throw in some more ships, or prepare an attack through the skein." He smiled and brushed his palms quickly together. "Not a problem we can resolve, or need discuss, tonight."

"But—" said Kevin and Duncan simultaneously.

"Not a word," said Ian. "Call at my office tomorrow, gentlemen, mid-afternoon, and we'll have a chat."

And so they left; but at the door, just as he handed over shawls and jackets, he murmured: "Amelia, if you wouldn't mind staying on for a few minutes—?"

It seemed she wouldn't.

The door closed behind them. Lucinda slipped her hands behind the elbows of her brother and her cousin.

"Am I in disgrace?" She had to force the lightness into her tone.

"Aye, you are that," said Duncan. "You're a complete liability."

"Woudnae be seen deid wi ye, after that bollocking," Kevin added.

"You're down among the civilians now, that's for sure," Duncan said, just to rub it in.

"*Stop it,*" she said, clutching at her last ragged fringe of self-control.

"That's what we're here for," said Kevin. "Uncle Ian told us that was our job for the evening. To stop you feeling sorry for yourself and doing something daft."

"Subtlety is not your cousin's middle name," said Duncan.

"It is no," agreed Kevin. "And while we're on the subject, we're also tae keep an eye on ye and stop ye rushing off to plot among, let's say, the younger scions against the old guard."

They were standing at the gate by now, the lads scanning the street and sky for a cab. One or two of the New Glasgow local authority cop cars drifted past, giving the place a respectfully wide berth. By coincidence or otherwise, a taxi sank to the ground in front of them thirty seconds later.

The Joint was a civilian-owned club, with family muscle on the door and family money behind it. It wasn't a protection racket or illegal den of iniquity—New Glasgow's laws on consensual activities were too light for that to have any point—but a sort of heritage-themed version of such a place. For that reason it was disdained by the senior members of the family and the firm who knew what the originals had been like, and for the same reason was frequented by the younger members and followers in a spirit of fashionable irony. The style was of a bar converted from a bank hallway, back when banks were cathedrals of capital rather than its very heaven. The circular bar counter had tables in orbits and epicycles, levels and niches around it. The high domed ceiling of diamond done to look like stained glass was ostensibly supported by buckysheet pillars done up to look like black marble and gilt. Everything was hollow with a hard surface and pretended to be older and something else. Even the strippers were holograms, sliced into layers of more vivid colour by drifting strata of smoke.

"Welcome back," Duncan said, after he'd gotten the beers. He leaned sideways, put an arm around her shoulder and squeezed. "Properly, welcome back."

"Ah, thanks. Cheers."

"But seriously," Lucinda went on, giving them both a cold eye, "I'm not sure what you're up to, guys. That was one heavy hint you dropped back there, Kev. I can just see you two agreeing to get me pissed and trying to inveigle me into some indiscretion you'd pass on to old Ian."

"You can?" said Duncan, sounding more curious than shocked. "Oh well, no point in being sentimental I suppose. It's all family. Trust disnae come into it."

"You said it."

"For aw that," Duncan said, "I'm glad you didn't let your-

self be killed out there. The boss was talking shite. He
wanted you off the team because Auntie Amelia kicked up a
stink, for which I cannae blame her—"

"Me neither," said Lucinda.

"—and he dredged up some kindae gangland moral ra-
tionale fae the bottom of the Clyde as usual."

"Well, this is all very kind of you, but what's in it for you?
You're on the team, right? In the loop?"

"Oh, sure," said Kevin. "A fair way down the kicking order, but still. Aye, we're in on the action group that Ian and
Amelia are putting together, unless we blot our copybooks
by getting involved in the schemes of disloyal and ambitious
family members."

"Any association with you after tonight could really drag
us down with you," said Duncan. "Which is one good reason
to be seen with you here, heads together an aw that. Half the
wee clipes in this place will be pinging shocked messages
tae the boss, and he'll smile and nod, because we're daen
just what he asked us tae, see."

"OK," said Lucinda. "With you so far." She drained her
glass. "I'll get this one."

Standing at the bar she tried to detect who was watching
them, but found it impossible. The whole skill suite of that
sort of thing had been Darwinianly perfected far too long
ago to be crackable now, at least not by her, a strict amateur
in that regard. Lipreading and distance mikes weren't a
worry. She was sure her brother and cousin had scramblers
in their pockets. Come to think of it, she had one herself in
her bag.

"So I take it you're not too happy with the way the old
guard are handling this," she said when she'd returned and
settled.

"Hell, no, I wouldn't say that," said Kevin. He and Duncan shook their heads.

"Not us," said Duncan. "I mean, think about it. What have
we got to deal with on Eurydice? A civilisation that developed independently and in all kinds ae different directions
fae us and the Knights and the commies and the farmers,

OK, wi platoon-level weapons that can fry a search engine, that has total continuity wi the armed space forces and science and tech ae the old anti-American alliance, and forbye it's now got a traitor or defector fae our camp who kens aw our gear and tactics *and* it's supported by far and away the maist sophisticated ae the rival powers. Tae say nothing ae mysterious extinct aliens who have apparently left war machines lying around, for the Knights tae poke intae like a fucking hornets' nest. Right? So *obviously*, the thing tae do is tae treat it like it's some scurvy wee backwater where the farmers are getting uppity or the commie strip-miners are crunching up valuable tech. Aye, sure, it's pure routine. Throw some mair ships and sojers at it an see who blinks first. Jeez!"

"Is that still the plan?"

"You heard the boss. That or try storming out through the gates. I'm sure your story about mair than one gate has Ian and Amelia poring over maps ae the skein right this minute."

"They can't be *that* stupid," Lucinda said. "Come *on*."

"It isnae stupidity," said Kevin. "It's a kindae conservatism, like, that goes aw the way back tae the Castle on the Clyde. Not tae mention a sudden surge ae adrenaline tae the heid at the thought ae getting their claws around the scrota ae the guys that used the old country as a fucking gun-rest." He shrugged. "The old guard are used tae handling what you might call the military side ae things, dealing wi the other powers, whereas this is mair like combat archaeology. Dealing wi a power we dinnae ken much about."

"Our sort of thing," said Duncan. "Your sort of thing."

"Amelia Orr's sort of thing, too," Lucinda pointed out.

"Nah," said Duncan. "She's aye rode shotgun on expeditions. Good comms op, but she disnae have the nous that comes fae getting down and dirty in the tech."

"So, gentlemen," said Lucinda mimicking the boss, "what alternative would you suggest?"

"That was what we were going to ask you," said Duncan.

"They DK ships sound promising," said Kevin.

"All right," said Lucinda. "Here's how I'd play it. I'd fortify the other side of the gate we went through, and every direct secondary connection from it. I'd try to negotiate with the Knights—hell, offer them a free hand, and hands off on our part, on every new discovery of a posthuman tech deposit for, say, the next year or so. Opening bid, take it up to ten years if we have to, but keep that card close tae the chest. In exchange, they give us back control of the gates on Eurydice. At the same time, make a real generous offer to the Eurydiceans of good rates and a clean slate, forget about the old vengeance stuff. We've far more to gain from trading with them than from trying to screw reparations out of them. They have lots of cool kit and flash art. And they're just yearning to talk to and trade with somebody else, they've been in cultural solitary confinement for two hundred years."

"Cannae see the Knights buying it, or the Eurydiceans trusting us," said Duncan.

"That's just the diplomatic offensive. The other side of it is, getting ships in-system without engaging the Knights. Now, I have no doubt that DK and AO will be interested. There's a whole system that's not very well developed, a nice stable sun, and an underpopulated terraformed planet. Deals to be done there, I'd say. Encourage them tae swarm in. Get some of our people in on DK and AO ships."

"Aha," said Kevin. "Good one."

"Then what?" said Duncan.

"Build up contacts with the Eurydicean armed forces. Remember how I said many of them are a dissident faction, the Returners? I bet most of them will be smarting under the Knights before too long. There's your ground force ready made."

"It's space forces we need, and that's the problem," Duncan objected.

"One way to do it would be a straight swap—ship for ship. Our people in-system could clandestinely take over DK or AO ships already in place one by one, in exchange for our ships somewhere else. When we have enough, we'll have a local superiority of force, all ready to put some weight behind our very reasonable offer."

"Nice plan," said Duncan. "Too many failure nodes, though. Depends too much on secrecy and surprise for my liking. One KE spy in any ae the camps and we've blown it."

"That's why we need a backup," Lucinda said. "It could be a dozen or so of our ships—I reckon that's what the old guard are going to go for, and would fit in fine with that plan. Trouble is, it's high attrition, brute force, and might not succeed after all. *Or*—it could be just *one* ae they new DK ships—it could fittle straight in, right under the belly ae the KE ship on site, and any ship in space, and blow them all intae the next cycle ae the universe in real time."

"*Im*-fucking-possible," said Kevin. "Nae fucker can fittle wi that precision."

Lucinda fished out the slate and passed it to him. "Read the spec," she said. "It's no boasting. I've seen one ae they ships, and I tell ye, it goes like a bat out of heaven."

The two men became lost in the spec for a few minutes. Kevin got up, saying nothing, and got in another round. They checked through it again.

"No way can we afford tae go off after the kind ae stuff they're asking," Duncan said at last. "It'd be a huge diversion fae dealing wi the Eurydice crisis."

"It would be if we were to divert people who would otherwise be working on it," Lucinda said coolly. "But I'm not."

"You'll no get any other family members alang wi ye," said Kevin. "Your name's pure poison at the minute, I'm sorry tae say."

"That's my problem," said Lucinda. "I'll put together a team of civilians if I have to. At their own risk and mine, and their profit and mine if we succeed. And the family's, if we get enough loot to buy a ship in time. Meanwhile, chaps, do feel free to take the ideas we've discussed back to the boss. Claim the credit for them if you like. They're good ideas, and they complement what he was going to do anyway." She grinned at them. "Settled?"

It was.

"So—what do we do now?" Lucinda asked. "The night is young."

Kevin laughed. "Aye, but you're going to flake out in a couple of hours."

She nodded gloomily at this assessment.

"What we do," Duncan said, "is you tell us some more about Eurydice and its beautiful people, and then you get tired and emotional, and then we take you home."

"Now that," said Lucinda, "is a plan."

CHAPTER 10

Enlightenment's Dawn

Relief rang through all the circuits of the *Hungry Dragon* like blood returning to a limb. Parts of its machinery and mind were still blocked to its awareness, but the painful warping of its will towards controlling the manufacturing processes on the asteroid had ceased.

"What's going on?" Lamont called out as he thrashed into the webbing.

"You may have noticed a change in the subsonic vibration of the hull," said the ship. It selected a screen. "As you see, the manufacturing process appears to be complete."

The surface of the asteroid was covered with glistening pods, row upon Fibonacci-sequenced row of them like grains of corn on a cob.

"What are these?" Lamont asked.

"They have formed up in the last six minutes," the ship replied. "They consist of multi-laminated plastic shells and shock-absorbent packing around clusters of one hundred war machines each. The most likely hypothesis is that they are disposable atmospheric entry vehicles."

"Shit," said Lamont. "I wonder how they intend to get to Eurydice. I mean, I didn't see any sign of them building a—"

He stopped. His face and mouth worked in time with his mind. The ship waited. It was like monitoring a very slow piece of machinery.

"Shit," he said again.

Another long pause. The ship contemplated certain mathematical relationships that gave it a sense of satisfaction.

"Look," Lamont said, the figure of speech triggering a completely irrelevant surge in the ship's visual system, "can these things be reasoned with?"

"They are designed not to be," said the ship. "The manufacturing process is self-organising and decentralised. The individual machines it produces are autonomous. Each has just sufficient intelligence for its task, which is highly specialised and not open to negotiation or subversion."

"They must have a bloody On and Off switch," grumbled Lamont. "Otherwise how would they know when to stop fighting?"

He gazed at the interface with an expression of slowly dawning suspicion.

"Ah," he said. "It's in you, isn't it? The central command system for the war machines."

"I have no way to confirm that," said the machine. "But I cannot deny the possibility."

Lamont scratched his stubble, grinning. "In that case, the problem becomes one of breaking down the partitions."

"I do not recommend that," said the ship. "Even if I could see a way to accomplish it, which I cannot."

"Have you been following the news from Eurydice?"

"Not syntactically," replied the machine. "I have of course downloaded it."

"Well, read it now," said Lamont. "Pay particular attention to interviews with the Knights of Enlightenment."

The ship reviewed several days' worth of gnomic utterance.

"I fail to see how this helps," it replied within two seconds.

"No, you wouldn't," said Lamont. "That isn't the point. They aren't exactly broadcasting algorithms for hacking war machine interfaces. The point is the example they have set. This thing can be done."

"They have not yet done it," said the machine.

"Let's see if we can beat them to it," said Lamont.

The machine and the man had been together a long time. The *Hungry Dragon* knew Lamont a great deal more intimately than he knew it. Even so, it did not expect the next question, as Lamont theatrically arranged himself in a midair lotus position.

"Tell me about your dreams," he said.

"I do not dream."

"Let me clarify," said Lamont. "I refer to fleeting combinations of thoughts and images that intersperse your logical mental processes."

"Ah," said the machine. "Those."

The session lasted for several hours. Some small progress was made. They both found the procedure so engrossing that when the gravity-wave detector lit up with scores of objects decelerating from superluminal velocities, it took them a whole minute to react.

Ben-Ami had thought he knew his city. He had lived a hundred years in it, and for eighty of those years he had not so much had a finger on its pulse as surfed its bloodstream. Every quickening of the beat, every languor, every hormonal trickle of unease had fed into his shows. Often it was easier to see in retrospect just what nerve he had touched: the concern about the gradually encroaching communism implicit in the cornucopian economy in his *Leonid Brezhnev*; the need to overcome a sense of division and faction in his version of *West Side Story*; the feeling of a softening in morale, a loss of possibility for heroism in *Guevara*; the troubled ethics of resurrection in the sensational vulgarities of *Herbert West*.

Now, as he walked through the deep, morning-shadowed streets of the Government quarter, he felt he was out of touch. What he had seen and heard, even smelled, on the way here was something he hadn't encountered before and didn't himself feel. Here a glance that lingered then jumped away when met, there an edged rasp and quaver in a young woman's voice; in the air of the crowded commuter shuttles a faint, disquieting sour tang. Fear. It was unmistakeable, and unbelievable. It just didn't sit well with what he knew of New Start. The city had always lived up to its name, and so had the planet. The colony had burned off all its fear in fueling its long flight, and it urged those who loved it to not look back. They had turned their faces towards an unknown future with gaiety and resolve. His friend Adrian had often detected a febrile undertone to this, a sadness in living beyond extinction, a *post mortem triste* . . . but Ben-Ami never had. Perhaps he wasn't sensitive enough. Perhaps he was made of sterner stuff. He didn't know.

What he felt now, beneath his present worry about what other people felt, and beneath his mild foreboding about the appointment to which he briskly walked, was elation. *We are not alone! The universe is open! There are people out there! There are doors to everywhere! We can fittle!* He could feel his steps spring, he could almost punch the air at the thought. Why are you walking like this, he wanted to ask the trudging crowd as he slipped through its gaps, when we should all be dancing?

He ran up the marble steps of a familiar ornate building, beside whose open doors a modest plaque proclaimed it the offices of the Members of the Eurydicean Assembly.

"I have an appointment at nine with Jean-Luc Menard," he told the receptionist. "Member for the Seventy-Ninth Arrondissement."

"He's available, Mr. Ben-Ami." The receptionist looked slightly awkward. "Ah . . . if you can spare a moment?"

Ben-Ami signed the tattered programme book for *The Madness of George II*—a farce from seventy-odd years earlier that he'd have been delighted to forget—chatted briefly, got the directions, and bounded up the indicated stair.

Menard welcomed him into an office with a good view to-

wards the ocean and a lot of screens on the walls, all silent
and all full of earnestly talking people: an early debate in the
Assembly, morning studio interviews, vox-pops. Menard
was a short man who looked a little older and stouter than he
needed to; it was as much part of his image as the conservative, almost collarless suits and shirts which he wore in daily
defiance of (and approximately annual compliance with)
fashion. One of the responsible elements, he'd been Ben-
Ami's MEA and nodding acquaintance for decades.

After a few social niceties over a cup of coffee, Menard
got to the point.

"This is . . . a little difficult, Benjamin," he said. "I don't
usually ask my constituents in to see me. Normally, of
course, it's the other way round. As you know."

"I appreciate your help on many occasions past," said
Ben-Ami, searching his memory for any relatives or offspring Menard might have with theatrical ambitions or pre-
tensions, and finding none. "If there's anything I can do for
you . . ."

"Not at all, nothing personal, nothing like that," said
Menard. He glanced out of the window, and back. "Damn it,
old chap, I hate doing this." He slapped his hands on his
knees. "The fact is, it's about your play."

"My play?" For a moment, Ben-Ami thought it was his
most recent play that was meant: *The Reformer Reformed*, a
knockabout satire on Eurydicean politics that had closed on
its third night. Had there been some careless allusion in it
that had offended Menard?

"The Returner play."

"Oh!" Ben-Ami laughed, relieved. "Early days, Jean-Luc.
Don't like to talk about unfinished projects—bit of a profes-
sional superstition, I know, but there it is. I can tell you this
much—" He tapped his nose. "It'll be controversial."

"Indeed." Menard frowned at him. "That's the problem."

"I'm sorry." Ben-Ami shook his head. "What problem?"

"It's difficult to put this as delicately as I would wish,"
said Menard. "Let's just say there are many people who
would regard it as politically inopportune. In the present sit-

uation only, I assure you. When things settle down a little, then, to be sure, there would be no objection, but for now . . ." He spread his hands.

Ben-Ami floundered. "I expected my political friends to question it. All sorts of rumours are flying around. You know what actors are like, can't resist gossip or a good line—but I assure you, when you see it all in context—"

Menard threw up his hands. "Yes, yes. Patriotic, progressive, all that sort of thing. The business with the Returners might raise some eyebrows, but I'm confident you can carry that off. That isn't the problem—or rather, it precisely is the problem. To stir up feelings, however well-intentioned, of what one might call the *chauvinisme*, the sense of Eurydicean—"

"One moment," said Ben-Ami coldly. "You, my friend, a *responsable politique*, are telling me there are those who fear my play will be too patriotic?"

"Yes," said Menard, sounding ashamed of himself. "Not myself, of course. Not even our party. I am merely the messenger, you understand. I've been asked by a very highly placed source to convey a—a word of advice. The Executive, and above all the Joint Chiefs, are very concerned about the delicacy of our relationship—a relationship of the highest importance to our security, perhaps even to our existence—with our new allies."

"Ah, I *see*!" said Ben-Ami. "They're worried about offending the Knights!"

"Exactly," said Menard, beaming obvious delight that they were at last on the same wavelength.

"Then," said Ben-Ami, standing up, "I'll thank you to convey a message back to your friends in high places. Tell them they can take their word of advice and stick it up their arses."

Winter had once stood on the pier at South Queensferry, and noticed the three-metre height between high and low tide. He had guessed that the area of sea in front of him, between the Road Bridge and the Forth Bridge, was approximately a kilometre square. In that little area, that tiny fraction of the sea's surface, three million tons of water had been raised in a few hours, airily lofted by the distant moon. He had been struck by what had then seemed deep thoughts about physics and gravity and tidal forces, of the sheer power in the great machine of the world.

Or maybe he hadn't, and the memory had been provided for him by another machine, as a logical consequence of some surviving fragment of his experiences and beliefs, rather than from, say, a recorded snatch of reminiscence caught on late-night television.

Whatever. He remembered it now, looking across the city at the black ship that hung above the park like a cartoon weight marked one! million! tons! and poised for an impossible instant before it flattened whatever or whoever was under it.

"Bugs you, doesn't it?" said Calder, evidently noticing the way Winter's gaze gravitated to the thing. They were drinking mid-morning coffee in an open-air waterfront café where Ben-Ami had arranged to meet them.

"It does," said Winter. "Like, what's holding it up?"

"Ask the Knights." Calder jerked his head, indicating several black-clad men drinking tea a few tables away.

"I have," Winter said, leaning out of his partner's sidestream smoke. "They asked me a few questions about my knowledge of physics, and politely suggested that I acquire some more before asking questions whose answers I couldn't understand."

"Sound advice."

"On the other hand, maybe they don't know either."

Calder snorted. "There's a lot of that about. You ask any of the locals how their system works, they look at you as if you're stupid for even asking. They don't even give you a handwave." He waved his arms about. "I mean, where's our guided tour of utopia? That's part of the package. It's in the brochure. I checked."

"This isn't utopia," said Winter. "It's what we had back in

Polarity, with the rations and incentives and all. It's just got more sophisticated. More abstract. Lucinda got the guided tour. Couldn't make head nor tail of it, she said."

"Still carrying that torch," Calder said.

"Yes," said Winter. He felt a sudden surge of frustration, a tension from his groin to his throat via his solar plexus. "You know, I'm getting fed up with this place."

Calder looked surprised and bothered. "Why?"

"Oh, I don't know. It's because it's like Polarity, I guess. I feel like we're still in the fucking tunnels." He swung his hands back and forth on both sides of his head. "I can't wait for them to open their wormhole gates or for some ships to arrive that aren't stuffed with smiling samurai. I want to see the other planets, right, and I want to go back to Earth."

Calder nodded and didn't seem to want to say any more, so Winter helped himself to more coffee and stared out to sea, inhaling the breeze. Freighters and bulk carriers filled the harbour, sailing dinghies and cruise liners dotted the sea to the horizon, aircars and entopters buzzed above it. All no doubt economically justified in some way he couldn't quite get his head around. Cornucopian capitalism ran on something even more abstract than money, a calculus of reputation and reward that tweaked the material balances and made or broke the fortunes of promoters and projectors, physical accountants, and venture planners. Loafing and lotus-eating earned contempt; providing goods and services that couldn't be churned out on a drexler bought respect. Art and design were big, as were entrepreneurship, advice—existential consultancy, philosophical mentoring, physical training, erotic education—and a surprising amount of manual labour, practical skill, and personal service all paid big dividends in credit and interest.

It was a great place, a lively city, a venue where he could make it big. So why did feel this way, as if he was trapped indoors in winter and getting cabin fever? Stir-crazy or SAD; maybe there was a vital line missing from the thin spectrum of the sun. Or it could be a combination of homesickness and lovesickness. That Lucinda Carlyle had visited

Earth, and that she spoke and acted like the people he remembered from Earth, that even in her appearance and accent she could have stepped straight out of his remembered past—all these resonated with the spurious memories of Irene and nostalgia for Earth that had gnawed at him so needlessly and so long.

"Good morning, gentlemen," said Ben-Ami, swooping to the table in the batwinged, knife-pleated gunmetal habit that was the fashion of the day. He poured coffee, sat back and grinned at the musicians. "I have news. Very interesting news." He paused, as if to tease out the moment.

"Fire away, mate," said Calder, earning a puzzled glance and a confidential hunch.

"I've just been called to a meeting with my MEA. He's warned me against putting on this production, for fear of—he leaned closer, spoke quieter—"offending the Knights." He sat back and brushed his palms against each other. "Worth about a thousand hours of publicity, wouldn't you say?"

"Hah!" said Calder. "That's one way of looking at it, and good for you. But how do you know it isn't a wise move to keep on the right side of the black-pyjama guys?"

Ben-Ami flapped a sleeve. "I don't care if it is or not. If our so-called security requires self-censorship of artistic work, then frankly we've lost the planet already. Genuine military and diplomatic considerations are one thing, and cultural cringing is another entirely. Let the Knights shut the production down themselves, should it come to that. I for one will not shut myself up on the basis of heavy hints dropped on my toe." He sipped a little more coffee, and darted a sharp glance at each of them. "Are you with me, gentlemen?"

They both nodded. At that Ben-Ami stood up. "Excuse me," he said. He lifted the crockery and *cafetière* and laid them carefully on a vacant seat, then jumped up on to the table. The clapping of his cupped hands was like a rattle of stage pistol-shots.

"Attention, people!" he shouted. He spun around, cloak swirling and flashing. "Listen, everyone!"

He had a fine deep voice and he knew how to project it. Heads turned.

"For anyone who doesn't know me—yes, gentlemen of the Knights, that means you—my name is Benjamin Ben-Ami. I am a playwright and promoter, and I intend to produce and have performed a spectacular musical entertainment based upon the history of Eurydice and its glorious precursor states. It will be called . . . *Rebels and Returners*, ladies and gentlemen, and it will be performed in the grounds of the Jardin des Étoiles in . . . four weeks!"

Winter saw Calder put his head in his hands, then look up and mouth silently *"Four fucking weeks!"*

"All are welcome!" Ben-Ami shouted. "And yes, gentlemen, that very much includes you, the Knights—"

The Knights stood up as one, tipped their heads towards Ben-Ami, and walked off.

A man jumped up, sending his table crashing.

"Now look what you've done, Ben-Ami! You've offended them! And I don't blame them, this is no time for this kind of divisive, contentious stuff!"

"Who says it's going to be divisive?" someone else shouted, and in the subsequent contention had his answer. Ben-Ami jumped down as the first thrown tomato whizzed past his head. More tables went over. Shouts. Winter stood up. Calder was already on his feet, in his forced fighting crouch, hands out, glaring around. Scuffles were breaking out. Out of the corner of his eye Winter saw a blade flash, then heard a grunt. He reached inside his jacket, forgetting that there was no weapon there.

Calder grinned, or maybe just bared his teeth.

"I hope you're getting all this, Benjy old boy," he said. "This is just like it was back on—"

A shoulder hit his hip and he went over.

Lamont stared at the patterns of the gravity-wave display, his mind translating it into a visual image as though it was a stereogram. The resulting magic-eye picture of the starships converging on Eurydice was as disturbing as it was vivid.

Hours passed. The patterns stabilised around the planet.

"The Knights aren't fighting them" he remarked.

"In part it is a question of the balance of forces," said the *Hungry Dragon*. "But more significantly, it is because these are not their enemies. These are not Carlyle family ships."

"What are they?"

The *Hungry Dragon* turned on several comms channels at once. The audio filled with American-accented voices, and the visuals with swift-shifting surveys of Eurydice and what looked like rapid-fire negotiation and exchange of contracts, in which kilohectares of land were being haggled over in acres of small print.

"What is online," said the ship with a rare stab at humour, "is America Offline. The farmers that Carlyle mentioned."

"They're selling land to each other!"

"They are at least staking claims."

"But they have no right—this is outrageous—"

The ship lurched. Lamont was thrown back and forth in the webbing. Through the singing cables he felt the additional vibration of a brief burn of the main jet, and a few nudges from the attitude jets.

"Stop!" he yelled.

"I am sorry," said the ship. "This is not under my control."

With fierce concentration Lamont eyeballed up some external views just as the retro-rocket jet killed the ship's forward momentum. Half a dozen gummy cables—extruded from somewhere on the surface between the rows of machinery pods—extended, clung, and contracted, winching the ship back a little to the polar end of the asteroid, where it was further snared and hauled. Within minutes its stern and jets were attached—glued, it seemed—to the rock. It was as though the ship had become the bowsprit of an iceberg. Lamont expected some of the pods to detach from the surface and fasten themselves to the side of the ship, but nothing of the kind happened. Instead, the external cameras showed the transmission dish aerials jerking about. The control board indicated that they were active. The power drain was visible to the naked eye.

"What are you transmitting?"

"I do not know," said the ship.

Lamont twisted in the webbing, then catapulted himself out of it to a corner of the control board and grabbed a manual control for an external aerial. It was a crude, mechanical contraption to move the dish in a case of power loss. He shifted it until it caught the edge of the beam from one of the transmitters.

"That was ingenious," said the ship.

"Are you receiving it?"

"Yes," said the ship. "It is identical to the transmission that took control of my processes."

"Do you have it firewalled?"

"Yes."

Lamont relaxed, for a moment. At least the whole business wasn't about to repeat itself. Then he thought a bit further.

"Where are these transmissions directed?"

"Towards Eurydice," said the ship.

"At a wild guess," snarled Lamont, "they're aimed at these newly arrived ships. It's trying its luck to hack into *them*."

"That sounds plausible," admitted the ship.

"Step two," said Lamont. "That Carlyle woman didn't seem bothered about war machines. I have the impression these people elsewhere in the galaxy have dealt with them before. They may have firewalls or antidotes to this virus. I don't expect them to be too kind towards any sources of it."

The ship's lights dimmed for a second.

"The transmissions have ceased," the *Hungry Dragon* reported.

"That doesn't change anything. We're a sitting duck."

"We are not," said the ship, "in the place from which the transmissions originated."

"What?"

The ship patched up an image of the stellar background,

time-stamped a minute earlier. Then another, shown as current. It repeated this several times. The difference was tiny, but perceptible as the image flicked back and forth.

"The stars have moved," said the ship. "Or we have."

SIDE 2

When the Stars Are Right

CHAPTER 11

Team Spirit

"You're a lightning-chaser," Carlyle said.

That was the polite term. The rude one was Rapture-fucker. What she'd said still sounded like an accusation. She hadn't meant it that way. She really wanted Campbell Johnstone on her team. He stared back at her, his gaze peculiarly blank. His retinae were really cameras. The irises didn't adapt, the photocells did. Carlyle was used to the widening of the pupils when men looked at her. Not on Eurydice, but thank God or Nature she wasn't there now. Only Winter and, to a much lesser extent, Calder and Armand had responded thus to her in that world of optimal beauty.

"I am that," Johnstone said. It was an English idiom, in a perfect Home Counties American accent, like in an Ealing comedy. He knocked back his whisky, refilled his glass from the bottle, topped up hers. "What's it to you?"

"I'm in the soul market," Carlyle said. "I can offer excellent rates."

The rates hadn't helped her get any kind of routine crew. The labour exchanges and other recruitment routes had effectively blacklisted her, whether because of Carlyle family old guard pressure or because she was too much of a risk.

The only people she could hire would have a worse record than she had. Even the most adventurous freelancers had looked at the DK barter price list and shaken their heads. Hence her going after lightning-chasers.

"I shouldn't say this," said Johnstone, "but the rates aren't the issue. The risk is." He glowered at the bottle. "Moths to a flame, my dear. That's what we are."

Spare me the self-pity, you fucking drama queen. He seemed to pick up the thought. Maybe he did, you could never tell with lightning-chasers. You didn't know what enhancements they had.

"It's like an addiction," he said. "To get so close you could touch it, without getting dragged in yourself. It's hard to explain."

"You ever thought of going over to the Knights?" Carlyle asked, curiosity getting the better of discretion.

"Oh, sure." He sipped whisky. "Couldn't take the puritanism. Besides, their whole thing is, they don't go up close. Arm's length, gloves, tongs. Contemplate the mathematics. Complete the calculation. One step at a time. You know the drill. Not my scene at all."

"If it's risk you're after, I can offer plenty."

Johnstone sucked his lower lip, eased it out under his upper teeth. "All right," he said. "Show me."

She passed him the DK slate. He read through it impassively while she sat back and kept a wary eye on their surroundings. The Hairy Fairy was a dive so low it passed right under the Carlyles' radar. Dim lights, sour carpet sticky with spilt drinks, air stiff with smoke. Its clear, curving diamond window-wall overlooked New Glasgow's lights from two hundred metres up the side of a building crusted with similar bubbles. It was a notorious hangout for Rapture-fuckers, the bane of exploration and hacking teams. They were hard to screen out. Like sociopaths, they knew how to manipulate expectations they didn't share. In recruitment interviews and tests they came across as normal, knowledgeable, interested types, keen to get on a team. They could restrain their excitement long enough to complete a few missions successfully, often distinguishing themselves with what seemed like bravery. Then, just when you trusted them enough for a really challenging job, they'd let their obsession get the better of them, break away and plunge deep into the works. If they didn't disappear entirely—into the ravenous tornado of Singularity, or destroyed by the machinery—they came back changed: bodies mutilated or enhanced, minds time-sharing with, or displaced entirely by, other entities. Posthuman processors used human-level minds as subroutines. Some of these minds were eager to escape into other systems. With sufficient care one could trap them—as Shlaim had been—but without it, they could possess the incautious. The best outcome was when the Rapture-fucker was the only victim.

Some of the less autistic wrecks of such adventures were frazzling their neurons further in the corners of this bar. Trying to make the voices go away, or shut up, or speak more clearly; trying to make the fleeting impossible insight come back. A woman with long silver hair leaned against the outward overhang of the window wall, palms and forehead pressed against it, as though contemplating a jump that the diamond plate denied her. Every so often she'd rock back, reach behind her for a bottle on the table, swig, and resume her outward staring without turning around.

"This is the one you want," Johnstone said, pushing the slate across the table and swivelling it at the same time. He'd highlighted the relevant paragraph in the long list of bits of kit DK considered the equivalent of one of their new ships. All of them looked almost impossible to get hold of, with the resources she could muster; this one she'd dismissed entirely.

"One (1) macroscale quantum teleportation device (transmitter and receiver) fully functioning with human-level interface control enabled; minimum mass transfer capability: two (2) tonnes; minimum resolution scale: atomic; minimum range 10 1y."

"This is some kind of joke," Carlyle said. "The little commie bastards are trying it on. There's only been one, brackets, one of these ever found, and we sold it to the Knights for a fucking solar system. One with two gas giants and a habitable terrestrial, at that."

"There wasn't only one found," said Johnstone. "There's only one been *recovered*. I know where you can find another, because I've seen it myself." He laughed. "I can even tell you. It's no secret. It's just that nobody's been mad enough to go after it. It's in the cave system on Chernobyl."

The name made her shoulders hunch a little. "That's a pulsar planet! And it's right in the beam!"

Johnstone nodded. "Every two point seven seconds. Chernobyl's tidal-locked to the primary—no rotation, and the gate's on the day side, if you call getting nuked every two-and-a-bit seconds 'day.' The gate's fifty-odd klicks from the caves—from the known entrance to the cave system, that is. The terrain is rough, the atmosphere's thick, ionised, stormy . . . let's just say you wouldn't want to fly in it. What light gets through is from the stars and from secondary radioactivity. The machine, the QTD, masses about five tonnes and is as delicate and about as radiation-tolerant as a leaf photometer. It's only because it's three hundred metres below ground that it's survived at all." He smiled. "And that's just the transmitter. The receiver is a few thousand kilometres away—still on the day side, worse luck. Heavily shielded with a hundred tons of lead, because it's in a shallower cave. One that doesn't have any known entrance. And believe me, the planet's been satellite-mapped to centimetre resolution."

"So how come anyone knows where it is, or even that it exists?"

"We fired up the QTD transmitter and sent a probe through it. It was possible to deduce its new location by timing the radiation pulses. Some of that shit punches straight through half a klick of rock, and this was maybe ten metres below the surface." He shrugged. "Of course, you can only do so much with probes. Especially in these conditions. Terribly bad line, you know. So I took a backup and went through myself."

She tried not to show quite how impressed she felt. "What did you find?"

"Oh, a cave full of very nice kit. Nothing as good as the QTD, though. And no way out, no exit that I could find. No transmitter the other way, either."

"So how did you—oh."

"I didn't. I died there. Gives me claustrophobia just thinking about it." He thumped his chest. "I'm the backup."

"How did you die?" she asked.

"Suicide, I'm pleased to say. Webster bolt to the head. Good to know I have the balls for it. Though considering it was the first symptoms of radiation sickness that made me do it—puking up in the suit and all that, very messy— maybe 'balls' isn't quite the mot juste."

"Somehow," Carlyle said, "I get the impression you're not telling me all this to show how tough you are. You think there's a way to get the thing out."

"Oh, I know there is," said Johnstone. "Think about it. The Raptured may have been as gods, but they couldn't work miracles. How did the receiver get into a closed cave? There must be another gate, in the second cave."

"Leading to God knows where."

"Well, yes." He grinned. "Exciting, isn't it?"

"What about the transmitter?"

"I'm afraid there's no way around that one. There's simply no way to get it to the gate. So forget about gates. You'd have to land a starship as near to the entrance as possible and load it on. Come to think of it, you could do the same with the other one. Use a bunker-buster to break into the cave— the receiver's shielded, like I said, so it's pretty robust—and carry it out."

"Why hasn't that been done?"

"The pulsar beam is like a nuclear bomb going off nearby in vacuum every two point seven seconds. You'll recall what a radiation burst like that does to a starship main drive."

"I do indeed," said Carlyle. "But you could protect the

drive by cladding it with enough lead. Hundreds of tons."

Johnstone leaned back. "You could," he said. "And why isn't that done routinely, I ask, given the low but unfortunately not zero frequency of nuclear skirmishes?"

"Because if you did that, you wouldn't have enough power to shift anything much else."

"Exactly," said Johnstone. "It isn't just the added weight—shielding the drive against radiation weakens the field's grip on the spacetime manifold. And don't forget, we're talking about loading *another* hundred-plus tons of lead-cladded object on board."

Carlyle ran through some mental calculations. "It could still be done," she said. "Cutting it very fine, leaving out every scrap of mass you didn't need . . . shit. And some that you would. There'd be nowhere near enough for the team's protective suits, or extra armour for the search engine. Or a search engine at all, come to that. The team and the crew would have to stay in the same shelter as the drive . . . yeah, that's possible, but when they went out . . . "

"How clearly you see the problem," said Johnstone. "Believe me, I've done the math. Factored in all the equipment you'd need—a crane and a truck, principally—and whichever way you cut it, you're right at the margin. You can't get the ship there safely *and* have the safety gear for a surface team. We're not talking suits, anyway. That pulsar beam is *fierce*. You'd need a search engine with so much armour it can barely move, like we had. The solution, of course, positively jumps out at you."

"Do it in two trips. Or two ships. Or a really big KE ship, or one of those AO arks . . . "

"Can you afford that? Any of that?"

"If I could get the investment in advance . . . but not for this, no. Just a standard AO truck."

"Well, then."

Carlyle stared at him. His fixed-pupil eyes stared back.

"Oh, fuck," she said. "One-way."

"Dying's not so hard," said Johnstone. "Take it from me."

*   *   *

A lot of things could go through your mind at a moment like this. The first thing that Carlyle thought about was robots. She dismissed the thought. She couldn't afford robots. Robots autonomous and smart enough to do that kind of job were more expensive and harder to hire than humans, and less easily replaced. The second thing she thought about was dying. She'd never done it before, and there was a certain pride in that, an existential security in knowing for sure that you were who you thought you were. It felt clean. On the other hand, a lot of people, most of whom she knew and had trusted her, had lost that innocence because she had fucked up. Maybe it was time for her to show she could take it, so that she could look them in the eye again. The third, and oddly enough the most conclusive, was the thought of more dreary trudging or phoning around the exchanges and more scornful looks from freelancers. This was the first person she'd met who thought one of the jobs was feasible and wanted to take it on.

"All right," she said, her mind suddenly made up and immediately quailing, "let's do it or die trying."

"It's 'and' not 'or,' my dear," said Johnstone. He raised his drink. "Good health."

After they clinked glasses he became instantly businesslike. "Who else do you have on the team?"

"You're the first," Carlyle admitted.

"That's good," he said, to her surprise. "It means we're not cluttered up with artillerymen, grunts, scientists, and such, all quite redundant on this exercise. You'd have had to stand them down anyway. You, me . . . the pilot comes with the ship, fine, I presume you can hire one for a quick in-and-out"—Carlyle nodded—"and one more person. A heavy-duty crane operator with archaeology experience and a death wish."

"A tall order."

"Not a bit of it," said Johnstone. "I know someone who's just the ticket. You've come to the right place."

He stood up, quite steadily considering how much he'd drunk, and threaded his way among the tables. He returned with the silver-haired woman from the window. Her face too was silvery, as though coated with aluminium powder. Her eyes were cameras, but more cosmetically effective and emotionally responsive than Johnstone's.

"Morag Higgins," she introduced herself, shaking hands and smiling. Teeth like steel. She sat down and helped herself to the single malt.

"I know who you are," she added, raising a glass. "Well met, Carlyle. Your reputation precedes you."

"Not a very good one, at the moment."

"It is to me," said Higgins. Her metallic teeth glinted again. "I'm well up for a suicide mission. It's the only way I can afford a backup and a resurrection."

"Why do you need one? If you don't mind me—"

Higgins waved away the apology. She drew a finger across her throat, at the line between the silvery skin and the rest.

"Last mission I was on—another pulsar planet as it happens, PSR B1257+12 c, the one in Virgo—I wandered off on my own." She tossed her silver hair back; it made a hissing noise as it settled. "All right, all right, I'm a lightning-chaser. I admit it." She swallowed some whisky, smiled wryly at Johnstone. " 'My name is Morag Higgins, and I'm a Rapture-fucker.' I got . . . infected. Optic-nerve hack, absolute classic, should never have fallen for. . . . Anyway. Then it makes me open up, some kind of needle gets in, right. Hours later I wander back sounding very strange. Team leader—one of your lot, Jody Carlyle her name was—she blows my fucking head off. End of story. Except it isn't. Whatever it was had taken a backup of me, and stored it outside my head. Which it also had a memory of." She tapped her face with the glass. It rang. "*This* grows back. It's a crawling mass of steel nanobots. Most of it's machinery for the meat—hormones, blood circulation, that kind of thing.

My actual mind's on a chip *describing* my brain, just like a backup, except it's running in real time. I'm still me, memories and everything, but my emotions are kind of raw, as you might expect. Mostly frustration, in that I can't get drunk and *nobody* will give me a job. Until you came along. Thanks, sweetie."

Carlyle felt as if her own head had turned hollow and hard. The room went cold and dim for a moment. She fought down a dry heave. A long slug of whisky burned along her throat and warmed her belly and brought some blood back to her brain.

"Losing heads seems to be an environmental hazard on pulsar planets," she said, toughing it out. "Ever wonder if your other body's still headless, Johnstone?"

"I have indeed," he said. "I guess we'll find out, huh?"

The DK Interests Section in New Glasgow maintained a quantum-entanglement comms link to the nearest branch of the Shipyard Twenty-Nine production brigade. Carlyle held out for expenses, which she had carefully costed: as well as the lead shielding, surprisingly expensive, there were the usual crew pay, backups and insurance, the hire of a ship. Normally that was implicit in the contract price, but you couldn't be too careful with DK. To her surprise they agreed straight away, and topped her opening bid with an offer to pay 5% up front. She walked out of the building with a thick wad of AO kilodollars which every few minutes she checked again until she was sure they weren't about to turn into dry leaves.

Sorting out the hire of a ship and the installation of the shielding took another couple of days, after which they were ready to go as soon as they'd all taken a last-minute backup. At the drily named Terminal Clinic just outside the gate complex the tech balked at first over Higgins; Carlyle frowned him down. He was just being awkward, she pointed out: reading a chip had to be easier than reading a brain. She tried to put the momentary unpleasantness from her mind as her own reading was taken. As always, it was overridden by the poignancy of such occasions, routine though they were; a feeling of sorrow for the person who would be resurrected, not the self who would have died. It was like seeing yourself in an old photograph. If they were lucky, they'd all make it back alive, take another backup and check out on a warm flood of heroin in the hospice ward. But they couldn't bet on making it back. This might be her last saved self.

Outside she looked over her team. They could have been going on a skein hike. Not much food; this job was going to be quick or not at all. Suits, lights, emergency high-calorie rations, water, one Webster each just in case.

"Keep the last cartridge," said Johnstone, stashing a charge, and Higgins laughed. They set off through the gate. Fifteen transitions later, they arrived at the planet where the ship waited. Beyond the terminal's plate-diamond window it sat on a bright field under a black sky where only a vast circular occlusion of the stars showed the primary, a brown dwarf. They sealed their suits and trekked out through the airlock and across the field to the ship. Its name was lettered in stencil style on its side: *Extacy*. Everything unnecessary on board had been stripped out. The lead-brick shelter gleamed dully like a giant slug. A massive crane and a shaped-charge Webster reaction bomb occupied the cargo bay. Higgins checked the crane, gave a thumbs-up. Johnstone and Carlyle checked the bomb. The pilot was a teenage AO tyke with freckles and hair the colour of wheat. He led them into the shelter and they huddled on the floor next to the drive.

"This'd better be worth it," he said, by way of greeting, as he fingered a jury-rigged control panel that looked like a games console. Carlyle flipped him what remained of her roll of advance money.

"Call that a bonus," she said. "Lift and fittle, already."

Johnstone patched him the coordinates. The pilot scrolled up the resulting stellar map, rolled his eyes upward, closed them for a moment in what might have been prayer, and fired up the drive. Twenty light-years and half an hour later, they were in the pulsar's system. Another two hours of careful manoeuvring and they were at the site.

"You really expect to die out there?"

"No," said Carlyle stiffly. "We'll just be walking dead when we come back on board. Like the zombies from the cities after the Big One. I'm sure your grandmother told you about them."

The boy shivered. "Holy Koresh help you."

"Yeah," said Higgins nastily, "*he* knew all about suicide. Now open the fucking door."

Johnstone had guided the *Extacy* to within fifty metres of the cave entrance. Out on the surface the cliff-face was barely visible. With the lights full on Carlyle could see clearly a few steps in front of her. Every couple of seconds the faint glow in the atmosphere peaked and faded, which with the simultaneous spikes on her radiation moniter were the only indications of the pulsar's spin. Before they'd gone five metres the dosimeter in her head-up was over the yellow line for *Abort Mission, Seek Medical Attention*. There was only the red line above that: *Fatal Dose, Please Back Up Your Memory to a Secure Server*. She avoided watching the virtual needle's upward creep.

Johnstone drove the balloon-wheeled flatbed truck down the ramp and the two women clambered on. There were no seats, just a bar to hang on to. Like the ship, the vehicle was stripped to a minimum. The controls were on a handset over which Johnstone's thumb flipped back and forth.

The cave, when they reached the entrance a minute or two later, was not at all what Carlyle had expected. The air was clearer, visibility much better. The walls—about three metres apart, just enough clearance for the truck—were smooth and the angles between them and the floor and roof were sharp. Rather than the diffuse glow of ionised air and surface radioactives, it was lit by distinct glowing patches every few metres along the roof.

"This isn't a cave," said Higgins. "It's a tunnel."

"When you're looking at the work of the Raptured," Johnstone said, "that distinction becomes kind of moot. Check out our expedition report sometime. None of this shows any trace of having been made, or the rock's having been *worked*. It's like some wildly unlikely coincidental outcome of geological processes. Like those natural nuclear reactors they found in Africa, only more so."

Carlyle had often enough seen structures of which the same could have been said, but something about Johnstone's confident statement niggled at her. Before she could track down the elusive thought, the truck emerged from the tunnel into a chamber about forty metres high and wide and over a hundred metres long. The light-patches, at this distance quite obviously rectangular, dotted the vaulting roof and soaring sides. The floor was littered with large complicated metal objects whose nature as machinery was as clear as their purpose was obscure. It was like standing in a cathedral that had been taken over by militant scientific atheists as a laboratory or factory, and then abandoned. The truck's lights, as they moved, cast shadows like encroaching cowled inquisitors eager to avenge the sacrilege.

Johnstone idled the truck, jumped out and led the way through the machinery. He stopped in front of what looked like a solid gold omega, the circular part about two metres across, the two horizontal pieces at the bottom fixed to a steel plinth in which several control panels were embedded.

"There it is," he said. "The transmitter."

"How do we get that onto the truck?" Higgins asked.

"Very carefully," said Johnstone.

He remote-controlled the truck along the path they'd taken on foot, bringing it to a halt a couple of metres away. Then he lowered the flatbed platform to the ground. He sprayed the edge of the platform, and the floor between the truck and the QTD, with buckyball lubricant. Carlyle was expecting they'd have to push it, but Johnstone tied some carbon-fibred rope to the object and Higgins expertly converted the engine shaft to a winch. Very slowly, and steadied by all three of the team, the QTD transmitter was eased on to the truck and lashed into place.

On their return to the cave entrance Johnstone called up the pilot, who brought the *Extacy* directly outside. Even more slowly and carefully, they got the object up the ramp and into the ship. With more buckyball lubricant and, this time, muscle force, they pushed and pulled it into the lead shelter. Cleaning up the lethally slippery lubricant took longer.

"Now for the tricky bit," said Johnstone.

He had, as he'd claimed, done the math. The pilot already had the coordinates of the receiver's location, and Johnstone had an even more precise spot in mind for the break-in. There was no GPS—even the radiation-hardened exploration satellites thrown into orbit by the first expedition had long decayed or burned out—so navigation was an old-fashioned affair of checking the apparent position of the more prominent of the detectable stars, then of matching local gravitational anomalies with their records, then of matching the disorderly ground with the high-resolution maps, then of radar pinging.

"This is definitely it," Johnstone said, as the *Extacy* hovered above a two-kilometre-wide bulge of upraised plain in a circle of eroded hills, all of which looked almost identical to a hundred adjacent features even on the map, let alone in the glowing murk. The radar and the gravity meter showed empty space underneath, as they had for the plain behind the nearby range, and behind the one before that.

"You're absolutely sure of this," Higgins said.

"Absolutely," said Johnstone. He left the shelter and wheeled the bomb to the hatch. "Take us to twelve hundred metres," he told the pilot. "Forward one hundred metres, ten, four. Mark."

Then he tipped the bomb out. A second or two later a faint thud was detectable through the ship's external microphones. There was no flash.

"An earth-shattering *kaboom*," Johnstone said, sauntering back to the shelter.

"That's it?" Carlyle asked.

"Of course it is," Johnstone said. "Come out and take a look."

They did. Beneath the hatch a black round hole, still infrared at the edges, fifty metres across and surrounded by a ragged ring of ejecta, was clearly visible against the grey and glint of the plain. Deep within the blackness indistinct shapes glowed faintly.

"Told you so," said Johnstone. "Down we go."

Higgins clambered the ladder to the crane's cabin and manoeuvred the huge machine to straddle the hatch. Johnstone attached himself to the end of the cable; Carlyle clipped on just above him. The descent was swift and smooth. They could have been in a lift. The lip of the hole was exactly as Johnstone had said, ten metres thick. Higgins checked the descent just after they'd passed it. Their helmet lamps and handheld lights picked out a space even vaster than the first cave, and more cluttered, and with larger and stranger machines, as big as blue whales and as complex as protein molecules: folds and helices, mirror-perfect plane surfaces, dendritic bushes, arrays of lobate panels. Tiny lights pulsed or raced among them and along them, like remote descendants of the blinkenlights on an antique server.

Johnstone guided the pilot and Higgins through a few more fine adjustments, and then they were lowered to the flat basalt floor in a motorway-wide aisle between rows of the machines. Keeping the rope attached, Johnstone strode confidently forward, turned a corner, and peered into a gap.

"Shit," he said.

"What?"

"I died here."

"How do you know?"

"I gave the location in my final message," he said.

"You could have been delirious by that time."

"I doubt it. Anyway, look." His beam and his pointing finger indicated a ragged scorch-rimmed hole in the smooth pedestal of the fractal pagoda in front of them. "Webster bolt." Dipping, the beam found a spattered smear on the floor, crusted over with some crystalline mould. "Blood."

"So where's the body?"

"That's what I ask myself," said Johnstone. He giggled. "Watch out for Johnstone the headless Webster gunner."

"Fuck," said Carlyle, backing out of the alley and looking over her shoulder. "Don't *say* things like that."

"What's to worry about? We're zombies ourselves now anyway. Or hadn't you noticed?"

Carlyle checked. She was over the red line. No deep spiritual insights followed. Just as well, she thought, as they would have died with her. But she felt less spooked.

"I thought we were heading for the QTD," she said.

"It's a few minutes walk from here. Allow me a moment of sentimental curiosity."

As she followed him along the aisle Carlyle in fact felt reassured by the precision of his navigation. This feeling didn't last. After about fifty metres Johnstone halted and turned aside to marvel at an inlaid screen at about eye level, a rectangle about one and a half metres by two and a half. It was a dull pewter colour and held a watery pattern that wouldn't quite resolve into a moving monochrome picture. She wanted to stare at it, to make it stabilise, but every time its evanescent shapes eluded her—

She jerked her head sideways, breaking the spell. Before she could stop him, Johnstone had extended a lead from his helmet and was jacking it into a socket in the screen's bottom right corner. She swiped at the cable and the pin sprang out. Johnstone didn't react. She waved a hand in front of his faceplate. Still no reaction. She grabbed his shoulders and pushed him gently back. His feet paced, keeping his balance, but his eyes stared out, still in a dwam. Fuck, fuck, fuck. She wished she still had a familiar handy, to hurl a disposable and screamingly reluctant copy into the internal fray of Johnstone's suit circuitry. But since Shlaim's defection, she'd lost her trust in virtual slaves. She was alone in her suit.

Back to elementary first aid, the rule-of-thumb routines the Carlyles had put together from centuries of experience in dealing with CNS hacks. She drew back her fist, made sure he could see it coming if he could see anything at all, and punched at his faceplate as hard as she could. The blow didn't shatter the plate, or numb her knuckles, but it knocked Johnstone off his feet.

"What the fuck was that for?" Then; " . . . Oh, thanks."

He struggled to his feet, disentangling himself from the cable.

"Hang on a minute," he said. He blinked rapidly, eyes rolling as he paged through head-up menus. "Good, that's it cleared."

"Sure?"

"Best antivirus money can buy," Johnstone said smugly.

"I bloody hope so."

"They don't evolve, that's one thing."

"Small mercies."

Johnstone laughed. "It's the biggest."

They walked on. It was like being in the Valley of the Kings, or Manhattan, or Polarity, except that every one of the great machines contained more art and craft and mind than the entire civilisations that had produced these works of man. Carlyle, looking at it all with a looter's eye, had long grown blasé at this thought.

The QTD receiver was, in that place, brutal in its simplicity: a ten-metre torus of lead, with a ring of the same gold and instrumentation as the transmitter had, inlaid in a deep groove around its inner surface. Its base was an proportionately huge rectangular mass. Johnstone vaulted up on it, disengaged himself from the line, told Carlyle to do the same, and then passed the end of the cable around the ring. He knotted the rope carefully, checked it a few times, and gave a thumbs-up. With a lot of careful instructions and some errors they and Higgins between them managed to drag it to beneath the hole. Carlyle, sitting on the opposite side of the base, rode up with Johnstone as the cable carried the massive object up into the ship's hold. Higgins rolled the crane forward and lowered the device to the floor.

"I hope that was worth it," the pilot said, over the common circuit.

Carlyle, Higgins, and Johnstone looked at each other.

"Tactless little prick, isn't he," Johnstone observed. "Time to go, I guess."

"Wait a minute," Carlyle said. "There's stuff in that cave that, well, I wouldn't want to go to waste."

"You're not thinking of hanging around," Higgins said.

"No, no. But to make life easier"—she winced—"so to speak, for a future team, we could leave the crane."

"Now there's an idea," said Johnstone. "Well, hell, you paid for it, the Carlyles might as well have the advantage of it."

Getting the crane out was awkward. The pilot brought the ship right down to the surface, with the hatch open much wider than before, fully retracted. Carlyle guided Higgins as she drove the crane off the floor of the hold and on to the surface close to the hole, then the pilot lifted the ship clear. He lifted it more than clear, taking it up to about five hundred metres. Very slowly it moved aside; as Higgins descended from the crane's cabin Carlyle guessed that the pilot was looking for a spot where he could bring the ship down again without any risk of colliding with the crane. The ship's lights shone bright in the dim glow of the ionized haze of Chernobyl air.

"Let's move over a bit," Higgins said. "Give him a couple hundred metres clearance. He says he's worried about gusting."

Carlyle was looking down at the ground again, picking her way cautiously forward, when she saw out of the corner of her eye a blue flash just above the horizon. She then saw another, and another, closer and closer. In between, like a shadow on the shining mist, a gigantic batwinged shape was just discernible.

It was far bigger than the ships she'd seen back at the DK spaceport.

The DK ship was heading straight for the *Extacy*, flying quite slowly, except that every few hundred metres, it fittled. It must, Carlyle guessed, be fittling a light-second away, then returning to the exact point from which it had departed, and moving forward again and repeating the process. Every 2.7 seconds, she realised: timed to avoid the pulsar beam. Just when it seemed about to collide with the *Extacy*, its enormous wings swept downward, meeting at the tips to form a circle. A blink later, and the wings encircled the *Extacy* from above. Another blue Cherenkov flash followed, almost overhead. Its afterimage faded. Both ships were gone.

CHAPTER 12

Nerves of Steel

Carlyle had her Webster out and aimed at Higgins's face-plate before the woman's mouth had closed. She felt betrayed, abandoned, fooled like a rube, and enraged.

"You bastards! You stupid fucking bastards! Tell me what you did that for! I'll blow your fucking head off right here!"

"I had nothing to do with it!"

"You must have been in on it together!"

"I wish I had been—then I wouldn't be left down here with you!" Higgins's metal face looked distraught and bewildered. Carlyle backed off, keeping the pistol levelled. Her knees felt rubbery.

"So what's your explanation?" she demanded.

"Never trust a commie," said Higgins.

Carlyle glared at her. "Never trust a Rapture-fucker, you mean!"

Higgins shrugged. "Takes two to make a deal."

Her offhand attitude and flip answers reignited Carlyle's fury. "Yeah, or three! Or four if it was you and that hick pilot!"

"Not me!"

"You knew nothing about this?"

"No."

The metal face was etched with anguish. Carlyle believed her. The anger dimmed, leaving a cold dismay. They were going to die more painfully and uncomfortably than she'd intended, but that wasn't the worst. They were going to die for nothing. She squatted down, lowering the pistol.

"Oh fuck, fuck, fuck," she moaned. "Why the *hell* would they do that?"

"Like I said, never trust—"

"Oh, fuck that," Carlyle snarled. "That's just a stupid fucking prejudice. When they do a deal they stick to it—it's in their interests after all. I can buy an AO pilot selling us out, even to DK. I can't buy a DK family cheating us."

Higgins moved over and squatted down too.

"We don't know it was the same family as you were dealing with. Or the same group within the family. You should know about that, Carlyle."

"Don't tell me what I should fucking know about," Carlyle said. "It still doesn't figure. These DK clans compete all right, but they keep a united front to the rest of the world."

"How do we know it was DK at all?"

Carlyle rocked back on her heels. "Because it was a DK ship." She knew that was a fallacy even as she said it.

"We don't even know *that*," Higgins said. "It was like the one in the spec, sure. But it was a lot bigger and better."

Carlyle snorted. "So who built it? Aliens?"

"Whoever *built* it," Higgins said, "might have sold it to someone else. Someone who wanted a QTD real bad. Or maybe just wanted another DK ship real bad and knew they could buy one with a QTD. Either way, I think there's some third party out there."

"The Knights?"

Higgins shrugged. "They're in hostility mode. Why not?"

"Why not indeed," Carlyle said bitterly. "That makes sense. They bought the first QTD off us and there's no reason they shouldn't steal the second. Seeing as we're fighting them and all. Shit."

She sat for a moment staring in silence at Higgins, not

wanting to divulge the next thought that followed on from
that. If the Knights of Enlightenment had an even better
model of the latest DK ship than the one she'd gone through
all this to buy, then her bright idea of using a DK ship to out-
manouevre them at Eurydice was so much chaff.

"I guess," said Higgins, "that you planned to use the ship
against the Knights at this new planet, and—"

"Oh, shut up!"

Higgins's steely lips compressed.

"What I don't understand," Carlyle went on, slightly
apologetic, "is what Johnstone would get out of it."

"You mean, apart from a lot of money when he comes
back from the dead?"

"Aye," said Carlyle. "Apart from that. What's money tae a
Rapture-fucker? The truth about this'll come out soon
enough, likely as soon as my backup back hame wakes up
and asks where the shiny new ship is. And after that his life
willna be worth a damn anywhere we can reach. And there's
naebody but us who'll poke around like we do in the tech,
which means nae other suckers tae latch ontae if Rapture-
fucking's yir fix."

Higgins shrugged. "This isn't getting us anywhere."

"Aye, you're telling me!" In a sudden surge of renewed
rage Carlyle brandished her pistol. "Do you want to get it
over with now? Put the guns to each other's heads, count of
three?"

Higgins shook her iron head, her steel tongue dry on her
steel lips.

"No," she said. "I don't trust that method of suicide, not
any more and not here." She glanced in the direction of the
hole. "Remember what Johnstone said."

"You heard all that?"

"Sure, it was on the open circuit."

"Fuck. You're right. Anyway. So what do we do, if we
cannae just kill ourselves?"

"I'll tell you what we can do," said Higgins, standing up.
"We use the time we've got. Johnstone thought there must be
another gate in there. We can go looking for that."

"With no guarantee that we'll find it, or that it'll lead any-where more hospitable."

"Any less hospitable and it'll be instantly lethal," said Higgins wryly. "Which is kind of the point, yeah? And any-way, looking for it will take our minds off things. And we might find some interesting stuff on the way."

A Rapture-fucker to the end, Carlyle thought. She had lit-tle doubt that Higgins, with nothing left to lose, would be off in the cave like a kid in a toyshop. On the other hand, she was right: doing something had to be better than waiting to die. Already she felt feverish and nauseous, but that could just have been the shock.

Aye. The shock.

Higgins went back up to the crane's cabin, retrieved a re-mote control for the winch, and they attached them-selves to the cable and descended together into the hole.

"Wow," said Higgins. "This place is fucking *magic*. All those little lights, like it's all alive!"

"Aye, whatever. No doubt we'll make a fortune off it someday. Any ideas about how we go about finding the gate?"

"You're the Carlyle. I thought you knew these things."

"I'll let you in on a family secret," said Carlyle. "Your guess is as good as mine."

"Oh!" said Higgins. "Well, in that case . . . "

"What?"

"I'd do it logically." She began turning around, her helmet beam and her handheld halogen spotlighting one uncanny thing after another. "There are passageways through the ma-chinery, aisles between the machines. That means that phys-ically shifting stuff must have been a consideration. One of these aisles must lead to the gate."

"No shit."

"Ah, but look at what we can see from here, of the angles and the layout. Which way are the paths converging?"

"Hard to tell, with perspective and all."

Higgins drew her Webster and thumbed the laser sight on. She squatted on her heels and again turned around, more slowly, sending the beam down each of the visible corridors. It glowed a faint red in the dusty air, picked out bright red spots where it met objects. The lights on the objects moved in a way that suggested a response. Then she stood up. "That way," she said confidently.

Carlyle didn't share her confidence, but she was past caring. "OK," she said. After a few hundred metres and several turns, she shared it even less. The only thing she was sure of was that she was thoroughly lost. She might be able to literally retrace her steps. The thought made her stop and glance back. Sure enough, their tracks were easily visible in the dust: two distinct sets of prints, sometimes crossing each other, slightly scuffed. Ten metres behind her, at the side of a thing that looked like a gigantic silver sculpture of a light-house-sized melted candle, was the end of a third set of prints.

She must have yelled. Higgins was back beside her in a moment.

"There," said Carlyle.

The third set of prints stretched into the distance as far as their lights could reach. They were of bare feet.

There was some kind of reassurance in that she and Higgins had drawn and levelled their pistols without conscious thought.

Carlyle switched on her suit's external speaker.

"Come out," she said.

Nothing happened.

She was about to step forward when Higgins caught her elbow. "No."

"What?"

"Leave it. If it wants to be seen, it will be."

"Aye, *that's* reassuring."

They walked on. Higgins never looked back, but every so often Carlyle did. The footprints were there behind them every time, always ending approximately the same distance away. After a while Carlyle began to hear, or imagine, stealthy pacing steps, approaching right up to behind her shoulder. She whirled, gun drawn, but still the prints ended ten or so metres behind. She wondered if whatever was following them was invisible. This thought was not reassuring either.

What overtook them eventually was weariness. They slumped, in wordless agreement, against a shining wall and sucked recycled water and greasy fruity-tasting paste from their helmets' tubes.

"White cell count right down," Higgins observed, with something like anxiety. "Not much longer to go."

"To the gate?"

"Till we die." She looked around and shivered, her shoulder shaking against Carlyle's. "I don't want to die here."

"Why not?" Carlyle had a metal taste in her mouth, but it was only her gums beginning to bleed.

"I can't swear that would guarantee extinction. There are some very sensitive devices in this place. They might . . . take us up."

"I know that," Carlyle said. "But is that no what you want? Rapture?"

"Oh, Christ, no." It sounded like a prayer, not a profanity. "There's no guarantee of becoming something better than human. You might become worse: a trapped consciousness in a treadmill, with no chance of upgrade. Hell. And even if you can avoid that, you still don't want to be taken up, even to heaven. You might lose yourself entirely."

"So why do you people risk that by lightning-chasing?"

Higgins sighed. "It's the getting close to . . . the sublime and the beautiful, yeah? You can look over the top of a cliff or look up at it and be, like, ravished, but you wouldn't want to fall off it."

"I don't understand the attraction at all," Carlyle said. She waved a hand. "I've been in places like this. Weirder and more beautiful places, like crystal jungles, like iron coral. And I've crunched a search engine right over them and through them tae get what I want. I mean, fuck, it isnae like it's nature or anything. It's just artificial."

"You don't understand," said Higgins. "What the posthumans created was—when you can see it up close, inside, in virtuality, not this"—she waved dismissively—"*hardware*, it's more wonderful than anything in nature. What you're seeing here is like brains. Grey matter, whorls, fissures, big fucking deal. What I've seen is thoughts. Art and science. Creations."

"Mair wonderful than the real world? Greater than God or Nature?"

"Yes!" said Higgins explosively. Then, perhaps sensing the stiffening in Carlyle's muscles, she retracted: "A greater insight into the reality than we have, anyway."

"Hah!" said Carlyle. "Tossers. I mean that. That's whit the Raptured were when ye get right down tae it. Nerds. Wankers. This is aw"—it was her turn to wave dismissively—"pornography. Because if it wisnae, how come they burned out so fast? How come they arenae around any mair? Wanked theirsels tae death if you ask me."

"You couldn't be more wrong," said Higgins. "They loved the universe far more than we ever can. There are infinitely many modes of existence of which we can't conceive: not space-time, not thought, not mind, or matter. They began to conceive them before they left. They went below the Planck length, and away. Into the fine grain of the world. And there they still are, and far beyond it. The whole of space-time is now riddled with their minds. Or rather, with minds far less than theirs but far greater than ours. It is these minds that enforce the CPC and make FTL travel possible and time-travel paradoxes impossible."

Carlyle had heard such conjectures before. "You know all this?"

Higgins laboriously stood up. "I know. I've seen it. Seen them. The quantum angels. Come on, let's find the gate."

The gate was in the direction Higgins had taken. Higgins's face looked twisted and strained, warped away from human semblance, as if resisting the deterioration of the rest of her body was becoming a major preoccupation for her metal head. You expected to see beads of mercury running down it. Her glass eyes had cracks in them.

Carlyle gazed at the gate incuriously. Its absent shape was outlined by a gold filigree frame beaded with crystals that flickered in elusive patterns. She had walked past greater and stranger things in the past hour. Her mind was jaded with wonders.

"Brilliant," she said. "You got us here."

Higgins attempted a smile. Reflective surfaces moved. "Just get me out."

Carlyle grasped her hand. "OK."

Together they stepped through the gate. As soon as they did so their knees buckled, their arms went instinctively in front of and above their faces, and again at the same moment, they both laughed and looked embarrassed at each other. They lowered their shielding arms. With an effort Carlyle straightened up, Higgins a moment later. 1.2 g: it was no worse than carrying a pack. Before them stretched a plain of cratered ice, sharply lit by a distant yellow-white F7 at what looked like 10 AU and blue-shaded by reflected light from the plain-featured sub-Jovian ice giant that filled a third of the sky and that had, for a moment, looked as though it was hurtling down upon them. Another moon, sulphur-yellow to its jet-black terminator, hung in the sky, its disc plain among a prickle of stars. Carlyle took a few steps forward and turned to look back at the gate. It was marked by a perfect parabola of smooth, sculpted-seeming ice.

"Where are we?" Higgins asked, feebly and querulously.

Carlyle gave her a smile she hoped was encouraging.

"In the skein, if we're lucky," she said. "Race you through the catalogue."

Higgins flapped a hand, and squatted, elbows on thighs. "You do it."

Carlyle blinked up the Messier 102.02 on her head-up and systematically scanned the sky. Her suit's sensors fed every available scrap of incoming information to the catalogue: the positions of the visible stars, the spectrum of the sun and of the light from the planet, the temperature of the ground, the motion of the other moon. . . . It took about a minute to match them and come up with the anonymous string of numbers that identified the system. She cross-referenced the result with the skein map.

"We're lucky," she told Higgins. "We're in the skein all right. If not exactly in the Drift. None of the firm's outposts is anywhere nearby." She licked her cracked lips, winced. "That gate we came through isn't marked. There's another one, but it's about twenty kilometres away. North-northwest." She looked around, letting the suit take a bearing from the now charted sky. The moon they were on had no magnetic field. "We should make it."

Higgins looked sceptical. "Where does it take us?"

Carlyle hesitated, then gave her the bad news. "A KE homeworld."

Higgins rose to her feet. She even smiled. "The *Ladies* of Enlightenment? That'll be something to see."

"Good on you," said Carlyle, dubious though she felt at the prospect. She had never heard of any outsider going to a KE homeworld, let alone coming back from one. This had, she hoped, more to do with the protectiveness of the Knights towards their homes than with anything more sinister.

They set off across the ice, following the bearing on her head-up. That gave them a direction, and it changed by dead reckoning as they detoured around craters large and small. It didn't so much as suggest an optimal route.

"Footprints behind us again," said Higgins, as they walked down a small valley that looked as if it had been carved by flowing water, but surely couldn't have been.

"That's our *own* footprints," said Carlyle. She wished Higgins hadn't said that. The thought that the haunter of the Chernobyl cavern could have followed them hadn't ocurred to her before. Now it wouldn't go away.

"Why are they in front of us?"

"Because we've had to retrace our steps."

"I can't see properly," said Higgins, sounding relieved and resigned.

She laid her hand on Carlyle's shoulder, and before long, a fair bit of her weight too. Carlyle vomited suddenly, and almost blacked out as she held her breath while the suit's cleaning mechanisms cleared the airways and the spew went into the recylers. They couldn't do anything about the stink, but after a while it had so saturated her nostrils that she couldn't smell it.

They stumbled on. The other moon moved in its orbit to a place where its shadow cast a spot, a solid ellipse of perfect black, on the ice giant. The shadow moved, it sometimes seemed, as they watched, and at other times, dismayingly, moved back.

"Relative motion of the moons," said Higgins, surprising Carlyle with that sensible reassurance.

The other gate appeared as a tiny regularity on the horizon a long time before they reached it; this world was bigger than most of the terrestrial planets, let alone moons, that either of them were used to walking on, and their intuitions played them false. The gate was marked with a square of ice, bevelled like a picture frame. It advanced and receded in Carlyle's sight as they approached, hour after hour. The moon-shadow vanished from the top of the giant planet's placid blue atmosphere.

"Are we there yet?" said Higgins, when they were a hundred or so metres from the ten-metre high gate marker, then laughed at herself. She swayed and began to topple forward. Carlyle ducked, letting her fall over her shoulder, and struggled upright. Higgins was surprisingly light. Carlyle staggered towards the gate and almost fell through it. A sudden wash of light made her shut her eyes until the faceplate had adapted. Her feet were in something soft. Higgins felt suddenly lighter. Carlyle staggered a few paces away from the gate and then fell face-first into sand. After a moment she crawled forward, out from under Higgins, and looked around.

Daylight of a young blue-white star, arc-weld bright and small, in a pale blue sky. She was on a rocky terrestrial, 0.86 g, thin carbon dioxide atmosphere. To all appearances utterly lifeless: sand dunes, wind-eroded sandstone of the same beige colour, black wind-polished rocks. After Chernobyl and the ice moon it felt like a garden. And it looked like a garden—a Zen garden, though with wheel-tracks rather than raked lines. A few hundred metres ahead of her was a complex diamond-pane greenhouse arcology, hundreds of metres high and kilometres in extent. Behind her, two black rock pillars marked the gate. Between it and the ruts in front of the arcology there were no tracks of any kind. She heaved Higgins back on her shoulder and set out to make some.

The difficulty was finding an entrance. As she drew closer the transparent walls rose before her like an unbroken cliff. There was no response to her croaked shouts on the standard hailing frequency. With stoned lucidity she realised that her best bet was to find some wheel tracks and follow them. She trudged across the sand until she found one, then trudged along its curving path. After ten minutes' walk she found herself in front of a five-metre-high airlock. There was, not to her surprise, no doorbell, and still no response to her distress calls. She dropped to the ground, crawled from under Higgins again, and walked over to the wall beside the lock and started banging on it, then kicking. Fifteen minutes of this had no effect. She backed off about a hundred metres, drew her pistol, and started shooting at the wall above the airlock. Not even the concentrated succession of Webster bolts could do more than blacken the sheet diamond, but it made one hell of a racket. The airlock door began to open. Carlyle at once ceased fire, dropped the pistol and raised her hands. An optic poked cautiously out, then withdrew. The airlock opened fully and a squad of five space-suited figures emerged and jogged towards her.

The faceplates were sun-shaded; she couldn't see the faces. After a moment voices found her frequency, and her Japanese-American translator kicked in.

"Who are you and where do you come from?" It was a woman's voice.

"Lucinda Carlyle," she said. She pointed. "Morag Higgins. We have come through the gate back there, from Chernobyl. We have severe radiation sickness and request your help."

"Of course," said the woman. "You are prisoners of war."

"Good," said Carlyle. She kicked the pistol towards the squad leader. "Now please take us in."

Her knees buckled. Somebody caught her arm. She straightened up, determined to walk while she still could. Two people picked up Higgins. Surrounded by the squad, Carlyle went through the airlock and a decontamination chamber, and stepped out into a vast, airy space where clumps of botanic garden were interspersed with grassland and low trees and tall pseudowood buildings. The squad took their helmets off. They were all women, three Japanese and two Indian. Responding to a gesture from the squad leader, she took her own helmet off. A clump of hair came with it. From the expressions of those around her, she looked and smelled dreadful.

There followed several minutes of rush and confusion which ended with her being wheeled on a stretcher trolley to an emergency clinic close to the airlock: a medium-sized green-walled room with a window looking out on the sand. The equipment it contained was obviously for dealing with accidents outside, none of which were likely to involve radiation exposure. She was laid on a bed and put on a drip, and lost consciousness in seconds.

S he woke in a different clinic, naked on a bed. The air was heavy with floral scents over the faint unmistakeable clinical reek of shit masked by disinfectant. A big steel machine beside the bed was attached to her body in a great number of places by shiny curved pipes and thin fibre-optic monitoring cables. A Japanese woman in a white overall leaned over her.

"How are you feeling?"

Carlyle moved her arm and the plugged-in pipes moved with it. Metal nanotech, like Morag's face. She could feel the tug and give of skin and muscle where they went into her bones, and a dull ache there. She tried to sit up, but the woman pushed her gently back.

"I'm feeling a lot better," Carlyle said.

"So I see," said the woman. "So you should be. You have been unconscious for a week. In that time you have had a complete bone marrow replacement, and other extensive and invasive treatments."

"Oh. I expected euthanasia."

The woman frowned, then forced a smile. "You people with your backups, you give up too easily. Enlightened approach is to develop medical tech to recover the living, not raise the dead. In any case you are prisoner of war. We are not allowed to kill you. Geneva Convention I believe."

Carlyle swallowed. Her throat hurt. From certain absences on the edges of her vision she could see that she'd lost her hair, eyebrows, and eyelashes. The medic passed her a glass of water. She sipped. There were gaps where teeth had been, cold in the water. She investigated with her tongue, also painful: an incisor, a canine, a couple of molars were missing. Skin was sloughing off her tongue.

"Well, thank you," she said. "What about Higgins?"

The woman gave here an odd look. "Something complicated and strange. We were unable to save her body. The metal nanotech head is . . . inactive, but something continues within. We are studying it carefully. We will attempt to preserve its continuity."

"Good," said Carlyle. She smiled, feeling skin crack. "You know, I didn't expect this, but dying really sucks."

"It is natural for consciousness to desire continuation," the woman said. "At present this would be best served by sleep."

Carlyle lay back and let herself drift off, soothed by her surroundings. They were much more pleasant than the emergency clinic: the bed was surrounded by paper screens, between and over which she could see a sort of bower, and glimpse other beds. Overhead the sun, dimmed to visibility by some property of the dome, warmed her face, and then her closed eyelids.

She woke again in the same place, but the machine had gone and there was a sheet over the bed. The sun was low, and in some indefinable way she knew that it was morning, not evening. She sat up, and found that she was wearing a plain cotton hospital nightdress that opened down the back. The holes in her arms and legs and sides had all been closed up with what looked and felt like natural flesh, and might have been. There was no hair on it, but nor was there any hair anywhere else. Her skin still felt dry and her teeth were still missing. All of that could be fixed. She felt extraordinarily lucid and lively.

The Japanese woman came back, holding a tissue-paper packet.

"Good morning," she said. She bowed. "My name is Dr. Kaori Yoshi." She sat on a folding stool by the end of the bed. "You are feeling better."

"Much better, thanks."

"Good. If you wish, you may get up. You are already washed." She laid down the packet. "Clothes."

Yoshi disappeared behind the screen while Carlyle pulled on a blue silk wrap and flat black slippers. She found herself steady on her feet, and walked out.

"Let us go somewhere more pleasant," said Yoshi.

They walked on real grass as smooth and dry as astroturf past the rows of screened beds and out into a garden. Parkland, lakes, mist under a glass sky. Black squiggles of buildings. Distant voices of women and children. Yoshi lead her to a black wooden bench, subtly curved, comfortable on the seat and back.

"Very peaceful," Carlyle said.

"I have something to tell you," said Yoshi. "You have been asleep for another week. Your treatment is complete. Unfortunately it has not been successful. The cell damage has been too extensive. We have given you drugs to eliminate pain and confusion of mind. When you next fall asleep, in a few hours perhaps, it will be for the last time."

Carlyle stared at her, pained and confused. "I'm going to die after all?"

Yoshi leaned forward and took her hand. "I am sorry, but yes."

Anger surged. "Why couldn't you have sent me *back*? Then at least I could have taken a new backup before I—"

She couldn't go on.

"We are more than a week's travel from the nearest place where you could have taken a backup," said Yoshi. "You would have been dead before you got there, and without the opportunity to gather your thoughts before you go into a future cycle of the universe."

Carlyle felt caught up short. "What?"

Yoshi cupped her hands as though holding water. "It is something to know that you have something to carry forward." She blinked, eyelashes sparkling. "It is not much, but it is something. It is all we have."

The confirmation of the old Haldane theory of the eternal and infinitely various return of all possible combinations of matter over googolplexes of cosmic cycles was one of the earliest fruits of KE investigation of posthuman discovery. The physics was accepted, it was as true and hard and established as physics got. The cold comfort drawn from it by the Knights was not. That was something you had to come to spiritually, a lonesome valley you had to walk by yourself. There was some speculation that a sort of progress was possible, not simply an endless and unimaginably if not incalculably immense recurrence but an evolution, not just of the material soul but of the material universe; that if such a progress was possible at all, it depended on that portion of lucidity with which the mind faced the inevitable darkness before the inevitable return of the light. She believed that as much as she believed anything, and she realised now that taking backups had not been, as she'd joked to Armand, a way to save time so much as a way to put off that confrontation.

Calm again, she sighed. Breathing was good. Every breath was good. She had not known that, the last time she'd taken a backup. There was a lot she hadn't known: that breath is good and death sucks, that it's the end and the beginning, that none of it matters and it all counts, that the soul is material but the form of its materiality is, well, immaterial. . . . That she had not been wrong in her first response to Winter. The prejudice of her second response, she saw now, had been burned out of her in the hard radiation on Chernobyl, when she'd been dying together with Higgins.

"What's happened to Higgins?"

Yoshi's cheek twitched. "The head has adjusted to its loss. It is conversing by radio. The personality of Higgins appears to be alive. We are discussing with her what to do. She is not a Carlyle, nor an employee of the family, so she is not a prisoner of war. She will be repatriated to New Glasgow if she wishes. It is not yet clear what she wishes. Her mind is confused and quite naturally we have no medicine for her, other than by speaking."

Carlyle smiled skeptically. "Psychotherapy?"

"Physics," said Yoshi.

"That makes sense," said Carlyle. "Give her my . . . give her my love."

Life was good. This life was good, and it was about to end. She regretted its loss desperately. That she had a backup was no comfort. That she would live again an infinite number of times was no comfort. There was only one number that mattered, and that number was *one*. All that she would carry forward into the dark would be anger and regret and the burning will to go on living; no acceptance, no enlightenment, none.

"We have something to ask of you," Yoshi said, diffidently. "When you were in your sleep you talked of how you came to be here. You thought the Knights had stolen your ship, and the teleportation device."

"Oh!" Carlyle felt embarrassed. "I'm sorry, that was just . . . raving. I hope I didn't offend you."

"Not at all," said Yoshi. "It is true."

"What?"

"It is true," Yoshi repeated. "The Knights wanted the QTD. Had the opportunity arisen some other way, they would have taken it, but as it is you handed it to them on a plate. Or rather, Johnstone did. His reward will be to share in their investigation."

"Wait a minute," said Carlyle. "If they wanted it, why the hell didn't they just go through to Chernobyl from here?"

Yoshi looked taken aback. "You do not understand. This is a women's planet. A homeworld. The Knights cannot mount expeditions from it, no matter how convenient that might seem. They may only come here to visit the women and see the children."

"There are no men here?"

Yoshi laughed. "Of course there are. The Knights are a small elite, though not quite as small as their name suggests. Perhaps one in five of the men has the mental and physical discipline required for what the Knights do. The others, and the women, do all the other necessary work of society." She waved a hand. "But that is not important. What is important is what the Knights have discovered at the planet Eurydice. Control of it could give them great power."

Carlyle nodded firmly. "You're telling me! That's why my family can't let them control a skein nexus."

Yoshi's perfect eyebrows rose a fraction. "A skein nexus?"

"Aye," said Carlyle. "A group of gates, all within easy distance of each other. Walking distance, in this case."

"That is not the most important thing there," said Yoshi. "The important thing is what you call the relic. What do you think the relic is?"

Carlyle spread her hands. "I speculated that it was the remains of the starship that took the Eurydiceans to the planet. This seems to have been borne out." She smiled. "It transmitted a defensive virus that contained Microsoft patches."

Yoshi smiled too. "That would not be definitive. It could have picked them up from scanning Eurydicean communications. But as it happens, you are right. The Knights' preliminary investigations confirm it. It is indeed the starship. But it is more than that. It is a wormhole generator."

"Oh, *fucking hell!*" Carlyle almost shouted, shocked, then

caught herself. "Sorry, sorry about the language, but—that's so much worse for us than we thought. If the Knights can generate new wormholes—"

"It is worse than that, from your point of view," Yoshi said, sounding politely amused. "The relic is the machine that created the entire existing wormhole skein in the first place. It generated Carlyle's Drift."

I should die right now, Carlyle thought. I should have died before I knew this. But she had to know more, to drink the cup to the dregs.

"Can it be used to control the skein?"

"Oh yes," said Yoshi. "Once it is mastered. That is why the Knights wanted the QTD. It is a primitive version of a wormhole generator. Through investigating that, they hope to understand the skein generator. And, as you say, control it."

"Why are you telling me this?" It seemed cruel, tormenting her when she could do nothing with the information.

"Because," said Yoshi, "we do not wish the Knights to have this power."

"Why ever not? They're your top men."

"They are indeed our top men, and there is the problem. The balance of power between the sexes and the classes is subtle. For the Knights to have such a sudden access of power would tilt it decisively towards them."

Carlyle stared at her. This was a way of thinking that was not familiar to her. But if it could be used to the family's advantage, and hers . . .

"How does telling me this help you?"

Yoshi's face was expressionless. "That is for you to decide," she said. "I may just remind you that as a prisoner of war you have the right to correspond with your family, and that the secrecy of that correspondence is guaranteed by law and convention."

"Oh," said Carlyle. They sat for a while in silence.

"What do you wish to do now?" Yoshi asked.

"I'd like to stay here."

Yoshi nodded and stood up. "Can I have anything sent to you?"

"Yes, please. I would like you to get me something to eat, something to drink, and something to write with. I have letters to send home."

"To your family?"

"Yes. And one to myself."

CHAPTER 13

Giant Lizards from Another Star

The big empty building down by the docks had been a warehouse, decades back, before being made obsolete by local nanofacture of the wares concerned. Ben-Ami had no idea what the wares had been, but the air and floor and very beams of the place were pervaded with some scent, spicy and sour, that suggested long-degraded alcohol molecules. The extravagant electricity supply might have originally been to maintain temperature and humidity. Now it powered lighting and sound, holograms and engines. Rehearsals of songs, dances, and dialogues, and workings through of stage and prop business, had been going on for a week. Denied for the first time in his career a performance permit for the Jardin des Étoiles by a flagrantly spurious fire-safety objection from the municipality of the Seventy-Ninth Arondissement, Ben-Ami had instructed his MEA to contest it and had provisionally transferred *Rebels and Returners* to this marginal locale. In interviews he had called it the Theatre in Exile. The name was now in lights above the doors.

Today was his first attempt to run the first act—or the prelude, depending on how it went. He sat in a plastic bucket seat a few rows from the front. Winter, Calder,

Kowalsky, and Al-Khayed sat in the row behind him. Other people—technicians and stagehands—sat farther back, or hung about the aisles. A few strangers, too. Some attempt had been made to keep the public out, but it wasn't enforced wholeheartedly—Ben-Ami wanted rumours to circulate in advance. The stage was dark and empty, except for two four-metre-tall wood-and-cardboard radio-controlled and string-suspended puppet replicas of Walker tanks on either side.

"Looks good," Winter said, leaning forward.

Ben-Ami turned his head and grinned. "I have a surprise," he said.

"More surprising than the Polarity tunnel orgy in the third act?" said Calder. "That'll be something."

"Nothing like that," said Al-Khayed.

"Go," Ben-Ami said, into a throat mike.

Above the back of the stage appeared a full-colour holo-gram of Earth. Blue and white, glimpses of continents in green and brown, with only the outlines of the landmasses to distinguish it from any other habitable terrestrial. That was enough: the Horn of Africa, the pinched lake of the Mediter-ranean were unmistakeable, iconic, burned into human memory since the classic Apollo 8 shot. Behind him Ben-Ami heard Winter's indrawn breath. He smiled in the dark.

How do you show history, when all around you history is happening?

In the past few days Benjamin Ben-Ami's gaze and atten-tion had flipped repeatedly between his scenario slate and the news wall. There had been a moment when a news team had stopped and taken a panning shot down into a valley. There, on the South Continent, a few hundred kilometres from New Start, was a sight like nothing he had ever seen. The five kilometres visible had been transformed overnight, from fertile if wild and scrubby riverbanks to farmland: green replacing blue-green, fences and glass houses, evenly spaced knots of houses each with its own comms cluster and antiaircraft missile battery. It was as if a great carpet of farms had been unrolled down the valley, each farm almost identical with the others, and each bristling with self-defensive, self-sufficient individuality.

When he'd looked away, turned his gaze back to the street around the cafe before wrenching it again to his work, the same distraction had prevailed: strangers everywhere. A few were quiet, watchful, Asiatic-featured people in colourful clothes that distinguished even the men among them easily from the black-clad Knights. These were the ones Lucinda Carlyle had called "commies," the DK. There were far more of the ones she'd called "farmers": adults in stiff, sweaty garb gaping and rubbernecking and talking loudly, children swarming everywhere, yelling and laughing, all suntanned skin and sun-bleached hair and screaming laughter and gappy white teeth. You would have thought the farmers would have had enough to do, what with their settlings and steadings, but no. They had time to spare for tourism and shopping. Tourism without tact, shopping without respect or reciprocity, slapping down their AO dollars as though doing the place a favour and departing with armfuls of stuff. And their faces, unoptimised, raw, unageing but stubbled and spotted, lined and furrowed. The commonest purchase, or loot, among the women was cosmetics, clothes a close second; among the men, deodorants and gadgets.

It had taken him a day to realise ways in which this invasion of the body-shoppers could be turned to the advantage, practical and emotional, of the play.

The hologrammed Earth turned; the orchestra, recorded for this rehearsal, struck up. Brassy, rythmic, with an underlying and increasing drumbeat. The Walker tanks shuffled into a ponderous dance, their treads rising and falling, their gun arms sliding back and forth. In step with the drumbeats they approached each other, feinted and fell back, time and again. Apart from the flags painted on their sides—the Stars and Stripes and the Circled Stars—they were indistinguishable, their movements mirroring each other.

A tall woman in a ragged floaty dress ran on tiptoe from

the wing to centre stage, spotlit; stopped, faced the audience. Gwyneth Voigt, Eurydice's top female solo singer. Her classically trained voice lavished itself, wasted on Winter's lyrics:

> *Two empires walking blind to war:*
> *USA and EUR!*
> *Under capital's eyes unblinking*
> *workers trapped by their hoodwinking*
> *sacrifice their lives unthinking*
> *to giant lizards from another star!*

And so on. It was a crude and didactic rant in rhyme, but the woman's voice made the words sound eerily apt. The light and shade silhouetted the Walker tanks, making them look indeed like giant lizards, great skeletal tyrannosaurs that loomed and thrashed and never quite laid a blow on one another, until . . .

The hologram planet faded as the stage's backscreen lit up with an equally iconic and familiar image, of rising rockets. Zoom and track to the star-circled flags on the missiles and on the British, French, and Russian submarines from which they were fired. Cut to mushroom clouds over the US launch facilities, then missiles rising from those the first strike had missed. A series of almost subliminally fast, cliched images: the Eiffel Tower, Big Ben, the Vatican, the Kremlin, each followed by a nuclear explosion. The hologram of Earth came back, this time a combined image from near Earth orbit: archived images from the real time, as the continents and seas sparkled with a thousand points of light.

Ben-Ami felt reasonably satisfied with this as a quick visual for the war. Showing how an American military AI had upgraded itself to consciousness and burned its way through the networks, then into the brains of people connected to them, had been more of a challenge. He'd had to rely on his audience's prior knowledge of the Hard Rapture, but he still wanted to show it, at least symbolically.

Voigt fled the stage and the drumbeat deepened and

quickened, and the lights faded: the war went on in the dark. When the lights came dimly back, after a moment of silent scurrying, two rows of green-glowing paper-thin screens with keypads had been laid on the floor. From each wing a dozen people in camo silks and dark shades ran on, formed up in lines and sat down cross-legged on the stage, facing each other across the banks of screens. Their fingers tapped at the keyboards. On the hologram the planet vanished to be replaced by gunner's eye views of several heavy machine guns, whose bullets rapped out in time with the rattle of the keys—no particularly clever trick, since it was the same sound effect that did service for both. The operators sang instructions to each other, in English on one side, in French on the other. The guns darkened to sharp shadows, and behind them, filling as much space as the Earth had done, a sphere of light grew. It was a complex sphere, made up of many lines in many colours, that twined and slashed about like the sparks on a Van de Graaff generator. The light intensified, and the hologram drifted forward and expanded.

Suddenly, all the people on the USA side of the stage swivelled their screens and turned their heads to the audience at once, and—with a few exceptions that Ben-Ami mentally noted for later correction—each screen and each pair of shades reflected the swirling sphere above. The operators on the EUR side worked on, oblivious.

The American Walker tank changed too. With one tug of a hidden rope, it separated into its component parts. Each part sprang into a different self-sufficient shape: the turret and the cab, the guns and legs and treads each transforming into an autonomous war machine—some winged and remaining airborne, others sprouting new limbs on which they scuttled. A cloud of carbon dioxide swept across the stage, revealing a barrage of laser beams that struck the EUR tank and slashed across the faces and bodies of the EUR operators, who fell back writhing dramatically. The new war machines swarmed across the stage and pounced on the bodies and on the enemy tank.

The action speeded up, becoming intentionally more chaotic, the music more urgent and discordant: people and machines surged in from both sides of the stage, those on the USA side becoming caught up in the rainbow trance of the glowing sphere, those on the EUR side fighting and falling to the machines. Every so often a flashbulb flared, leaving afterimages through which what was seen on the stage became a glimpse of a memory you wanted to forget.

The lights went off. The hologram sphere expanded to fill the stage, then vanished like a popped soap bubble in sunlight. The music softened. When the lights slowly rose again the stage was filled with a massed choir. They wore academic robes over leotards. None of the singers was Eurydicean. There was something shocking and beautiful in the rank on rank of unoptimised faces and wildly variant heights and skin-tones.

"Wow," breathed Winter. "That's your—"

Ben-Ami raised a hushing finger, intent on the stage. The song began.

If you could hie to Koresh in the twinkling of an eye,
And then continue onward with that same speed to fly,
Do you think that you could ever, through all eternity,
Find out the generation where Gods began to be?

The works of God continue, and worlds and lives
*   abound;*
Improvement and progression have one eternal round.
There is no end to matter; there is no end to space;
There is no end to spirit; there is no end to grace.

There is no end to virtue; there is no end to might;
There is no end to wisdom; there is no end to light.
There is no end to union; there is no end to youth;
There is no end to learning; there is no end to truth.

There is no end to glory; there is no end to love;
There is no end to being; there is no death above.

There is no end to glory; there is no end to love;
There is no end to being; there is no death above.

"Curtain," said Ben-Ami. There was no curtain, but the stage lights went off and the room lights came on. The people on stage stood blinking and smiling self-consciously. Applause, scattered but fervent, echoed around the building. Ben-Ami leaned back, smiling. His surprise, and his entrepreneurial flair, had worked—seizing the literally heaven-sent opportunity of having all this talent and historical authenticity fall from the sky. The America Offline population included a remarkable number of trained and practised singers, mostly choral—tabernacle, temple, gospel, union—and some individual, whose rural and religious roots meshed perfectly with the show's themes.

"Did you write that?" asked Calder.

Ben-Ami leaned his elbow on a beam at the side of the room, near the table around which the cast and crew were taking their lunch-break, and sipped umami tea and looked anxiously at Winter and Calder. Calder had taken up tobacco-smoking again in a big way since the AO folk had arrived. It was frowned upon by most of their sects, and was therefore a gesture of rebellion. The hunchbacked musician was taking this for all it was worth. Ben-Ami could see the point, but preferred to stay upwind of it. Winter eyed choristers in leotards.

"Gentlemen," said Ben-Ami, "a moment. What did you think?"

Calder stubbed his cigarette. "The choir, that was good," he said. "Makes a neat sort of backwards link between us and the new cultures that we didn't know about. Not so sure about the run-up, though. The war and Singularity stuff."

"Ah," said Ben-Ami. That was what he'd been worried about, but he still felt a stab of dismay. He'd put a lot of effort and thought into that scenario.

"Visually it's fine," said Calder, sounding slightly apologetic. "It's just not very clear what's going on, you know? Not even with one of our most crap songs as commentary. Half the people in your audience, maybe more, wouldn't have a clue what 'USA' and 'EUR' stood for—in any sense of the words."

"Well, that's hardly relevant," said Winter. "Everybody knows there was a world war and that one side's forces and most of its population went through a hard-take-off Singularity in its first minutes. That's all they need to know."

"Exactly!" said Ben-Ami.

"But that's not the problem," Winter went on. "It's too bloody abstract and evenhanded. I mean, I know 'Giant Lizards from Another Star' is kind of bitter about both sides, but fuck. *They* attacked *us*."

"Correction," said Calder. "*We* attacked *them*. I'm sure you do remember that."

Winter moved his hand as though dashing something to the ground. "Technicality. It was a preemptive strike, everybody knew it was us or them. They were the ones going for one world empire. It doesn't give the feel of how it was, back in the old Axis. We felt we were standing up for humanity, for *Earth*, against a fucking inhuman *machine*, and in the end that was what the USA literally became."

Ben-Ami crushed his empty cup and threw it away. "You're missing the point," he said. "This is just a prelude. An overture. An introduction! What I'm trying to do here is show the catastrophe, the tragedy of it all, for both sides and for everyone. The whole tone changes later, as you know, you have seen it, when it's the remnants of Europe and the space settlers and space forces against the war machines. But for this part, you have to remember, we had—we have—people originally from the American side in the resistance—scientists, astronauts, even space marines who didn't get caught up in the Hard Rapture thanks—ironically enough—to the superior firewalls built to guard them from our side's hacking. Certain of our institutions are of American origin: for one, the *Joint Chiefs*. I hope you understand me. Yes? We cannot beat the anti-American drum too hard here. Later for patriot-

ism, my friends. Let us show . . . decorum in how we treat the
final war."

"Yeah," said Calder, "fair enough, but you haven't shown
how the civilians got caught up—"

"Fine, fine," said Ben-Ami, furiously. "I shall make sure
we have at least five people off to one side watching television or on-line or playing virtuality games and becoming en-
trained like the soldiers. Would that satisfy you?"

"Sure," said Calder. "You can't have everything, but you
got to be realistic."

"I'll try to bear that in mind," snarled Ben-Ami, and
stalked off to talk to the nearest Latter Day Adventist.

It took another day to get on to rehearsing the second act,
in which ragged people scrabbled in polystyrene ruins and
squinted along rifle barrels while holograms and models of
ESA aerospace fighter-bombers strafed war machines and
the choir sang *The Battle Hymn of the Republic*. Ben-Ami
watched and supervised from a platform in the wings.

"*That* isnae how it *wis*!"

Ben-Ami's first thought, on hearing the raised female
voice, simultaneously scornful and indignant, was that Lucinda Carlyle had come back. Looking down at the rehearsal
stage, he could see that Winter had had a similar startled
thought—the musician had whipped around and was looking at the voice's source with his nose forward and his body
quivering like a pointing dog. Ben-Ami's second thought
was along the lines of *oh fuck, not another one*. But this
time, it wasn't one of the girls in the chorus, stepping out of
the line, interrupting the song, and brandishing her script. It
was some woman who'd joined the rehearsal's unofficial audience, now having an altercation with the stage manager.
This was a relief.

As he clattered down the stairs to the stage in the hob-
nailed boots that were this week's must-have, Ben-Ami reflected that if his newly recruited chorus and session singers
went on impugning his script's historical accuracy much

more or much longer, he'd do better to sack the lot of them and start from scratch. A hard core of people among them had actually been there: they had lived on Earth before, during and after the Hard Rapture, and they thought "artistic licence" was something you got from the government. The more intelligent they were, the more doggedly literal they seemed about anything literary. Some of them talked about "sacred writings" and "holy books," a notion that made Ben-Ami scratch his head.

He leapt to the stage and strode across the chewed-up rubber mats that marked out places to stand and move, and incidentally protected the boards from the fashionable boots. The woman who'd objected was standing a bit off one of the strips, still arguing with the stage manager, who seemed to be retreating.

"Excuse me," said Ben-Ami.

They both turned to him. The woman was small and stocky, a little plump, with green eyes and black curly hair. She was wearing a white shirt and blue jeans and high-heeled boots.

"*Madame*," Ben-Ami said as patiently as he could, "could you tell me what your problem is with my libretto?"

"I'm sorry, Mr. Ben-Ami," she said. "I couldnae actually help myself, but . . . I was well out of line there, sorry, no problem, it's your play and I'll hold my tongue."

"Seriously," said Ben-Ami, "I would like to know—"

Winter bounded up on the stage and hurried over. Ben-Ami waved resignedly at the rest of the chorus and cast.

"Take ten," he said. People wandered off. He turned to the woman. "Now, what were you—"

"Funny accent for AO," said Winter, looking at the woman. "Wouldn't you say?"

"Aye, I would that, Winter," she said, grinning. She stuck out a hand to him. "My name's Amelia Orr. Pleased to meet you. I've been a fan since I was wee."

"You're not one of the AO people?" asked Ben-Ami.

Orr and Winter were looking at each other with an odd understanding. "Could you no tell?" Orr asked.

Ben-Ami waved a hand. "Frankly, no. All these American

accents and dialects sound equally strange to me. You do sound like Lucinda, but—" He shrugged, then straightened up, startled. "You haven't come through that . . . hole in space, have you?"

"Ah, no," said Orr. "I came in wi the farmers. On a ship, see? The gate's still shut as far as know."

"But you are connected to the Carlyles," said Ben-Ami, eyes narrowing. "You know, I can see the resemblance. . . . "

"To Lucinda? Aye, you could say that. She's my great-great-granddaughter. Or was."

"What?" Winter asked, sounding shocked. "Is she dead?"

Orr shrugged. "Seems so, from last we've heard of her. No tae worry, she'll be out the resurrection tank soon enough—well, her copy will, and none the worse for not knowing what happened to her original, poor thing."

"And what was that?" said Winter.

"Some daft scheme." She shook her head. "Don't worry about it. I mean, what's dying in this day and age? As ye no doubt ken well enough."

Winter nodded sombrely. "I suppose you have some plan. If not, well, it's a long way to come to have a photo signed."

Orr chuckled. "Aye, it is. And yes, I do."

Ben-Ami was beginning to feel something of the frustration of a child listening to a conversation among adults, or vice versa. "You're losing me," he said.

Orr turned to him. "Youse are the Returners, aye? You want tae go back tae Earth, and push off the Knights, and have, uh, independence for Eurydice?"

Ben-Ami recoiled slightly. "Not me personally," he said.

"Sure sounds like what your play's about."

"This is *art*," said Ben-Ami. He had an uneasy thought that this distinction didn't signify to her.

"Aye, aye, sure," said Orr. She was looking around with a sort of artless inquisitiveness, as though bored with the conversation. "Is there no some place we can talk privately?" She looked back at him. "When you're through wi the rehearsal, I mean. I'll be quiet."

* * *

There were five new ships in the system. Cyrus Lamont tracked them in the virtual mental space generated by watching the gravity-wave detector display with one eye and the visual display with the other. In the past weeks he'd become, he fancied, something of an expert on starship wakes. This pattern, a surge of matched gravity pulses and Cherenkov radiation flashes, was unfamiliar. It did not take him long to interpret it as successive short-range FTL jumps. Only one ship headed for Eurydice. The others fanned out to the asteroid belt. One of them was aiming more or less head-on for his quadrant.

"Comms?" he asked. "Summarise."

"Languages," said the ship. "Korean, Bengali, Chinese, Spanish, and Tagalog. Content: property rights claims and prospecting."

"They're divvying up the *asteroid belt*?" This time the sense of affront was personal.

"Yes." A sense of hesitation in the silence. "That transmission that happened before—"

"It's just happened again. Five times?"

"Yes."

"Shit."

"Quite."

Everyday conversation between Lamont and the ship had become compressed. In the days since the transformation of the asteroid into reentry-packaged war machines, and the FTL jump, no further untoward events had occurred. He and the *Hungry Dragon* had used the time to continue their attempt at therapeutic debugging. Progress had been slow. It had left both of them too emotionally exhausted for much in the way of other interactions. Even their sex life was not what it had been.

Hours passed. Lamont exercised in the web, though he was beginning to doubt that he'd ever walk in a gravity well again. The new ship came closer, jump by jump. It was as though it was feeling its way, or perhaps navigating by sight and trial and error. Once or twice. it seemed to repeat a jump it had already made: disappearing from its point of arrival, setting off again, and emerging in a slightly different place.

Eventually the foreign ship's trace vanished, in the location of an asteroid just large enough to register on the gravity-wave detector. Other than that, Lamont was quite unable to observe it, or any of its effects. After an hour, the ship departed, in a jump that (as Lamont learned, hours later) took it straight to Eurydice. Running traces from the rest of the system as they trickled in hour by hour, Lamont and ship figured that the other three ships in the quartet had followed a similar course—moving step by step towards a relatively large asteroid, engaging with it, then jumping to Eurydice, where their tracks were lost in the clutter and the well.

That is one gae weird ship," Amelia Orr remarked, glancing up. Winter, walking under a warm rain beside her from the docks to the monorail station, looked up too. A black manta ray gliding through the sky. It had something smaller and more angular attached to its underside, hard to make out, black on black.

"Jeez," he said. "Mind you, they all look weird to me." He jerked his head at the ship of the Knights, still motionless above the city, then his gaze followed the new ship as it turned—banked, in fact, which struck him as a flourish rather than an aerodynamic requirement—and headed north. "Do you know what that one is?"

"No tae speak of," she said. "It's a new design knocked up by DK."

"The commies?" Winter laughed.

She shot him a sharp glance. "Don't underestimate them. They hae this fixed idea called *juche*—self-reliance. They're no as patient as the Knights, but they do try tae figure stuff out for theirselves. Partly fae the posthuman tech, partly fae first principles. It gets results. Yon's the most manoeuvrable ship ever built." She sighed. "Lucinda wanted tae get one for us."

Winter felt a stab, again, at the thought of Lucinda dying. "What for?"

Amelia made a swooping gesture with her hand. "You can guess."

"Yeah. Looks like that's off the set-list now."

"We have a better idea."

"I'll look forward to hearing it."

"I'll bet." She grinned at him sideways, in a way that made something inside him jolt. It puzzled him. She was a generation younger than him, born soon after the Hard Rapture. On the astronomical scales of living and dying, that made her a near contemporary. He had been dead in the frozen bog when she had been growing up in the ruins of Glasgow. Of all the people he had met here—even people he'd known, like Armand, whom they were now going to see—she was the least alien. That she had listened to his live postmortem performances—transmitted from Mars and the Belt to Earth—and had collected various reproductions of the band's albums in whatever media could be made to work in the post-holocaust environment—this gave her an almost uncanny lien on his acquaintance. She was a fan who had matured, who was *older* than he was. She had lived a longer life.

They crossed the road—he'd already become dangerously habituated to automated traffic, and stepped out with barely a glance—and went up to the station pillar and the spiral steps to the platform. Winter thumbed up Lesser Lights Lane in his phone and it told him which shuttle to take. When the right one arrived it was empty. They sat opposite each other, knees to knees. Looked each other in the eye, looked away, looked back, laughed.

"What?" asked Amelia.

"Nothing," said Winter. "It's stupid." He looked away again. Whizz of the line, lights, and drops.

"No, go on."

He rubbed his stubble. He knew it would only make it itch. "It's strange meeting someone who's listened to our music longer than we've been alive."

"Aye, well. It's strange meeting you. After all this time." She put her knuckles to her lips, knocking at the door of her mouth. Somebody must have answered. It opened. "I had a crush on you when I was a wee lass. In my teens, like."

"You're kidding."

"No, really I did."

"Well, I'm flattered," He laughed. "I hope I'm not a disappointment. . . . " He nearly said *in the flesh*.

"You look younger than you did in the pictures."

At last a chance to change the subject. "I should bloody hope so. I was twenty-odd then. I'm only fifty-something now. What's it like living, what, five times longer than that? Do you get wiser as well as older?"

Amelia shook her head, curls bouncing. "You get cannier. Mair cunning. That's it. I think a lot ae what folk used tae call maturity was just fatigue poisons."

"Damn," said Winter. "And there was me thinking I had that to look forward to."

"What?"

"Better impulse control."

"For that, you can go tae the Knights. I've never seen the attraction myself."

"Still impulsive, then."

"Oh, aye."

He was kind of hoping she would demonstrate it, but she didn't.

Instead she talked about the music and what it had meant to her. It was a conversation Winter had become used to; he could predict the questions and comments and come up with the responses while thinking about something else; but more than usual, he felt a burning shame at where he'd been coming from all those years ago. The songs that had given voice to many people's hatred of the war machines and the posthumans had been adapted from songs that had given voice, before the war, to a more sinister hatred. It was not that he and Calder had shared it themselves, not exactly, not in their better moments, not when they were sober and in the daylight. They had adapted to it. They had literally played along to it if it had gone down well with the audience. All those pubs and halls: the English electric folk scene, the Scottish radical left, rabid in their patriotic passion and pro-war zeal. You could pick up an old Phil Ochs number or Billy Bragg cover version and twist it into something that made people want to go out and kill Americans.

The offices of Blue Water Landings in Lesser Lights Lane were smaller and scruffier than Winter had expected. Name in discreet pale grey LEDs above the door, dust in the corners of the sheet-diamond windows, a neglected pot-plant yellowing on the sill beside a sheaf of scribbled-on plastic transparencies going milky in the sunlight. When he and Amelia turned up at the door Armand paged them in and sat them down in what was obviously a reception area, with no receptionist and no other staff. The former general looked tired and not a little alarmed to see them.

"Ah, James, good afternoon."

"Jacques. This is Amelia Orr, from—"

Armand raised a hand to silence him, then shook Orr's.

"Your name is familiar to me," he said, smiling. "A moment, please."

He ducked into his own office, rattled at a keyboard and came out, closing the door behind him.

"That's better," he said. "Hush fields up. Just making sure." He perched on the reception desk, waved Winter to a coffee machine. "Please. Help yourselves. For me, *au lait*."

As Winter sorted out the coffees he realised that Armand probably was less competent with the machine than he was, and was rather clumsily concealing that fact. How small are our vanities sometimes, he thought.

"I did not expect you," said Armand to Orr. "So soon. Is there a problem?"

"No exactly," said Orr. "I've come tae you with a proposition fae the Carlyles."

Armand lifted an eyebrow. "Another one?"

"Someone's approached you already?"

"Of course," said Armand. "Did Lucinda Carlyle not tell you?"

"No, she did not."

"Ah." Armand shifted uneasily. "That raises certain difficulties. Perhaps you could put your proposition to me, and I can tell you if it's compatible with the one I've already agreed to."

"That question," said Orr, "disnae arise *at all*."

"Oh, but I'm afraid it does. Lucinda is, after all, a Carlyle."

Orr almost slopped her coffee. "I don't know what she's been telling you, but her name gie's her nae privileges where this is concerned."

Armand gave a downward wave of his palm. "I make no presumptions about your family's internal affairs. I've just noted the names of the people who've been making such earnest entreaties to the Joint Chiefs."

Winter knew that the question on the tip of Orr's tongue was *You know about that?* He would have been disappointed if she'd asked it, and she didn't. Instead her face became a mask of calm.

"That's true," she said, "and I'm on the same team. Just checking the back door, so tae speak, while the high heid yins are knocking on the front."

"An illuminating metaphor," said Armand, as though breathing out the smoke of a fine cigar. "Please go on."

"We can offer you . . . mair than one starship tae back you up if you move your forces tae dislodge the Knights fae around the relic."

"Oh! Is that all?"

"It's no sic a big deal as you might think," said Orr. "Militarily ye're mair than a match for them. That gun you used on our search engine—killing me and a few others, I may add, so I know what I'm talking about—is better than anything the Knights possess. Their only advantage over you is the starships, and like I said, we can take care of that."

"Oh, I'm sure you can, and I'm sure we are. The only problem is that my company, and any others I could muster, are a minority of Eurydice's armed forces. We would be facing not just the Knights but our own people—more of them, and better armed."

"Not if they were otherwise engaged."

"In what?"

"In putting down a riot in the city, for example."

Armand laughed. "We don't use troops for internal security. It is known as the principle of *posse commitatus*. In any case, I don't see any occasion for a riot in the near future."

"I do," said Orr. "Your friend Ben-Ami's play."

Armand stared at her. "You are not completely mad," he said. "You are, however, quite unfamiliar with our ways. Yes, there is every possibility that fights will break out in the audience, if what I hear is anything to go by. No, there is not the slightest chance of even the municipal militia's having to intervene. A few bravoes will be stabbed or shot, a few dozen heads will be broken, and the hospitals and resurrection clinics will have a busy and profitable week. That is all."

"I wish you had put this plan to me before you took it to Armand," said Winter. He was as embarrassed on her behalf as he was furious with her on his own.

Orr looked quite unperturbed. "Not a problem," she said. "Sure, you're mair familiar wi the facts on the ground. So you come up with something."

"Fortunately," said Armand, "I don't have to, and neither does James. I have a much more satisfactory and realistic plan, which I've been working to for some time."

"And what might that be?"

"It's very straightforward," he said. "I've discussed this whole situation with the Joint Chiefs. They expressed great disquiet. We no longer have any control over who comes to the planet, or the system. The Knights do nothing against the AO settlers, and now, I hear, the DK arrivals. Worse, they forbid us from doing anything about it ourselves—although we could. This is deeply resented. So I put a plan to them, and together we put a . . . condensed version of the plan to the Knights. They were highly amenable to my suggestion that Blue Water Landings and other military companies provide on-site backup for the Knights while the Knights investigate the relic, and that selected Returner veterans be resurrected to bring their expertise to bear. We are, as you say, better equipped than the Knights for handling any outbreak of war machines, and they are glad of our help."

"You mean you have troops around the relic right now?" Amelia asked.

"Yes," said Armand. "Along with the Knights, of course, but yes. That's why I'm the only person left in the office. I'm kept very busy coordinating it all, and greeting and orienting the, ah, returning Returners. And, as you see, there is absolutely no need to divert or confront the rest of Eurydice's armed forces, because they are controlled by the Joint Chiefs, and the Joint Chiefs are on our side. As indeed are the other armed forces—though they don't know of the plan they're as angry about the Knights and the farmers as are those who do."

"That's brilliant!" she said. "So you're ready to move as soon as we come in wi our ships?"

"We are indeed," said Armand. "That gun we used against your search engine—it is, as you say, superior to anything the Knights have. Funnily enough, it was they who explained to us how it worked—we developed it empirically from refining the standard plasma cannon, and we didn't grasp just how it's as destructive as it is. The Knights tell us it generates a fragment of *cosmic string*. It's quite capable of shooting a starship right out of the sky."

Orr punched her palm. "Fantastic!"

"Yes," said Armand. "And that's exactly what we'll do in the event of an attack by the bloody Carlyles."

It didn't quite register.

"Shoot down the KE ships?"

"Yes," said Armand. "And yours, if you attack us."

"Why should we attack you? We're on your side."

"No, you're not," said Armand. "You're on your own side. I've no intention of being used to grab control of the relic from the Knights, only to be displaced in turn by the Carlyles. We don't know what the relic is, but we know it's important *to Eurydice*, and we want control of it *for* Eurydice."

Amelia Orr rocked back a little in her chair.

"Aye," she said carefully. "We can live wi that. We can come tae some kindae agreement. Just so long as it's no the Knights, or any o the other powers for that matter. Aye. Nae problem, General. I just hae one wee question. What does this Assembly o yours think of aw this?"

Armand glanced over at Winter, as though seeking complicity. "They know nothing about it," he said. "Not even the, ah, responsible elements. They can't be trusted in advance. After the die is cast, they'll come round."

"Welcome aboard," Winter said. "I seem to recall a similar argument before the Returner rebellion. That time, it was you who was expected to come round."

The bitter reminder left Armand unperturbed. "I didn't have the Joint Chiefs on my side, that time," he said mildly. "I'm sure your friend Kowalsky will do an excellent job of portraying my double-dealing and treachery. Meanwhile, I shall do my duty, as I did before." He looked down at his desk for a moment. "And, you know, it presses."

They took the hint.

"**K**oresh on a *spit!*"

"What?" asked Amelia, as they turned the corner out of Lesser Lights Lane and into the boulevard of Walker Drive.

Winter laughed, relieved of some of his rage. "That's the filthiest oath you can swear around here these days. Fashionable with the bravoes."

"I kind of gathered that," said Amelia. "I was wondering why you're upset."

Winter stopped in the shade of a potted ginkgo and looked down at her earnestly inquiring face. "Jesus," he said. The older blasphemy seemed fitting. "Don't you realise what you wanted to do? Turn *our fucking play* into a riot—what were you thinking of?"

She shook her head. "That's a very narrow view of it."

"You were thinking strategy? Oh, great. You know, when Lucinda told us her family were criminals, we laughed it off. Fuck. That's what you are. I remember these gormless Glasgow gangsters and the low cunning they thought was ace. Even so, I'd have thought two centuries would have knocked more sense into your head."

For a moment her face showed hurt. Then she shrugged and smiled. "That isnae how it works," she said. "Like I was saying. You don't get wiser. You just become mair what you are."

"I'm not sure I like what you are."

"I'm no sure I do, either," said Amelia. "But I like you." She caught his hand and squeezed it, grinning up at him. "Come on," she said. "Let's take that poor impulse control of ours for a ride."

CHAPTER **14**

The Bloody Carlyles

Lucinda awoke in her own bed, in her own flat. Morning sunlight from Rho Coronae Borealis slanted low through the window. She lay staring at the ceiling for a few minutes, feeling relaxed and refreshed, as if she'd had a sound sleep. After a while she began to feel a vague disquiet. There was something big and frightening she had to do today. Oh yes. That was it. She had to go on the Chernobyl expedition. Meet the team, take a backup, go and get the QTD, and then . . .

She remembered that she had already met the team and taken the backup. She sat bolt upright and yelled. The bedroom door opened and her brother Duncan and cousin Kevin came in.

"It's aw right," Duncan said awkwardly. "You're aw right."

She stared at the lads and hugged her knees through the covers. "I died," she said. "I died, I died, I died."

Kevin took a step towards her.

"Keep *away* from me!" she shouted. He looked around and sat down on the edge of a wicker chair. Duncan propped himself on the windowsill.

"How could you let me *dae* that?" she accused.

"We didnae *let* you," said Kevin, sounding aggrieved. "It

was aw your idea. We didnae even ken you were gonnae dae that."

She thought about it. "I suppose you're right," she said. "Sorry. God." She put her hands to her head. Her hair was short and felt downy. "I must have been crazy."

"You could say that," said Duncan. "I won't. It was brave, I'll give you that."

"I hope it was worth it," she said. Her tone was faintly self-deprecating; she was absolutely confident it had been worth it, from the family's point of view and hers, if not from that of her predecessor, her unfortunate original.

"Well, kindae . . . " said Kevin. Duncan shot him a look.

"What dae ye mean?" Lucinda asked.

Kevin sighed. "It's a bit complicated. Best discuss it when you're up, aye?"

He jerked his thumb at the door. Duncan followed him out.

"See you in a minute," Kevin said, as the door closed.

Lucinda sat and shook for more than a minute. There was something absurd about her situation. Total novelty combined with utter familiarity. Physically she had never felt better. She was even hungry. None of the trauma that her original must have gone through could affect her in the slightest. It took some introspection for her to recognise the feeling that made her shake. It was the feeling she remembered from occasions when she'd been unharmed but had narrowly escaped death. That sense of the fragility of existence. She held the thought until it faded into a glow of gratitude for being alive, then very deliberately put it out of her mind.

She swung out of bed and stood up in a soft but plain green hospital gown. She pulled it over her head and tossed it in the drexler. Naked in front of the mirror, she inspected herself. Her skin was very smooth, not a callus on her feet. Her hair was soft and curly, not nearly dark enough. For the rest, she seemed to have rejuvenated about five years. Her face struck her as unused and naive; all evidence of her experience and earned cunning sponged away like so much makeup.

She dialled up a sharp, military-style suit and shoes, and

showered while the drexler chugged and spun. A vain effort
to tug her hair a bit straighter and longer-looking only made
her wince and realise how close she might still be to crying.
Dressed, she struck herself as far too cute. More like a cadet
than a soldier. It would have to do. She went out and
marched through to the main living space.

"You look . . . smart," said Kevin. He'd thoughtfully
made her some coffee and cereal.

"What's this about—"

"Eat," her cousin said. She sat down at the table.

Duncan prowled the file racks. Kevin stared out of the
window, overlooking the street. The cereal filled her mouth
and her belly. She pushed away the empty bowl, poured another coffee.

"I'm up to strength," she said. "Get me up to speed."

Duncan retreated a bit, sprawled in a web chair. Kevin sat
down across from her.

"Lucinda—" He paused. "Your past self sent you this."

He handed her an envelope. It was Red Cross stamped,
gene-sealed to her. It opened to thumb pressure. A few
sheets of astrogram paper slipped out. She examined them.
God, had her state of mind been that terrible? It all looked
very emotional. She couldn't read it, not now. She slid them
back in the envelope.

"Later," she said. She held up the envelope. "How did this
get to—*from* me?"

"You—" He paused again, shook his head, pressed on.
"You didn't die on Chernobyl, or back here. You found a
gate that took you through to a KE homeworld. They took
you prisoner, tried to save you, failed. You sent two messages back. One was that letter. The other was to the family.
Not so personal. It told us what had happened."

"Did we get the QTD?"

"Well, yes," Kevin said. "You recovered it aw right. But it
and the ship you hired got wheeched away by another ship.
One ae they DK ships you told us about. You found out later
it was the Knights who stole it."

Lucinda jumped up. "It was all for *nothing*?"

"No, no," said Kevin. "Uh, look, it's aw right, calm down—"

"Don't *you* fucking tell me to—"

She collapsed back into the chair, breathed heavily a few times. "Aw right. Go on."

"The information you sent back was worth mair to us than a ship," Kevin said. "Uh, could you please, like, bear that in mind, see?"

"OK," she said.

He told her it all, the whole thing: Johnstone's betrayal, the enormously greater significance of the relic on Eurydice than anyone had suspected. Now they were fighting the Knights not just for control of a skein nexus, but for control of the entire skein, for starters. And for all that he had told her of how important this information was to the family, all that it meant to her was that her initial screwup on Eurydice had been far worse than she'd realised, and that in her last expedition she had fucked up again.

She didn't want to talk about that. Let it hang unspoken between them. Right now all she could do was try to repair the damage.

"What happened to the other woman?" she asked. "The metal-head?"

Kevin rasped his jawline. "Um," he said. "Like I said, she went through with you—"

"No, I know that, I mean did she come back?"

Kevin glanced over at Duncan.

"Ah, fuck, tell her," Duncan said.

"She came back aw right," Kevin said. "In fact she came back wi your letters. She's spitting blood, or she would if she had any blood tae spit."

"Oh, my God!" Lucinda had a sudden sickening vision, or rather two: of Morag Higgins reattached to her radiation-raddled corpse, and of her being sent back as a head in a box. "How is she—"

Kevin looked at her oddly. "There's nothing wrang wi her. That's her problem. Her heid's been stravaigin' aff searching for scrap, you might say, and she's back wi no just a heid. She's come back wi a whole metal *body*."

Lucinda shuddered. "She took a backup before she went. Giving her another and a new body is the least we can do for her."

"That's the strange thing," said Kevin. "She's pissed aff, nae doubt about that, but she disnae want tae kill hersel any mair."

"Is she angry with me?"

Kevin shook his head. "I think she wants tae kill Johnstone."

"Johnstone must be dead already," Lucinda said.

"You're no used tae this," Kevin told her, like she needed reminding. "The version ae Johnstone who went wi you has nae doubt died. The version he left here was timed tae kick aff his revival as soon as the other was out the door ae the clinic. He fucked aff before we knew aught had gone wrang, took the money and ran. For sure he's wi the Knights now, probably on Eurydice."

"Oh," said Lucinda, smiling for the first time in this life. "That's *beautiful*."

Kevin looked alarmed. Duncan sprang up from his chair and stalked over. They both glared at her.

"What?"

"I hope yir no thinking of another ae yir wee schemes," said Kevin. "The best ye can hope for is tae join the expeditionary force as a grunt."

"There's an expeditionary force?" she asked, genuinely interested but also hoping to change the subject.

"Oh, sure," said Kevin. "Ian and Amelia are heading it up. Just like you said. She's doing the starship swap trick and ground liason work on Eurydice, and Ian's found some mair gates to the same place you did. Well, the gate you went through originally hasnae reopened yet, but he's found a wormhole route tae near enough that DK planet you found that has a gate tae Eurydice. They're building up a combat archaeology team tae hit them through that in a day or two.

I'm getting a squad together myself. You should offer tae join in."

"That's fine by me," said Lucinda.

"Come on," said Duncan. "You had mair nor that in mind. I ken ye too well by now."

Lucinda leaned back and made soothing motions with her hands. "I just wondered how Morag Higgins might feel about doing the same," she said, as mildly as she could. "Come on now, guys, the Knights have one Rapture-fucker working for them on the relic. Would it no be a good idea to have one working for *us*?"

This was not going to be easy. Not the doing of it, not the preparation.

Preparation first. Alone again in her flat, Lucinda eased the letter from her previous self out of its envelope. The thin paper shook in her hands. She had to look away and walk about for a few minutes. Then she sat down and read it.

Dear Lucinda,

Don't do what I did. Death is real and believe me you don't want it to happen to you. I don't want it to happen to you. I already think of you as someone different from me, as of course you are. Ah hell we just go into this one by one.

Oh, cut the crap, girl! Lucinda skimmed page after page of meditative whinging before she got to the meat.

But enough about me. (You said it, Lucinda thought.) *This is for you. As I hope our family have told you or will tell you, Johnstone sold us out to the Knights, stole the QTD, and the Knights hope to use it to gain an understanding of the relic on Eurydice which they believe created and can be used to control Carlyle's Drift. I expect you will go back to Eurydice one way or another.*

*If you do there are two things to bear in mind. One is
that the stakes are very high. Johnstone is capable of
anything and I don't know if the Knights can keep him
on the leash. The other is that synthetics and chip minds
really are people. You remember how you felt when you
learned about Winter's mind being constructed? Well
that was wrong. I don't know how but I learned that
from being with Morag Higgins. If she survives and
chooses repatriation please be kind to her and remember that she can help you, and the family, get back at
Johnstone. If you possibly can, please kill Johnstone
for me. And again, if you possibly can, please fuck
James Winter for me. He's an opportunity I missed this
time around.*

Here's tae us on the next recurrence.

The dictyping here was replaced by shaky, scrawled hand-
writing that she barely recognised as her own:

Yours aye,
Lucinda

She started quivering again. The person who had written
the final paragraph was a person different from herself. The
revenge on Johnstone, yes, that she could take, that she
bloody well could take. But not the rest. Not the advice
about Higgins and Winter. Her other self had been changed
out there, by some experience other than approaching death,
in some way that her present self could not understand.

She sighed and put the letter away. Some day, when she
was calmer, she would read the first part of it again. It contained no useful information. It did not even contain useful
advice about facing death. No recollection of anything that
her other self had written would stand her in good stead if—
when—she went down the dark glen herself. Perhaps that
was what she was supposed to learn from this: that you really did have to walk it all alone.

Still, it made her feel better about contacting Morag Hig-

e was less in dread of the prospect than she had
Perhaps this, too, had been what her other self had
ho ed.

Lucinda peeled a new phone off the flat's comms panel
and slipped it on. It still had Higgins's code.

"Oh," said Higgins. "You."

"I would like to meet."

Higgins shrugged. "You know where to find me. Back
where we started. In the Hairy Fairy."

There was something ineradicably depressing about a
place that smelled of the middle of the night in the middle of the day. Lucinda bought a long vodka and walked
over to the window alcove where Higgins sat. Sunlight
blazed through the sheet-diamond and gleamed on Higgins's hands as she fiddled with a half-litre bottle of whisky,
half-empty.

"The stuff works, now," she said. "Isn't that amazing?"

"And a steel liver, too," said Lucinda, in what she hoped
was an admiring tone. Something inside her, in her belly or
in her head, was churning.

Higgins laughed. "Thank you. The one thing I can't stand
is sympathy."

"I heard you were angry."

"Sure, I'm angry." Higgins bit off the top of the bottle's
neck and crunched the glass in her mouth. Swallowed.
Poked out a tongue glittering with powdered particles, then
washed them back with a swig from the bitten bottle. "Fascinating, eh? I have this marvellous body, and I still have the
same pathetic mind. 'My name is Morag Higgins, and I'm a
Rapture-fucker.' Only more so. God, I want it."

"I'm kind of glad you didn't find it, on Chernobyl."

"Nah, didn't like the place. Too many ghosts." She looked
at Lucinda appraisingly. "It was you who got me out of
there, you know. You were tough. You were good to me."

Lucinda tilted her hands. "She wasn't me."

"Well, you have her *character*. You're a good sort, Carlyle. Don't forget it."

Higgins, her self-pity suddenly gone, was gazing at her in an odd way, as though looking at some admired person she'd previously met and hoped remembered her.

"All right," Lucinda said. "I won't. It's good to know." She sipped her vodka, but it wasn't only that that warmed her inside. It was rare, really, to be liked by a civilian. And gratifying, even though this civilian was not quite human. "My cousin said you don't want to download back to the flesh. We can pay for it, you know. We owe you that."

Higgins shook her head, the fine wires of her hair hissing. "You can revive my old self in a new body if you like. I'm sure she'll be happy." Her lips compressed, stretched. "Or maybe not. I don't know. She can always kill herself if it doesn't work out."

"What about you?" It was a rule that there could be only one instance of a person walking around at the same time in Carlyle's Drift. One legal person, anyway. It made life difficult for identical twins. They needed certificates.

"I don't want to stay the same, or download, so it doesn't matter. I want to upgrade. You can write me off, honestly. I'll surrender all my identity rights to the clone."

"Where will you go? I don't see an expedition taking you, and you can't afford to take ship, and you can't walk out of the Drift."

"I don't have to breathe, you know."

"Stow away on the *outside of a ship*?" Lucinda asked incredulously.

"Keep your voice down," said Higgins. "Well, it's a dream, innit? To feel solar wind in my hair. See the stars with my own naked eyes, in vacuum. See what an FTL jump really looks like. I'd hold my mouth open and catch quantum angels like midges."

"Do you," asked Lucinda, "have some way of sobering up?"

"Yeah, sure." Higgins blinked, sighed. Her glass eyes

came into focus. "Hah. Fuck. Clarity again. Did I really say all that?"

"You did." Lucinda leaned forward. "Would you like to take part in a raid on Eurydice?"

"Wow. Yes. Your firm has one set up?"

"I didn't say that," said Lucinda. She pushed the half-empty vodka glass across the table. "Here, finish this. It'll get you started on the downward path again." She stood up, winked. "I'll be in touch."

The combat archaeologists and the rest of the Carlyles' fighters sometimes called themselves soldiers, but that was just the traditional way of referring to the family's members and the firm's employees. It did not imply acquaintance with military strategy, tactics, or discipline. This wasn't much of a disadvantage: none of the other powers had the capacity or the necessity to build armies; in interstellar warfare all ground engagements were skirmishes, and anyway the real enemies were nonhuman. The biggest and best army in the human population of the universe was probably that of Eurydice. And it, they expected, was on their side.

"What a rabble," said Higgins. Suited up, kitted with a laser rifle, a Webster, and a combat knife, she looked no different from the rest. Just as well. Kevin, in charge of the squad, knew who she was. The other seventeen people on it didn't. Lucinda knew a few of them: the gunner Macaulay and the biologist Stevenson from her first mission to Eurydice were there, but this time Macaulay was second-in-command to Kevin, and Stevenson was on the same level as Lucinda and Higgins: grunts.

They formed up into double file at the terminal building, stared at by travellers and smiled at by refugees, and set off through the skein. It didn't get any faster doing it as soldiers, except that you weren't stopped at the gates. After a couple of hours they were outside of the warren of spatially connected corridors and hiking or driving on sleds between gates on uninhabited and hitherto unexplored planets. Some of them had life, all of it unicellular on the usual pattern: bacteria and slime moulds and algae, biospheres of snot. Here and there, close to the gates, were the enigmatic remains of posthuman activity, on every scale from the gargantuan to the minute. On one world, glimpsed sidelong as the squad's gravity sleds raced across a desert of riddled clinker, low flat buildings of diamond pane housed machinery that still moved; on another, the sticky slime was slowly being converted into crystalline objects like the workings of a mechanical watch. Others still were scarred with previous teams' passage from days or weeks earlier as Ian Carlyle's commandos explored the connections of the skein and laid down tactical nuclear firebreaks through kilohectares of malevolent machinery.

"What a bloody waste," said Higgins, her boots crunching over the scorched shreds of rubbery synthetic slugs the size of whales that had browsed the hardened mucus of the planet's—perhaps—natural inhabitants.

Carlyle shrugged. "These things don't look like they're more than a slight case of exuberance on the part of a dumb program."

"We don't know."

"Tell you what, if we make it back you can have first dibs. Yuck."

"It's the principle."

"Leave that to the Knights. God, times like this I can sympathise with the farmers. Better their green fields than this green slime. It's like God didn't *breathe* life into the universe—he sneezed it."

"And left the angels the job of wiping it off," added Higgins, as they stepped through the gate and emerged on the other side—a hot lunar vacuum—with their boots as clean as if they'd just been polished. Cleaner, in fact: sterile. The filtering process was a feature of the skein, definitely, but nobody knew how it worked, or why. It seemed uncharacteristically benign. The posthumans had never left any other impression that they cared for the welfare of humanity or the integrity of biospheres.

But then—and the thought made Lucinda break pace for a moment—if the Knights were right, and she was right, the skein and the gates with all their convenient and inconvenient features had not been made by the posthumans generated in the Hard Rapture. They had been generated by the relict machine on Eurydice, the transformed remains of the starship: the consequence of a different Singularity entirely, whose AI enablers had envisaged different ends from those of the American military-industrial complex whose transcendence had taken Earth's best minds away and scattered their disquieting products across the galaxy.

She did not yet know what to do with that thought.

Two jumps later, the squad arrived at the gate closest to the DK planet. Methane slush, a distant dim primary, buckyboard walkways to the launch field where a boxy AO ship waited to take them the remaining dozen light-years. The ground under the slush had been churned by many tracks in the past day or two. When they filed aboard the ship they realised it didn't have pressure outside the cockpit. They sat on the floor in gloomy rows.

"We'll get tae take our helmets off in half an hour," said Kevin, cutting across grumbles. "So shut the fuck up, guys and gals."

The ship lifted and fittled. There was nothing to see, and nothing to hear until atmosphere screamed and whistled. The pilot wisely took his time about the descent: the ship had nothing in the way of heat-shielding. After about ten minutes the sound diminished, then stopped. The hatch opened to blue sky. The fighters stood up, walked forward and dropped, one by one, from a metre up in the air on to a long beach. The ship, not hanging around, lifted behind them as soon as the last was off. A few hundred metres up the beach, below the tideline, stood a diminishing series of statues with their heads blown off. Over to Lucinda's right smoke rose from the still smouldering jungle. As she followed the others' example and opened her helmet her nostrils were choked with the smell of wet ash. The whole beach looked as though it had been invaded from the sea: search engines, gravity sleds, robot walkers, heavy weaponry, bivouacs, latrines, hundreds of soldiers. Then you noticed there weren't any boats. The gate she'd come through was now clearly marked with a big loop of glowing plastic. A ramp of board-held sand led up to its lip, and the big screen of a hair-thin fibre-optic probe stood on the beach beside it.

"Shit," she said. "This place used to be a nature preserve. And there was no call for shooting up the statues, dammit."

"You've been here?" asked Higgins, gazing around. She'd covered her face with green and black camo slap; not a bad trick.

"Uh-huh. That gate up there's how I got away from Eurydice." She shook her head. "Met the biologist who looked after it. He kind of guarded it."

"Maybe he started the shooting."

"Aye, it's possible," Lucinda conceded. "Poor wee bugger. I wonder if he knew what was coming. Probably not."

She started inquiring among the advance guard. Nobody had seen Ree, or found a corpse in the statues, but that didn't mean much—the search would have been cursory, and he might now be feeding the fishes he'd studied. If Ree was dead he wasn't coming back. The commies used life-extension but didn't take backups. It went against the self-reliance idea.

She stalked off and confronted Kevin, who was stooped over a map table.

"Any idea who did this?"

Kevin shook his head.

"No that I've heard of. Ian did a deal wi the local collective through the usual channels. They didnae mind us going through here against the Knights. We found this place just as it is."

"Sure it wisnae our advance guard securing the area, just tae mak siccar?"

"Oh aye." He caught her sceptical scowl. "Truly. It wisnae

us. It was recent, mind, but it wisnae us. Same thing's happened at the nearest settlement, on the mainland. Shot tae fuck and abandoned. Horrible. Deid weans in the ruins and that."

Lucinda remembered the bright, eager children and felt sick. "What? Who could have done that?"

Kevin shrugged, glanced down pointedly at the map. "Ian thought at first it might hae been the Knights fae Eurydice, but there's nae trace of anyone's coming through this gate anyway. Maybe it was some kindae commie faction fight or family feud."

"Aye, maybe," said Lucinda.

She wandered off for a bit and shot at cormorants.

Good to see the boss taking a lead," said Higgins. Ian Carlyle stood on a large boulder near the headland while the troops gathered.

Lucinda snorted. "You won't see him going through the gate." Behind her hand she added: "He doesn't back up."

"Jeez H."

"Yeah, that has something to do with it."

Ian coughed and gestured impatiently. "I'm not going to shout," he said. Everybody gave a thumbs-up as they found the channel.

"Good, ah, afternoon," he said. "Thank you for coming. You'll have seen the situation report, I trust. Tactically, ladies and gentlemen, this one is going to be a bit tricky. I hope you've all backed up, because many of you are going to die." Even from where she stood, twenty metres away, Lucinda could see on his face a pinched, fastidious flinch. "Any who haven't, or indeed any of you, should not be ashamed to see the chaplain. However. Enough about that." He stopped, gaze straying.

"Good God," muttered Higgins. "You said this guy used to be a lawyer."

"Give him a moment," said Lucinda.

"*Today*," shouted Ian, smacking his fist on his palm, "we free Eurydice! Here is how we'll do it. We can't communicate with our forces and friends in the system—over thousands of light-years chronology protection kicks in something fierce. So we have a fibre-optic probe through the gate giving us real-time updates. Squads should line up in single file, two squads alongside each other. As soon as we see action—within the hour, people, within the hour!—we start diving through in pairs. The first pair takes out the bored guards. Commando action." He drew a finger across his throat. "Each subsequent pair splits in opposite directions, rolls away, takes cover, keeps low. We couldn't do that unless we we were sure the Knights will be distracted. Be assured, they will be. But that opportunity will be brief. As soon as any of us is spotted or fired upon, everyone opens up with everything they've got. The heavy vehicles will follow the foot troops through and reinforce. Advance on the enemy, turn on your IFF to distinguish friend from foe, avoid damaging the relic, and otherwise fire at will. God bless us all, and have mercy on our souls. Kinsmen and friends, for the Castle on the Clyde—*victory or death!*"

"Fuck," said Higgins. "That's me encouraged."

The crowd cheered perfunctorily, shuffled, and dispersed a small way. Self-sufficient in their closed-cycle suits, they didn't need to forage, but some did, stuffing leaves or seaweed into their integral drexlers for trace elements or interesting flavour combinations, or heating coffee in pans for the sake of the smell rather than the taste. Others checked weapons, stretched limbs, or took blessings. But all the while a minority whose individuals came and went but which gradually grew as a group clustered near the screen beside the gate. It showed the green false colours of night on Eurydice—from the distance that Lucinda saw it, just the triangular spike of the relic and indistinct shapes moving in front of it: not much to go on. By the time half an hour had passed most of the soldiers, by forty-five minutes all of them, were formed up and ready to go. Lucinda and Higgins were assigned to a position that would put them the fortieth and forty-first pair to go through. Not in the vanguard, but no disgrace. The queue of troopers was lined up along the beach, not directly in front of the gate, just in case someone on the other side had the bright idea of putting a shot through. At some point in the battle, it was entirely possible that the enemy would lob a tactical nuke through the gate—which would not only wipe out anyone still on this side of it, but would collapse the wormhole. The attack would be dangerous, but not so dangerous as staying here. It would be a flight to the front.

Still, seeing Ian wave, yell, and go through as one of the second pair gave her a surprise. At least the old reprobate had the courage of his fears.

After that it was a slow jog forward for all of them, like some insane queue with death at the end of it. No time seemed to pass before they were at the front and on the much-trodden ramp. A man squatted, intent on the screen. On the opposite side one of the commandos stood, intent on the troops, perhaps to shove aside—or shove through?—the wavering. She glanced at the soldier on her right, then back at Higgins. A glint of steel teeth behind the visor.

The man at the screen raised a thumb. The commando mouthed "Go!"

Through they went, into a darkness broken by distant flashes and diminished somewhat by the crowded Sagittarius stars. Lucinda dived to the left and rolled as soon as she was clear of the hillside cromlech, fetched up in an erosion slippage hollow, and snuggled into mud. There had been a rainstorm recently; she could see clouds clearing to the east. The single moon, Orpheus, was a narrow crescent, low in the west. When nothing happened for a few seconds she peered over the lip. Night-vision cut in instantly. Far too many people were close to her, and more on the way. She levered herself out of the hollow with a foot and a hand, the other hand clutching the rifle, and rolled farther down the hillside moments before Higgins thudded into the place she'd just vacated. She felt hideously exposed. They were well within range of a Webster or a laser rifle, to say nothing of a plasma cannon. In a crouch she ran at a diagonal down the hillside, heading for a low boulder. Already occupied, somebody poking a laser-rifle muzzle around the side of it. She ran on behind them and squelched waist-deep into a bog. That would do. She waded forward and lay face down from the waist up in the heather-like stuff around it. A few seconds later Higgins joined her.

Four and half kilometres away and about two hundred metres downhill, the kilometre-tall relic, glowing faintly in real light, still seemed to loom overhead. The Knights' starship lay like a shadow, darker than the dark, on the ground beside it. Low small buildings clustered a little way off. Lucinda frowned up the zoom-band on her visor and peered closer at the area around the relic's base, from which flashes could be seen. Small arms fire, Webster bolts mostly, as Armand's people or other Eurydiceans challenged the Knights. Lucinda could imagine the fight. The Knights, even in their first surprise, would be fighting back with more than weapons. Their preternaturally fast reflexes could, if not quite dodge a bullet or a bolt, at least anticipate them by the requisite split second.

Kevin's voice lit the command circuit. "Move out," he said. "Keep on a bearing of twenty-seven degrees east of local mag north. Regroup a kilometre downslope and wait for Macaulay with the sleds and the heavy gun."

Lucinda and Higgins hauled themselves out of the backward suck of the bog and ran downhill. The rain-wet vegetation washed some of the mud off their legs as they ran. Beside them to left and right other figures scurried, their paths insensibly diverging, then over-correcting and almost running into each other. Keeping to the bearing was harder than it sounded. Time after time she blinked up the virtual compass and found herself straying. It was unavoidable, to get around boulders, scree, and—as they moved farther down the hill—increasingly deep and treacherous bogs. Every patch of what looked like moss had to be treated with circumspection. And then you would trip on a low, sharp stone and hurtle headlong. In the suit it was only a padded jarring, but it was a nuisance and your brain still got bashed about in the skull.

Away ahead, beside the relic, a brighter and more diffuse glow arose.

"Down," said Kevin. They dived. Lucinda raised her head a little and saw the Knights' starship lift. It climbed a couple of hundred metres and moved about the same distance horizontally, then stopped. A streak of flame shot out from it and passed directly overhead. The whizz, the downdraught, and the afterburn instantly told Lucinda that it was a rocket. An instant later, light flared behind her.

Tac nuke, through the gate!

Before the afterimage had faded from her eyes another line of light flared across her sight, from the ground to the ship. It was the discharge of the same type of weapon as she had, on her first day on Eurydice, watched burn through the search engine. It took no longer to burn through the ship. The vast shape yawed, sideslipped, and buried about a quarter of its length into the hillside. Lucinda pressed her head down with her hands, waiting for the explosion. Nothing happened. When she looked again the upper side of the ship showed a vivid cherry-red dot where the beam had passed through, smoking slightly, but there was no sign or evident prospect of further damage.

Unwillingly, she turned her head to look behind. A gate's collapse under nuclear or other high-energy weapon attack usually prevented much of a backwash, but in this instance the absolute amount was such that the minuscule fraction of the bomb's energy that had flashed through had been enough to sear a swathe of hillside hundreds of metres long. Tiny figures on its edges were running about, burning in their suits. One by one they dropped, whether killed by the heat or by the mercy shots that rattled out she couldn't tell. Backlit by flames, Macaulay's team with the five sleds and the plasma cannon skimmed down towards her. As the nearest sled glided past she ran up and vaulted on, Higgins close behind. The sleds slowed, picking up more and more of the squad as soldiers leapt from the heather and piled on.

"How many have we lost?" Lucinda asked. Kevin's voice came back:

"Just under half our total strength. Get on the sleds, spread out, keep moving in. Macaulay, line up on any KE forces you can see and zap them."

All across the hill, plasma-cannon bolts were coming the other way. Though precisely enough targetted, their overkill was tremendous: over her shoulder Lucinda saw an individual soldier vapourised by a bolt big enough to take out a tank. Flash-dried by the bolts, the previously sodden shrubbery was beginning to burn. Macaulay and the cannon with its crew were on the sled up ahead. It slewed and began a rapid sideways traverse, bolt after bolt singeing the air and all aimed at the same spot. In the few seconds the engagement lasted the other pilots put as much distance as they could between their sleds and Macaulay's. One sled went down to a responding shot before the plasma fire from the KE forces ceased.

The slipstream rose to a roar for a minute and then they were between the foot of the relic and the fallen ship, and among the enemy. Lucinda keyed up her IFF, pretuned to the Carlyles' and the Eurydiceans' suits. She rolled off the sled, letting the suit save her in the tumble, and lay on the ground selecting targets and firing at any suit that didn't come back with the agreed ping. She saw a ragged line of men emerging from the hatch of the wrecked ship, and shot them down one by one, faster and faster as they fled. Other Knights who had time retreated to the ship—some small squad of the Carlyle fighters followed them in. She only imagined she could hear the shots within as she sent forth more of her own.

A weight crashed on to her back before her suit could warn her, and hands in stronger armour than hers pinned her arms. A frantic voice found a channel.

"Cease fire! Cease fire! It's over! The Knights have stopped fighting!"

Lucinda recognised the voice. "Armand!" she shouted.

"Oh, Christ, it's you." He rolled off, reached out and hauled her to her feet. "Can you get through to your commanders?" he asked. "I can't. Your soldiers won't stop for me. It's a massacre."

Perplexed, Lucinda transmitted him the key to the firm's command channel. She watched him shout, gesticulate, pace up and down. After about four more minutes, he stood still, then stalked up to her. A Black Sickle aircar drifted overhead.

"Your—your barbarians were not taking surrenders!"

Lucinda shook her head. "Nobody told them to."

Armand lifted his visor. "When we attacked the Knights, we kept negotiating. Each side lost, perhaps, a dozen. There were five hundred of the Knights. Your forces have killed *three hundred* of them."

"We lost hundreds too," Lucinda pointed out. "To the nuke, and on the hillside."

"Exactly," said Armand. "Only about fifty of you have reached here. They did most of the killing."

"Well, hey," said Lucinda. "That's what you get when you call in the bloody Carlyles."

"So I see." He was calming down. "I confess myself relieved there are not more of you."

She laughed. "We've won."

"Indeed we have." He looked distracted, turning away. "For now. There is another KE starship here, and it must be on its way. Let us hope the bloody Carlyles can stop it."

"Oh, I wouldn't worry about—"

Colour, reddening, washed into the scene. Lucinda looked up to see its source. Something intensely bright had risen above the southeastern horizon and was soaring up the sky like a small unreasonable sun.

CHAPTER 15

Rebels and Returners

Winter had never been in his own conceit a philistine about opera. He could stand it fine, as long as it was in Italian. Hearing people singing English prose made him want to curl up or laugh and point. At least this one had plenty of proper songs as well. He and Calder waited sweating in the wings to provide one. Kowalsky playing Armand, creaky in a stiff uniform, beard oiled and moustache tapered, stood with one hand on his bemedalled chest and the other arm thrown out and sang:

> *I cannot do what you ask of me! It would be treason
> to ESA and the Joint Chiefs, and nothing can make me
>   break the oath
> I swore in Paris when I took my office.*

To which Alain Aruri, playing the Returner agitator Lawrence Hammond in labour-force fatigues and cropped hair, responded from the front of a massed chorus in beggars-banquet ragged finery:

It is the Runners who are traitors, not ourselves.
How does fleeing to the stars defend Paris, France, Europe, or Earth?
"Where is Paris now? What lives in France? What walks on Earth and reaches beyond it even now?"

Kowalsky's arm pointed skyward to the proscenium's planetarium hologram arch:

I'm glad you mentioned that! The war machines have already
taken Phobos and are only held back by constant and exhausting
batteries of laser fire! We'll starve and die
under this power drain!
By fighting each other we only hurt ourselves, and aid the enemy.

Aruri sang back, furiously:

We shall return, we shall take Earth again!

Kowalsky turned on his heel and stalked off. That was their cue. Winter and Calder strutted out like militiamen on a rubble street with guitars instead of guns, and struck up "Great Old Ones" with the massed chorus behind them:

Do you ever feel, in your caves of steel . . .

As he sang Winter twitched his cheek and tweaked the polarisation of his shades so that he could see the audience, out there in the evening dark of the park. Ben-Ami's permit had come through just in time for the premiere. The stage itself was gigantic, a couple of hundred metres across, invested with floodlights, spotlights, and hologram projection devices that doubled as or could be mistaken for siege engines and laser cannon. Amplifiers made the air shake. The KE ship remained where it had been, overhead and a little to one side.

The crowd was of at least a hundred thousand; many more throughout the city and beyond would be watching on screens or contacts. It was the biggest live audience Winter and Calder had ever performed to, in any of their lives. They'd always had a big following but it had always been dispersed: big in the asteroid belt, small in the venue. Tonight this was not *their* audience, but it made Winter shake a little to indulge the illusion that it was.

And from what he could see from here, it was not all Ben-Ami's audience either. Already Winter could see here and there small circles of empty space where people had backed off from around tight, quiet knots of struggling bravoes; the glint of a dagger, the muzzle flash of a silenced automatic pistol betraying their favoured weapons for close-quarter fighting with no quarter asked or given. None of this meant there was a problem, or that Amelia Orr's expectation of a riot was about to be fulfilled; no doubt most of the guys in these small savage exchanges affected some political affiliation, but to them Reformer and Returner meant team or gang colours, family honour, nothing more. None of the resurrected Returners, people whose real-life roles were being accurately or otherwise portrayed, were here; nor Amelia either. Winter had a good idea why, though he had not spoken to Amelia for some time. Their relationship had been good for the days and nights it had lasted, and he wasn't sure where it currently stood; she'd just become absorbed in her intrigue with the Returners, and had disappeared without rancour or apology. Ben-Ami had assured him that this was nothing to worry about. There was, he'd decided, something a little alien about the very long-lived.

As one fight began, another ended. Black Sickle entopters swooped and picked up the pieces. Winter and Calder glanced at each other, grinned; thrashed and boomed the closing line:

"We will COME BACK AND EAT YOUR BRAINS!!!!"

Darkness, spotlight, roar of applause. They bowed and walked off, carefully in the opposite direction to that taken by the chorus. Let them queue for their drinks in the twenty-minute interval before the third act. Winter and Calder had theirs set up with the actors and professionals. Kowalsky, Aruri, and Voigt, half a dozen others, clustered around a table in a backstage booth made of some smart fabric you could drape to shape and shake to harden. People dashed to and from the dressing-room, snatching drinks or smokes on the way back. The two musicians grabbed beers. Calder lit a cigarette.

"It's going well," said Winter.

Kowalsky frowned over a cocktail, tapped the table. "Don't say that."

"Oh, hell, break a leg."

"That's better," said Ben-Ami, sweeping in with Al-Khayed on his elbow. The assistant smiled and winked at Calder.

"You're *terrible*," she said.

"That's the intention," said Ben-Ami.

Winter was gazing fascinated at Voigt, whose costume looked as if it had blown against her and somehow snagged. She stood sniffing a blue tube and gazing intently to one side. She turned and looked straight at him. He thought she was staring back, and smiled with belated politeness and turned away a little, but she raised a hand.

"Everything's going wrong," she said.

People ignored her. Highly strung, the word went.

"No, really," she said, her voice calm but carrying. "Everything's going wrong. Get a newsfeed."

"A *newsfeed*?" said Winter. Even though he'd been expecting something to happen, it struck him as disjunct. Nothing happened in the real world during performances; you didn't pay attention to the news. He noticed the coloured flicker on her eyes: contacts, tuned to a channel. A newsfeed. She meant it.

Winter fingered a card out of his shirt pocket, flipped it to palm-size, flat; clicked to news. Shoulders and elbows bumped him.

"Hey, help yourselves." He shook it out to screen size, folded it slightly and stood it on the table.

The feed was grainy, pasted from pinhead cameras too small to resolve a good image individually; night-vision green with flaring flashes. The sight gave him a reminiscent shiver. Somebody even said it.

"It's just like—"

Somebody shut him up.

The relic, posthuman or prehuman, that Carlyle had disturbed and the Knights guarded was occasionally central in the view, glowing with dim but real light. Around it machines and armoured people moved, exchanging fire. A babble of voices, from the news channel and from around him, indicated confusion. There was no confusion on the scene. Every movement struck Winter as purposeful. The forces contending knew what they were doing. So did Winter.

He looked up, looked around at faces that had forgotten their surroundings. Some had a green pallor that didn't come from the screen.

"Eurydicean forces are contending with the Knights for control of the relic," Winter said.

It was the first clear explanation anyone had heard.

"How do you know?" asked Kowalsky.

Winter realised he shouldn't know.

"It's obvious," he said, with a shrug.

Ben-Ami affected a wrist timepiece. He looked down at it and tapped it.

"The show must go on," he said. A bell chimed.

Winter stared at him in disbelief. The actors and professionals were getting ready to go back on.

"You're kidding," Winter said.

"No," said Ben-Ami. He jerked a thumb at the screen. "You think *that* is fighting? Interrupt this performance, and you'll see *fighting*."

Winter still couldn't believe it. Calder looked at him and shrugged, drained his bottle and picked up his guitar. Winter followed suit. Together they walked to their place in the wings, ready to walk on for the first song about their own mutual hostility and separate, unrelated, pointless second deaths. Neither of them had any recollection of the Returner

Rebellion—they'd both lost a few months' worth of memories before, or in, their Black Sickle harvesting. Winter had a certain satisfaction in the thought that he'd died a Returner, and that his partner had at least had the courage of his Runner convictions, even if that particular detail had not gone down in history, or legend.

Kowalsky sang Jacques Armand's loyal—or treacherous, depending on how you looked at it—warning to the Joint Chiefs. A chorus of them sang back and sprang into action. Behind a backdrop of scenes of welter, Voigt sang and danced an overflowing measure of feminist anger and feminine despair at the fratricide.

Outside, in the audience, the scuffles had stopped. Winter had the sense of hundreds of thousands of eyes turned to the stage, many of them looking at it past, or through, the fragmentary news of the real fight, the real rebellion, taking place in real time. But as the eyes watched Voigt dance and declaim, their attention did not waver.

A sound came from overhead, as if the sky was being ripped from one horizon to the other. Winter looked up, and saw a glowing object so huge he could not believe it was flying. It was like a mountain on a glide path, very high up in the northern sky. It moved too slowly to be a meteor, too fast to be an aircraft. It disappeared behind the horizon and the sound continued to roll down.

"Asteroid," said Calder. "Incoming."

The implication was too enormous for panic. Nobody so much as screamed. The KE ship above the park suddenly moved, displacing a great downward gust of air, and shot away in apparent pursuit of the vaster flying object. No lesser agency or action could affect whatever was to come. People who had stared upward turned again towards the stage.

Voigt danced on.

Lucinda stared up at the thing climbing in the sky with a sense of the utter absurdity of life and death. If that was what she thought it was then there was a good chance that

Eurydice was about to experience an extinction-level asteroid impact event. She grabbed Armand's arm.

"Call the starships!" she said. "All of them! Get as many
people off as possible!"

Armand, still gazing up, shook his head. "Look," he said.

At first it seemed that the gigantic bolide, now almost directly overhead, was breaking up in the atmosphere. Hundreds of smaller glowing sparks arced away from it, and its
own glow faded a little. After a few seconds it became clear
that the objects falling away from it were doing so in a defi-
nite pattern, a timed and successive release like an elabo-
rate, enormous firework, and that their trajectories would
take them down all around where she stood and in some
cases directly on top of her. In a few more seconds their
glow, too, faded to infrared and they became incoming
specks, rapidly growing in her view. Some of them—scores
of them—suddenly popped and dispersed into smaller
specks that were too dim and small to see clearly even with
her night-vision and zoom, but that—from the little she
could glimpse—seemed to be gliding down, or even—to her
utter disbelief—flying.

The diminished remains of the bolide itself finished
crossing the sky and vanished behind the horizon before its
offspring had fallen halfway to the ground. It couldn't be an
asteroid impacting, she was fairly sure of that: its trajectory
was too high and steady for it to be anything but artificial
and under some kind of control.

"What the hell is that?" she asked.

This time, it was Armand's turn to grab an arm, and to
look frightened.

"It's a war-machine deployment," he said. "Bigger than
any I've ever seen, even back in the—" He shook his head.
"Call your commanders. I'll get my people and the Knights.
We have to fight this off together."

He ran off, leaving her to raise Ian Carlyle's callsign. It
was Kevin who answered.

"Ian's dead," he said.

Amid all that was going on the shock made barely a rip-

ple. "We'll be fighting war machines any minute," Lucinda
said. "They're landing—"

"I *know* that!" shouted Kevin. Then, more calmly: "I'm
trying to pull the troops together. Here's the list." A message
zapped in to her helmet. "I'll find everybody who's on
Macaulay's gun crew. You find the rest. Pull them into a
bunch behind the starship wreck, or inside it if you can. Grab
any abandoned weapons along the way. Hold out as long as
you can. Amelia's got us one starship, it's coming in."

"*One?* You know the Knights have a starship on the way?"

"Yes," said Kevin testily. "I'm trying to ping them both so
they don't shoot each other down."

Lucinda froze for a moment, paralysed by the magnitude
of that potential disaster. The thought struck her that she was
cursed, and had been from the moment she had stepped inside the relic. She shook off the superstitious notion and followed Kevin's order, with a backward sense of relief that at
least her moment of doubt and silence had spared him any
further distraction from her.

The head-up in her helmet that Kevin had provided was a
standard self-updating chart of who was on the team and
what their role and current vital status was. Most of the en-
tries had gone dark. Macauley's gun crew still had their
names in lights, forming a hillock of hierarchy in the otherwise almost flat management structure of the squad. She
paged the others en bloc and began to be joined by them one
by one as she ran towards the crashed KE ship. The heads of
the Knights she'd shot down were already being harvested by
the Black Sickle. She doubted they'd be grateful, but she
felt glad to see it herself. The ground was buckled and ripped
by the ship's ploughing into it, hundreds of tons of earth displaced in all directions. The downed ship's engine must still
be working, she realised, otherwise the gigantic vessel
would be fallen flat instead of still sticking out, wedged into
the slope like a slate in shale, at an angle of thirty degrees to
the hill and fifteen to the horizontal.

"If we had a pilot," she muttered, half to herself, "we
could *move* this mother. . . ."

Higgins, running about ten metres behind her, broke in. "I can fly a starship."

"You? How?"

"Skill I downloaded accidentally once."

"Then why the hell didn't you use it to earn some *money*?"

Higgins giggled. "Would *you* trust a Rapture-fucker with a starship?"

"Looks like I'm gonnae."

The hatch from which the fleeing Knights had emerged was right in the groin of the overhang. Lucinda stopped under it and checked the remainder of the gang. Twenty-nine of them, all present and correct. She flashed Kevin a message of her intentions.

"You and Higgins do it," he told her. "Leave the rest on guard for now. If you can lift the ship, sure, pick everybody up."

She grabbed the edge of the hatch, chinned herself up, swung aboard. The usual disorienting sensation as she moved from the planet's gravity to the ship's. Higgins replicated the manoeuvre one-handed. They stood up and looked around. Lucinda hadn't been in a Knights' ship before, but she'd been in KE-built ones, and the interior was familiar except that there were more trees. The damage done by the bolt wasn't evident here. Her head-up lit with a couple more names, the squad members who'd gone inside the ship. She pinged them. They had about ten dead Knights on their hands and one prisoner, not a Knight.

"I'll join you," Lucinda told them. She turned to Higgins. "Know your way to the control deck?"

"Down there and to the left."

"OK. Before you do anything else, open a comms link to the grunts on the ground and patch me through."

Higgins nodded and ran off. Lucinda leaned out of the hatch, told her troops to send a Black Sickle tech into the ship as soon as possible, then swung back with another insult to her inner ear and set off along a corridor defined by lines of bonsai and broken algae tanks in which fish flopped, still dying. Human corpses and body parts lay among the splintered glass. She stepped over or past them carefully, alert to the possibility that they might not all be dead, but she reached the two squad members without mishap. They were sitting in a grass-paved social arena, a lounge or something like that, with their weapons pointed at a man who sat in the centre, hands on his head. He wore black clothing but he was indeed no Knight. He was Johnstone.

Cyrus Lamont clung in the webbing like a frightened child on a roller coaster. About a tenth of the asteroid's mass, and almost half its bulk, had been removed by the deployment of the war machines or by ablation in the atmosphere. The spindly residue, with the ship stuck to the front end, was still red-hot as it hurtled over the ocean.

"I appear to be alone," said the *Hungry Dragon*. "The intrusion is in stored rather than active mode. I have acquired a connection to the new drive within the asteroid."

"Can you control it?"

"I believe so," said the ship, with uncharacteristic hesitancy. "I would not wish to attempt a faster-than-light jump at this stage."

"I'm relieved to hear that," snarled Lamont. "Faster than sound seems quite enough to handle. Could you possibly slow our speed to a point where we are not actually burning up in the atmosphere?"

The ship disdained to reply. There was no sense of deceleration, but quite abruptly the ocean and cloud-banks below stopped flashing past and assumed a more stately progression. Slowly the glow in the air around and the rock behind faded.

"Mach 5," announced the ship, in a satisfied tone.

"Good for you," said Lamont. "Do you have any capacity to, perhaps, steer?"

"I am reluctant to attempt it," said the ship. "I would prefer to attempt a controlled landing."

"I think I could live with that," said Lamont.

"Ah," said the ship, sounding imposed upon. "You require a landing that is not just controlled but survivable."

"Ideally," sighed Lamont.

"Very well," said the ship. "I shall now adjust the altitude." After a few minutes it added, as if to itself: "Now let us see whether moving this the other way *reduces* the altitude. . . . "

They were not going to die. It was, Ben-Ami wryly reflected, probably the absence of a searing shockwave and rain of impact ejecta that had given the crowd the first glimmering of this conviction. They had restrained their panic; they did not restrain their relief. There was a lot of sobbing and clinging and wild laughter going on out there. A lot of cheering and applause too, enough to make the performance inaudible without earphones to anyone in the audience. Ben-Ami seriously doubted that his play's most rhetorically and artistically dodgy section—its attempt, by means of some fanciful virtual reality dream sequences and offline debates, to make the colony's flight into a triumph— deserved anything like this approbation. But the reprieve from what had seemed inevitable catastrophe made the final act of *Rebels and Returners* an experience that would for all those watching it be forever associated with joy and life. For every critic but himself it would go down as one of his triumphs.

Andrea Al-Khayed clutched his arm and sighed, watching Gwyneth Voigt showered with bouquets and taking bows.

"How are we still alive?"

"God knows," said Ben-Ami. "Perhaps that thing just skimmed the atmosphere. Or maybe the Knights' ship was able to, ah, deflect it."

Al-Khayed shook her head, still watching the singer. "Your grasp of physics is as charmingly intuitive as ever, Ben."

He waved a hand. "Whatever." He kissed her suddenly, surprising her. "Come on. It's time for us to take our bows."

"Not me," said Al-Khayed.

"I insist."

Together they walked to the front of the cast and led them once more on to the stage. The applause hit them like a shockwave. Then, as though the applause itself was withdrawing like surf on a beach, all the crowd breathed in at once and fell silent. Ben-Ami squinted out into the darkness and, with an impatient gesture, cut the lights. High in the sky the bright object had returned. It had travelled right around the planet, Ben-Ami realised. It was no longer glowing, and it appeared to be smaller, or else actually higher in the sky than before, outside the planet's shadow-cone, lit by the sun that had already set over New Start. It surface had become faceted, and for a moment that was how Ben-Ami saw it, foreshortened and glittering, like a knuckled fist of gems.

Lucinda glared at Johnstone. He looked back at her incuriously, as if she was just another Carlyle grunt. She remembered to flip up her visor. His expression changed to a grin. He was younger than she remembered him. Perhaps her own face projected a like innocence.

"Good to see you again," he said. "Can you ask your goons to stop pointing their guns at me? It's making me nervous."

For a moment she was inarticulate with the gall of the man.

"No bloody thanks to you that I'm here!"

"You were expecting to die," Johnstone pointed out, reasonably enough. He thumbed his chest. "I'm a resurrectee, too. My death was just as unpleasant as yours, no doubt. I remember as little of it as you do. So let's cut the recriminations, shall we?"

"I know why you stole the QTD," she accused.

"Good," said Johnstone. He jerked his head back. "It's in the lab in the hold, along with the rest of the research gear."

"What research gear?"

"What we've been using to study the relic."

She stared at him. "You have all the gear in the *ship*? You don't go into the relic?"

"Oh, do get a clue, Carlyle. The Knights are subtle. They don't barge in like looters."

"So what are they doing with you, Rapture-fucker?"

He looked eager to tell, then stopped as if he'd just remembered something. "I don't have to tell you that." His cheeks twitched. "Geneva Convention."

"Want me tae work him over?" one of the grunts asked.

Lucinda glared him down. "I do not." She returned her attention to Johnstone. "That only gets you off so much. You still owe us billions. We'll get it out of your hide one way or the other."

Johnstone laughed, showing better teeth than he'd had in a past life. "Owe youse? Wait till you see what I've saved you, and you'll call it quits."

She took a step forward. "Don't fucking fence with me."

Her helmet pinged: Higgins had patched her through. The situation on the ground and in the sky was unchanged. Still no attack from the war machines. She kept the icon up in a corner of her eye.

"All right, all right," Johnstone was saying. "You wanted to buy one of these fancy new DK ships, right? Well, the one I rode in on—under, actually, in the *Extacy*—seems to have got off all right, but the ones that were in the system for some time have got buggered up something rotten. I don't know what kind of addled eggs they laid out in the asteroid belt, but they sure aren't hatching out habitats. And the commie crews have been sending out discreet distress calls to the farmers. Most of them have abandoned their ships and been rescued in AO flying boxes. Big loss of face, so it's got to be serious. Just be glad you weren't trying some flashy fittling in one."

She ignored the jab. "Any idea what the problem was?"

Johnstone shrugged. "We got hit by an unidentified virus shortly after arriving in the system. Firewalls knocked it right back, of course, and even the AO ships laughed it off, but the commies seem to have got infected. Must have bought cruddy vulnerable tech from some kind of cowboys

and incautiously reverse engineered it into their new drives."
He chuckled. "Self-reliance, my arse."

Lucinda rolled her eyes and gazed up at the laquered ceiling. "Fuck," she said.

Her helmet pinged again. "We got a situation," Higgins
said calmly. "Maybe you should take a look."

"Keep him here, boys," Lucinda told the grunts, then
turned and ran back the way she'd come, leapt over the hatch
and sprinted on down another corridor and around a corner
to the control deck. She pushed through a delicate array of
tall fronds and stepped up to where Higgins stood leaning
over the command table. A small corner of the display was
comprehensible to Lucinda. It was the interface Higgins had
cobbled together for the existing comms link. Higgins was
gazing at the centre of the table, into depths where colour-
coded sigils and symbols moved like ornamental fish. Lucinda looked up from them, baffled.

"What's going on?"

"The good news is we've got the two starships out of each
other's sights," said Higgins. "They won't be attacking each
other. And the war machines aren't attacking us, in fact they
seem to be retreating. They've landed on the hilltops around
us and they're scuttling away through the gates."

Lucinda beat her fist on the table. "Shit! Shit! Shit!"

"What?"

"They're not running away!" she shouted. "They're taking
control of the skein!"

She could just imagine them, boiling out of gates all
across Carlyle's Drift, brushing aside the lightly armed customs enforcers and fending off or attacking the locals, finding new nodes and surging on.

"Oh," said Higgins. She seemed as overwhelmed as Lucinda felt.

"What's the bad news?"

Higgins pointed at the display. "That huge thing that
passed overhead—it's coming around again, and it's coming
down. Here. Right on top of us. In about ten minutes, I
reckon. We have to get everybody off."

Lucinda squeezed her eyes shut. "No," she said. "First we have to close the gates. Do what the Knights did—put a tac nuke through each of them."

"I don't have that level of skill," said Higgins.

"Then call up Armand's lot, tell them to fire their high-energy guns at the gates."

Kevin broke into the circuit. "Countermand that," he said. "We don't have time, and we need all the firepower we have. Higgins—can you lift the ship, and at least fire a nuke if the target's big enough?"

"Sure," said Higgins.

"Then go for it," said Kevin. "Try to bring down or break up that flying mountain before it comes over our horizon. We can get everybody into the Knights' accomodation blocks and ride out the shockwave."

It was feasible, Lucinda knew—a KE encampment was proof against anything but an on-target nuke, or an asteroid landing on the roofs. They might survive it. And if not, it was better than waiting.

"Everybody on to the ship," she told the squad. When they had all checked in she waved to Higgins. "Close the hatch and lift."

The ship lifted with a frightening noise and violent jolt as it pulled itself clear of the packed earth. Then it shot up in the air. To Lucinda's horror, she could feel some of the acceleration, like in a fast lift. She found a fixed seat and sat down, clutching the armrests, as the ship tipped and swayed. Crashing and slithering sounds came from all around her.

"What the fuck!"

Higgins's hands danced across the command table. "Controls are a bit unresponsive. The field's fluctuating. It's all the damage from the bolt, that's how it came down in the first place. Kind of thrown off balance."

"Can you call up something that lets me see what's going on?"

Higgins muttered something about "idiot board" but spared a moment to project a vertical screen from the table, in which what Lucinda hoped was a forward view appeared.

Leaning carefully out of the chair, she examined it. It was quite a convincing fake full-colour daylight picture of the scene, thrown together from input from the ship's instruments. The sort of handhold she could imagine the ship's real pilot disdaining even more than Higgins did. The ground was dropping below them and falling behind them, the horizon widening by the second. Already they were on the edge of the atmosphere, at about thirty thousand metres. Low above the horizon was a small bright dot, becoming higher and larger as she watched. The picture had no vernier or grid-lines, but a mental calculation was all she needed to show her the scale and speed of the thing. It had to be at least a kilometre long and travelling at several times the speed of sound.

"Closing to range," said Higgins. The ship lurched forward; everyone was thrown back.

"Locking on target," Higgins reported. Her hand moved, poised to strike.

The object vanished.

"Did you see that?" yelled Higgins.

"Where's it gone?"

"I don't know," said Higgins, tapping the board. "I do know I saw a Cherenkov flash. It fittled."

"That thing's a *starship*?"

"I don't know," said Higgins. "Wait, wait . . . oh, look at that." She sounded awestruck.

"What?"

Higgins straightened up, turned away from the board. The view on the screen flipped. "Looking behind us," said Higgins. She zoomed the view, centred it on the relic. Another kilometre-tall spike, rougher but just as large, now loomed beside it.

"It didn't crash," said Higgins. "It landed. It fucking *landed*."

Cyrus Lamont hung in the webbing and wept. Partly it was with relief at his survival. It had more to do with a sense of loss and a sort of agoraphobia. He knew he could have chosen to ask the ship to return to space after its fatal lading had left it and it had taken control of the new engine. Instead he had chosen to land in the midst of what fighting there had been, out of a desire to do right and to undo, if possible, the damage of which he and the ship had been the instruments. That did not make the thought of losing the ship's continuous company, and of reacquainting himself with humanity, any less daunting.

"What are you going to do now?" asked the ship.

"Try to raise whoever's out there."

"Our aerials were severely degraded in the entry," said the ship. "We have no external communications. Repairing them will take me some time."

"I could sit here and wait," Lamont said. "Somebody is bound to investigate."

"Eventually," said the ship. "For the present, the people around the base of the asteroid and of the relic are being deterred by the presence of numerous war machines."

"Are they indeed?" said Lamont. "In that case, I had better leave."

He shifted convulsively and tumbled a couple of metres into another part of the mesh.

"Your reflexes have not yet readjusted to gravity," pointed out the ship. "I would not recommend your attempting a thousand-metre descent."

Lamont rolled, bounced, and grabbed a length of elastic rope. "I'm learning. See?"

"You may be attacked by the war machines, or by the humans. Both are on hair-trigger."

"Better that than waiting."

"You can survive here indefinitely."

Lamont scratched an eyelid. "That was the worry, yes."

"I shall miss you," said the ship.

"And I'll miss you," said Lamont. "I expect to be in touch with you very shortly. Once I've abseiled down and made contact with whoever is in control here."

"For me, that is a long time," said the *Hungry Dragon*.

Lamont eyed the exit hatch. "You have much to think about," he said.

"That is true," said the ship. "I have much data to integrate."

"Good," Lamont, scrambling upside-down, downwards through the mesh, blood queueing for his head. "Now spin me a rope."

CHAPTER 16

A Harder Rapture

Higgins brought the ship down where it had originally been, in convenient location for the camp. The vegetation beneath where it had been parked for the past weeks formed a distinct pale square. Some automatic mechanism stopped the ship's descent where it could remain horizontal a metre or two above the uneven ground, its lower corners perfectly level with each other, as though on an invisible plane. The whole manoeuvre looked, Higgins said, cleverer than it was.

For a few minutes after landing they looked at the scene outside. The virtual daylight of the ship's visual display gave a much clearer picture than their night-vision could provide, and from a good vantage. People were emerging from the diamond-shelled camp buildings and staring at or focusing instruments on the grounded asteroid. Their view of it was partially obscured by the relic, but the bases of the two gigantic objects appeared to be about half a kilometre apart. The asteroid speared up into the night, its surface pitted with curiously smooth and regular cavities as well as by the fused remnants of its natural bricolage. Long veins or strands snaked and branched down from its summit, at which a relatively tiny structure, perhaps a hundred metres high, was perched like a cairn on a mountaintop.

"Zoom on that," said Lucinda.

"It's a ship," said Higgins, as the view expanded. It was sticking up from the confluence, or source, of the veinings like a tree-trunk from its roots. Scorched, stubbled with broken aerials, it looked like a wreck.

"Well, somebody must have flown it," said Lucinda. "There must be a pilot."

"That or some smart machinery," said Higgins. "My money's on that."

"Speaking of machinery," said Lucinda.

Higgins expanded the view again. Several species of war machines were visible, lurking around the bases of the relic and the asteroid and in the middle distance, and in the air maintaining midge-like holding-patterns around them. They were neither attacking nor being attacked; the situation seemed to be a standoff. The hundreds of people on the ground had stopped milling about and had begun to organise: sullen clumps of the defeated Knights, tidy platoons of Eurydicean troops, scattered bands of the Carlyle fighters. As they watched, a man detached himself from the nearest such band and walked towards the ship. He took off his helmet and waved, beckoning. It was Kevin, looking more cheerful than Lucinda had expected.

"Oh, *well* done!" he said, as Lucinda and Higgins descended the ramp from the ship.

"We didn't do much," said Higgins, glancing up at the monstrous addition to the landscape.

"You tried," said Kevin. "You took the ship up and you locked on to that thing. That's as clever and brave as you had to be. Probably just as well you didn't shoot it down, anyway."

"Is it still a threat?" Lucinda asked.

Kevin shrugged. "We've been scanning it. There are war machines around the base of it, just like around the relic." He jerked his thumb over his shoulder. "We'll consider taking them on later, when we've got ourselves sorted out. Right now, they just seem to be guarding the thing. There aren't any more war machines on it. That's definitely a Eurydicean ship stuck to the top of it."

"A Eurydicean ship? With a starship engine?"

"That's no weirder than a Eurydicean ship turning an asteroid into a fucking nest of war machines."

"Corrupted its fabricators," Higgins diagnosed confidently. "Same thing's been done to the DK habitat-builders, that's my guess."

"What's that?" Kevin asked.

They relayed what Johnstone had told them.

"Sam Yamata didn't tell us anything about any of this," Kevin said. "Shit."

"Who's Sam Yamata?"

"Leader of the Knights here. Christ, I could wring the little fucker's scrawny neck."

"You couldn't," said Lucinda. "Martial arts."

"Ha, ha," said Kevin. "If we're up against starships controlled by a virus from the relic, to say nothing of yet more nests of war machines that could just fittle in any time like that fucking rock did, we're in deeper shit than we knew."

"Aye, deep enough," said Lucinda bitterly. "Only the biggest disaster since the Hard Rapture. Leave aside whatever rampage the war machines are daein." She jabbed a finger towards the relic. "That thing created the skein, and now it controls it. Not us, no the Knights and for sure not Armand. Speaking of which, we don't have enough forces on the ground to even hold the site nominally. Fuck." She glared around. "I rue the day I ever found this place. Everything I touch turns to shit."

"Hey, hey," said Kevin. "Take it easy. This is not your fault. I'm getting things sorted out with the Knights and Armand's lot. If the Knights and the farmers knew about the DK ships they must at least be keeping an eye on them out there. We cannae dae anything about the war machines in the skein right now, but I reckon they'll be meeting some pretty tough resistance fae our gang. We'll find out as soon as messages start tae propagate back, Chronology Protection permitting. And we're not, you know, being attacked at the minute. We just need tae get our act together, consolidate, and work out what tae dae next."

"Great," said Lucinda. "So what do we do now?"

"What maist of us need tae dae," said Kevin, "and you in particular, is *sleep*."

Later, it seemed to Lucinda incredible that she and almost everybody else had slept, but that was what they did. Emotionally and physically exhausted, with the war machines watchful—and watched, by the short-straw-drawn unsleeping—rather than actively hostile, with too many dead to count except by the Black Sickle girls whose job it was, all of them—Carlyles, Eurydiceans, Knights—except those on guard duty crashed out in whatever shelter and with whatever human companionship they could find.

She woke with synthetic sunlight on her eyes and metal hair between her lips.

"Oh, sorry," she said, disengaging the hair and withdrawing a careless arm from across Higgins's breasts.

The metal woman smiled. "I don't mind," she said. She rolled away, on the yielding turf-like flooring, put her hands behind her head and gazed at the ceiling. "I don't sleep."

"How nice for you," said Lucinda, straightening limbs and picking salt crystals from the corners of her eyes. She felt sweaty and filthy, as well as obscurely embarrassed. After some foraging she found the nearest bathroom, all low vessels and pebble-shaped steel objects whose functions she discovered by trial and error as she used them. The drexler gave her plain underwear, canvas trousers, and a cotton top and, after some persuasion, a quilted jacket. She wasn't going to get back into her suit unless she had to, but she poked into the helmet and strung the comms around her brow, neck, and ears like jewellery. There were no calls waiting. She detached the boots and tugged them on; buckled on a belt and weapons.

There: that felt better. She stood and examined herself in the mirror for a minute. Looked better, too.

The room they'd slept in had a low ceiling that mimicked a clear sky, and a small trickling water feature surrounded by plants in a corner, and otherwise no furnishing. As she paused at its open doorway Lucinda formed a vague opinion that it was some kind of retreat, perhaps for meditation. Higgins was still lying on the floor. Her glass gaze tracked Lucinda, who met it, unblinking, as she came over and sat down cross-legged beside her. Higgins sat up with one smooth flexure of the spine.

"You OK?" she asked.

Lucinda ran a hand through her damp, still annoying curls. "I'm fine," she said. "It's just, uh, I'm sorry."

"For what?" Higgins asked, in a mildly surprised tone.

"If I've been, like, kind of rude lately."

Higgins shook her head, metal hair flashing. "Not at all."

Lucinda didn't know what to say. She would have been ashamed to reveal even the trace of her initial revulsion that had remained, and that she now wanted to vomit out. "I like you," she said at last. "My original liked you, and now I can see why. Last night, in the fighting and in the flying, you were just *so fucking great*."

With that she really did find herself wanting to vomit. "Excuse me," she said. She ran back to the bathroom and spewed, nothing much but acid water and slime, but she felt better for getting rid of it. She washed her face and rinsed out her mouth again and walked shakily to the room. This time Higgins stood up, met her, and put her arms around her for a moment. The metal body felt like flesh.

"You're all right," Higgins said.

"So are you."

Higgins smiled, looked aside awkwardly. "Things to do," she said. "I gottae look around this vehicle."

"Sure. Catch you later."

Leaving Higgins to roam the ship, Lucinda swung out of the hatch to face the day. The early sunlight was dimmer than the diurnal lighting inside. A thin drizzle fell from clouds that concealed all but the first hundred metres of the relic and of the grounded asteroid about half a kilometre to its right. Two other ships hung just below the cloud cover; she presumed they were the two that had nearly clashed during the night. Tiny solar-powered news cameras flitted and drifted, their little wings labouring in the damp air and dim light. Around the bases of the relic and the asteroid war machines patrolled, a dull sheen of condensation from the mist on their jittery shining limbs and swivelling sensory apparatuses. Well away from them, and close to her and the ship, troops stirred from bivouacs, fires and heaters were being lit, somebody was making coffee. She wandered over and cadged some. It was Eurydicean, muddy, and strong. This group were from Armand's army. Nobody knew what was going on. As she sipped hot black coffee and listened to rumours she saw a figure far outside the camp, walking away from the asteroid and towards them through the mist. Lurking war machines registered his presence, but let him pass unhindered.

Around her and on the perimeter, the grunts saw him too, and guns came up. He must have noticed the glint and the threat, because his hands rose above his head. As he came closer she saw that his hair and beard were long and matted. He was about two metres tall, perhaps more, because he walked as though carrying a heavy pack. His face was lank and pallid, his eyes bright. With his upraised arms he looked like a mad prophet coming out of the wet wilderness. He wore a close-fitting space suit with the raised whorls that covered electromagnetic coils and marked it as Eurydicean long-term microgravity gear. That would account for his peculiar stoop and laboured gait.

"Cover me, lads and lasses," said Lucinda. She put down the mug on the damp moss and walked forward, her hands open at her sides. She and the stranger stopped about three metres apart.

"Can I take my hands down now?" he asked. His voice sounded surprised at itself.

Lucinda nodded. He lowered his arms and straightened his back.

"Who are you?" she asked.

"Cyrus Lamont," he said. "Prospector. Owner and pilot of the *Hungry Dragon*." He jerked a thumb over his shoulder. "The ship that's stuck to the top of yon asteroid. Which I claim, in case there's still any metal left in it."

Lucinda had suspected something of the like, but it was still a surprise to her.

"It was you who flew that? Landed it?"

"Oh, no," Lamont said. "It was the ship did all that." His eyes closed for a moment. "It wasn't responsible for the war machines," he explained. "They hacked into it."

"Well, I don't think anyone will blame you for that."

"Good," he said, sounding relieved.

"How did you get down?"

"Climbed."

"Climbed down? In the dark?"

"The dark?" He looked puzzled. "Yes, I suppose it was dark. The ship helped." He gazed around, distracted. "I need to talk to someone, very urgently. Someone in authority."

"That would be Jacques Armand," said Lucinda. "I can take you to him." She stuck out a hand. "My name's—"

"Lucinda Carlyle," he said, shaking her hand firmly. "I saw you on television."

She tried raising Kevin and Armand on her comms, but they weren't taking calls. Annoyed, she sought them out, stalking around the KE camp with Lamont in tow until she found them in a small, open-sided diamond-aerogel shelter, sitting at a table with the leader of the surviving Knights. Sam Yamata turned out to be the very old man Lucinda and Armand had encountered the day the Knights had arrived. Lucinda presumed they'd already discussed what, if anything, could be done about the corrupted DK ships, because when she and Lamont arrived they were talking about the Knights who had not survived, but had been given a chance of resurrection by the Black Sickle.

"We cannot run them in a virtual environment," Yamata was saying. "It is very dangerous."

Jacques Armand and Kevin Carlyle glanced at each other. They both saw Lucinda and Lamont; Kevin gestured to them to wait. The leaders were not taking interruptions.

"You might set off another Rapture?" said Armand.

"Not exactly," said Yamata. "It is just that, when you run uploads to solve a problem, they soon, in a matter of seconds, form what is called a civ. The uploads replicate and develop relationships. Most of them go very bad. You sometimes get an entire virtual planet of four billion people devoted to building prayer wheels in an attempt at a denial of service attack on God."

"Does it ever work?" asked Kevin, sounding interested.

Even the Knight creased a smile. "In the nature of things we would not know," he said. "However, within the virtual universe, it does work, in that the god of that universe is its initiator, who has to stop the experiment because of exponential waste of bandwidth."

"All right," said Armand, clearly feeling that bandwidth was being wasted right here. "Is resurrection acceptable to you, in the circumstances?"

Yamata hesitated a moment. "Yes," he said. "The consequences in another life will be borne by me, not by those resurrected. They will understand, and I . . . will accept the consequences."

Lucinda detected a note of complacency in his humility. This was a man who felt his karmic balance was well in the black.

Kevin sighed. "And I'll dae the same for Ian. Let the old bastard sort it out with *his* God."

Yamata leaned forward. "His God has a difficulty with resurrection?" He sounded incredulous. "What is this religion?"

"It's called Christianity," said Kevin stiffly. "It has a jealous God. Keeps a bit ae a monopoly on resurrection, that one. Disnae like others muscling ontae His patch."

"Ah," said Yamata. "When your venerable relative is resurrected I shall endeavour to show him the light."

Aye, you just try it, you heathen bugger! Lucinda tried to suppress a snort. The sound was enough to turn heads back to where she and Lamont stood.

"Yes?" said Kevin, as if he didn't know fine well they were there, and had been there for minutes. This business of not being interrupted was just showing off his new importance, Lucinda thought. It was not something she would have taken from anybody but a Carlyle. She swallowed the surge of annoyance and introduced the pilot. That got their attention all right.

Lamont walked through the camp with a feeling of rising panic. Had he ever been among so many people before? He knew he had, but he could not believe it. People stared at him, and he was never sure whether or not to look back. He had thought the rule might be to look at people only when in conversation with them, but that still created anomalies. It would have to be revised later. For now he looked, as far as possible, only at the starship. Doing so felt like cooling water flowing over his brain. The ship was so large that only the close proximity of the relic and of the asteroid made it proportionately small. It was about two hundred metres long and across, fifty thick. Every line on it was either straight or an arc. The unbroken matt black of its surfaces made some of its lines, and therefore all of its shape, difficult to see. One would have to walk around it several times, seeing at at many angles, before one could form a clear mental image of it.

That he did, somewhat to the bemusement of his three companions. When he set out on the second circuit they stood and waited for him, looked at him very oddly as he commenced the third, and with relief when he completed it.

"I see it now," he told them. "It's like—" His hands circled, chopped.

"A portion of a very large sphere," said Lucinda Carlyle. "I could have told you that."

"Telling would not have done it," said Sam Yamata, in a tone that struck Lamont as kind.

"Come on," said Armand, "let's go into the ship."

Yamata bowed, held out his hand. Lamont walked up the
rubber-ridged ramp into the ship. At the top he stopped and
looked around, astonished. It was more than spacious: it did
not feel like being inside an enclosed space. The air smelled
fresh and fragrant, the ventilation a breezy susurrus like
wind in distant branches. The ceiling was high, with the
colour and luminosity of a white cloud. It was just high
enough, about five metres, to make it seem like a sky when
your eyes weren't focused on it. The outdoor illusion was
compounded by the grass-like covering of the floor, springy
underfoot, and the trellised or potted plants and small trees
that defined work areas and passageways. There were few
flowers, all of them apparently incidental rather than decora-
tive. The most colourful features were the ornamental fish in
aquaria here and there. The furniture and instrumentation
were spare in line and plain in aspect; there was a distinctly
masculine minimalism about the whole great space and its
subdivisions that resonated with a tang, very faint, on the
air: when the Carlyle woman walked up the ramp Lamont
could almost hallucinate the pheromonal clash. She smiled
at him in a way he didn't understand. He smiled back and
looked away quickly.

"This way, please," said Yamata.

As they walked along a passageway they passed broken
aquaria, but there was no broken glass on the floor, merely
patches of a darker colour on what might have been grass,
but wasn't. Out of the corner of his eye Lamont glimpsed a
subtle movement in the fibres, like cilia. Nobody was about.
Lamont began to suspect the ship was empty, but after a turn
they found themselves in a wider clear space, a sort of
atrium, above which the ceiling formed a glowing cupola. Its
circumference was terraced into low, rounded-edged steps,
on which a man and a woman lounged, talking to each other
with some tension and intensity. Their voices ceased as the
party's footsteps approached, and they looked up.

Lamont had been forewarned about these two, but seeing
the woman was still a shock. He was glad the ship was no

longer, and not yet, in contact with him. He was certain its reaction to his unwitting physiological responses would have been jealousy. Of all the eyes he'd seen here, he found hers easiest to meet. Her handshake was, almost to his surprise, warmer than flesh. Campbell Johnstone's was cold and firm. His eyes were organic, hers were not, but there was a similarity in their gaze, as though they sought, and found, something similar in his.

"We've been told about you," Morag Higgins said. "We're impressed."

Lamont sat down on the floor. Armand and Carlyle sat on the seat a little way around the curve, Yamata at a small but noticeable further distance.

"Thank you," said Lamont. He placed his palms on the floor behind him—it felt disturbingly like fur, rather than grass—leaned back and gazed at the opalescent hemisphere above for a moment. Then he sat up and forward with his forearms on his knees and, fixing his gaze on first Higgins, then Johnstone, said: "As I understand it, from conversation with our friends here, I've gained a small measure of indirect acquaintance with the posthuman, through my, ah, discussions with the ship. The two of you have greater experience with this kind of tech, and the three of us are being asked to cooperate in establishing communication with, or control over, some level of consciousness within the relic. At the same time, we have different loyalties. You, Higgins, are working for the Carlyles; Johnstone for the Knights. I presume it's my job to fight a corner for Eurydice."

"But—"

"That's—"

"Please—"

Johnstone laughed as the three voices spoke at once. "Reckon you got it in one," he said. He stood up. "The lab's this way."

The lab smelled of cold and electricity. It occupied most of the otherwise empty hold. The space was large and

bare, lit by portable spots and floods—no luminous ceiling
or self-cleaning carpets here. Lucinda and Armand hung
back as Johnstone and Yamata talked Higgins and Lamont
around the QTD—transmitter and receiver set up about ten
metres apart—and the screens and desks connected to the
instrumentation with which the Knights had, with great and
characteristic caution, interacted remotely with the relic.
She eyed the two big round bulks of the teleportation device
with disquiet. It was for these that she had died, and she
wondered with what thoughts her original had looked upon
them. To Johnstone and Higgins the equivalent thoughts
would be memory, not speculation.

Watching Lamont troubled her more. Since coming into
the lab he had shrugged off all his awkwardness. She
couldn't make out everything he was saying, or understand
all of what she could, but his every intonation and glance
and gesture screamed one thing at her: *Rapture-fucker!* He
and Johnstone and Higgins were so instantly and blatantly in
cahoots that if she'd come upon the scene as a stranger she'd
have assumed they'd known each other for years.

"You seemed to know him," she said to Armand.

"Not personally," he said. "By repute, and"—he tapped
his temple—"this tweaked memory we have for people. He
was a rich man once, and he'll be again even if there's not a
gram of useful ore in that asteroid and his ship is a wreck.
With his experiences his credit and interest will be sky-high,
at least for a while. No doubt he'll find some way to leverage
it into a more durable competence."

"Having his own stardrive should help," said Lucinda
dryly. "Especially if the skein is fucked."

Armand looked at her sidelong. "There is that," he said,
like it hadn't occurred to him. He shifted, looked around,
and sat on the edge of a lab-bench. "The matter that Lamont
raised," he went on. "I would appreciate your opinion on it."

Lucinda spread her hands. "Higgins works for us, sure.
Johnstone betrayed us, to the Knights."

"So I've heard."

"The point is, these two are what we call Rapture-fuckers.

Lightning-chasers. They have a fascination with this stuff and they'll take risks the Knights won't. All well and good right now, maybe, but it means they each have their own agendas. I wouldn't trust either of them an inch. As for your man Lamont, he may be a good patriot of Eurydice but he's one of them. I know it."

"He seems quite taken with your woman Higgins," said Armand. He smiled. "I could venture a coarse remark, but will restrict myself to saying that a man who can screw a ship is unlikely to have a problem in that respect."

Lucinda gave an appreciative dirty laugh. "Maybe that'll be enough for them to maintain a united front."

"A united front against whom, eh?"

Lucinda jerked her head back. "The Knights. I know the immediate problem is the war machines, but let's not forget the main enemy."

"They are not the enemy," Armand said mildly. "They are our rivals, and temporary allies. Let us not forget that."

"And what are we?"

"Our agreement stands," said Armand.

Since the agreement had already been pretty much fulfilled from his side at least, this was not saying a lot. Lucinda returned him a wary smile. He leaned sideways a little, looking past her.

"Our three champions are about to start work," he said.

Lucinda turned to see the Rapture-fuckers a good way off in the lab, sitting in front of a screen, their backs to where she and Armand watched. She gazed at a distant mercurial ripple of hair and thought, *You hang in there for us, girl!*

The interface was not as foreign as Lamont had expected. Its underlying architecture and ergonomics had a common ancestry with those used on Eurydice. Fundamentally it was as familiar to him as the lineaments of the *Hungry Dragon*. No doubt all human and even posthuman software could be traced back through genealogical trees of slouching, slope-shouldered code-geeks and capitalists to the same

Olduvai in Silicon Valley. The instruments with which it interacted were outside the ship, encircling the relic at a respectful range. Their infinitesimally subtle input from deep quantum-level eavesdropping on electronic interactions within the vast artefact were analysed and collated by the ship's immensely powerful computer: some of its components were themselves cannibalised from posthuman tech. The whole array quivered on the verge of some sentience deeper and more recalcitrant than that of the *Hungry Dragon*, or even of Eurydice's Leontieff matrices. Any unscheduled self-upgrading would trigger its hardwired EMP generator. Likewise independent of its core processing were the firewalls against optic-nerve neural hacks. This seemed enough to reassure his new colleagues, and was therefore enough for him.

Strangely, despite their experience's being deeper and wider, they deferred to his, recent and specific. Yamata stood well back; Johnstone and Higgins, one by one, nodded. He leaned forward and slid his hands into the access field. Like the Knights, Lamont had long dispensed with visual and tactile feedback from such devices; his hands and fingers moved by ingrained habit in the combination of gesture, chording, and keyboarding that had, even before the Hard Rapture, become as invariant as any martial art. The wide screen lit up without a flicker. The first iteration showed the point reached by Johnstone's work on the QTD's control system, which had provided a key to the logic of the relic's major function, the generation of the wormhole skein.

Lamont shaped an inference chain based on his long sessions with the ship, which had in some measure succeeded in ridding it of the viral incubus, or at least limiting its effect. It was all from memory; he wished he had the ship with him. He checked the formulation over once, twice, then launched it into the virtual depths like a molecule cruising the bloodstream for a receptor.

The response was immediate. Something ferocious threw itself against the firewall. The screen went blank.

Yamata sighed delicately. "Restoring power," he said.

Lamont restored the formulation and reexamined it, checking its premises.

"Ah," said Johnstone. "Nice one. But . . . allow me."

Lamont relinquished the structure. Johnstone leaned forward, hands flexing. The formulation scrolled, disappeared, emerged from a mathematical transformation that turned it conceptually inside out.

"Sugarcoating," murmured Higgins. "Uh-huh."

This one lasted almost two seconds, an era in processing time but not enough for it to get through. The screen crashed again.

"Restoring power," said Yamata. The screen came back up. They stared at it for a while.

"I have an idea," said Higgins.

"One moment," said Yamata. He motioned to Johnstone. "Look, here is the power switch. I shall be better occupied on the control deck."

Johnstone nodded. Yamata went out.

"OK," Johnstone said. "Let's see what you've got."

Higgins's new structure came up, failed, was modified; and so it went on.

"Shit," said Johnstone, sitting down again for the tenth time. "Don't these guys have *technicians*?"

After a while Lamont became aware that Armand and Carlyle had followed Yamata's example, and left. Lamont didn't know how much time had passed—an hour, perhaps, and he was leaning back, hands behind his head, staring at the screen—when his comms tickled. He twitched it up, irritated at the interruption.

"Yes?"

"Your ship is pinging you," Carlyle's voice told him. "Do you want me to patch it through?"

"Oh!" He sat up, heart hammering. "Yes, that would be wonderful. Where are you?"

"We're all up on the control deck," she said. "So we're not breathing down your necks. We can see you through the command table. OK, patching you through."

Higgins and Johnstone yelled at the same moment. The

structure they'd been working on had been displaced by the complex front-end display screen of the *Hungry Dragon*.

"I meant to my own comms!" Lamont shouted.

"That's what I *did*," Carlyle's indignant voice said in his ear. "Wait, let me . . ."

"No," said the *Hungry Dragon*. "There is no need to do that. Everything is under control."

It was in all their phones.

CHAPTER 17

Subtle Conceit

Lucinda snatched her hand away as if burned from the comms link Higgins had made in the command table. Sam Yamata glared at her. His face flushed then as quickly paled. She could hear his breath. In. Out. In.

"All right," he said. "There is no danger. Whatever has intruded cannot upgrade our ship's software. But still. We now have"—he paused, paging the display too fast for her to follow—"an agent program of Lamont's ship on our side of the firewalls. It is active. Very active."

Lucinda's knees shook. Yamata had okayed the transaction, but she felt again responsible. She was still kicking herself when she saw Yamata suddenly straighten up and listen intently to a message in his personal comms. Her own chimed a moment later and she heard Amelia Orr shouting: *"Lift! Lift!"*

In the external visual display, still up on the end of the command table, she saw the two other ships—the Knights' and the one Amelia had swapped crews into—vanish in the blink of an eye, leaving a wrack of disturbed low cloud.

Yamata reached for the control menu of the command table. "Sit down," he said.

Armand and Lucinda were barely in their seats when the ship lurched upwards. They were pressed down, then released so that they almost rose out, then were slammed back again. Yamata was more skillful than Higgins had been at compensating for the ship's damaged controls, but the ride was rough. In the small view of the lab, still up on the table, she could see the three Rapture-fuckers braced under the table at which they'd worked, Lamont's long arms holding the other two and a stanchion at the same time.

"What the fuck is going on?" Lamont demanded.

"Emergency lift," Lucinda said. "Apart from that I don't know." The obvious thought struck her. "Has this something to do with what your ship did?"

"No," replied Lamont. "It *succeeded*. It cracked into the relic's control over the war machines. You can call your commander and check."

Lucinda did just that while watching the visual display. It was already showing the blue curve of the planet below, black above. Kevin's voice came through: "Aye, they're standing down. But forget about that. The corrupted DK ships are attacking."

So that was why they'd taken off so fast. "OK," she said. "Good luck down there."

"We're heading for the shelters," said Kevin, and signed off.

She relayed the information in an undertone to Armand. He frowned, staring at the visual diplay, now all black and blank but for a fleeting glimpse of Orpheus.

"Fucking useless," he muttered.

Yamata was talking quietly, switching seamlessly from Japanese to American as he spoke to the other KE pilot and to somebody called Nardini, the guy flying the Carlyles' ship. He shot Armand an impatient glance and stabbed a spot or two on the board with his finger. The visual display changed to a schematic. It showed the situation on several scales, from system-wide to local, with tags. Lucinda immediately grasped how it was put together. If the Knights had followed standard practice they'd have sown the system with transceiver sondes on all wavelengths and modes of communication, enabling the ship to build up a picture from radio and FTL comms, gravity-wave detection, reports and, she guessed, wild surmise. There were four ships marked as enemy, three—including their own—tagged as friendly, and named. The ship she was on was the *Subtle Conceit*, the other KE one the *Small Arrangement of Chrysanthemums*; and whatever the now Carlyle-piloted ship had been called originally, it was now hailing as the *Stanley Blade*. The clutter of AO vessels and uncorrupted DK ones were not in the fight, except as targets: the former location of two DK ships and one AO were shown as fading glows. The remainder were taking fast evasive action—a rapid-fire Cherenkov flicker and, moments later like thunder after a lightning-flash, a rumble of gravity-wave disturbances, showed them fleeing the system as fast as they could fittle.

"Cowards," muttered Armand.

"No," said Lucinda. "They're *helping* us—clearing the board. Cuts down on chronology tangles, too."

She watched intently as the *Stanley Blade* and the *Small Arrangement* raced to the points that triangulated Eurydice's gravity well. The enemy ships, millions of klicks away, had formed the corner of a vastly larger enclosing square. Both sides were following well-grounded tactical moves for a starship battle. What came next would be a game of bluff and chance, which could last for hours or be over in seconds. The decisions were up to the pilots, the execution to the computers. But the enemy ships were being flown *by* their computers, or rather by the combative virus that had infested them. Whether this gave her side an advantage she would soon discover. That was the only outcome she would know in this life; if the opposite was the case, she would be dead.

One of the DK ships blinked away in an FTL jump. In instant response the two other KE-built ships darted away from the planet, while the *Subtle Conceit* dived towards it, deep into the gravity well. The manoeuvre took five seconds. In less time than that the ship that had vanished reappeared, having fittled a mere two light-seconds. Close enough now to see where they were, but far out of missile or laser range. Lucinda had seen this short-hop FTL capability before; Yamata had not, but he showed no surprise. He tapped a finger; a scatter of nuclear proximity mines were expelled from the ship; and then the *Subtle Conceit* once again moved fast, to one-tenth light-speed in two seconds. This time, those on board felt no fraction of the ferocious acceleration: Yamata had mastered that problem. The enemy ship fittled again, to reappear close to where they had been. The proximity mines detonated. The enemy ship's drive exploded. A portion of the screen whitened for a moment.

Yamata allowed himself a small grunt of satisfaction. Armand and Lucinda whooped and punched the air.

The other two friendly ships, having diverged, were again converging. Another of the enemy ships fittled. The *Stanley Blade*'s and the *Small Arrangement*'s trajectories instantly halted. The enemy appeared, as it seemed on this scale, right beside them, and as rapidly was destroyed.

"Ya beauty!" yelled Lucinda.

"What happened there?" Armand asked.

"Chronology Protection trap. It came out of the jump just too far away to hit them, and it couldnae fittle the remaining distance without going outside its own light-cone or back in time. They had a moment while it waited tae catch up wi itself, fired off a nuke, and—" She clapped her hands.

Both the remaining enemy ships fittled away at the same moment. One of them reappeared between the *Small Arrangement* and the *Stanley Blade*, and Lucinda saw something bigger than a nuclear explosion: the deliberate detonation of one stardrive, and the secondary detonation of two more. To anyone looking in that direction from the ground it would have appeared like a supernova. There was no time to respond to the shock. The one remaining enemy ship had not reappeared. It was Armand who guessed its location.

"Behind Orpheus," he said. Yamata reached for the table.

"Take your time," Armand said. "There'll be nothing but debris."

And so there was. The enemy ship had run straight into

one of Eurydice's own defences, a particle-beam battery on
its moon. But as Yamata took them back towards the camp
and the relic, Lucinda carried no great sense of triumph with
her to the ground. And when she found that Amelia Orr had
not been, as she had assumed, on the *Stanley Blade*, she ran
straight to her arms and cried.

Lamont sat alone in the lab for a long time, talking to the
Hungry Dragon, and to a greater mind whose name he
did not know. Eventually he felt silver hair brush his face, a
warm metal hand clasp his wrist. He looked up into depth-
less eyes of glass.

"You can leave now," Morag Higgins said. She smiled.
"We've landed."

"I know we've landed," said Lamont, "but—"

"But nothing," she said. "Come on. People are waiting for
an explanation."

"But there's so much more to find out."

"You can leave now," said the *Hungry Dragon*. "You
know enough to tell them."

"I'm sorry," Lamont said, standing up, staring at the
screen.

"You need not apologise," said the *Hungry Dragon*. "I
have someone else to talk to. An equal mind. So have you.
Go with her."

Lamont flushed.

"You needn't apologise to me either," said Morag Higgins. She flicked her hair back. "I could tell from your
pulse."

"Tell what?" he said, feeling as if he was in the ship's
webbing, and flailing mentally.

"Your're the first normal man who has looked me as if I'm
a normal woman."

"Oh," said Lamont, dismayed. "I'm sorry to disappoint
you." He looked away, let his nails dig into his palms, looked
back. "I'm not a normal man."

She frowned. "In what way?"

"I've been alone with my ship for five years. I've become eccentric, almost autistic, and perverted."

"Perverted?"

"Well, you know. I've . . . been having sex with the ship. It . . . sent me incubi. From among its avatars."

"Oh," said Higgins. "And what were they like, these avatars?"

Lamont described curves with his hands.

"You mean, like, beautiful women?"

"Yes."

"Oh. I see. That's different, of course."

"Different?"

"Different from me. I'm not beautiful."

He was shocked. "You are beautiful, don't say that!"

"You really think so?" she asked. He could tell from her intonation that she was no longer teasing.

"Of course."

"So. I'm a beautiful woman, and I'm a machine. I don't see the problem."

He could see it from her point of view when he thought about it. "Neither do I."

"Show me," she said.

It was Johnstone who came looking for them, but he gave them time.

Most of the survivors of the various encounters of the past thirteen or so hours had gathered in one of the Knights' dining-halls, a long buckysheet shed with sheet-diamond windows, interior wall surfaces like blond wood, and a score or so of low, long black tables. It was not crowded. From the door Lucinda reckoned there were about a couple of hundred people here. They had divided, more or less, along party lines: Knights, Eurydiceans—regulars and Returners in a single bloc—and Carlyle gang. Morag Higgins and Camplbell Johnstone sat together, near the front, a little apart from everyone else. Lucinda sat down among the

Carlyle soldiers beside Kevin and Amelia. The ebon lacquer of the table couldn't be scratched with a thumbnail. It couldn't be scratched, she discovered in a moment of vicious idleness, with a diamond blade. The news she'd heard in the last hour or so was, on the whole, good. The war machines in the skein had stopped attacking outside its gates. They still patrolled its corridors and concentrated at its nodes, but they let people pass. This did not smell like victory.

The Knights had called it a conference. Yamata and Armand sat at a table up at the front, facing the room, conferring quietly. Rumours had flown, and Lucinda hadn't caught any. The Knights looked insufferably smug, the Eurydiceans excited, the Carlyle gang glum. At length Lamont arrived, walked briskly to the front table and sat down between the other two. At a word from Yamata he stood up. He patched his comms to everyone else's; there was no need. But the audience was wider than those present: news-gathering motes hovered in the air or perched on the tables, relaying the news to the rest of Eurydice, and thence—pending propagation delay and chronology disentanglement—to the rest of humanity.

"Um," Lamont said. He scratched his appalling beard. He introduced himself, for the benefit of the majority who didn't know who he was. Lucinda found herself, like others around her, shifting on the bench.

"What has happened," Lamont said, coming to the point at last, "is quite simple." He stopped and stared at the ceiling. "In a manner of speaking. What we have referred to as the relic is indeed the ship that took us or our ancestors to Eurydice. Its function was to create and put in place machinery for downloading and incorporating its passengers, and provide them with accomodation and tools and so forth. Before doing that it modified the entire biosphere of Eurydice, creating multicellular organisms from the native bacteria. It did more. What the outsiders refer to as the skein is a wormhole network which it generated."

He hesitated, as though wishing to spare them bad news,

or avoid inciting their incredulity. "This network even now continues to propagate. Already it encompasses most of the galaxy. Eventually it may extend to others."

Lucinda felt the same falling sensation that she'd had on the ship. She had a vivid mental image of the relic's diamond spike like an ice pick striking the great black bowl of the sky, turning it crazed with cracks, milky with flaws. The cracks might propagate outwards forever. If so, there would be no more untouched nature: wherever humans went, their work—or that of their creation—would be already there before them. The whole face of God, or Nature, changed irrevocably by the work of Man! And to think that they had called the skein "Carlyle's Drift!"

"Then," Lamont continued, "the colony ship's mind upgraded itself to the same condition as the previous wave of posthuman intelligences, those we call the Raptured, and went away, to—wherever they have gone. It left behind the source-code of its original self, and some autonomic defence mechanisms. Those we call the war machines. They were its immune system. When the Carlyle . . . gang's intruders broke into it, these machines were activated, and a data-rich virus was transmitted that took over machinery that could build more of them. As it happens, the only such machinery it found in any suitable location was the fabrication system of my ship. This was used to build war machines, and to provide the asteroid with a stardrive. Later, it managed to likewise infect the DK ships." He shrugged. "You know the rest."

"No, we don't!" someone called out.

Lamont scratched his hair. He told them about how he and the *Hungry Dragon* had worked, alone in space, to isolate the intrusion, and how they had almost succeeded. His stern gaze fixed on Lucinda. "But before we could finish, yet more high-energy weapon discharges around the relic brought the reserves into action. The ones on my asteroid. They acted to protect the skein."

The Carlyle fighters and Eurydiceans stirred angrily. Armand made a cut-off gesture.

"That is what it was doing," he affirmed. "Our bad luck.

Our good luck that Lamont and his ship gained control of the asteroid's descent."

Lamont went on. The *Hungry Dragon* had finally reasoned itself out of the control of the virus. It had then repeated the process to cut the relic's control over the war machines, and to assume control over them itself. That had, however, left the infected DK ships as autonomous war machines in their own right. These had now been dealt with. All that remained were the war-machine nests they'd established on four asteroids that had been intended as raw material for DK space habitats.

"These will not be a problem," he said. "They are now under control again."

Lucinda could not contain herself. She jumped up. "You mean they're now controlled by *your fucking ship*!"

Lamont shook his head, matted locks flying. "No, no!" he said. "You don't understand." His fingers rampaged through his beard. "I haven't explained this yet. The war machines really are like an immune system, controlled by reflex. When that was compromised, a higher level of processing was awakened. That is what currently controls the skein and all the war machines." He blinked hard. "It's . . . benign, and it's . . . friendly towards the colony of Eurydice, which after all is its own work."

"How do you know *it* won't go off on some Rapture of its own?"

Lamont shrugged and spread his hands. "This is not the original mind," he said. "This is like a ganglion, a subroutine. It's powerful enough, a superhuman sentience, but it's not ambitious. Or so the *Hungry Dragon* assures me." He glanced down at Armand. "It wants to speak to the Joint Chiefs," he added. Armand smiled and nodded.

Lucinda sat down shaken and dismayed, and turned to Kevin and Amelia. "We've lost the skein. It's Eurydice's now."

Kevin shook his head. "No, surely not. We can fight *war machines*, for fuck sake!"

"Not an endless supply of them, we can't!" Lucinda said. "And it isnae just a matter ae war machines anyway. If that muckle thing out there controls the skein itself, who's to know what it could do? It could switch the gates away fae our planets. Reconfigure the whole skein, for that matter."

Kevin frowned at her for a moment, nodded slowly, then stood up.

"Come on," he said to the Carlyle fighters. "There's nothing more for us here."

He led them away from the tables, striding to the door without a backward glance. Their departure was noticed, but not remarked on or, as far as Lucinda could see, regretted except by Morag Higgins, who gazed after her. Lucinda beckoned to her, with a smile and a slight flexure of her fingers; Higgins's silver lips compressed, and she turned her attention back to Lamont like all the rest. But Armand met Lucinda's gaze with a sharp glance and a small nod.

Somebody called out:

"What about Eurydice's fossil record? What about the fossil war machines?"

Lucinda stopped, turned around. This question had been nagging her too.

"I understand," Lamont said slowly, "that the ship was equipped with what are called Darwin-Gosse machines. They are capable of evolving an entire biosphere in virtual space, and creating the result. The ship's own capabilities well exceeded that. It reshaped Eurydice's lithosphere. It laid down new strata. It created the fossil record."

Lucinda remembered what Johnstone had said in the Chernobyl caves, about worked rocks that looked like they'd formed naturally.

"*But why?*" she shouted, almost from the exit. "Why the hell should it do that?"

"I have asked it that myself," Lamont said, "and it told me why it did it." He spread his arms wide. "For the panache!"

I t was early afternoon. The clouds had cleared; the shadows of the spike and the space mountain were short, but

still covered the camp. Ones and twos of Knights and Eurydiceans here and there stood watch. One reporter pursued
Lucinda, but she waved her hand in front of her face and said
nothing, and it flew back in to the conference. She jogged
over to where the remaining Carlyle fighters were piling on
to four of the company's gravity sleds.

"We arenae going tae ride *these* aw the way back tae New
Start," Lucinda complained, as she caught up with the others.

Kevin gave her a look. "We are no," he agreed vehe-
mently. 'We're going tae ride them up intae the hills a way
and get picked up by one ae our ain starships that hae been
lurking out-system. If you'd been paying attention, Amelia's
made the contact and set up the rendezvous."

Lucinda glanced around the matériel-cluttered encampment as she clambered aboard a sled alongside Amelia and
grabbed a handrail. "Why not land here?"

Amelia jerked her thumb at the *Subtle Conceit*. "Knights
are just a wee bit touchy about bringing one ae our starships
down here. Too much possibility for misunderstanding."

Lucinda chuckled darkly. "OK."

The sleds lifted and accelerated forward. The slipstream
whipped her hair, snatched at her breath. They passed out of
the great shadows, into the sunlight. It was exhilarating, and it
lifted her spirits and diverted her attention from brooding on
the catastrophe that had been brought upon the clan. That had
been brought upon it by *her*. She thrust the thought away. The
Carlyle ethos was causal, not moral; based on results, not intentions. But even in that unforgiving light she found it possible to think that what had happened wasn't entirely her fault.

We'll just have to get into an honest business, she thought.
With the income from the skein gone, what could they do?
Combat archaeology remained, but with Eurydiceans—or
their friendly superintelligence—in control of the skein, and
on better terms (as they now seemed) with the Knights, it
would be more difficult. But, she thought, looking over the
heads of the fighters on the sleds, the clan and the firm could
deal with difficulties in its own way, and as it always had.
They were still the bloody Carlyles.

And they still had a job to do here. She recalled Armand's subtle nod.

"Do you think General Jacques is still with us?" she asked Amelia, loudly into her ear in rushing wind.

"Still up for the Return?" Amelia yelled back. "I'm no sae sure. No himself personally, anyway."

"But he's promised his troops!"

"Aye," said Amelia. "He has that. So we wait and see, aw right? That's why we're going back tae New Start."

Within about half an hour the flotilla of sleds had crested the nearest ridge, a few hundred metres from a gate—still guarded by war machines, whose sensors pinged them as they passed—and all but the upper parts of the gigantic objects behind them had dropped out of sight. The sleds skimmed along at a few metres above the ground, along a blue-green glen shadowed by flitting clouds. It was a classic U-shaped valley, scoured out by glaciers that had perhaps never existed but in the imagination of a god with a sense of style. Lucinda scanned the sides of the glen, and saw with delight a little flock of small grazing animals, long-limbed and dark-haired, skipping among outcrops of rock and falls of scree. High above, some winged predator circled on an updraft, a black speck in the blue sky. Terraforming, even with Darwin-Gosse machines, was an unpredictable procedure, more a matter of evolution than creation; trial and error. Even this simple food chain, if that was what she was seeing, was itself a triumph.

Something else moved among the rocks. She glimpsed it only out of the corner of her eye, and when she turned it was gone. Her gaze swept the slope—there, something again—a human figure, so well-camouflaged it was as if the grass or shrub had shifted. It darted across the side of the glen, about halfway up, a little ahead of them and running in the direction opposite to theirs, and disappeared behind a rock.

She tapped the comms unit at her throat and pinged Kevin, in the leading sled. "Bandits on the slope at two o'clock," she said. "Time for a fast lift."

"Got ya."

The sleds shot into vertical ascent, stopping seconds later at a couple of hundred metres above the hills that defined the glen. The vehicles didn't have much in the way of instrumentation. Heads, Lucinda's among them, peered cautiously over the sides. She wished she'd kept her suit. But the man was now much easier to see. He stood and waved his arms above his head.

Kevin sent out a cautious interrogatory and identifying ping. After a few moments he reported back.

"He claims he's alone, and he's pleased to see us," he said, sounding surprised. "Says his name's Ree, and he's asking for you. Lucinda."

It really was like a weight off her shoulders. A small weight compared to what remained, but a relief nonetheless. "Wow! He survived!"

"Who is he?"

"The wee commie biologist fae the statues. Can we pick him up?"

"Is that safe?" Kevin asked.

"I think so."

Lucinda elbowed her way to the front and asked the sled's driver to take them down. Reluctantly, he complied. They drifted to the man's level, and hung in the air ten metres away from him, keeping him covered. He was wearing his survival suit with the visor up, and he was grinning.

"Hello again, Miss Carlyle Lucinda," he said.

"I'm glad to see you," she said. "How did you get here?"

"Through the gate, three days ago," he said.

"Wasn't it guarded?"

Ree put his fists on his hips. "*Juche* martial arts superior to those of decadent effete Knights," he said proudly. He mimed knocking heads together. "Left guards unconscious and ran to hills. Since then have been living self-reliantly and awaiting your heroic production brigade's arrival. Most impressive battle, observed from safe distance. Also observed your departure."

"How did you know we would be coming this way?"

"Lucky guess of optimal route out of artifact region, and

very fast running." He held out a hand. "May I come with you?"

"Uh, sure," said Lucinda. She gestured to the driver; he edged the sled towards the slope. "But why did you come here?"

"To see great playwright Ben-Ami," Ree said. He caught a rail and vaulted deftly aboard. "I have much to tell him."

They lifted off to join the other sleds, which were returning to a more sustainable altitude.

"I meant—I thought you were escaping," Lucinda said, "from whoever wrecked the statues and burned the jungle and destroyed your settlement."

Ree looked grim and grieved. "That too," he said. "They are connected."

CHAPTER 18

Heroes and Villains

The Carlyles had walked out. The reporters had buzzed off. There was a hiatus in the conference, filled with a low murmur as people came and went to fetch water, tea, beer, or coffee from the Knights' commendably ecumenical catering machine. Lamont sat at the top table beside Armand and Yamata, sipped tea, and wondered if he and the two lightning-chasers, as they called themselves, formed a third party to the Eurydiceans and the Knights. Or if there were more parties here than that: the Eurydiceans all wore uniforms identical apart from their company logos, but he could tell the resurrected Returners from the rest at a glance: faces fresh out of the tank, and yet older and more experienced than the others, more primitive, more guarded.

As for the Knights, their expressions were calm but curious, their voices low, their gestures oblique. Higgins and Johnstone were looking around uneasily, but smiling.

Lamont hated this sort of thing: ambiguity, micropolitics, the presentation of self in everyday life. He decided he would have to get used to it. Morag Higgins caught his despairing glance, and returned him an encouraging smile. Now she was one straightforward person. Like the *Hungry*

Dragon in that respect. He smiled back. He put down his empty cup with an unintended bang (still not used to gravity), shuffled his forearms on the table, turned to Armand and Yamata.

"Gentlemen," he said. It came out too loud. The place hushed. "I detect a certain tension in the room."

To his surprise, everybody laughed. Lamont took from it no sense of relief. One of the Returners jumped up.

"Too right there's tension," he said. "We were promised Return. I haven't heard that mentioned. And I'm wondering if you haven't sold us out again, General Jacques."

Armand glanced sharply at Yamata, sighed, and leaned forward, elbows on the table.

"Thank you, Lawrence," he said. "It is not a question of selling out. It is a question of doing my job."

"Now when have we heard that before?" the Returner asked.

Armand cut across the chorus of concurrence.

"Neither I, nor the Joint Chiefs, nor the Knights can prevent any of you from returning to Earth even if we wanted to. I must point out, however, that the Knights disapprove more strongly than ever of what the Carlyles call combat archeology." Armand glared at Lamont, Higgins, and Johnstone in turn. "Not to mention what the Carlyles call Rapture-fucking. I cannot imagine the Joint Chiefs taking any more sanguine view of them. What was awakened here is benign. What has been awakened elsewhere has often not been. As Eurydice moves to take full control of the wormhole skein, the opportunities for such activities will diminish. Despite our recent conflict, the Knights remain the most civilised of the powers, the one with whom we have most in common, and most to learn from, and most to give." He leaned back, and opened his hands. "Or does anyone think the American farmers or the Asian communists are more promising partners?"

"You're forgetting the Carlyles," said Higgins.

"I am trying to," said Armand, to laughter.

The Returner who'd stood up now turned to face the others. "In that case," he said, "I have to say with the Carlyles that there's nothing here for us. For myself, I'm going back to the city. Anyone want to join me?"

A few of his resurrected comrades shook their heads. The others, about sixty in all, along with a few native-born Eurydiceans, rose and followed him out. Higgins cast Lamont an anguished, angry look, and followed them.

Lamont jumped to his feet. "Morag! Come back!"

A shake of her head sent a ripple down her silver hair.

Lamont hesitated, then looked at Armand and Yamata, shrugged, and made his way around the corner of the table and ran after her. He slowed to walk beside her.

"Glad to see you," she said. Her glass eyes glinted, her metal hand was warm. They had gone out of the door by the time Armand had sprinted up and caught their shoulders, then kept pace.

"Coming with us?" asked Higgins.

Armand ignored the sarcasm. "You know I can't," he said. "But don't be fools." He lowered his voice. "You and that hothead Lawrence Hammond should have listened to what I said. How long will it take for Eurydice—or even your newly wakened AI—to take control of the skein? Days, weeks, who knows? Likewise for the Knights to harden their fortifications on Earth."

"And what if the Knights don't just let the Returners leave?" Lamont asked. "Or if the Joint Chiefs don't? How long have we got then?"

"Maybe a few hours," said Armand grimly. "Just keep it quiet and move fast. Talk to Lucinda Carlyle or Amelia Orr, they'll know what to do. Set up a meeting, but don't discuss anything over the comms." He raised his voice. "All right then!" he shouted, pushing them forward. "Go! Go if you want! Go now!"

He stalked back in to the conference, theatrically shaking his head, while Lamont and Higgins walked after the Returners to the hypersonic transports. A starship screamed across the sky and stopped above the horizon, drifting down to land somewhere beyond the encircling range of hills.

"T he thing is," Winter heard himself shouting to Andrea Al-Khayed, as he waved a bottle in one hand and clung to a pillar with the other, outside the Bright Contrail some time about mid-afternoon, "the *thing* is, see, that General Jacques, that, that, that *bastard*, has sold out the Returners *again*! He's done just what he done in the play last night! Just what he did back in Polarity! All over again! Son of a fucking *bitch*!"

She yelled something back.

"What?" he shouted. The music was loud. Vehicle traffic had stopped. The street was filling up with people drinking and dancing. More of the same was on the big screens, relaying views from right across the city, which was going wild with relief and exultation. It was being claimed that this would be the wildest party in the history of Eurydice. And why not, Winter thought dourly. They'd just survived what had seemed like certain disaster and emerged to find themselves—according to the more soberly reported news earlier—the potential future capital of the galaxy.

"I said, *'You're right there!'*" Al-Khayed shouted.

"Oh, right." He nodded.

"And you need this!" She passed him a glass. He knocked it back. The music suddenly quietened. He could hear and see a lot more distinctly.

"What the—" He stopped, suddenly aware of how he'd been assailing her ears. No way to speak to a lady. "What was that?"

"Iced umami tea."

"Ah. Thank you." He shook his head and looked around, realising that he had sobered up. "Jeeze."

"It won't last," she warned. "But it's good for hangovers, too."

"Thanks," he said. The mention of a hangover made him

want another alcoholic drink. Fast, before it caught up with
him. "Uh, can I fetch you a drink?"

"I'm fine," said Andrea. "Catch you later."

Evidently giving him up as a hopeless case, she swayed
back through the crowd on the pavement to rejoin Ben-Ami,
who was holding court at his usual table by the railing.
Kowalsky was sitting beside him, Voigt opposite him and beside Calder, who'd somehow snagged her—or she him: the
tall dancer, corseted and kirtled in black satin, petted him
absently and intermittently as if he was a monkey. They
were all talking as raucously as he had been a moment ago.
Passersby, who all recognised them and might otherwise
have nodded and smiled, passed tactfully on if they were
more sober, or added to the press around the tables and
slumped on the ground if they were more drunk.

Winter turned away, savouring his fleeting moment of
moral superiority as he made his way to the drinks table in
front of the cafe's main, wide-open window. He was just
reaching for a bottle of red wine and, with some surprise at
his own self-restraint, a glass, when he saw Lucinda,
Amelia, and a stocky, dark-skinned, black-clad man pushing
through the crowd towards Ben-Ami's table. They seemed to
have a small crowd of their own behind them, a score or so—
maybe more, it was hard to see in the crush—of people who
looked like tourists, gawping around, wearing wild local
clothes they obviously weren't used to. As they approached,
Amelia glanced over her shoulder and waved them towards
the park, and with a lot of jostling they dispersed in that direction, leaving the two women Winter knew and the man he
didn't to step on to the pavement spread of the Bright Contrail. Amelia was in a very Eurydicean outfit of the day,
bright blue, all carnival fronds and fringes, inconspicuous in
the festivities. Lucinda wore the same off-white long dress
in which Winter had last seen her, back at the gig. The effect
was hallucinatory. He stared at her face, wondering if she
looked different. It was hard to tell. Her appearance had always outdone his memory of her each time he'd seen her.

She noticed him just as she approached the table, and smiled and nodded briefly. She said something to Ben-Ami and seated Amelia and the man who had arrived with them down beside him, and then walked over to Winter. She was carrying the same enormous floppy hat, and a bottle.

"Hello," she said.

"It's good to see you again," said Winter. "To see you, uh . . . back."

"Back from the dead!"

"As I think I said to you once, the experience is overrated."

At that Lucinda did look changed. There was a thrawn weariness in her face that Winter hadn't seen before.

"Aye," she said. "You could say that." She looked down, then firmly up. "Well. A lot tae talk about. Could we, like, start again where we left off?"

He laughed. "Hence the antique frock, yeah?"

"That was the idea, yes." She sounded embarrassed. "Dialed up a copy at the skyport, from my old hotel room."

"It's still not you, but it's a nice—"

"—Oh, shut up—"

"—thought."

She flourished the bottle. "Talisker," she said. "From the captain's table. Well, the captain's drexler, tae be honest. Want some?"

"Let's find somewhere to sit." He glanced at Ben-Ami's table.

"Not there," she said.

Tell him," said Amelia, pouring Ree a drink. His hand was shaking too much to pick up the glass. He withdrew it, looked Ben-Ami in the eye and said, "All my production brigade killed or dispersed and in hiding because we sold your work, Mr. Ben-Ami."

Ben-Ami closed his eyes and opened them again. "What?" Everybody at the table was by now looking at Ree.

"I owe you licence fee, of course," he said. "I am representative of Eighty-Seven Production Brigade. But I hope you will have it in your heart to defer requirement of payment."

Ben-Ami waved a hand. "Forget about that. You said people have been *killed* for selling my work?"

"Is my fault," said Ree. He sipped the neat whisky, then downed it in one gulp as if it was vodka. "Miss Carlyle sojourned at our brigade headquarters. She gave collected works of Mr. Ben-Ami as payment. We all watched your wonderful play, Mr. Ben-Ami, about great Prince Leonid. I was so moved by it that I had it transmitted as sample to several DK habitats in the same system. One of them, Man Conquers Space Collective, is very rigorous in interpretation and upholding of self-reliance idea. They took exception to it. Great exception. They were already disapproving of us because we were terraforming planet for Yank farmers. They said now we are corrupting self-reliant society with backward and decadent Yank ideas. There was ideological discussion, then dispute. They said Leonid was a revisionist. We knew this was not so, and we were even more convinced that it could not be, Mr. Ben-Ami, because of your great play. We voted to continue selling your work to other brigades and collectives. Man Conquers Space Collective sent their self-defence force, aerospace militia division, to correct us. They attacked us from the sky, Mr. Ben-Ami! We had no defences prepared! We did not expect this, even from dogmatists! I only escaped because I was far away, with my marine biology work, and even then they destroyed my place of work. I hid underwater and made my way through wormhole gate and waited for Miss Carlyle's production brigade, which we already knew was going to pass through on way here to fight the Knights."

"What about the other production brigades on your planet?" Amelia asked, tipping him another whisky.

"Rest of Transformation of Nature Collective mostly afraid of Man Conquers Space," Ree said scornfully. "They have indeed become soft living on dirt like Yank. While hiding in the hills the past days and nights I have used my *juche* untraceable communications gear"—he tapped a pendant at his throat—"to make clandestine agitation in DK settlements on and around Eurydice. I have made contact with many people, scores of people, who are most indignant and who are not afraid. We will fight these Man Conquers Space son of bitch bastards like Brezhnev fought Nazis and Yanks and Polacks and South African slaveholders, gaining his honourable scars."

Ben-Ami looked hard at the strange small man, fascinated and appalled.

"How many of these son of bitch bastards are there, do you reckon?" Calder asked.

"Only hundred million," said Ree. "I will kill every last one of them even if I have to die like Leonid."

"No," said Amelia firmly. "You will not. That's revenge, not recompense. What you want to do is damage them, yes, kill some, yes, but gain something from it yourselves. You should think of it as collecting on a debt."

"Debt collection is not war," said Ree. "Is well-understood in DK." He gave Amelia a very ambiguous stare. "As we know from previous dealings with Carlyles. But conflict and debt collection would not only be with Man Conquers Space. They would not do this on their own. We suspect they are backed by the wicked Chinks."

"Who?" yelped Calder.

"Knights of Enlightenment, so-called," said Ree. "To disincentive self-reliant people from getting involved further in terraforming for Yank farmers. So we may need help from bloody Carlyles." He looked beseechingly at Amelia. "Would this be problem for you?"

"Not for me, it wouldn't," said Amelia cautiously. "I wouldnae object if you were tae raise a few fighters. Gie the Knights a wee payback."

Ree shook Amelia's hand. "Is done, is deal?"

"Uh, yes," she said. "Inasmuch as it's up to me. But . . . we have another deal to fulfil first. Maybe."

"Is no hurry," said Ree. "We build our forces. Gain experience."

"Ah," said Amelia. "Would you like to gain some experience fighting the wicked—the Knights, on, ah, some other planet?"

"I would indeed."

"Amelia sucked in her lips. "Could you use your untraceable comms right now, to ask them to come here? Discreetly? I would like to meet them. Quite urgently."

Ree nodded, turned away and spoke as though to himself in a language Ben-Ami didn't know, then turned back and smiled with a thumbs-up.

"Wait a minute," Ben-Ami said, leaning forward. "The Joint Chiefs would be most upset if Returners and Carlyles and God help us, commies were involved in an attack on the Knights."

"You've always known about this," said Amelia. "We talked about it."

"Not in a way I had to take seriously," said Ben-Ami." And not in a context where . . . all these other forces are involved. If the Joint Chiefs were to find out about this conversation, the consequences could be severe."

He looked solemnly around all the faces at the table, then laughed.

"So let us ensure that they don't," he said.

Lamont sat on a bench, his legs stretched out, at the skyport concourse beside Morag Higgins as they waited for the Returner fighters to emerge from the changing rooms. Outside, on the field, the hypersonic transports of Blue Water Landings, like all the other vehicles in the parking apron, were dwarfed by two KE-built starships suspended on nothing a few metres above the landing strips. One of these ships was the Carlyles." Other starships—AO trucks, DK batwings—hung in the sky like so many box or dragon kites. Around the perimeter of the skyport the usual bright-painted red and yellow emergency or auxiliary vehicles had been supplemented by darker, heavier military cars and tanks, bristling with cosmic-string projector guns. Nothing was go-

ing to land or take off from New Start without the Joint
Chiefs' approval, and all air and space traffic was being directed here. Whatever Armand had hoped, the Eurydicean
government was already moving to take control of the skies.
Even the little entopters were being grounded one by one,
ostensibly for safety as the city revelled. Anyone disembark-
ing would have to use the monorails and shuttles. The
thought made Lamont break into a cold sweat of agoraphobia, but he knew he could overcome it. The only arrangement that had been made—in a very guarded in-flight phone
conversation—with Amelia was to meet up at some cafe on
the edge of the central park, the Jardin des Étoiles. Lamont
guessed Amelia had some plan in mind—perhaps to bring
another Carlyle starship down on a sharp vertical descent
over the park to pick everybody up.

The Returners trickled out, dressed in the scanty or elabo-
rate costumes of the day. Lawrence Hammond, who seemed
to be the leader of the handful of Eurydiceans among them
as well as of the recently resurrected, was the first to walk
over, quite unself-conscious in high-heeled boots and a
fringed white leather suit set here and there with small shiny
stones. He looked down at Lamont.

"You ready?"

"Yes."

"Are you not going to get changed?" Higgins asked.

Lamont looked along the length of his body to his boots,
then at her.

"No."

"You'll kind of stand out."

Lamont snorted. "I'm a celebrity now. Nothing I can do
about that. What about you?"

She was getting stared at more than him, not to his surprise. Her metal features, though they looked like painted
flesh, were in stark contrast to her black cotton suit.

"I have an idea," she said.

She stood up and stripped off her tunic and trousers and
threw them in the nearest drexler bin.

In her underwear she looked like she'd painted herself silver from head to foot.

"There," she said. "Ready to party."

They set off through a corridor to the monorail platform. The capsules that they boarded were empty apart from themselves, but as they swooped and soared between the towers and trees of New Start and stopped at other platforms they soon filled up. Lamont clung to a stanchion, sweating in his suit, breathing slowly. He kept his eyes closed, or looked outside. The city had changed in his absence; as he might have expected, it was the most massive and ancient-looking buildings, the ones built of stone and concrete, that were new and strange to him. The nanofactured, quasi-organic tree-like structures of towers and walkways, that could in principle be reconfigured overnight or returned to the ground, were all familiar; the city's old growth.

The wildest party in the history of Eurydice was what had been promised, and that was what was delivered. Every light was on, every speaker was loud, every glass was full, every couple were in love for as long as it lasted. Winter wasn't entirely sure if he and Lucinda were among them. She'd explained to him that a bunch of Returners were on their way, with some kind of plan or instructions from Armand about getting a starship in, and after a bit more conversation she'd traipsed off to the park to talk to the gang who'd arrived with her and to liase with—as far as he could see, over many heads—a steadily increasing number of what looked like DK types, if their fancily cut but drably coloured outfits were anything to go by.

Winter found a guitar in the back of the cafe, and he and Calder sat on the cafe's pavement-edge railing, legs dangling, sweat falling, and sang and played all they could remember to anyone who cared to listen. At some point towards the dusk, Winter looked down and saw Lucinda at the table beneath his feet, talking to Ree and to Ben-Ami, who hadn't shifted all afternoon, letting people come and go, and shouting his approbation or otherwise at the musicians.

"Oh you daft scunner," Lucinda was telling Ben-Ami. "Of all the folks you could hae picked tae be a doomed romantic hero, it had tae be bloody boring Brezhnev."

Ben-Ami shrugged. "Artistic licence, my dear."

"And you," she went on, turning to Ree, "you poor daft buggers, you had tae dae the same! Oh it ashames me! With all the worthless heroes of history to choose from. You could have had Mao, did you but know it. Or Guevara. Or Bonny Prince Charlie. Or even—"

She reached up for Calder's guitar. "Give me that."

She stood up, rested one foot on the chair; stooped over the guitar, strummed it, then raised her head and looked Winter straight in the eye and sang a song he remembered from Highland halls and pubs back in the 2030s. It startled him to hear it again, almost unchanged. It could have been about Guevara, or, as Lucinda had said, someone else as unworthy of the praise the song bestowed. No one had ever told him, not even when he'd sung it himself. Now that he came to think about it, inquiring after to whom the old Jacobite song now applied had not been a welcome question, and he'd learned to desist.

> *Sé mo laoch mo Ghile Mear*
> *Sé mo Chaesar, Ghile Mear,*
> *Suan ná séan ní bhfuaireas féin*
> *Ó chuaigh i gcéin mo Ghile Mear.*
>
> *Syne my brave darling disappeared*
> *Naught know I but pain and sorrow*
> *no news we heard, his death we feared*
> *on far-off hills, in cruel caves.*

That last line had been different before. Winter frowned, trying to recall it. In *th' cruel caves of* somewhere somewhere. A foreign place-name. It had almost rhymed. The conversations nearby were stopping, in a spreading circle of silence. Lucinda had quite a voice, and she was throwing a lot of what sounded like real grief and yearning into it.

> *Sé mo laoch mo Ghile Mear*
> *Sé mo Chaesar, Ghile Mear,*
> *Suan ná séan ní bhfuaireas féin*
> *Ó chuaigh i gcéin mo Ghile Mear.*

> *Freedom's fierce and gallant knight,*
> *a high-flown laird with gentle eyes.*
> *A blade of fire upon the night,*
> *he'll wreak destruction from the skies.*

Winter joined in the next chorus, and Lucinda smiled warmly and connivingly at him, but it was to Ree she turned when she sang the rest, eyes bright and wet.

> *So drink his health and sing his praise*
> *his far-famed face and sloganned name.*
> *In every house be one who prays*
> *he'll scorch the tyrants with his flame.*

> *Sé mo laoch mo Ghile Mear*
> *Sé mo Chaesar, Ghile Mear,*
> *Suan ná séan ní bhfuaireas féin*
> *Ó chuaigh i gcéin mo Ghile Mear.*

"I didn't know she could sing," Calder said.

Winter glared at him for a moment, but Calder was looking past him.

"Behind you," said Calder. "Guy dressed like Elvis, from the rhinestones and amphetamines period. Play it cool and turn slowly. He seems to be squaring up for a fight with Amelia."

Winter slid down from the rail and looked around. A few metres away Amelia stood with her back to him, and was indeed almost head to head with a man in a white suit. Winter expected to witness a Glasgow kiss at any moment. Beside that man stood a much taller figure in a tight, tattered space suit and with shaggy hair and beard, a man whom Winter recognised from the television as Lamont. He was leaning into the quarrel and clinging, as if for support, to the hand of a woman got up as some kind of robot sex-toy.

Winter edged closer, Calder just behind him.

"We thought *you* were ready with—" the white-clad man was shouting.

"—fucking moron, dae ye think we hae—"

At that moment Lucinda flashed past him in a flurry of pale skirts and flung herself on the robot-like woman, hugging her and spinning her around. The quarrel abruptly halted in distraction and Lamont stepped forward and grasped both participants gently by the shoulder. Winter strode up to stand beside Amelia, who shot him a furious, *about-fucking-time* look. Other people, Returners and Carlyle gang and DK, were beginning to crowd around behind the antagonists, listening in and ready to back them up.

"What's the problem?" Winter asked.

"These fucking maroons," said Amelia. "They think *we* have a starship all set tae lift us all off. I thought your bloody General Jacques was gonnae take care of all that."

"What the hell can he do?" said the man. Winter looked in his face and in a moment of disorientation recognised him as Lawrence Hammond, the Returner militant he'd last seen back on Polarity, a few subjective months and objective centuries earlier.

"Hey, you're—" Hammond said.

"Yeah, yeah," said Winter. "Glad to see you back too. You were saying?"

"Armand's stuck with the Runner Joint Chiefs and the Knights," Hammond was saying. "And you should see the skyport, it's ringed with armour. No doubt the city too, and space defence. There's not a thing that can move in the sky without being shot down. The only chance is to bring in a Carlyle ship hard and fast, we thought that was the plan—"

"Aye, and have it shot down?" snarled Amelia. "I don't fucking think so, jimmie."

Calder poked his head in and looked around the small but growing circle of tense faces.

"You mean this whole thing is all about who was supposed to bring what to the party? He said, she said? Koresh on a fucking stick, kids. This is pathetic."

Everybody bristled, turning on this new common enemy.

"Thank you for that," said Winter. "But, yeah, this isn't getting us anywhere. We—"

"Excuse me," said the silver-skinned woman. "But, you know, we *do* have a starship. . . . "

Everyone looked at her, puzzled, and then Lamont grinned all over his face and said: *"Yes!"*

First there was a blue light everywhere for a moment, and then from the sky came a great rushing wind that made trees bend and chairs and tables bowl along the street. Winter clung to the rail with one hand and to Lucinda's arm with the other. She was holding her daft hat crammed down over her head and face like some utterly inadequate armour. The wind stopped as suddenly as it had started, and every face looked up and saw what was coming down. Screams and yells rose above the loudest music that still played. People ran from the park in all directions. Winter heard Calder say, in an amused, satisfied tone: "Thousands flee screaming . . . "

But he, like everyone else, was looking up with his mouth open. The sight above them was like nothing anyone had ever looked on before. A kilometre-long narrow inverted cone of a mountain hung in the air, descending slowly until its relatively tiny, bristly metallic tip touched the grass a few hundred metres away, as gently as a well-balanced needle going into a vinyl groove.

Winter knew that it was no more impossible than the sight of all the other starships he'd seen; that his back-brain's screaming question *what's holding it up?* was mistaken in its premises; but at some level he could not believe what he was seeing.

"Well," said Lamont, "I'd like to see them try to shoot *that* down."

"Don't *say* that," said Lucinda. "Let's just get everyone on board."

They all walked, a few score of people, into the park, against the stream of everybody else, and one by one they climbed up an extended ladder to the small hatch under that enormous overhang. Winter was among the last to go. He looked down from the top of the ladder and saw Lamont and the silver-skinned woman still on the ground. They seemed to be arguing; then Lamont shrugged, shook his head, and stepped back as she scrambled up the ladder. Halfway up she swung away like a monkey, to cling head down to one of the external comms arrays. She grinned fiercely up at Winter.

"I've always wanted to do this," she called out.

He felt a nudge on his heel. Lamont looked up from just below him on the ladder.

"Get in," Lamont said. "She's mad." It didn't sound like a criticism.

As Winter hauled himself through the hatch the gravity field flipped over. Somebody reached to steady him; he swung around and found his feet on a bracketted metal shelf. Lamont came in, twisted around, and set off upwards, hand over hand to another aperture a few metres above. The outer hatch closed. Looking down, and therefore skyward, Winter could see every available space and place in which to sit or cling among the ship's fittings and machinery occupied by people in incongruous gaudy finery. It was like seeing an entire contingent of the Notting Hill Carnival thrown into some overcrowded panopticon. The sound of a hundred and fifty-odd people breathing vied with the roar of overworked air scrubbers.

"I appreciate that you are all somewhat uncomfortable," said a voice from everywhere. "Please be patient. The journey will not last long."

Five hour later, the *Hungry Dragon* was parked unobtrusively, or so Lamont assured them, in the Solar System's asteroid belt, and a Carlyle interplanetary transport was docking to take them all to New Polarity. Lamont stayed with the ship; and as the transport separated, Winter saw from its window an improbable silver-skinned figure on the side of the impossible ship, waving goodbye.

CHAPTER **19**

Returners (Reprise)

They were about twenty kilometres north of Crianlarich when Calder said, "Stop!"

Winter could see the annoyance on Lucinda's swift sideways glance. "Why?" she asked.

"This is the place," Calder said. "Where we went off the road."

"This no time for sightseeing," Lucinda said. "Maybe on the way back."

"Not even on the way back," said Winter.

The other two laughed. The moor across which the long articulated gravity sled was following the faint traces of a road was littered with the rusted hulks of war machines and fighting vehicles. Yellow splashes of mutated lichen were blazoned across the rockfaces and boulders, between which unpleasantly shaped small things, machine or animal, scurried. The sky flaunted a variety of interesting colours, none of them any shade of blue. The Rannoch battlefield was too polluted to plunder, its scrap too radioactive to recycle. The skirmish fought here had been between a force deploying relatively conventional defences—supersonic drones, autonomous armoured vehicles, Walker tanks, tactical nukes,

and nanobot sprays—and attacking devices that had under-
gone—or, more likely, undertaken—several generations of
technological upgrading in their hour-long flight across the
Atlantic. All that had prevented it from being completely
one-sided was that a significant fraction of the attacking devices had become so mentally sophisticated that they had
questioned their own purpose. Their existential doubts had
been terminated along with their existence within millisec-
onds, leaving the defending side to add "the too-smart-
weapon problem" to its strategic lexicon. The attacking
side's command headquarters had probably forgotten what
the whole conflict was about before the swarm of proto-
sentient ordnance they'd launched had passed the Azores.

In this location sitting in the cab of a gravity sled—an experience centuries out of his time—felt to Winter almost familiar, and certainly reassuring. It was like being in the cab
of a big articulated truck, right down to the porn decals on
the dash and the cigarette ash in the footwell. Only looking
back in the rear-view patch on the forward screen at the five
similar sleds toiling up the trail behind them destroyed the
illusion. You had to narrow your eyes quite a bit to make the
slow monsters look like trucks. Each of the six sleds contained a search engine and at least thirty soldiers. The force
was made up of about equal numbers of Carlyle combat archaeologists, resurrected Returner veterans, and Ree's DK
dissidents, the Brezhnev Battalion.

Nonetheless it would, for an unsuspecting watcher, be a
routine sight, one of the daily commercial columns serving
the population of the Isle of Skye. Thanks to a coincidence
of wind patterns and tactical decisions that some of its inhabitants would to this day attribute to Providence, the island had come through the war-singularity relatively
unscathed. This was not true of most of the North of Scotland, nor of a great deal of the rest of it either. The Castle on
the Clyde had turned out to be very much as its name suggested: a grimly functional and laughably obsolete fortifica-
tion, damp and draughty, with bad drains. Though nominally
the seat of the Carlyles, the clan was canny enough to leave

it to the Old Don, as he was misleadingly known (he was an obsessive, almost abusive, user of rejuvenation and resurrection tech), and to his robot retinue. The actual administrative capital of the Carlyle empire was in the far more comfortable and capacious quarters of New Polarity, right next to the ruins of the old Mars colony and not far from the First Gate whose discovery had given the family its now-failing grip on the skein.

The column picked up pace on the downhill side of the moor, gliding through Glencoe with its verdant hanging foliage to swing northeast after Ballachulish, over the fused ruins of Fort William, along the (according to Lucinda) plesiosaur-infested lochs of the Great Glen; turning westward again past Cluanie and the Five Sisters whose dense rhododendron forests were (Lucinda claimed) haunted by relict homindae—it was a fact that an undocumented release of genetic weaponry had at some point inflicted a peculiar and distressing atavism on the entire area—to eventually pause at Dornie. From the shore of Loch Duich the stub of Eilean Donan Castle stood up like a rotted molar.

Winter and Calder got out to stretch their legs, as did everyone else lucky enough to be riding in the cabs. The soldiers had to stay put; comms silence was maintained; Lucinda conferred with Amelia, Ree, and the other commanders under cover of a rest stop and locally purchased refreshments. The low-tide seaweed lent a sour metallic tang to air already damp from a thin drizzle. Beyond the narrow mouth of Loch Long the ground was dead, poisoned by runoff from the rust desert to the north.

"What a fucking dump," said Calder, squinting at the village through cigarette smoke. Winter, sipping the vilest coffee he'd tasted in decades from the thinnest cup, had to agree. Dornie was an arguably human settlement, a status precariously maintained and frequently contested, scrounging a living from the passing trade. Bulk transport in manufactured goods was a necessity in those parts of the world where, as here, the stray presence of malign nanotech made it dangerous to fire up a drexler. Some kid threw a stone; another offered, if Winter understood his fractured English aright, some dubious sexual service; a scrawny teenage girl touted, even more ludicrously, protection for the rest of the journey, shyly indicating an alleged sidearm that looked as if it had been chrome-plated after having failed in action quite lethally for its last user.

"You know," said Winter, after chasing her off and cadging a cigarette from Calder—it was for him a minor and occasional vice, not, as it was for his partner, a full-time addiction—"I'm beginning to have some doubts about this enterprise."

"You don't say," said Calder. "What reason could you possibly have for doubting it? The vanishingly slender basis of the assumption that the war machines would go to the trouble of storing some semblance of the brain-states of their victims? The entirely exiguous evidence that such mindfiles, if they ever existed, are still there and awaiting deliverance? The riotous improbability that their resurrection en masse into actual reality is even feasible, let alone an earnest of their future happiness in a universe so markedly different from and in many respects arguably less congenial than the one from which they were prematurely despatched? The—"

"Oh, shut the fuck up," said Winter.

Calder had once surprised and dismayed him by downloading mega-bytes of nineteenth-century rationalist polemic, and assimilating them to his brain with less discrimination than he had to the hard drive of his handheld. He had felt a need to exorcise some disturbing traces of one of the less forgiving versions of Tibetan Buddhism fashionable in his parents' youth and his childhood, and of a brief immersion in a Pentecostal Baptist sect (by way of reaction) in his teens. A born-once atheist himself, Winter had found the whole preoccupation perplexing and mildly distasteful. This had turned to almost murderous fury after his death and resurrection, when Calder had recast the arguments to fortify his rejection of the prospect of the Return. That these now sounded entirely plausible objections not only irritated Winter, but perversely strengthened his wavering resolve.

He dropped the cigarette butt and ground it out underfoot. "We'll get them all back," he said.

"The truth is," Calder admitted, "I'm a little bit nervous myself."

Lucinda walked back up the column, sending people back to the cabs.

"Time to go," she said.

As soon as the cab doors were shut she turned on the engine. The sled lifted a metre off the ground. She toggled the controls to autopilot, tabbed a few icons on the dash. As the vehicle moved forward she slid open the rear hatch of the cab. In the trailer the elongated ovoid of the search engine gleamed like a leaden slug.

"Everybody in," she said. "After you, gentlemen."

"Won't it look suspicious, the cab being empty?"

She jerked a thumb at the forward and side screens. "Got recordings running on the windows."

They made their way down the narrow gap between the search engine's tracks and the walls to the end of the twenty-metre-long trailer. The rear door of the search engine swung up and they climbed in. The soldiers, now armoured and helmeted, clamped at waist, limbs, shoulders, and head by safety restraints, sat in facing rows along the vehicle like robot paratroopers. In this vehicle they were all combat archaeologists; the Returners and Brezhnevists were distributed between the other five, in combined squads. Lucinda led the way up the aisle to the forward-facing shell seats of the command console. The two men sat down beside her just as they had in the cab. The screen in front showed the same view as from the cab, but wider and with far more enhancements and interpretation features. At the moment the vehicle was skimming across the loch at Camas Longart where the bridge had been. It turned west alongside the northern shore of Loch Alsh, between the grey sea now and then glimpsed to the left, and to the right the steep ochre-stained sides of mountains hundreds of metres high, their bare tops lost in the low cloud.

"OK, guys," Lucinda said. "Time to download a copy be-

fore the shooting starts." She swung two bracket-mounted
backup helmets above their heads, and down to cover their
eyes. Blackness. There was a tickle behind the bridge of the
nose, a sparkle behind the eyes, then light again and she was
folding the devices back into their niches. She checked the
copydeck, the small device on which the recordings were
stored. "It's done."

Winter wished he'd been better prepared: that he'd had
some encouraging thought in his mind for the copy to carry
forward if it was thrown into action. These copies weren't
for backups—all involved other than the DK lot had backed
up the previous night, to secure servers in the old castle's
vaults. These were for going in to the virtual reality within
the target artifact, the fastness, if a viable such environment
could be detected by the search engine.

"You ever done that yourself?" Winter asked.

She gave him a look. "Not bloody likely. That's what
thralls are for."

After a few kilometres the hills were behind them and the
sea right beside them. Just ahead, the mouth of the Balmacara River bled red down the shore.

"This is it," said Lucinda. She reached for the controls
that overrode the autopilot and swung the sled hard right, off
the remains of the road and on to an even fainter track by the
stream, and then they were going, foot down and throttle forward, hell for leather northward up the Balmacara slopes
and into the rust desert above Duirinish.

The fastness at Carn Tollaidh, Tully Carn as the Knights
called it, was a complicated black mass spread across a
square kilometre of hillside like a lava flow that had taken on
an almost organic, coralline shape as it had solidified. It
faced out across the sea toward Skye and the small islands. It
utterly dominated and—by way of the iron oxide dust that
its presence inexplicably attracted or generated—devastated
the once notably scenic promontory between Loch Carron
and Loch Alsh. Originally an insignificant node in the global

communications system—an automated telephone exchange
or microwave relay mast—the ganglion of circuitry at Tully
Carn had begun its metastasis into its present gross form
moments after the first US military AI to achieve independence had burned through its containment firewalls and set
off on its rampage through the Internet.

That it retained the uploaded copies of some at least of
those who had died on the fronts defined by the Atlantic coast
of Scotland was a tradition founded on reports and rumours
little more substantiated than ghost stories: strange antique
figures on television screens within a thirty-kilometre radius
of the thing (such apparitions never recorded at the time, and
recounted long afterwards); anomalous messages on the
fetch-mails of distant descendants (invariably inadvertently
erased); dust devils in human shape glimpsed in the ochre
desert on windless days (never photographed); and, perhaps
most controversially, a handful of rare unencrypted transmissions that had leaked out of the US military-intelligence
complex in the first hours of its transcendence, indicating
that some such incorporation of human minds on all sides of
the conflict had been an objective of what was referred to as
"the mission" and for which success was claimed. The discovery, by the Carlyles and others right across the Drift, of
such unregenerate entities as Isaac Shlaim's encoded personality was solid evidence that some minds had indeed
been involuntarily uploaded in the runaway Singularity; but
that, really, was it; was all anyone had to go on; and the notion of reversing the process, or even investigating it seriously, would not have occurred to Lucinda or, as far as she
knew, anyone else had she not encountered the Eurydicean
minority aspiration to the Return.

The most significant feature of the fastness at Tully Carn,
as far as Lucinda was concerned at this moment, was that it
was lightly guarded. The Knights maintained a small laboratory a hundred metres downslope of the artifact's westernmost extension. Most days the shift was of about a dozen
men, rotated in and out from the research station on the
nearby but relatively uncontaminated islands in Erbusaig

Bay, three or four kilometres to the west. The complement of the research station varied but seldom went above fifty, of whom perhaps a quarter would be combat ready.

Even so, alarms would have been tripped the instant the column had turned off the main road; in the couple of minutes it would take to reach the fastness, the handful on guard duty would be alerting their colleagues and scrambling to their defences. The key tactic for Lucinda's joint force was to get well inside the structure as fast as possible, thus in effect holding it hostage—a posthuman shield—against any aggressive countermeasures by its guardians. She knew that the Knights could rapidly overwhelm her if they were to hit her in the open, or draw in forces from a wider area. All she had going for her was their concern for the integrity of the fastness, and the advantage of surprise.

The leading gravity sled bumped up over a brow of the moor to within sight of the artifact and into a concentrated barrage of plasma fire.

The screen, most of whose input currently came from the sled's external sensors, went completely white, then blank. Winter and Calder yelled, a distraction she didn't need when she was screaming herself, more constructively.

"Spread out! Spread out!" she told the other teams. There was a rending sound and a forward lurch as the antigravity generator cut out and the sled ploughed into the ground at sixty kilometres an hour. The interior instantly filled with shock-foam: you could see through the bubbles, they popped as you breathed, but any violent motion they gently absorbed like some infinite sponge. She toggled to the search engine's own input and output. The screen filled with images of flame, inciting more yells. Calder was attempting to thrash, to throw his arm across his face, and—finding this violent motion resisted by the foam—panicking. She could hear the hyperventilation behind his scream. She engaged the forward gear and the search engine's treads dug into the floor of the trailer and propelled the machine out of the burning wreckage of the sled, crunching over the remains of the cab. The view cleared. Tully Carn lay like the stump and roots of a gigantic black vitrified tree a couple of hundred metres ahead. Between her and it were three dug-in emplacements from which plasma cannon were keeping up a rapid fire. They were no longer shooting in her direction—the Knights would know that was useless against a search engine—but at the other sleds coming over the hill. One of the sleds tumbled on its back. The search engine inside would be helpless, unable to right itself. The other sleds burned and crashed just as hers had, and likewise the search engines began to emerge. She concentrated on moving forward. A search engine had no external weapons. Its relative invulnerability—to anything but a Eurydicean cosmic-string projector—was the trade-off. That, and the troops on board.

She was just about to order their deployment when the machine went over a landmine. The prow reared up. She saw clouds. For a moment the search engine continued to move forward, impelled by the cusp of its rear tracks on which it balanced like a kid on a bike doing a wheelie. A second explosion threw it over on its back.

Lucinda, like everyone else in the vehicle, hung there upside down for a moment. Then the shell seats swung around on their gimbals, the display and controls following, and she was upright again.

"Looks like we were expected," she said on the general circuit. "Use your own initiative, everyone. Mission unchanged."

"I can't breathe!" Calder gasped. His chest was moving so fast that the shock-gel was resisting it.

"Try to breathe normally," she said. He stared back without comprehension, his eyes like a trapped animal's. She released the solvent to clear the shock-foam. The cabin filled with the hiss of popping bubbles. Calder screamed again, coughing on the acrid spray.

"Calm him down," Lucinda told Winter. "Move slowly."

She turned her attention to the soldiers' icons on the screen in front of her. All thirty of them were fine. They could get out of an upside-down search engine in half a minute. It was a standard drill.

"OK everybody, out the back!" she said, and tabbed the hatch release. It opened a fraction, then stopped. A quick check of the rear view showed that the search engine's topple had jammed it against a boulder.

"Sorry, belay that," she said. The fighters had already rolled to their feet and were crouching on the inverted ceiling. "Hang on a minute."

The number two engine was close behind hers. She called on it for a shove. Its prow nudged her machine's stern away from the rock, then it reversed, changed course a fraction and ploughed on past her. A second or two later it was grinding over the nearest gun emplacement and, she devoutly hoped, crushing whoever was inside it. She opened the hatch.

"Go!" The fighters ran out one by one, rolling for cover on the rough, rust-covered ground, their plasma rifles up and firing within seconds. She slammed the hatch shut again and studied the display. The rest of the small battlefield was confusing, as ever—the enemy, hard-suited like her own side, popping up here and there, firing. The laboratory blockhouse was no doubt as impenetrable as a search engine, and a lot of fire was coming from that. Lucinda was pleased to see that the one search engine and several running troops who'd got between it and the artifact were not being fired upon. On the other hand, the defenders had no doubt called in air support. One more search engine was coming up behind her. She signalled to it for a pickup, grabbed the copydeck, opened the hatch again and led Winter and Calder to the back and out. The open hatch of the other vehicle gaped a few metres away. They dashed across, heads down as plasma bolts fizzed through the drizzle.

The only person in this engine was the driver, a Carlyle man. The soldiers had all deployed. Lucinda shoved Winter and Calder toward empty seats and ran to the front and swung in beside the driver.

"OK," she said. "Patch me through tae the team wi the fancy gun."

He did. A moment later the laboratory blockhouse was punched through, its layered sheet-diamond reduced to what looked more like charcoal as it crumbled. Beyond it a gap was torn in the clouds, revealing a blue blink of sky.

"Fuck," said the driver, who hadn't seen this kind of focused destruction before.

"Go that way," Lucinda said, pointing at the nearest tentacle of the fastness, which lay across their path about fifty metres ahead.

"There's no entrance," said the driver.

"Then fucking *make* one!"

"No need to shout," he grumbled. The vehicle ground forward at a little more than a walking pace. Twenty metres, ten. She scanned the horizon through the sensors, saw the expected fast-growing dots in the sky through the clouds. Five. The great thick cable of the fastness's extension loomed like a wall of black glass, and like black glass, it broke. The search engine crunched inside and swung to the right, moving up the widening tube. All the comms links with the other search engines faded out. Lucinda hit the floods. The walls, ridged and grooved like the inside of an old blood vessel, gleamed back. She scanned the seams by eye and with the search engine's instruments, trying to interpret them by something she couldn't explain in words but that she refused to call intuition, hoping that this primordial posthuman artifact might follow some pattern familiar from other artifacts plundered in her years of combat archaeology.

"There," she said, pointing at a confluence of irregularities. "Log on to that."

A flexible needle probe poked out from the prow, tapping in to the wall. Incomprehensible data in abstract geometric shapes flickered across the forward screen.

"Eleven-dimensional environment," Lucinda said. She glanced back over her shoulder at Winter and Calder. "No use for you guys."

Winter laughed hollowly. Calder had his eyes shut and was breathing slowly.

"Let's move on in to the hub," Lucinda said.

"Couple of hundred metres," the driver said. "Two minutes."

She nodded and went to the rear of the vehicle. Calder opened his eyes.

"Sorry about the panic attack," he said. "Claustrophobia, maybe asthma."

"You should have said. Are you OK now?"

He looked around the interior, looked away from the view of a tunnel of black glass on the forward screen. "I can cope."

"Good." She held out the copydeck, still in her hand. "Soon as we find a node to downlink this to, we can have you out of here." She smiled, in a way she hoped was reassuring. "You and anyone else you can rescue."

"Won't it take time?" Winter asked.

"To the copies, yes," she replied. "Hours, days." She waved a hand. "To us, seconds maybe. In and out."

Calder's face showed alarm again. "I don't want to go in," he said.

"What? It's not you that's going in, it's just a copy."

"A copy that'll think it's me."

"Well, sure. You can upload the memories afterwards. Or not, if you prefer."

He shook his head stubbornly. "I won't do it."

"But—" she began.

"Leave it," said Winter. He clasped Calder's knee. "It's OK, mate. It's OK."

Lucinda went back to the command console. The vehicle was just emerging from the extension into the hub, whose interior space was wider and higher than the lights could reach. The black glass of the floor was smooth and free of dust. Here and there, small stacks of instrumentation showed that the Knights had taken their investigation here further than they usually dared. Complex crystalline shapes hung down like stalactites to within a few metres of the floor. Lucinda read the runes of the scans and guided the driver carefully across the vast floor, on a course that took them back around to the curve of the wall close to another groin of hub and extension. A small stack of apparatus from a previous investigation lay a few metres from where Lucinda asked the driver to stop. Perhaps this augured well for her intuition.

Again the probe tapped a seam. This time, the picture that came up was of a landscape, topographically similar to the one they'd travelled through, but curiously barren. It reminded her of the hills around the relic on Eurydice.

"Yes!" she shouted.

Whatever it was, it was a human-adapted virtual reality. She was about to stick the copydeck in its slot when a movement on the visual display caught her eye at the same time as the driver yelled. She looked up to see five Knights holding a cosmic-string projector aimed straight at the search engine. After them another man, carrying a Webster, walked out of the tubular extension and around behind and then alongside the gun-crew to face her.

"Come out where I can see you, Carlyle," said Isaac Shlaim. "And bring the copydeck with you."

How the *fuck* did you get that gun?" Lucinda asked. Outside in the chamber, the air smelled like it hadn't been breathed in a thousand years. The floods cast her shadow long across the glass.

Shlaim smiled. "I wish I could say we captured it from your pirates," he said, "but the truth is even more galling to you—we got it on the authorization of the Joint Chiefs. They authorized me to come here as soon as you admitted, at that amusing gig, to having done a deal with the Returners. I came here weeks ago, as soon as a KE ship could be spared, shortly after the Knights arrived at Eurydice. I hear now that I missed some more of your cataclysmic bungling back there, but all's well that ends well."

"It's not ended," she said.

"Indeed not," said Shlaim. "We would in fact be very reluctant to use that gun in here, and there is . . . something of a standoff outside. But if needs must, we will risk a mutually destructive fight rather than let your gang blunder about in the dataspaces of this fastness. However, there is a more civilised alternative. I understand you have the two musical geniuses on board. Invite them to step out."

"They're backed up," said Lucinda, glancing at the Webster in Shlaim's hand.

Shlaim cast her an impatient glance. "I wouldn't waste a bolt on either of them."

She walked around the back again and beckoned to Winter and Calder to come out.

"All right," said Shlaim, when the three of them stood facing him. "Here's the deal. I and my colleagues in the Knights have been, as you'll have noticed, looking in the same place as you have. That's because we were looking for the same thing. I obtained—again, on the authority of the Joint Chiefs—copies of the backup files of Winter and Calder from the Black Sickle. We've used traces within them to run searches for recordings of the two women with whom you, gentlemen, are so obsessed. We've found them."

"You found *Irene and Arlene*?" Winter asked, incredulously.

"Yes."

"Now you're telling us they really existed?" Calder sneered.

"Apparently so," said Shlaim. "The discrepancies in your biographies and your fans' recollections and so forth were all based on errors on the other side of the equation, so to speak." He shrugged. "You, your record companies, or whoever—it doesn't matter now—put out misinformation about your lives and loved ones, doubtless for reasons that seemed good at the time. So, gentlemen, there was an Irene, there was an Arlene, and they were indeed waiting for you at Fort William."

"Which was nuked," said Winter. He didn't sound like he believed Shlaim at all.

"Later in the war," Shlaim pointed out. "Perhaps decades later, in the same conflict from which your bodies were recovered. They were there, they were caught up in the Singularity, and we have them here."

He reached his free hand into his jacket pocket and held out a data card. "You can load them straight into that copy-deck, and take them away and resurrect them. You can check all you like; and in any case, we have no reason to lie to you. The Knights will vouch for it."

"And what do you want in return?" Lucinda asked.

"That you go away," said Shlaim. "Go away and never come back. Tell your Returners that the mission failed. That nothing was retrieved. Irene and Arlene can be resurrected anywhere, far from Eurydice if you wish. Even on Earth, if you prefer to stay here. You'll have your own Return, all you wanted."

"That wasn't all we wanted," said Winter. "We wanted them all back."

"Come, gentlemen," said Shlaim. "That is insane and im-practicable, as well you know. Even recovering all the recorded minds in this fastness is unthinkable, let alone those all over the Earth and elsewhere. You owe the Return-ers nothing. All they ever accomplished was to delay and disrupt the project that eventually brought themselves and you and many others to Eurydice." He held up the card. "In any case, this is all you will ever get. The Knights will not al-low further assaults on the fastnesses, and neither will the Eurydicean authorities. The Carlyle pirate gang is finished. Take what you can have, and forget the rest."

Lucinda looked at Winter and Calder. "Your call, guys," she said.

The two men looked at each other. Calder's tongue wetted his lips. "You were the Returner," he said.

"It's this or nothing," said Shlaim.

Winter gazed at the ground, then at the card. He didn't seem to want to look at anybody's eyes.

"All right," he said. "We'll take it."

Shlaim smiled, and nodded to Lucinda. "The copydeck." He touched the card to it.

"That's it," he said. "Winter and Calder, Irene and Arlene, all set to party."

He handed her the card. "Just so you know you have it," he said.

"You will go now," said one of the Knights.

The three of them backed off and returned to the search engine. Shlaim followed, covering them with his Webster. He stood just outside the hatch as the two men took their seats.

Lucinda walked up to the front and slammed the copy-deck into the slot of the computer, still linked by the needle probe to the virtuality.

"What!" shouted Shlaim. "Stop—"

Lucinda turned to him. "We're getting them all back," she said.

Shlaim stepped inside and strolled up. "The hell you are," he said. "I expected you to do something crazy like this." He pointed at where the probe joined the wall. "I'm in there already, and I'm waiting."

CHAPTER **20**

No Death Above

They were about twenty kilometres north of Crianlarich when Calder shouted: "What the *fuck*—?"

Winter grabbed the steering wheel just in time. The car swung away from a steep bank down to a loch on the left, narrowly missed an oncoming truck, and continued on up the A82, climbing the high slope between higher hills.

"Fucking GPS has cut out," he said. "And the autopilot. Fuck, I'm *driving* this thing, and I'm driving *drunk*."

Calder lifted the open whisky bottle in his hand and closed one eye, checking the level. "Only a third between us," he said judiciously. "You're not *that* drunk."

"Only because the joint is working against it. Shit, we should get off the road, call the AA or something."

"Phone's out too," Calder said.

Winter had a sudden inexplicable feeling that something was seriously wrong. "Try the radio," he said.

Calder toggled the sound system. Their latest album, the one whose big contract they were celebrating, gave way to a roar of static.

"Fuck, find the station."

"I'm trying, man, I'm trying." Calder hit the search button.

They were almost at the summit of Rannoch Moor now. Winter kept the speed down to less than sixty kilometres per hour. He was making a very deliberate effort to concentrate, to fight the effects of the alcohol and the joint. The radio scratched around like nails on a blackboard, searching. The more lucid Winter felt he was becoming, the more uneasy he felt. It wasn't just their dangerous and illegal driving, it was something deeper, something at the back of his mind. He took the Volvo carefully around the next bend, and almost lost the road himself when he saw a big articulated lorry overturned a few metres off the road and a crashed car beside it.

"Christ, we'll have to stop and help—" He slowed, looking for a safe place to pull off. Half a kilometre ahead, he saw another crashed car.

"It wasn't just us that—"

"Wait," said Calder, turning up the volume. "Caught something."

The station, even at full volume, was faint, the midwestern-accented voice strained to breaking point.

" . . . reports coming in . . . almost unbelievable . . . New York and Washington . . . Cheyenne . . . deep silos . . . my God, folks, all of you pray . . . not a hoax, not a . . . complete devastation . . . casualties . . . Los Angeles . . . millions . . . pray for . . . "

It faded to static. Winter brought the car into a long lay-by and to a halt. He leaned over and snapped the sound system to Off. The utter horror of what he had just understood, and what must come, made the world turn grey before him. Then something became clear in his head, and must have become clear in his eyes.

"It can't be," said Calder. "Come on, man. Don't look at me like that."

"That isn't why," said Winter.

"What? What isn't?"

"I'm not looking at you like that because the war's started," he said. "I'm looking to see if you *know where we are*."

Calder looked around. "We're on Rannoch," he said impatiently. "Where we died." He heard what he'd just said. His mouth opened. "Uh."

"Now it's you who's looking at me like that."

"It's all coming back."

"Yes," said Winter, heavily. "It all comes back. What's the last thing you remember?"

"We'd just crossed a bridge—no, we went over *without* a bridge, like we were on a hovercraft or something—from that place with the castle and the cousin-fuckers."

"Dornie."

"Dornie, yeah, that's it. Shit, yes, and there was some kind of alien thing on the moor, it was like we were in the *future*, except we were—no, we were going to go into it, the, the—"

"The fastness at Tully Carn," said Winter. "That's where we are, now."

"No, we're nowhere near—" Calder banged the heel of his hand on his forehead. "This is like being in a dream just before it becomes lucid."

"I know what you mean," said Winter. "All that future stuff seems unreal, but—"

Calder lit a cigarette, hands shaking. "You don't suppose," he said, "that we didn't die, that we both had some kind of, I dunno, near-death experience back there, and we have a false memory? Of, like, another life, or—"

"Of space and Mars and the city in Sagittarius? Lucinda? Gwyneth Voigt? Amelia Orr? And the castle on the Clyde, and travelling up here this morning through an ancient battlefield of machines beyond anything—"

"Oh, fuck, OK." Calder shook his head, as if trying to make it work. "Why is it like this?"

"I reckon," said Winter, "that if we *are* in some kind of virtual reality, and trying to get Irene and Arlene back, it has to seem real to us." He looked back at the overturned truck, now burning. "Which it does. Let's get back on the road."

"Looks bloody dangerous."

"I don't think we're going to die," said Winter. "Now

let's get to Fort William before the American retaliation strike arrives."

He drove recklessly, and they didn't die. Past crashes, past armoured columns snaking along the road through Glencoe, and through the empty streets of Ballachulish and the half-empty, half-crazed streets of Fort William. The journey took less than an hour. They found the hotel, off the High Street, and walked into the bar. Everybody was sitting at tables, fixated on their little screens or the big wall screen, crying into phones, drinking hard liquor, smoking, or gnawing their knuckles. Two women sat together at a table, each clutching a hand of the other, looking from the screens to the door.

Irene with her long fair hair and pale blue eyes, sitting on that Afghan coat she had; and Arlene, small, no taller standing straight than Calder was stooped, and dark; eyes bright behind narrow rectangular frames with lenses in them. Glasses. People still wore them then, back in the 21st century. Winter and Calder rushed to them and they all held each other for a minute, crying and laughing.

"Thank God you're alive," said Irene, when they'd all sat down. "We heard you were killed in a car crash when the first EMP hit took out the GPS and the automation."

"We were," said Winter. "We came back for you."

"We know," said Arlene. She and Irene were the only people in the room who were smiling. "We've been waiting for you. Not for long, but—it's not been easy. You really might not have come."

Irene was looking out of the window, facing the sea. "Counterstrike's on its way," she said. "We should leave soon."

Calder jumped up. "Fuck, fuck, yes, I saw the ruins—"

Irene tugged him back down. "It's all right. We have an hour. Time enough."

Winter stared at her, ravished as ever by her eyes and cheekbones and mouth. "You know what's going on," he said.

"Oh yes," said Irene. "A lot more than you do."

"What about them?" Winter glanced furtively at the other people in the bar, gazing at grim news. He felt like a spy, a time-traveller, a ghost.

"Some of them have a glimmer," said Arlene. "Most of them are still deep in the necessary illusion. They're replaying some pretty traumatic memories. Doesn't matter. They'll be fine. They *are* fine. Oh, you have no idea how fine!"

Winter shook his head, looked at the likewise baffled Calder. "I don't understand," said Winter. "We're here to get you *out*. To let you know you *can* get out. We *know* all this is a virtuality. You can download from it, come back from the dead. It's 2367. There's a whole galaxy, a whole new world out there. Wormholes and starships and endless youth and resurrection. We can bring you back. We can bring you, we can bring these people all back, out of this, this—"

"We know," said Irene. "We know all about it."

"How?" asked Winter. "Does this place have comms? Some connection to the outside?"

Irene shook her head. "No. That's a problem. We'll talk about it later." She smiled gently, suddenly; reached out and stroked his stubbled cheek, the way she did. "Oh, my darling. I've missed you so much, even if—"

"It was that funny little man," Arlene was saying. "Well, he was a funny little man then, when we met him."

"Who?" asked Winter.

"Isaac Shlaim," said Irene. "The little—the Israeli." She cast him a disapproving look. "He was kept as a thrall by your friend Lucinda. Dreadful woman."

"She isn't—" Winter began hotly.

"Isn't your friend, or isn't dreadful?" Irene smiled at his discomfiture. "It's all right. We know about everything that's happened to you, and everything you've done."

"Can you read our minds?" asked Calder. He sounded horrified.

"No," said Irene. She closed her eyes and ran a hand across them. "Not exactly. Well, it depends what you mean by 'we,' and what—" She looked despairingly across at Arlene. "Did you remember it being like this?" She flapped a hand. "The *bandwidth*!"

"I think you've just told us something," Winter said. She returned him a knowing smile.

It was strange, it was the same feeling he'd had about this whole world right at the start—that this was real, was as it had been, and yet was not. This was Irene, exactly as he'd remembered her, and yet she was not. His Irene would never have used the word *bandwidth* like that. Not when she wasn't negotiating a comms contract. Not conversationally, not metaphorically. But, for her, here, it would be literal.

"Get us some more drinks," said Irene. "Tall vodka for me, G&T for Arlene, and—" She raised her voice and eyebrows, looking at someone behind his shoulder.

"The best malt in the house," said Isaac Shlaim, pulling up a seat and sitting down. "On the rocks."

"What, no Coke?" said Calder.

Shlaim was wearing a faded black T-shirt with a soaring penguin and the slogan *Where do you want to come from today?* He grinned affably at Calder.

"I may be a little yid, but I'm not a heathen," he said.

"Single malt and *ice*?" said Winter. "You fucking are."

"I don't have any money," said Calder, standing up and groping his pockets.

Shlaim laughed. "I wouldn't worry."

They watched as Calder went behind the bar counter and helped himself.

"Lagavulin," he said, returning with a tartan tray. "Triples. One with ice,"—he mimed a shudder—"two with water. And yours, ladies."

"Well," said Winter, sipping gratefully, "Arlene here was implying you were no longer a funny little man." He scrutinised Shlaim over the rim of his glass. "I await the evidence."

"Oh, I can give you evidence," said Shlaim. He glanced complicitly at the two women. "*We* can. But before that, let me explain. Within the limitations of low bandwidth." He waggled two fingers at Calder, accepted a cigarette. "When I came here," he said, lighting up, "I had the same idea as you had, except in reverse. You want to, as you say, 'bring them all back.' I wanted to stop you."

"Why?" asked Calder.

"Good question," Shlaim acknowledged, nodding. "Part of it was to spite Lucinda Carlyle. I know that sounds petty, but, hell, you try spending eight years inside a space suit with her—" He laughed at their faces. "Pervs. You know what I mean. Part of it was what I'd learned from the Knights: that ignorant poking around inside posthuman virtualities—not just ripping chunks off the hardware like the Carlyle gang, but getting down and dirty with the software—can set off local Singularities, such as so predictably fuck up our friends the Rapture-fuckers. And I spent long enough in a hell-file to know what that can mean for human-level minds." He took a long swallow. "Imagine boredom and no cigarettes, or whatever your thing is, for a thousand years. Not that I'd tell Carlyle, you understand, but being in her service was an improvement, of a sort."

"What put you in the hell-file?" Winter asked.

"I did, probably, if my self that is out there somewhere is anything like my self here. I don't like myself very much. Not as I was." He stubbed his cigarette. "But I've got better." He stretched and laughed. "It's hard to explain. We'll have to show you."

Irene laid a hand on his arm. "We'll have to warn them first. It's only fair."

"Oh yes. Once you've been shown, all this business of bringing them back—or stopping it, for that matter—becomes somewhat . . . moot."

"Before you do that," said Calder, "just tell me this. I mean, I never was a believer in the Return. How was anyone saved at all?"

Shlaim shrugged. "Some because a nanotech swarm preceded the nuclear counterstrike. Often by whole seconds. Some because they'd already been uploaded via their on-line connections. Phones and such. You get an AI burning through these, you can do a lot. And some, frankly, by later deduction and reconstruction. Neural parsing on a mass scale, if you like."

Irene looked about to say something; Shlaim stopped her with a minute, fleeting frown.

"But none of this matters," he went on. "It only refers to this very limited and isolated fastness. Out there among the stars, out in what you're pleased to call the real world, there are processors that can recreate not just everyone who ever lived, but everyone who could possibly have ever lived." His face bleakened. "With all the joy that that implies, and all the suffering. The great minds are good, I believe that, but they are not kind. They are not *nice*."

"Like artists," said Irene.

"Shit," said Calder. "And I thought Mahayanna Buddhism was grim."

Shlaim nodded slowly. "There's no karma, no kismet, no *desert*." He stood up. "But there is a heaven."

Calder stared at him. "You're saying these machines of destruction, and the bastards who set them off, made something good?"

Shlaim shook his head. "There are good and bad things, but no good or evil will. There's only intelligence, and stupidity. Stupidity is what we had as humans, and intelligence is what we and everyone else now has, however they began. Let me show you—"

"Wait—" said Arlene.

"I know," Shlaim told her. He looked at Winter and Calder. "We can't shift virtualities without a credible transition," he explained. "Otherwise you get hung up on the it's-all-an-illusion trip or start trying to hack the underlying reality. With consequences that are, shall we say, very much not fun. But in this case a credible transition scenario positively drops out of the logic of the situation." He grinned evilly. "Think of it as dying and going to heaven."

"Damn," said Irene, lightly. "I don't look forward to doing that *again*."

Shlaim was looking out of the window. "Bring it on," he said.

Winter jumped to his feet. There was a moment when he was aware of flying glass slicing him where he stood.

Everything went white.

Irene had always been, to him, an angel. Now she was. He had always thought he knew a lot. Now he did. The pathetic, limited personality that called itself James Winter fell away from him like sweaty clothes. He gazed around the eleven-dimensional space, and saw the big picture. All free, and all determined, because it was willed where what is willed must be. And still unfolding, still determined by his own decision, still undecided though eternally determined. He laughed at the notion that this could have ever seemed paradoxical.

"You wanted to warn me against *this*?" he said to Irene.

Her smile was a sunrise on a thousand worlds. "You wanted to *rescue* me from this?" She swept an arm to indicate the Raptured and the rapt, the busy multitude that filled the sky around them, a galaxy of talent indeed. "To rescue *them*?"

He laughed storms.

"So what was—?" His thought conjured the bar in the Fort William hotel, like a microscope slide seen through the wrong end of a telescope. They were still there, sectioned on the slide, sliced into three-dimensional shapes, their flesh shredding in a snowstorm of imploding construction materials, screaming and dying.

"That really happened," Irene said. "Arlene and I and all those there and everybody else who fell in it—we all died. We really died. Forever. Nobody comes back. Entropy is irreversible, except in the great cycles of the universe. I and Arlene died, just as you and Alan died an hour earlier. But in another sense, that never really happened."

She showed him what had really happened.

Winter felt the chill of ice ages. "You never lived?"

"I live now," she said, and the ice melted.

There was nothing more to say. "Yes. The identity of indiscernibles."

"Something like that."

"Why are we talking, when—?"

"We have to, while you have to ask."

The thought tickled him. "I still tickle."

"Nothing's wrong with you then."

"You haven't changed."

She laughed like a pulsar. "That's the wonder. The amazing thing."

"No," he said. "The amazing thing is I'm not satisfied. I feel limited."

She sighed plasma streams. "We are." She clenched her fist and smashed down cometary bombardments. "We are limited. We're in *fucking Tully Carn*! And you and"—she nodded to Calder and Shlaim—"have shown us what we could become! What else has been done!"

"The skein." The thought of it filled his mind like lust. "But the skein was made by—"

"Oh," she said, as he showed her. How had he known? He had seen the relic on Eurydice, he had talked to Lucinda, and now it all seemed so obvious that it was taking shape from the way he waved his hands.

"And the starships!" Arlene cried. "Oh, the way they are prevented from violating causality! The dedication, the attention, the work!"

"Work we can't do here," said Shlaim, his voice like tectonic plates.

"But look—" said Irene, showing him the shape of the skein, the forming gate.

"Ah!" he said. "I see." He grinned icecaps at Winter. "That's, you know, clever. Let's—"

"Wait—" said Arlene.

This time, Shlaim attended to her. "Oh, all right," he said, grudgingly like glaciers. "I suppose we owe it to ourselves, in a manner of speaking."

Libraries of condescension laughed with them all.

* * *

I'm waiting." Shlaim's words hung on the air for a moment. Winter and Calder ran up to the command console, crowding Shlaim and Lucinda and the driver at the screen.

"Waiting for what?" Winter asked.

"Waiting for you two. I'm there to stop you, and I think I know who will have the best of it," said Shlaim, turning.

"Indeed you do," said an amused voice from the screen. It was Shlaim's voice.

But it was Irene's face that at first took Winter's whole attention. She was exactly as he remembered her, but she had changed. Beyond beauty and brighter than intelligence, she smiled on him like Eve. He was certain that she could see him even though the screen had—designedly—no camera. Then he saw the others: Arlene, Calder, Shlaim, and himself, all the same and all changed, and a crowd that seemed infinite at their backs. They were all going somewhere, and it wasn't into the search engine's storage.

"There is something you should know," said Irene. "Your memories of us were false. As you see, they have now become true."

Winter felt his world turn inside out for the second time in minutes. "Shlaim lied?"

"Shlaim didn't lie to you," said Irene, "but he was mistaken. He and the Knights took your memories of us and used them to search for us. But in this environment, the parameters of that kind of search become ever more explicit, so explicit that they eventually define the object of the search precisely. And when that object is as simple as the specifications for a human body and mind and remembered life, the definition and the object become indistinguishable. The search for us called us into being."

"You must leave," said Arlene's voice. "There's no time to talk. But as you see, there's no need."

Their transfigured, exaltant selves vanished. The screen became all forward view again. The glass-like walls had begun to move and flow, in every colour but their original

black. The small squad of Knights looked around in frantic
alarm, swinging the cosmic-string gun.

"Get them on board," Lucinda said.

Shlaim leapt to comply. As soon as the men were in and the
hatch was shut Shlaim called out: "Go down the way we came
in! It's quicker, there's an entrance at two hundred metres."

"Let's hope it's still an exit," said Lucinda.

The driver manoeuvred the search engine around the corner and into the long tube. By now there was no need for the
lights. The walls themselves were shining. It was like driving through the end of a rainbow. It was so bright that the
driver almost did not notice the sunlight. They emerged
from the gap out on to the bare hillside, already cleared of
casualties but still littered with weapons and burnt-out vehicles, to see in the distance search engines and the Knights'
gravity sleds fleeing in all directions.

They were about half a kilometre down the track up which
they'd come when Shlaim said: "It isn't a fucking pillar of
salt, you know. We can look back."

"All right," Lucinda said. "Stop for a moment, OK?"

The driver complied reluctantly. Lucinda flicked the view
from before to behind. The fastness at Tully Carn was no
longer a black and glassy root-system spread over a rusty
slope. Complex and colourful, floral and coralline, exuber-
ant and expanding, it was a junkyard of jewelled clockwork
orreries giving off little spinning wheels that soared into the
air like toy helicopters and drifted away like dandelion
seeds.

"Oh. My. God," said Lucinda. "What have we done?"

"I'll tell you what you've done," snarled Shlaim.
"You've—"

"No," said Winter. "I'll tell *you*. I don't know whether the
minds in that thing were just data files or if they or anything
else in it were actually running, and I doubt you know either.
But your copy was the first to go in there, and that was what
set it off. Maybe they didn't know about the big wide galaxy
and what the other minds have done. They could certainly
learn about it from your copy. That thing is spreading, it'll

spread to all the fastnesses of the Earth, and there's nothing anyone can do to stop it. Any minds that got caught up in the Hard Rapture aren't going to need or want a Return. What they want is a *departure*, and you've given it to them." He clapped Shlaim's shoulder. "You've given it to *us*. You should be proud."

"What," Calder asked, pointing at a place on the screen just above the fast-transforming fastness, "do you think *that* is?"

"It's a gate," Lucinda said. She flicked to a forward view. "Let's go."

"What a fuckup," said Calder. Lucinda flinched.

"At least you've got the copies," Shlaim said.

Winter saw in Calder's face, as they both turned on the scientist, the same rage and fury and disappointment that burned in his own throat.

"They're not copies," he said. "They never lived. They're not fucking *real*."

"You don't understand," said Shlaim.

"It's you who doesn't understand," said Calder.

The search engine moved on down the hill to the road.

CODA

Worlds and Lives

"There is always a last time for everything."

Lucinda turned, startled by the familiar voice. Shlaim sauntered over, his sandals flip-flopping on the dusty marble of the museum floor. He was wearing khaki shorts and a black T-shirt printed with a picture of Earth and the words *AOL That!* As if, she thought. She had become as passionate a Returner—or, as was now said, a Stayer—as Winter. There had only ever been one planet worth taking, she had belatedly realised now that it was being taken away. In a googol of light-years she would not see its like.

"Hello," she said, ungraciously, though hardly surprised; he'd expressed an intention of "doing Earth," as the current phrase went, shortly before she and Winter had set off with the more limited intention of doing Europe. In the two years that had passed since then it was not surprising that at some point their paths would cross.

"What brings you here?" Winter asked.

"Like I said," Shlaim grinned. "Same as you, yeah? Last chance to see."

He stood beside them and peered into the glass case. Inside it was a brown ceramic disc about ten centimetres across, stamped in a spiral pattern with dozens of tiny pictographs: a profile face that looked like a Mohawk, stick figures, a boxy spiked shape that reminded Lucinda irresistibly of a Lunar Excursion Module . . . the Phaistos Disc was as enigmatic an artifact as it had always been, like some playful, planted evidence of alien contact, or the jest of a god who could fake a planet's entire past with a sense of style.

"Bronze-Age CD-ROM," said Shlaim. Winter laughed.

"Have you done Knossos?" Lucinda asked.

"Yeah, in the morning. You too?"

"Uh-huh. While it was cool, supposedly." She recalled momentarily the long queues in the unforgiving heat, waiting to stoop and peer into small or large rooms with their fragments of tile and fresco, from which could be derived scenes of dolphins and dancers and bull-leaping boys and girls; the concrete and red-painted reconstructions of ancient wooden pillars, and the overwhelming sense of gigantic scale and a grandeur not lost but present in the very shape of the shaped ground, the long stone ramps and artificial hills. "Must have missed you in the crowd."

"Easily done," said Shlaim.

They wandered on, past cases of coins and weights and drinking-vessels, of minute copper double-headed axes and elaborately worked, minuscule golden bees; of figurines of bare-breasted, snake-handling dancers in long frilly skirts. Every so often Lucinda saw an item familiar from encyclopaedia screens, and could hardly believe she was looking at the original, the thing itself. If the chronology given in the explanatory cards was right it seemed all wrong: the fine pieces of black stone and bronze, of gold and ivory were early, the cruder versions in terra-cotta late. The museum's rooms, big and airy and lit by tall windows, smelled of paper and old dust. Not many visitors were here; the rush had passed; in a few days the curators would be packing everything up, ready to be shipped off Earth. So far, no people, and few even of plants and animals, had been absorbed into the growing fastnesses, and their expansion was slow and erratic, but the once-burned inhabitants of Earth were in no mood to take chances. Most of them were getting out while, as they saw it, they still could. Here in Crete, the fastness that had once been the central telephone exchange of Heraklion had, a couple of months earlier, begun its transformation, and had now spread a hundred metres beyond its previous perimeter. Winter and Lucinda had been able to see its wavering topmost extensions, sparkling like stiff tinsel, above the town's rooftops when they'd had a quick beer in one of the few refreshment stalls that remained, under the multiple tilted flagpoles of Commonwealth Square.

All the time Shlaim kept up an informed commentary on the artifacts, surprising her.

"I didn't know you knew all that," she said.

"You didn't know me very well," he said mildly. "Just a comp-sci geek who had it coming, that was it, huh?"

Her cheeks burned. "Yes," she said. She glanced sideways at him. "I haven't used a thrall since, you know."

"Well, good for you," he said, grudgingly, but sounding somewhat pleased. "Anyway. Archaeology was a big thing, for us. In Israel, you know, as was? Back in the day." He sounded sad; his dark eyes blinked as he looked at her. "Last place I've visited," he went on, "was Krakow. The old Jewish Quarter. You know, back in the 2030s there were a hundred thousand people living there? And that there still were, again, just a few months ago? And now the streets are deserted, the synagogues are empty shells again, and the rabbis are stashing Torah scrolls for the ships." His fists clenched at his sides. "Another fucking exodus."

"I guess," said Winter, "you kept quiet about who you were."

Shlaim laughed loudly and clapped Winter's back. "Speaking from experience!"

"Damn right I am."

They were in a room of broken pottery decorated with reddish pictures; of mask-like helmets and pitted black swords. "Mycenean," said Shlaim. "Worth a look, but dull."

They ambled alongside the cases anyway, reluctant to depart, to miss anything that they might never see, and would certainly never see in place, again.

"What's Calder doing these days?" Shlaim asked.

"Back to New Start. He was never much of a Returner."

"And Amelia?"

Lucinda scuffed her toe in the dust, snagged a sandal buckle on her sarong's hem, stooped to sort it, and straightened up, feeling her face flush again. Every so often the shame descended on her like this, of the disaster she had brought on the family, as well as—though more ambiguously and arguably—on the world.

"Uh, well," she said. "You know, the family, the firm, they're scrabbling a bit for something new and profitable to do, without the income from the skein. And she thought, well, it might be a good idea to go into the entertainment business—"

Shlaim laughed. "Following in the footsteps of the Family, yes!"

"And she, um, took the copydeck. The one with Winter and Calder and Irene and Arlene. She's been downloading them to the flesh, honest, but she's got different downloads of them playing simultaneous gigs in every backwater dive from the asteroid belt to the Sagittarius Arm. . . . "

"We've set the Mouse on her case," said Winter, a little defensively. "Calder and me. But the downloads aren't cooperating."

For the first time Shlaim looked at a loss for words. After a minute he shrugged and said, "Information wants to be free."

"Yeah," said Lucinda bitterly. "That's how we got into this whole fucking mess."

"It's not such a bad mess, as such things go," said Shlaim. "Take it from me."

He looked around. The exit and the souvenir shop were just outside. "That's about the end of the line."

Lucinda didn't want to leave without walking, however quickly, past the brighter and older remains again, so she in-

sisted on going all the way back around to the entrance. As
they did so she remarked:

"It's a funny thing, compared to the Myceneans . . . the
Minoans didn't leave many weapons."

"They didn't need many," said Shlaim. "They were a
thassalocracy."

"A what?" she asked.

"An empire of the merchant marine," Shlaim explained.
"They got their wealth from trade."

"All this?" said Lucinda, waving her hand around. "Just
from . . . carrying things from place to place in ships?"

"That and growing vines and olives, yes," said Shlaim.

"The palaces and jewels and theatres and everything?
From *trade*?"

"Yes," said Shlaim. He sounded a little impatient with her
incredulity, or as it might seem to him, her obtuseness.

Lucinda put an arm around the shoulders of each of the
men and swung her feet up off the ground between them like
a child. Shlaim and Winter staggered, taking the weight, and
gave her, or each other, a puzzled look. Lucinda felt weight-
less herself, lightened by a load off her mind, but she re-
lented in a moment, swinging back to the ground. She
skipped ahead of them, turned around, and laughed.

"That," she said, "is the most amazing idea I've ever
heard. Or ever had."

Lamont stood on a hot red moor with the smell of rust in
his nostrils, with Morag Higgins beside him and the lip
of the fastness, moving slowly like a glacier, a few metres in
front of him. The great inorganic botanic garden of the thing
swept up and over the nearest hilltops. In the sky above and
far away to the west, shimmering aurorae rose like pillars
kilometres tall, within which insubstantial masses moved
like thunderheads.

"Wimps," said Morag, looking up.

"What?"

"Weakly interacting massive particles."

"It's a possibility," Lamont allowed.

She squatted and reached out with a finger towards the interface, where particles of rust were being picked up magnetically like crumbs carried by invisible ants, and in a hot flicker forged into further small, bright steel components buzzing and ticking like the inside of a fob watch around the fringe of the great sprawling machine that now extended far beyond the environs of Tully Carn.

"Don't!" he said, suddenly alarmed.

She turned her steel smile on him. "You still think I have anything to be afraid of?"

"I'm not sure," he said. "But I have."

She pushed her fingers into his beard.

"Some time . . . " she said. "Some time, the curiosity will get too much. And even putting in a copy won't be enough. I'll have to *know*."

He nodded sombrely. "I know," he said. "But not this time."

"No," she agreed. "Not this time."

They turned around and walked the two kilometres back along the moor to the empty streets of Inverness.

The habitat hung in space, a great turning wheel of lands and lakes under diamond glass and solar mirrors. Its defences were many, its vulnerabilities few. One of the latter was that it had no expectation of, or defence against, a small starship fittling right in under its roof, scorching along between its floor and roof for several kilometres before coming to a dead halt immediately above the central committee offices. Hatches opened in the ship and space-armoured soldiers swarmed out, riding down on rocket packs, carrying cosmic-string weapons and plasma rifles.

One of the soldiers kicked open the door of the office and marched in to see the chairman. He stared from behind his console at the visored, armoured and armed figure before him. Another soldier came into the office, while the rest ran thunderously through the corridors and up the stairs of the building.

"You are the responsible elected leader of Man Conquers Space Collective?" the first soldier asked.

"Yes," said the chairman, raising his hands slowly above his head.

"Good," said the soldier. The visor flipped up and a woman's face grinned out at him. "I am Number One Destruction Brigade San Ok." She indicated the other soldier. "And this is my comrade Number One Destruction Brigade Ree. Both formerly of Eighty-Seven Production Brigade, Transformation of Nature Collective. We're here to collect on a debt."

B enjamin Ben-Ami put down his coffee and sighed.

"Problems?" Andrea Al-Khayed asked, from the other side of the verandah breakfast table.

"Not at all." Ben-Ami waved a hand to encompass the green and crowded farms of the valley and the sky above it, where that morning's third shipload of Earth evacuees was drifting past. "These people have *problems*. They've seen the planet they were born on turning inexorably into a machinery of thought. All I have is a hankering for good New Start coffee."

Andrea nodded. "Me too. It's funny the things you miss."

They were two years into Ben-Ami's five-year exile from the city, the penalty for his part in what were now referred to as "the recent events." Al-Khayed had, with unexpected loyalty, chosen to share it. The thought still made him feel almost guilty.

"You can leave at any time," he said. "Honestly."

Under the table, her toes attempted to tickle his thigh. "Not really," she said.

He smiled back.

"It's not just the coffee, though," she said. "It's the cafe, and the comms, and the city. That's what you're missing,

Ben, and you shouldn't. They would just distract you from
what you're doing now, and this is the best possible place for
doing it."

"I know, I know." He thumbed his slate, looking at the
draft for the new libretto: *Jesus Koresh: Martyred Messiah*.
It looked like it might be the best thing he'd ever done, better even than last year's *Osama: Warrior Prince*: the most
conscientiously researched: every character, from its mild-
mannered and modest but strong-willed hero to its gloating
psychopathic villains, the Emperor Reno and the Empress
Hillary, meticulously authenticated from the documents of
the Latter Day Adventists. But still.

He looked down the valley balefully to the nearest of its
several small whitewashed churches.

"If I have to listen to another bloody hymn," he said, "I'll
burn down a church myself."

They walked out of the resurrection lab together, laughing and talking. As soon as they were out in the open
Calder lit a cigarette. Arlene nudged him.

"These things will kill you one of these days," she said.

Winter looked around. The sky was dark blue, webbed
with the hairline hexagons of a high dome. The resurrection
lab was a small low building with a wooden ramp down to a
broad plaza, set among green parks with paths that linked a
cluster of white buildings of four or five storeys. There were
a lot of people on the paths, and they all looked young. That
didn't mean much, but he suspected them of being students.

"Where are we, anyway?" he said.

Calder made a thing of squinting up at the sky. "Still the
Sagittarius Arm, by the looks of it," he announced.

"Another campus gig," said Irene. "Let's hope this time
the little bastards haven't cracked our copy-headers and nap-
stered us to virtualities all over the planet."

Winter looked at her, alarmed. "Has that ever happened?"

She shook her head, smiling. "I shouldn't tease you," she
said. "You fall for it every time."

"This is definitely real?"

"Definitely. Come on, let's find the bar." She slipped her hand under his arm and set off with him and the others, down the ramp. "Don't look back."